The Whipple Wash Chronicles

Book II

Mom & Dad Fraser
Enjoy the Journey
Susan

Also Available:
The Whipple Wash Chronicles: The Valley Time Forgot

The Whipple Wash Chronicles

THE SHADOW OF EREBOS

S.D. FERRELL

ELSBRIER INK

Where my family and friends have been given characters in the story, by no means are they a true characterization of said people or events that have taken place.

First published in Canada in 2014 by
Elsbrier Ink, Simcoe, ON
eslbrier.ink@gmail.com
www.whipplewashchronicles.com

FIRST EDITION

ISBN-13:978-1502609334
ISBN-10:1502309335

For my parents Kay'lon and Jack,
my fellow Sic Lid Sistas
& my brother Bob

Prologue

Since the beginning of time two Supreme Beings, the Light of Goodness and Chaos, have laid claim to this world and the humans that dwell within it. Where Chaos rules the mind and flesh of man, the Light of Goodness rules their heart and soul. They are always at war, as each feels that only one Supreme Being should reign over man. However in the character of a man there dwells both light and darkness; you cannot have one without the other. When a soul descends and embodies a human form, it has free will to decide which is the greater of the two and at what degree it will affect them throughout their life. According to the First Law in 'The Book of Truth'; "Neither Supreme Being can interfere with the decision. However once chosen, they can assist them along the journey to their determined fate and if need be, strategically place them throughout time to gain an advantage over the other. When this transpires a shift occurs which puts the balance of mankind at risk and the fate of the world in jeopardy."

So it is written in the 'Scrolls of the Ancients'

A long time ago in a far off land, when the earth was young and mankind still believed in magic and miracles, a beautiful, impetuous maiden named Fairbethia, the only child of Lord Henrik Canvil and heir to his vast holdings, went adventuring in the moors northeast of her home.

The moors were a dangerous place, especially for one so young. From the time children could understand the concept of danger they were warned of the evils that lurked in the massive area that lay south of Lake Gull; a large body of water that emptied into the Northern Sea. The moors were a labyrinth of bogs. Some were filled with murky water- the veridict vines that grew from the bottom would wrap around your legs and pull you to the depths of the pool. Other bogs had spongy soil that looked solid until you step on it. It would then separate, making you fall through. Once submerged, it would cover over again, making it difficult to break back through. And then there was the worst of the pools; quick sand. That too looked like solid earth until you stepped in the middle; the sand would slowly swallow its victim whole.

The bogs were connected by hard-packed dirt pathways that forked in several directions. Tall sedges in varying colours of green, deep purple and bold yellow lined the pathways, hiding the pools from view. One misstep off the pathway and a weary traveler would find his quick demise. If that were not enough to make one want to stay clear of the area, folklore told of an evil entity that haunted the moors by night. If a traveler walked too close to the edge of the moors, the entity would entice them to enter with an enchanted song and the traveler would never be seen or heard from again. To ward off travelers from entering the moors, signs were staked at every entrance which read: "Beware: Evil Resides Here!" Since the signs were posted no one had lost their life to the moors for over five hundred years.

The folklore had indeed rung true, an evil did reside in the moors; Erebos was its name. Erebos, son of the nefarious Supreme Being Chaos, had been trapped on the moors by a spell that had been casted a thousand years before by Ardrich, the son of The Light of Goodness. His heart had been broken after Erebos entranced Pamalina to lay with him. Pamalina was a virginal maiden and Ardrich's true love; that he planned to marry even though she was mortal. In order to break the spell, Erebos needed the unconditional love of a virginal maiden. The love had to be pure, without enchantments. Only then could Erebos return home and rule alongside his mother, Chaos.

Although she had been warned of the dangers, Fairbethia, just fifteen years old, thought she knew better than the elders in the Kingdom. 'Oh that is just a silly old wives tale,' she was often heard saying. 'The moors are no more dangerous than a baby lamb and one day I will prove it.' That day soon came. Fairbethia entered the moors with the false bravado of youth, without heeding the warnings or thinking of the consequences of her actions. Quickly however and much to her dismay, she was lost in the maze. As night descended, an eerie, thick fog rose, blanketing the moors in a grey darkness. No one heard her cries for help and no one came looking for her.

Her father and his army had left the day before on a crusade to take over the northern Kingdoms and would not be back for five years. Fairbethia's handmaiden Constance and the matron housekeeper Madam Buchanan would not come to her rescue. They greatly disliked Fairbethia and had had enough of her childish, mean-spirited and disrespectful manners; the true character that she let reign when her father was not in residence. So when Fairbethia did not return home by nightfall they did not raise an alarm.

Most of the staff had been released of their duties before Lord Canvil left; leaving only a handful of people to take care of the castle and his darling daughter. Madam Buchanan was an outspoken woman who could persuade the others to agree that Fairbethia had died of a fever if Canvil should survive the crusade and inquire upon them what had happened to his daughter. However it would not come to that, for no one knew that the tides of change would soon be upon them. Not even their God would be able to save them from the wrath that would unfold; all because a young maiden would not listen to her elders.

For six days and nights Fairbethia wandered alone trying to find her way out of the moors. Fevered, fatigued and chilled to the bone, she stumbled and fell to the ground. In the silence that followed, as she waited for death to come for her, she heard a sweet melody in the distance. With what little strength she had left she crawled on her belly along the rough path towards the direction of the song. Tiny sharp stones dug into her tattered, sweat-stained clothing, gouging her tender skin until it bled. Fairbethia did not care; hope gave her the energy to keep moving on. She soon found herself at a wooden bridge. Through the fog she could see the faint glow of a light. Fairbethia stood and staggered across the bridge; the wooden planks groaned under her feet. As soon as she set foot off the bridge the fog lifted. To her amazement a quaint cottage lay nestled in the middle of a clearing. It was surrounded by well-manicured gardens. The light she had seen in the fog came from a lantern that hung by the door of the cottage. She could see smoke rise from the chimney.

Fairbethia welled up with emotion and tears blurred her eyes as she made her way to the door. Thinking only of her plight and the need for food and shelter, she knocked hastily on it and cried out hoarsely for help. To her surprise a tall, darkly handsome, young man answered; Erebos in his human form. Knowing right away that Fairbethia was the one who could break the spell, he welcomed her in. At her wits end, Fairbethia did not care if he was the dark entity that the elders had often spoke of; he was young and handsome, and his home was warm and lit with scented candles.

In the middle of the room was a table laden with all manner of food and drink. Erebos helped Fairbethia find a seat at the table where she ate and drank until she could not eat or drink anymore. Just after thanking Erebos for his kindness she fainted from the fever that ravished her body. There she dwelled in and out of consciousness for well over a month while Erebos nursed her back to health. Once she recovered, he wooed her with song, kindness and loving words. Fairbethia fell helpless to Erebos' charms and soon gave her love to him; unconditionally.

The spell was broken, but not even Ardrich could predict what happened next; Erebos had fallen in love. While tending to Fairbethia then wooing her, he grew to understand why Ardrich had been so angered with him. Erebos forgave Ardrich for leaving him stranded on the moors and Ardrich accepted graciously. Erebos now had a difficult choice to make; stay with Fairbethia and forsake his lineage or go home to his mother. Even though he knew his mother's wrath would be fierce, Erebos chose Fairbethia.

When Chaos learned of her son's decision, to say she was extremely displeased was mild in comparison to how she really felt. After all, Erebos was the Lord of Darkness not a troubadour for love. Beside herself with fury, Chaos set off a great explosion that rocked the land surrounding the moors for five thousand miles; nearly destroying it. As it were, countless fires raged across the land in every direction and many lives were lost. The one place that was not touched by the fires was the moors; Erebos' love for Fairbethia had protected it. This made Chaos livid beyond all accounts. Instead of trying to reason with her son, Chaos sent the fires south. If Erebos wanted to live like a mortal, he would do so in a world that was blackened with ash.

However, the Light of Goodness protected this part of the world. Within it lived a Great Tree that had been there since the beginning of time. The Tree was a symbol of faith, kindness and love; all the things that man holds dearest to his heart during his darkest hours. To destroy The Tree would destroy the hopes of man.

Before the fires could make their way south, the Light of Goodness sent his most trusted earthly advisor, Faywyn, to watch over it. She and her seven daughters had been living in the Valley of NeDe; a sacred place that the evil of man had not touched. The hidden valley was located between the northern and southern mountain ranges that divided the world in half. Faywyn and her daughters lived in a Crystal Cave in Mount Aspentonia. They watched over the valley and the three forgotten tribes of old; the Elfkins that lived in the Greenwood Forest, the Meadow Imps from the Outer Bound Meadow and the Tara Aquians of Lake Kellowash.

Not wanting to leave the valley unprotected, the sisters carved a likeness of themselves out of white crystals and placed them in the walls of the Crystal Cave. Faywyn then enchanted each of the statues with a powerful magic that protected not only the cave from evil, but the valley as well. Only a friend of the lost tribes could enter the valley. As long as the statues remained in the Crystal Cave no harm by outside influences could fall upon it. Over time the valley became lost to man and unknown by all but who lived within it.

Faywyn and her daughters quickly traveled to the southern hemisphere. Upon reaching it they found the Great Tree sitting on a hill overlooking a vast valley. They named The Tree the Whipple Wash Tree and named the valley after it. They made a home in The Tree and casted a spell over it as well as the valley, protecting both from the fires. Seeing this, Chaos became even more enraged and began to plot her revenge against the Light of Goodness.

As for Fairbethia and Erebos, Chaos could not destroy them; their love protected them from her wrath. She instead conjured up a pair of white birds with eyes made from the shards of a looking glass. Whatever they saw would reflect back to her through a mirrored orb. She then transported the diurnal doves, as she so called them, to the moors where they nested in a tree by the cottage. Through them Chaos spied on Erebos and Fairbethia who were none the wiser and thought the birds' early morning cooing was enchanting. Chaos watched and waited for the most opportune time to exact revenge not only on her son for his betrayal; but on Ardrich as well.

While the years went by, the land surrounding the moors healed and man repopulated it. For twenty-five years they lived blissfully in love in the cottage. Erebos' time with Fairbethia had been the happiest he'd ever experienced, however the happiness would not last. On her fortieth birthday Fairbethia gave birth to a healthy son. But like her mother before her, she died giving birth. Erebos, so distraught with the loss of his love, buried her beneath the stone floor of the cottage and sat upon it for three days while his infant son lay in his cradle. Through the eyes of the doves Chaos saw her son's weakness for the mortal woman and was disgusted by it.

In the dead of night Chaos came to the cottage. While the child looked on from his cradle she killed Erebos where he sat. Chaos then turned to the child and raised her hand to smite him down, but the child showed no fear. Instead he looked back at her with a calculating stare. Chaos looked closer; the child had eyes as dark as the night. They were rimmed with red and no light of life shone from their depths. Chaos grinned wickedly; the mortal child had her eyes. A plan quickly formed in her mind. While she could not destroy the world because the First Law forbade it, a mortal could wreak havoc upon it. With that thought Chaos put her plan into action.

She picked the child up, walked out of the cottage and called to the doves. They flew down from their perch in the tree and landed at her feet where they immediately bowed in reverence to their maker. Chaos then turned the pair of them into mortals. Two maidens stood before her. They had black hair to match their glass glazed eyes. They wore long flowing white robes. She named them Ibisha and Egreta and handed the child to them, who they took with great care. They would raise the child as their own and through their eyes Chaos would watch his progress.

Chaos then burned the cottage to the ground, with Erebos in it. With the ashes she raised a great fortress that she called Pherangull and gave the child all the land that once belonged to his mortal grandfather. Through Chaos' tutorage the child, who she named Gregor Canvil, would become the wickedest blight that had ever been set upon the land. Man would come to fear the dark eyed child who would grow to become known as Lord Canvil from the Moors of Erebos. He and his sons would become the misfortune of man for three thousand years as they methodically took over the Northern Kingdoms.

All was not lost however, for the Whipple Wash Tree still held within it the hope of mankind. The Light of Goodness had watched over the land and had put his own plans into action. It had started with placing Faywyn and her daughters in the valley. They watched over and protected The Tree. But the influence of Chaos was resilient and the will of man waned as Canvil grew stronger.

Seeing this, the Light of Goodness initiated the second step in his plan to vanquish Chaos from this world. From the arms of The Tree four fairies of light were born with a fifth for good measure. Young and lively, they knew their purpose and understood their place in the greater scheme of things; one day they would war against Canvil for the sanctity of mankind. However doubt and fear trailed after them for they were like mortals, with all the complicated nuances that a human embodies. They questioned, when the time came, if they would be ready to take up arms against a formidable foe. Would they be enough to save mankind when dark shadows from Erebos had already perpetrated their borders, capturing the souls of men one at a time? Would they, with the Light of Goodness within them, be able to stop Canvil from taking over the world before the war even began?

Chapter 1
The Wickedest Blight of Mankind

Nestled deep within a forest, in a valley surrounded by mountain ranges sat the charred remains of a once quaint village. Earlier that year it had been inhabited by a humble race of man that was small in stature; most adults only grew to be three to five feet tall. They had pointed ears, a pointed nose and large eyes. They were called Elfkins and had lived modestly in round huts with peeked grass thatched roofs. They survived on vegetables and various fruits that they grew in their well-tended gardens, as well as fish from the river. For the most part they were a happy lot that got along well with each other. With the influence of the Council of Elders, they stuck with tradition and rarely waivered from the way their ancestors had lived for thousands of years. They were also a naive race and believed that they were the only ones that survived a catastrophic event that killed everyone else in their world. However, the tides of change had proven that wrong and now standing in the middle of the village was the wickedest blight of mankind.

"What do you mean...he's gone?!" Lord Canvil roared ferociously. The sound that erupted from him rumbled through the Elfkin village like thunder across a turbulent sky. Even though the night before the Fall Equinox was clear and the breeze warm, the people surrounding him shivered as if they had just been doused with a bucket of ice water. The clearing became quiet as all eyes were on Canvil and what he would do next. Calm he was intimidating; in anger he was downright frightening. He clenched his fist in anger; he did not like it when things did not go as planned.

Lord Gregor Canvil stood eight and half feet tall, towering over many of his men. His muscular body was clothed in dark pants and tall leather boots that were laced up the front. A small dagger nestled in a pocket in his right boot; only the shiny silver hilt could be seen. His hair flowed in a wavy brown mass to his shoulders. His passively handsome facial features looked like they had been chiseled from stone. His shirtless chest expanded as he took a deep breath; behind it beat a heart of pure evil.

It was his eyes however that were the most intimidating aspect about him. In anger they could freeze you to the very spot you stood on with unrequited fear. They were blacker than the night sky and rimmed with red. However, no light of life twinkled from them. It was said that they had been conjured from the murky depths of darkness by Chaos herself. In the heat of battle, his eyes glow an eerie blood red.

Beside him with its tip stuck into the ground was the sword that he used to conquer his enemies. It was not like any other weapon, for it had a malevolent presence about it, as if a foul aura shrouded it in evil. His followers called it *Blood Thirst* in reverence to the thousands of lives it took without prejudice or mercy. Wielded with the right amount of strength, it could cut a full grown man in two with just one swipe.

The blade, made from the rarest of ore and unblemished black spiral crystals, was curved and thin as a piece of parchment. It was much like the ones his army carried, but it was at least twelve inches longer and three inches wider. The hilt of the sword was made of finely twisted black steel that Canvil himself fashioned to fit his hand perfectly. He was never seen without it. It either hung from his shoulder in a handmade leather scabbard or stuck in the ground as it was now, forever ready to battle at the blink of an eye and carry out with precision Canvil's intent.

Lord Canvil and his sword looked oddly out of place, standing as they were in the remains of the Elfkin village. Surrounding him was a third of his army; ruthless killers whom had become known as the Venom Horde. They too

2

looked out of place with their dark clothing, metal armored chest plates and shabby appearances. The trek to the valley had been strenuous. Even though they were seasoned warriors, they were only mortal after all and the hurried pace had taken its toll.

Some of the warriors had followed Canvil from the Castle Pherangull and the surrounding countryside. The others were from the lands that had been conquered by Canvil; men whom he personally had chosen to serve in his army over the alternatives; slavery or death. Not everyone that Canvil picked survived the *Ritual of Eradication*. It was a demonic ritual that lasted three weeks and nights. They were given a blue elixir that was conjured up by Padmoor Detera, Canvil's personal Alchemist. The elixir purged the intendant of all that they once were, leaving an empty canvas for Canvil to mold and manipulate into a merciless warrior.

The Venom Horde, three thousand fold, blindly followed Canvil as if they were sheep and he the herder. They carried out his orders with deadly accuracy; without remorse for the lives they took. Men, women, children; none were spared the wrath of Canvil and his army once he deemed them not worthy to follow him or enslave.

Canvil had been relentless in his desire to reach the Whipple Wash Valley and was eager to conquer it before winter set in. Theodoric the Oracle had foretold there would be a sudden change in the weather. Fierce winds would bring with it mountains of snow that would not let up till late spring. Although Canvil was fearless, not even he wanted to battle during a severe winter, so he pushed his men to near breaking point to reach the top of the mountain.

Canvil was disappointed however once they reached the top. The valley that lay on the other side of Mount Aspentonia was not the Whipple Wash Valley that he was told would be there. Rather it was a valley that was not marked on any of his maps, and he had in his possession every map drawn from the beginning of time. Canvil would not believe it existed if he had not seen it for himself. But there it was. A valley that time forgot stretched out before him, nestled between the mountain he stood on and the one he wanted to be standing on. He was helplessly ignorant of its knowledge, which did not bode well with him.

Canvil took pride in his intelligence, an innate ability that had taken him far. As a child he had been a quick learner and spoke complete articulate sentences before his first birthday. By his fifth birthday he was being tutored by the greatest scholars of the day; Count Artimus, the bi-speckled chubby Mathematician. He was never seen without a pastry in one hand and an abacus in the other. He had a nervous laugh that usually ended in him having a fit of hiccups afterward. And there was Lord Blodswell, the white haired Scientist whose face was horribly scarred from his first attempt at conjuring up a powerful explosive at the tender age of nine. He preferred to live in a small cottage on the outskirts of Burdanliegh- a large cluster of hamlets that surrounded the Moors of Erebos.

Canvil learned the history of the world through Samuel Green, who was deaf and unlike the others, had no distinguishing mannerism. He was a tall, spindly, grey haired fellow who stayed up most nights pouring over the books in the castle's extensive library. They all taught Canvil that knowledge was power and power over others was absolute.

The only teacher who contradicted the others' teaching was Sir George Stephen, the Philosopher from Drewand. Like Samuel, he had no distinguishing mannerism, but he vexed Canvil to no end. Unlike his other teachers, Sir George loved to debate. And every chance he could he corrected Canvil even if Canvil was correct. Often he and Canvil had heated arguments that went on for days. Normally they ended with Canvil breaking things when his tutor would not concede defeat.

Where knowledge gave Canvil the power over others, death by his sword gave him a passion that he could not contain. His first kill was at the age of fifteen. After a heated debate with Sir George which had lasted over a month, Canvil became so angry he cut off Sir George's head with just one swipe of a sword. Gregor's studies immediately ceased and were replaced with the art of sword play and battle strategies, which he learned quickly and with great skill. However, after killing Sir George, a dark shadow overcame his spirit and soon vagrants went missing from the villages that surrounded the moors. With each kill his heart steadily turned black until it was nothing more than a dark void in his chest. Chaos, with the help of Ibisha and Egreta, watched over him and kept him alive. And it had been that way for over three thousand years.

Canvil's cancerous thirst for power became unyielding. He had collected a mass fortune of gold, silver and rare jewels over the years. But that was not all. He also collected a menagerie of strange mythical creatures like: the fireflies from the Forest of Spingal that traveled with him in fire proof cages; miniature gold horned whales from the North Kasala Sea that he kept in great glass holding tanks in Pherangull; and Sanival, the rare white tigress from the snowcapped Kieroo Mountains, which he kept chained in his bedroom. The animals and riches was not what he treasured most however; it was the spiritual artifacts he collected that were his cherished possessions. The Gilded Hand of The Hawthorn Springs was just such a treasure. Yet it vexed him like nothing else he owned, for he could not unlock its powers nor could Padmoor or Theodoric.

This minor setback had his temper simmering beneath the surface. He recklessly quickened the pace down the mountainside eager to know whether the one that they also sought was in the valley below. It had taken them a month to journey down the sometimes shear slope and he had lost two dozen men in the process. His men became anxious with each passing day. The nearer they got to the base of the mountain the stranger, for lack of a better word, the scenery became. A more appropriate word might be eerie, weird or unnatural because on this side of the mountain there were no signs of wildlife anywhere. There had been plenty of trees, shrubs and flowers, but not one bug or bird to speak of, let alone a rabbit or two.

The men were seasoned warriors, however they were also a suspicious lot; a byproduct of the blue elixir. The absence of wildlife had them muttering amongst themselves of evil spirits. It didn't help that Canvil had brought with them two prisoners, one being a witch woman who took glee in staring the men down and muttering curses under her breath as she walked by them. The men quickly learned to stay clear of her. The other was a captive that Canvil kept continuously under armed guard along with the witch woman. No one quite understood why- she was an elderly woman who looked kindly and not very menacing. But then Canvil never did anything without strategic purpose.

With no game to catch the men were near starving and quite tired of trying to survive on dried fruit and smack cakes; a hard dough dumpling that they baked, boiled or pan-fried. The cakes could keep for several months wrapped in a lightly weaved cloth but had no taste to them and little nutritional value. They were meant to be served with a stew not to be eaten on their own. They were happy that they had made it to the valley floor. They hoped there were at least mushrooms or wild berries to eat even if there was no wild game to catch.

Rishtoph, Canvil's youngest son and leader of the scouting party that he had sent out months ago, stood before him. Out of two hundred and twenty five sons, only two survived, Rishtoph and his older brother Jaja. The others had died in battle or from old age. Rishtoph and Jaja and been the lucky ones. They were both over five-hundred years old, but did not look a day over twenty-five. They aged slowly like their father. That however was where the similarities ended between the brothers; who had been born from different mothers, as had all of Canvil's children.

Rishtoph was tall, spindly, had blond hair and fine facial

features, except for his nose which looked like Canvil's. His nose however was not the only thing he inherited from his father; Rishtoph also had his despicable demeanor; foul, conniving and ruthless.

Jaja, on the other hand, was tall, muscular, had good looking dark features, and an easy likable disposition, which he inherited from his mother. Like Rishtoph, Jaja had his father's nose, but he also inherited his supreme intelligence and his drive to succeed.

Lord Canvil favored Jaja over Rishtoph and made no bones about that fact, which didn't sit right with Rishtoph. Over the years that knowledge turned to bitterness towards his bother and hatred for his father. One day he would rectify it; he had sights on ruling the empire. So when Rishtoph stood before his father he did not cower from his anger; he instead used it to fuel his hatred for him. Half the scouting party stood behind Rishtoph. The rest of them were nowhere in sight. Canvil, to Rishtoph's surprise, suppressed his anger, but he had a feeling that he was not going to like what his son had to say next.

"Father.... my Lord" Rishtoph quickly corrected himself as Canvil did not permit his son's to call him father in front of his army. He preferred instead that they call him My Lord, My King or Your Grace. "After we arrived we interrogated the villagers, Elfkins they're called. They're a small statured clan like those of the Kengco Valley. We learned that many of them had already fled to the south." Rishtoph continued, "As did all of the forest creatures."

Canvil looked around for the villagers that he spoke of and seeing none, his left eyebrow rose in question. Rishtoph understood the expression and said without emotion, "They did not survive the interrogation." He then inclined his head to a dark charred mass at the far end of the ransacked village. Canvil, if curious or pleased about this information, did not show it outwardly and Rishtoph provided no other explanation. His silence and blank stare however spoke

7

volumes. Lord Canvil, understanding his sons better than anyone, knew that Rishtoph had more to say, but would not do so in front of the others; he taught them well.

Canvil looked around the clearing and barked out orders, "Don't just stand around; you know what needs to be done." The men did not want to be near their liege when he exploded and started to scatter. Rishtoph however stayed them with his voice.

"There is still fish in the river," he said pointing east in the direction of the river. A small group of men started towards the river; smiles lit their weathered faces. "In that direction," he said pointing south towards the other end of the village, "you will find several vegetable patches and berry bushes growing amongst the trees." Another small group of men left in the direction of the vegetable patches, they too smiled. "And over there," he said pointing to a large pile of timber, "is the wood to make your huts with. We have already started to build some in a clearing to the west of us." The remaining men walked back to the foot of the mountain to pick up the backpacks, the cages of fireflies and the prisoners; their steps were quick and light with anticipation. All of them were excited with the thought of having fish and vegetable stew for their evening meal. There would be no smack cakes on anyone's plate that night.

"Your Grace," Rishtoph addressed his father. "Please follow me I have set up your quarters over here." Canvil followed his son out of the village and through the woods to a large clearing just south of the village. There stood a large structure that had massive wooden doors. Canvil would learn that it was once the Elfkins' Gathering Hall.

A large wooden bed with a thick matt stood against the wall on the left side of the hut and faced into the room. On the back wall, a second door opened to a large bathing shed with a shuttered window and a door that led outside. Further down the back wall was an enormous stone fireplace. Hanging from a hook was a large black pot filled to the brim with a savory stew that simmered over a small fire. On the wall to the right was a long bank of cupboards filled with provisions. In the middle of the room was a large wooden rectangular shaped table with seven chairs; one large chair sat at the head of it.

Rishtoph clapped his hands and two elderly maidens came out of the bathing chamber. They had been preparing a bath and readying the hut for their liege's arrival. Seeing Canvil they smiled with delight. Canvil's demeanor softened upon seeing them. Ibisha and Egreta walked over to him and bowed. They had not changed much over the years they had been in Canvil's household. Their faces had weathered only slightly and tiny signs of age dotted their hands. Their hair however was still long and black as the day they were created. They wore the same style dress on the day they had been given Canvil to care for; long, white and flowing. Much like his soldiers, Ibisha and Egreta blindly did their master's bidding without complaint.

They often traveled ahead with the scouting parties making sure that Canvil's quarters were prepared properly. Rishtoph looked at them with disgust then dismissed them rudely. He never understood why his father kept them. They rarely said anything, nor did they do anything other than make sure that Canvil's quarters were readied the way that he liked. To Rishtoph, they served no purpose; there were a bevy of young maidens who could do their job. No one knew however that through them Chaos watched her grandson's progress. Not even Canvil knew that his guardians served a greater purpose. Canvil dismissed them with a gentle hand on their shoulders. They left for their own sleeping quarters, which were in one of the few Elfkin huts that remained standing.

Although Canvil was hungry and in desperate need of a bath, he knew that what his son had to tell him was more important. However, his thirst could not wait. He spied a large vat of honey mead on the counter. He walked over to it, poured himself a mug, and drank it down in one gulp. He poured himself another, walked to the table and sat down at the head of it; looking at his son expectantly.

Rishtoph chose to stand rather than join his father at the table and began his tale of all that had transpired since his arrival in the Elfkin village. He told him of how they tracked the deserting Elfkins through the forest and of the young boy they came across who had been following the path that the others had left. Canvil was not surprised to hear that they befriended the boy and kept him safe from harm as they traveled through the meadow. Canvil listened intently to every word his son said about the creatures in the meadow that had not fled like the others, as well as the carnivorous fish that lived in puddles. He didn't even twitch an eye when he heard that they offered the boy up for bait and threw him into one of those puddles to distract the Elfkins while they crept up on them. Lord Canvil continued to listen in silence, even when Rishtoph told him that the Elfkins got away on watercrafts that carried them across the lake to the mountains on the other side.

Rishtoph hesitated for a moment. He cleared his throat and took a deep breath that wavered as he exhaled. Canvil picked up the subtle change. He realized that there was more to hear of the tale. He knew he was not going to like this part. The anger he had kept in check thus far started to simmer beneath the surface just as the stew was simmering in the pot over the fire.

"There… are… others… that live in this valley," Rishtoph said slowly, trying to gage his father's reaction to this news. Seeing none, he continued quickly, "They are men-like creatures who live beneath the water and swim like fish, but can walk on land. They are as tall as we are- some even taller." A vision of Duntar and Kerchot flashed before his eyes. "They are cunning warriors like nothing we have ever come across before. They have foiled every attempt we have made to cross the water. Half of the scouting party lay dead at the bottom of the lake because of them."

"And of the one we seek," Canvil's left eyebrow lifted as he asked. "Where is he?"

"Like I said earlier, he is not here. I did not see him. He either perished on the journey here or fled across the lake with the others." Rishtoph stared straight ahead. His assignment was simple; he was to capture the Hummingmoth Messenger that got away before it reached the Whipple Wash Valley and raised an alarm, but he had failed. He waited for what he knew would come. However, when it didn't, Rishtoph looked at his father with a surprised expression on his face which he quickly masked. Lord Canvil was not known for his tolerance towards failure and often would personally beat those who failed to carry out his orders.

Canvil stood abruptly and scraped the legs of the chair he was sitting on across the stone floor. He walked with long commanding strides to the door and threw it open. The heavy wooden door crashed against the wall, fell off its hinges and clattered loudly to the floor. Canvil's fists were clenched tightly and his jaw twitched with anger as he walked back through the forest to the Elfkin village. Upon reaching it, he bellowed so that all could hear, "Bring me the Witch Woman!"

Chapter 2
Summeria the Witch Woman

As Summeria entered the clearing, she could hear catcalls coming from a group of Venom Horde as she walked by. She stopped abruptly, turned back and glared at them in distaste. They chuckled openly at her. She quickly took a mental note of where they stood and how many there were.

The two guards who had been escorting her each grabbed an arm and pulled her forward. She stumbled, tripping awkwardly over her long dress as the guards roughly pushed her towards Lord Canvil. He grabbed her arm before she fell to the dirt at his feet and held on more tightly then was needed. She did not wince from the pain, but looked up at him boldly with no fear in her eyes. If he had been a lesser man, he would have quivered with fright from the depth of hatred and contempt that shone from them. Her piercing gaze could cut a man down to size just as quickly as the sharpened daggers holstered in his belt could.

Canvil did not miss the look of distain for him. He wondered if he was finally breaking through her thick exterior. If he had, then he would have control over her, as he did everyone else. He doubted that was the case. He released his vice like grip on her arm; she refrained from rubbing the pain away. She would not let him see that he had hurt her.

Summeria rarely showed her hatred and contempt for him, but he knew that it bubbled just below the calm and composed demeanor she portrayed outwardly. How could it not? Three summers ago he stole her from her family, her homeland, the only life she had ever known.

Lord Canvil and a small raiding party had come in search of Summeria after hearing about her powers from a Spiedrux. A Spiedrux is an advanced scout that travels to distant lands.

They enter a Kingdom with great stealth, gather as much information as they can and leave without anyone knowing they were there. The most cunning of them is called The Shadow. He was given the name not for his ability to hide, but for his fearlessness. Bold, cunning and a master of disguises, he infiltrates a Kingdom and becomes a citizen. He befriends the locals and settles in for months and sometimes years, gathering all the information he needs about their past, their riches as well as what their most treasured artifacts are and where they are hidden. He then takes the information back to Canvil who then strategizes his attack from the information that was collected.

Canvil remembered the day they had taken Summeria like it was yesterday. It was a clear sunny day in the middle of winter; snow lay all about as deep as his knee. They found her swimming in a pool that was heated by an underground spring. She had left her village with no guard that day and was only accompanied by three maidens. It had been easy enough, he mused, to steal her away. It was even easier to have her do his bidding as he had sent half of the scouting party, one hundred in total, back with the three maidens. They were to deliver Lord Canvil's simple message: follow, she dies. Try and rescue her, she dies. He held her prisoner not with chains and bars, but with the knowledge that if she did not do his bidding, his army would destroy her people. She did not know however that when this last crusade was finished, when he finally wielded infinite power with the Gilded Hand, he would return to her village and destroy her people while she watched helplessly by his side.

Canvil looked at her placid expression then looked her over from head to toe. Summeria was a tall, slender woman with fine dark features. She was lovely to behold. Her dark thick brown hair hung down passed her hips and was straight as an arrow. Her eyes were dark blue and an extra twinkle of light shone from them. Her dress, fawn brown in colour, was a simple fare that hugged her body. It had a V-shaped neckline; a white leather pouch hung from a thin leather strap around her neck. The sleeves of the gown were long, flowing and fringed at the end. She wore a thick dark brown braided belt around her waist. On her forehead, she wore a thin leathery strap that tied up at the back of her head. Three feathers, midnight blue in colour, were said to have been given to her by the fabled Blue Mystic Raven and hung down at varying lengths. Intertwined with the feathers were thin straps that had tiny white stones tied to them. The straps dangled down to her shoulders.

Her people were of the Baltic Fern Clan, a nomad tribe from the most northern Kingdom of Kanloopus. It is a barren land for most of the year, covered in snow deeper than the height at which Canvil stood. They hunted the mighty humped-back Mackilack, a giant beast that lives under the water and ice. Their homes were simple. They were much like the Elfkins' huts in shape, but were taller and wider. Rather than a large fortress that was surrounded by smaller hamlets, Kanloopus was a series of outposts of only a hundred or so inhabitants. The outposts were scattered all along the shores of the Northern Sea. The Baltic Fern Clan are kind, gentle and honorable people with great resilience. However, unbeknownst to Canvil, when crossed, they were just as determined for revenge as Canvil was determined to wield the power of the Gilded Hand.

Summeria or the witch woman, as Canvil called her, was not a witch at all; for witches conjured up spells and potions. She was in fact a spirit guide among her people, whose power derived from the living forces of nature. She was able to read the stars, speak with spirits, and manipulate nature to her will. She could also, with help from the bones of Baun Berlot the Great White Bear of the north, see into the future.

Although Baun Berlot had passed on centuries ago, his spirit lived on in the Alpha Stones. They were small white bones with fine etchings engraved into them. The etchings were coded symbols of the ancient language of the Baltic Fern

Clan and when deciphered properly could change the course of time. Summeria carried the bones in the pouch that she wore around her neck. She was the only one of her people, for six generations, who could decipher the coded messages and speak with Baun Berlot.

Lord Canvil looked once more at the leather bag before he spoke. "I thought you said he would be here," he said in a deep voice that was calm yet held an edge of evilness to it. He did not need to say more. Summeria knew of whom he spoke of. His followers curiously gathered around after he had called for the witch woman. They knew better than to be placated by his calm demeanor. Lord Canvil's wrath was at its worst when he spoke this way.

Several of them slowly backed away from him and the witch woman. Their movements did not go unnoticed by Canvil and he smirked inwardly as he looked around. It was good that they were afraid of him. Fear produced obedience and he would not tolerate any other way in ruling his lands or his people. They quivered at the mere sight of him. He reveled in their fear and fed off it greedily. There was only one who openly defied him and she stood before him, looking bored.

"I told you, if you remember correctly, that Baun Berlot said he had fled to the valley past the mountain ranges to the south. I did not say that he would be here when you arrived." If possible, Summeria looked even more bored as she brushed wayward strands of her lovely dark hair away from her face. Canvil's temper began to boil.

"You also said that Baun Berlot told you that the Whipple Wash Valley lay beyond that mountain," Canvil said evenly as he looked up at Mount Aspentonia.

"And I told you that if you ask vague questions you will receive vague answers," Summeria smirked before she continued. "Baun Berlot cannot read minds, nor can I."

"This is not the Whipple Wash Valley," Canvil said. His voice had become deeper.

"Well now that is stating the obvious, isn't it?" Summeria smiled at him cheekily.

Canvil's eyes grew darker and his jaw twitched with anger. Several of his men, who could see Canvil's face, stepped further away. Canvil however did not notice. He only had eyes for Summeria and her impertinence. Beneath the surface his anger began to seethe. "You said the Whipple Wash Valley lay beyond that mountain." This time he jabbed his hand in the air and pointed at Mount Aspentonia. His breath grew heavy and the ring of red around his pupils began to glow. Canvil clenched his hands into a fist.

"Yes," Summeria said, ignoring the signs that Canvil's patience for her impertinence was about to end. "And it would seem that one as well," Summeria pointed a dainty finger to the mountain range to the south of the valley. "Must I repeat myself?" She clicked her tongue and in mock amusement said, "I hate repeating myself." She heard gasps from the onlookers and smiled.

With all their power, all their strength, the members of the Venom Horde would never speak to Canvil in such a demeaning manner. But here she was, a petite woman openly mocking him in front of his men while he stood before her seething with anger. Turning back to Canvil her own eyes darkened with anger as she leaned towards him and said pointedly, "Vague questions, vague answers."

Canvil now enraged with fury quickly raised his arm, unfurled his fingers and struck Summeria across the face so hard she fell to the ground. Looking up at him with extreme hatred, Summeria slowly stood and unflinchingly glared at him. He watched as he had many times before, the cut and swollen lip that had quickly formed when he hit her just as quickly vanished before his eyes. That is why he called her a witch. No matter what he did to her, she healed within seconds and looked as if he had never touched her. A group of Venom Horde who had never seen this phenomenon in action before, but had heard about it in hushed whispers, looked warily at her as they took another step back.

The group of men who had catcalled after she had entered the clearing did not see her face change. They were standing behind her. They called out and clapped their hands in agreement that their liege had struck her down. They urged him to do it again. Those standing near the cheering men that had witnessed exchanges like this before quickly stepped away from them. They knew Summeria's response would be instant and without mercy.

Suddenly and without her even having to look their way, a loud crack sounded above the men's heads; her rebuttal was indeed swift. The men cried out in horror as an enormous limb from the oak tree they stood under fell on top of them. It knocked them to the ground, crushing them beneath its weight. One died instantly while the other five, with broken bones, would never look at Summeria quite the same way again.

The energy spent to carry out such a feat had Summeria feeling weak; she could no longer stand and crumpled to the ground. Canvil ordered the two guards to take her back to her quarters. The guards warily stepped forward and half dragged, half carried her back to the small hut that housed the prisoners. All the while they watched for falling limbs. They opened the door to the hut and gently placed her on one of two cots that had been set up on the far wall. They quickly left and joined the other two guards that had been assigned to watch over the prisoners.

Someone standing at the counter preparing the evening meal waited until the guards had closed the door securely behind them before she ran over to Summeria. Quietly, so that the guards could not hear, she scolded Summeria with a soft motherly tone. "Oh, dear why do you taunt him so? One of these days he is going to realize that he does indeed hurt you, and then what will you do?"

The other prisoner dipped a cloth into a bowl of cool medicated water. She had prepared it when Summeria was summoned; knowing that she would come back hurt. She placed the wet cloth on Summeria's face; Summeria winced. The instant healing she had shown Lord Canvil had been an illusion. Summeria could change her appearance at will, but only for short periods of time. Gradually over the years of confinement with Canvil she had learned how to stretch that time out, several hours in fact. It was not her powers of manipulating nature that left her weak, it was the beatings.

Summeria looked up at the kind woman who was tenderly and expertly administering to her injuries. Queen Faywyn of the Whipple Wash Valley was a practiced healer and Summeria was thankful for it. Her face would be back to normal by daybreak and Canvil would never know of her injury. Faywyn did not need to ask why Summeria conjured the illusion. She knew that it caused unrest among the Venom Horde and unrest bred doubt. It also meant that they were left alone, because most of them were too afraid of Summeria's powers to come near her.

"Why do you stay child, you have the means to leave," Queen Faywyn tried to reason with Summeria. "There is no need for you to stay. Canvil will not harm me; he needs me as a bargaining tool."

Summeria tried to smile but the pain was too great. Her words slurred as she slowly said, "Queen Faywyn, it is my destiny to see you home." Faywyn clicked her tongue in disgust and held up her hand trying to stop Summeria from saying what she had said several times before. However, Summeria continued, "I cannot leave until I have fulfilled my destiny."

Faywyn lowered her hand and looked sadly at Summeria; she wished her words were not truth, but she knew that they were. Rayley, one of the Seven Elders of Elsbrier, can speak with spirits. She told Faywyn that she would meet Summeria and go on a journey with her.

Faywyn clicked her tongue again. *Spirits can be so evasive with their predictions*, she thought angrily. *Why couldn't they just say, 'an evil Lord is coming, prepare for war'?* However, she knew better. There was something her and Summeria needed to learn or someone they needed to meet on this journey. It would all make sense at the end of it. *Things were never easy*, she mused. *Why could it not be clear at the beginning of the journey?*

Summeria winced again and whimpered as she succumbed to the pain; tears welled up in her eyes. Canvil had hit her very hard this time. Not only did her lip and cheek hurt, her ears rang and her head pounded.

"I must remember," she said to Faywyn as the tears poured from her eyes, "not to vex him so well next time." Her breath caught in her throat as she tried to laugh; she sobbed instead.

"Hush child," Faywyn soothed her kindly as she picked up a cup from the side table that sat between the two cots. She helped Summeria to sit then held the cup to her lips so that she could drink from it. Faywyn had put medication in the warm water. It would numb the pain; she wished she had a sleeping draught as well. "Why don't you rest while I prepare our supper, then we will have a talk," Faywyn hesitated as she looked at Summeria's swollen mouth. "Well, perhaps you can conjure up Baun Berlot for me and he and I will talk. I would like a word with him about this nonsense of fulfilling destinies."

Summeria smiled then chuckled lightly. *That would be quite the sight to see*, she thought to herself; Faywyn scolding Baun Berlot. Seeing that her words had the effect she was hoping for, Faywyn stood, smiled down at Summeria and nodded her head. Summeria, understanding that Faywyn was asking if she was alright, nodded her head in response. Faywyn patted Summeria's hand before she walked back to the counter to finish making their supper.

The white leather pouch on Summeria's necklace began to

vibrate slightly. Baun Berlot had heard everything and felt Summeria's pain. The stones began to heat; the warmth emitting from them encircled Summeria in a warm cocoon, and she fell contently asleep.

After cutting the meager helping of freshly picked vegetables that one of the guards had brought them, Faywyn asked Summeria if she would like smack cakes with their meal as well. Hearing no reply, she turned and was glad to see that Summeria was sleeping.

Faywyn picked up the vegetables and placed them in a pot of herbed water that had been simmering in the fireplace. As she stirred the soup, her thoughts turned to the Whipple Wash Fairies. Summeria was much like them, just as strong willed and impetuous. She wondered if they too would be just as fearless when confronted by Lord Canvil. She then wondered of the prophecy and hoped that the fairies had continued with their training. If not, all would be lost and Lord Canvil and his army would reign over all.

As she started to roll several smack cakes in dried herbs her thoughts turned to Jasper; sweet kind Jasper. Through Baun Berlot, Summeria had given Faywyn the message that it was a Hummingmoth Messenger that Lord Canvil sought. Faywyn instantly knew that it was Jasper who had gotten away. She also knew that he had warned the people of this village of the invading army and convinced them to leave with him. Faywyn said a quick prayer to the Light of Goodness that Jasper and the others, who trusted him enough to follow him, would make it safely to the Whipple Wash Valley.

Chapter 3
They're Coming

Deep within the Hollow of Rock that led from Lake Kellowash through the southern mountain ranges, the band of travelers fleeing for their lives from Lord Canvil looked hopeful at the returning scouting party. Rangous and Septer, from the Elfkin Clan and the leaders of the party, stood before Zusie. She could tell by their sullen expressions that their report was not going to be a good one.

The two month journey through the crevice, although dusty, had been uneventful and not unlike the Elfkins' trek through the Greenwood Forest. They walked all day and only rested at night. If they were to survive, they needed to gain as much distance between them and the invading army. On the onset of their journey the crevice had been fifty feet in width and was easy to travel through. Now however it had narrowed down to just ten feet wide and was littered with large boulders that took up most of the pathway. To pass, they would have to climb over the boulders. It would not be a difficult task for the Tara Aquians; they were between six to eight feet tall and quite muscular. Nor would the Meadow Imps find it difficult; they were quite small, many of them were less than a foot tall. Being so tiny they would be able to squeeze or duck through the space between the boulders and the crevice wall. The Elfkins however would find scaling the large boulders quite difficult and they were too large to squeeze their bodies through the spaces.

"Well?" Zusie enquired.

"It goes on for a couple more days, and then bends," Rangous said as Septer nodded in agreement beside him. Rangous was the strongest and tallest of the Elfkins at five feet six inches. He and Septer, who was just a bit shorter, were best mates. Zusie respected them. They had also become quite fond of her and her daughters. They had something else to tell her, but didn't know how to put it into words so they both looked away from her instead.

Zusie, although she didn't think of herself as their leader, was the one that everyone turned to for guidance, took direction from and reported to. She was not an Elfkin. She had by chance or good fortune fled to the valley when she was but a child. She was tall and had long white hair, blue eyes and didn't age like the Elfkins did. No one knew for sure how old she was, but she and the others surmised that she was at least seven hundred years old.

Zusie sighed heavily. The journey through the Hollow of Rock had taken longer than any of them thought it would. The lack of vegetation of any kind had everyone's nerves on edge. All they saw day after day was grey; grey rocks, grey dirt and grey dust, and now great grey boulders. They couldn't turn back; surely Lord Canvil had made it to the valley. He might have even found a way across the lake and past the Tara Aquians who had volunteered to stay, giving the rest more time to get away.

Their food and water supply had been rationed on the offset. They had enough to see them through for another month. What they would do for food after that, they were not sure. Hopefully they would be on the other side of the mountain long before then. She thought frantically about what they were going to do about the boulders.

Zusie looked at a group of Tara Aquians who stood with Lindrella, their princess and her parents Queen Gando and King Aldus. They smiled at her and she returned it in kind. They were faring well considering that they had not been in water since leaving the lake. The Tara Aquians were amphibious. Before fleeing with the Elfkins, they lived in a series of caves in the mountain. Their home was called the Golden City of Awnmorielle. The Tara Aquians watched over Lake Kellowash. Besides speaking a language other than

Elfish, they could also converse with their minds. Lindrella had taught Zusie's twin daughters Saphina and Chrystalina to speak her language, which they picked up quickly. Saphina and Chrystalina in turn taught it to any Elfkin who wanted to learn it.

Zusie looked over to her left. Zeander, a Meadow Imp who rode on the back of a Great Oba snake named Paraphin, looked thoughtfully at her. Zeander was the leader of his people. They looked like Elfkins, but they had thick accents and rolled their "R's" dramatically. Zusie mused to herself as she looked fondly at Zeander; he would have been the better person to tutor the Elfkins, because he was quite fluent in both languages. Unfortunately Zeander did not have the temperament to teach. Zusie's smiled widened as Zeander jumped off of Paraphin's back and walked over to Lillian, his mate, and gave her a warm hug.

Zusie watched as Paraphin slithered over to a small group of forest creatures who were standing with their leader Bauthal. Bauthal was a badger. He, like the rest of the forest creatures, could speak Elfish. They, as always, fared better than the rest of the travelers. Nothing seemed to bring them down or tire them out. It had been that way from the moment they set out from the Elfkin village and the Greenwood Forest. Zusie often saw the forest creatures giving the wee Meadow Imps a ride along the path. They were so small it was difficult for them to keep up with the others. Bauthal, she noticed, was the only one of the creatures that learned to speak the Tara Aquian language.

What could they do about the boulders, she wondered? The flying forest creatures could have flown up ahead to see what was around that bend, but Zusie and the others thought it best for them to fly to the western and eastern mountain ranges instead. They carried with them Jasper's message of the invading army and were to share it with all they came across. They had left before the first group of travelers had made their way across Lake Kellowash.

She looked up at Jasper as he made his way to Saphina. As she watched him flutter down and sit on her shoulder, Zusie thought they could send him. But if something should happen to him; Zusie did not want to think about the consequences. Jasper was no bigger than the size of a man's hand. He looked very much like a large moth with a black and brown stripped body; the Greenwood Forest had been full of them, but not as big as Jasper. That however is where the similarity ended. Jasper had a very long thin snout that curled up and sat just below his eyes. His eyes were large and his mouth was full of even, tiny, white teeth. If that were not strange enough he also had hairy arms and legs that had fingers and toes at the ends of them.

Instead of asking Jasper to fly up ahead, Zusie stood quiet for a moment longer, trying to think of a way out of their present predicament. They had all been through so much. How much more could they endure before they called it quits? She was their leader, by no ambition of her own, but she was all the same. She mustered up a smile, but was at a loss for words. Seeing her difficulty, Janilli, Zusie's half-sister who had been living among the Tara Aquians since she was a child, stepped forward. She spoke loud enough for the ones standing nearest to them to hear, who in turn would spread the orders to the others.

"Let's make camp early and over our evening meal we will discuss what the best course of action is." Her words carried quickly through the caravan. Camp was made ready, even though there was still enough daylight to travel on for another hour or so.

Zusie smiled a thank you at Janilli. She was a valued member among the Tara Aquians and now too among the Elfkins. The discovery that they were sisters, whose father was the very same man that they were fleeing from, was difficult for Janilli and Zusie to digest at first. However, they had come to terms with it and now it was as if they had always known each other. The sisters however, were as different as night and day. Where Zusie was regal in stature and mannerisms, Janilli was earthy and had panache for dressing unlike anyone else in the caravan. She wore sleeveless shirts, long flowing skirts, bangles on both of her wrists and most days she walked in her bare feet. Although the sisters had the same nose, which they inherited from their father, Janilli's features were much darker than Zusie's and her hair was plaited in tiny braids that hung down her back. On very hot days she pulled the braids up into a bun and wore a colourful scarf on her head to keep the braids in place. Their mothers had been from different Kingdoms. Unfortunately neither of them knew which Kingdoms they were as neither of them had memory of their mothers, let alone their homelands.

Zusie sighed heavily once more before she found her voice. She thanked the scouting party who disbursed immediately and sought out their families Next she made her apologies to her daughters and Janilli, stating that she needed to see how Lizbeth was doing, but added that she would be back to share the evening meal with them. The three of them looked sadly at her as she walked away. The weight of responsibility was wearing on her, but they did not know how to ease it.

Lizbeth was the Keeper of the Woods before she fell ill. Jasper had bumped into her the night he arrived in the Elfkin village; the sting of a Hummingmoth is fatal without the antidote. The only antidote Jasper knew of was in Elsbrier with Orliff, the village healer. Although the venom had taken its time, a full moon rotation and then some, Lizbeth had eventually fallen into a coma-like state. To make her journey bearable they had built her a small trolley that also held the ancient scrolls, statues that they had found in the crystal cave and Aldwin's supply of medicine. The wheels of the trolley churned up the dry dirt on the path, creating large clouds of dust in its wake. The first day on the path they decided that it should bring up the rear. Zusie now wished the trolley was much closer as she had to pass everyone before she reached it. Although most of the Elfkins smiled encouragingly at her there was one who treated her as if it were her fault that they were fleeing for their lives. Paramo glared at Zusie as she walked by her, but said nothing about this latest drawback. She had been a thorn in Zusie's side since they had left the village.

Zusie paid her no mind as her thoughts trailed to Lizbeth's health. Lizbeth was Zusie's dearest friend. They had been keeping her alive with a Soothe Ease potion that Aldwin, the village healer, had concocted for her. They mixed it into a vegetable broth and fed it to her three times a day. Marla, Aldwin's apprentice, Chrystalina and Zusie exercised Lizbeth's limbs every day to keep her muscles toned. They hadn't given up hope that she would survive the long journey to Elsbrier. As Zusie came up to the last family of travelers, Mirabella, the mother, spoke to her. Mirabella was best friends with Marla, Rangous' mate. She and Pothos had seven underlings all under the age of nine summers old.

"Can you ask them to hold it down please; their arguing is scaring my youngest one," Mirabella said. Zusie looked down and indeed Mirabella's little one looked scared as tears filled her eyes. The rest of her underlings and Pothos were nowhere in sight.

Zusie looked over at who Mirabella spoke of. Several paces away standing beside Lizbeth's trolley was Barton, a Tara Aquian, and Marla. They were glaring at each other. It looked quite comical Zusie mused as she walked towards them. Barton was quite tall and very muscular; he was bent down looking at Marla who came up just past his waist. She however was standing her ground and did not fear him. Barton had taken it upon himself to watch over Lizbeth. He had carried Lizbeth up the great stone stairs that led to the Hollow of Rock and often pulled her trolley on his own. Once he learned the Elfkin language he often talked to Lizbeth as he pulled her trolley. When he thought no one else was looking, he would lean over and pat her hand or kiss her on the forehead. He had been in the scouting party with Rangous and Septer and must have come back to tell Lizbeth what they had seen.

"Don't be so silly. It was the wind you heard," Marla said.

Barton was about to say something when he realized that they were no longer alone. He looked over at Zusie as she walked towards them.

"Am I interrupting something?" Zusie asked looking from Marla to Barton. He stiffened and stood his full height and nodded at Marla. Marla cleared her throat before she looked apologetically at Zusie.

"Barton said that he just now heard Lizbeth muttering. I told him that it wasn't possible...." Marla abruptly stopped what she was saying as Zusie quickly stepped by her and climbed into the trolley. She sat down and looked closely at Lizbeth. She was still and didn't look any different then she had the last time Zusie saw her, which was during the morning meal.

"What did she say?" Zusie asked quickly.

"Surely Zusie, you don't think she spoke," Marla said.

"What did she say?" Zusie repeated harshly. Zusie never told anyone that Lizbeth had spoken once before. They were still in the Meadow Imps' village readying to cross the lake. Duntar, Barton's brother, had given Rangous a summoning whistle to practice on. The noise had been loud enough to disturb Lizbeth who sat upright and spoke. That was the first and last time however, until now.

"Well go on, tell her what you think you heard her say," Marla said. Seeing Zusie's response she now knew that it must be true.

"There'd com ingh," Barton said in broken Elfish. Zusie gasped as she looked anxiously from Barton to Marla. She had heard 'they're coming' before. Benly, a small Elfkin underling, had once spoken them. They had rescued Benly after Rishtoph or one of his men had thrown Benly into a muddle puddle. Muddle puddles are home to the pigmy muddle fish. They are small fish with sharp teeth that eat flesh and bone. Before she

27

could utter her worries that Lord Canvil was catching up to them, Bauthal came running up to the trolley.

"Zusie come quick, its Janilli," Bauthal said breathlessly.

Zusie jumped down from the trolley and she and Barton hurriedly ran after Bauthal, leaving Marla to tend to Lizbeth. The villagers looked up anxiously as they passed by and yelled after them, but they did not stop until they reached the head of the caravan.

Chrystalina and Saphina looked fearfully down at Janilli, who was sitting on the ground staring forward blankly. Aldwin had kneeled down in front of her; his left hand was on her forehead while his checked her pulse. She continued to stare blankly at Aldwin. Lindrella, Rangous, Septer, Zeander and Paraphin stood around looking tensely at the scene before them. Aldwin stood up and stepped to the side. Zusie instantly took his spot and held onto Janilli's hands. They were stone cold and Zusie looked up at Aldwin. All he could do was shrug his shoulders.

"What happened," Zusie said looking at her daughters.

"She just plopped down on the ground," Saphina said. "One minute we were talking and the next she was on the ground."

"That's it?" Zusie exclaimed.

"Yes," Saphina said as she looked at the others who all nodded their heads in agreement. "Like I said, we were just talking about what our next step should be and the next thing we know Janilli was on the ground. Her face was set in stone and she went rigid."

"Did Desamiha come forth?" Zusie asked as she continued to hold onto Janilli's hands.

"No," Saphina and Chrystalina said in unison. Desamiha the Truth Sayer often came forth to give messages to truth seekers. It was a special ability that Janilli had had from as long back as she could remember. She usually only came forward when prompted by Janilli. Once before however, she had come forward with no warning. It was the same day

Lizbeth had spoken. Zusie looked at her sister with great concern.

"Janilli, Janilli." Zusie called to her anxiously, but Janilli did not blink an eye nor move.

"What should we do?" Chrystalina asked. She was almost in tears.

"I don't know," Zusie whispered. She then looked up at Aldwin. He just shook his head as there was nothing he could do; she was breathing slowly, but normally and looked fine for all intended purposes, other than the blank stare and cold hands. "Why don't we grab a blanket for her," Zusie said as Janilli's hands had not warmed from Zusie holding them, "and set a fire near her to keep her warm. I think we will have to wait this one out."

A small fire was quickly lit and the others sat around it, occasionally looking at Janilli. An hour had gone by. They were finishing their meager meal when Janilli threw back her head. She then screamed up into the night sky before shielding her head with her arms as she moaned pathetically.

Everyone sitting around jumped up, grabbed their weapons and looked about frantically. Zusie ran over to her sister. "Janilli, Janilli!" Zusie shook Janilli's shoulders roughly. Janilli stopped moaning and looked pathetically at Zusie.

"They're coming," Janilli said in a ghostly whisper. Zusie and Barton looked at her in shock as she repeated the words that Barton had thought he heard Lizbeth say earlier.

"Who is coming?" Zusie asked. Janilli's head and shoulders slumped down, and did not speak another word as she tried to catch her breath.

Zusie looked frightfully at Saphina and Aldwin. They had been there the night the Venom Horde had thrown Benly into the muddle puddle and remembered his words. Aldwin looked at Rangous and Septer, who had heard the story. They nodded at Aldwin and picked several men from a group to scout the area. The rest were ordered to wake every male old enough to carry a weapon and stand guard.

An hour went by before they heard the footsteps of the scouting party. As Rangous and the others passed the villagers they frantically called after them for news, but they did not stop until they reached Zusie and the others. A half hour away, the trail through the crevice gradually slopped downward. It was still light enough out. If anyone was following them they would have seen them or at least their campfires. However, they had not seen anything. No one was following them, that they could see.

"Well?" Zusie asked impatiently.

"There is nothing," Rangous shook his head. Everyone standing around sighed heavily in relief. "We left a group of Tara Aquians to guard the back of the caravan just in case."

"I wonder," Zusie said, "if she was dreaming of the future." Zusie looked down at her sister who had slowly composed herself. Her words did not make any of them feel better.

Barton, standing beside Rangous, said quietly to him "I thunk we shud tell dem whad wed found." Rangous looked up at him and shook his head slightly. He wasn't sure that was the wisest decision, even though they would find out sooner or later. Zeander heard what Barton said and elbowed Rangous in the knee, nodding his head in agreement.

Rangous stepped forward, "I think we should scout ahead," he said slowly. Zusie and the others looked at them questioningly, but it was Saphina who spoke.

"Why?" She asked suspiciously. "You scouted the path earlier today. Did you see something?"

"There were sign..." Rangous picked his words carefully. But before he could finish, Saphina rudely interrupted.

"What?!" She cried loudly. "Why didn't you tell us this when you first got back?"

"Lower your voice!" Rangous said harshly. He looked around to see if the others had heard her. Aldwin stepped beside Saphina, put his arm around her shoulders, and looked crossly at Rangous. Aldwin and Saphina were mates and were expecting their first child. Aldwin was very protective of her.

Rangous sighed heavily. "I am sorry Saphina," he said quietly. Saphina nodded her head, accepting his apology. Giving no explanation as to why they hadn't mentioned it before, he spoke to them quietly. "There were," he hesitated, "signs that perhaps we are not alone." The others looked quizzically at him then quickly up at the sheer rock that towered above them. Not knowing how else to break it to them he said quickly, "About a half an hour away there are bodies that have been crushed under rock." Everyone looked at them in surprise.

"Who are they?" Zusie said looking around frantically. She had been preoccupied with how to get over the boulders, she didn't wonder if all of the scouting party had made it back safely earlier that day.

"No, Zusie it is not one of us," Rangous said. Zusie and the others sighed heavily again, but wondered who it could be. Seeing that Rangous was having a difficult time telling Zusie what they had found, Aldwin stepped forward.

"By their bone structure they look to be Elfkins, Zusie." He then walked over to her and took her hands in his. "I am sorry," he whispered to her. He then walked over to Saphina and hugged her gently. Zusie's breath caught in her throat and she looked quickly towards the path that led through the crevice. Tears welled up in her eyes as her thoughts immediately went to her mate Willham. He and Lizbeth's mate Horman had left the village in search of Zusie's homeland, but never returned. That was over fifty years ago.

She then looked sadly at her daughters; they never knew their father. They had been conceived the night before he left. Zusie plopped down on the ground and put her head in her hands. Janilli put an arm around Zusie's shoulders and quietly repeated Aldwin's sentiment. Saphina looked at Chrystalina and together they knelt down beside their mother.

They knew how desperately she had hoped that they would one day find Willham and Horman alive.

"I have to see for myself," Zusie said as she brushed the tears away with the back of her hands. She quickly stood and without waiting for anyone else, she walked over to the large boulder that blocked the path and started to climb it. Rangous, Barton and half a dozen Tara Aquians followed behind her. The word that Willham and Horman's bodies had been found spread quickly down the caravan. The Elfkins mourned the death of the two best friends.

Zusie and the others returned an hour and a half later. She was carrying a necklace in her hand, another one hung around her neck. They were the necklaces that she and Lizbeth had made for their mates before they had left on their journey. The one Lizbeth made for Horman had seven fine white soft stones on it. She had carved each letter of her name into them, along with tiny holes, and then strung them onto braided pieces of bimble yarn. Zeander recognized the necklace that dangled from Zusie's hand and nodded his head. He had met Horman and Willham on their journey across the Outer Bound Meadow. He had introduced them to the Tara Aquians who carried them across the lake. One day he would tell Zusie and her daughters his tale of the two best friends, their journey and the love they had for their people and their mates. For now, he wondered, was their death by accident or did someone bring them to their demise?

Zusie absentmindedly rubbed the single yellow crystal that now hung around her neck. Instead of staying to speak with her family, she sadly made her way to Lizbeth's trolley. As Zusie passed, the villagers and forest creatures looked sympathetically at her. Everyone that is, but Paramo; who had a satisfied smirk on her face. Zusie was too caught up in her anguished thoughts however to take notice of her or the others.

Upon reaching Lizbeth's trolley she hesitated for a moment before she told Old Barty and Marla that she would like a moment alone with Lizbeth. Understanding they quickly got down from the trolley. Old Barty looked up at Zusie. Before leaving, he patted her on the arm. He was an elderly Elfkin who had been seriously injured when he was younger. The injuries had left him with a limp that made walking difficult. For most the journey he rode in the trolley with Lizbeth. Before Marla left she gave Zusie a hug and then quickly went in search of her mate Rangous. They too were expecting. She couldn't imagine being without him or raising her child on her own like Zusie had done.

Zusie hesitated again before she climbed in beside Lizbeth. As tears welled up in her eyes she placed the necklace around Lizbeth's head. She sat beside her, reminiscing about Willham and Horman long into the night. Eventually tears replaced the words and she cried herself to sleep. Zusie did not see that as she lay beside Lizbeth, her arm securely around her waist, that Lizbeth had shed a single tear.

Chapter 4
The Elder's Task

The busy day was nearing to an end in Elsbrier, the main trading port in the Whipple Wash Valley. Many of the villagers had been making preparations for the Fall Equinox Celebrations that would begin the next day. The three day event would involve traditional dancing and music, folktales and food; lots of food and of course honey mead and wine.

On the outskirts of Elsbrier, nestled in a large meadow was the Lily Pond. It was a popular place for the younger inhabitants of the village to meet up and frolic in the cool water on warm days. This day was slightly different however; everyone who was in or near the pond was hard at work.

Water Lilys, the Keepers of the Lily Pond, were harvesting the last of the Lea-Ther plants for the season. The Lea-Ther plant grew abundantly in the shallow waters on the south shore. The plants' large, thick leaves are stripped off the stem and placed on a frame that stretches them flat. The frames are then placed in the drying hut to cure. Depending on the thickness of the leaf, it takes three to seven days to cure. Once cured, the leaves are used to make various garments like belts and footwear. They are also used for book covers and water resistant pouches. The pouches that are used for various purposes are favored by Orliff, the village healer. He uses them to transport medicine in whenever he travels outside of the village.

The Water Lilys lived in the Pond and were hundreds of years old. No one quite knew how they came to be as they are all female. One or two of them are born every one hundred years or so. They take care of the Lily Pond and the animal life that dwells within it. They also keep track of the stock of fish, making sure that it is not depleted. They have pale blue hued skin, long silvery red hair, bluish green eyes, petite noses and medium sized ears that are finely scalloped along the edges. They are the fairest of all the creatures in the Whipple Wash Valley. Airam Andiela is their princess; even though they are a part of Elsbrier they live by their own rules and council. Although they live in the pond they can survive out of it for several hours and are often seen in the village.

Not far from where the Water Lilys were working were the Elsbrier Eagles. They are the local Hawkeye team that is made up of young men from the village between the ages of fifteen and twenty-five years old. Hawkeye is a game played on ice, with sticks and a hard rubber puck. The *9 Games in 9 Days* event would soon be upon them and the team often came to the Lily Pond to do their daily workout routine and practice. Although the game is played on ice during the winter months, in the off season and the weeks prior to the year-end competition, the game is played in open fields using a hard shelled, dense ball. After their practice the team members often take a dip in the water to cool off.

Several paces away from them and just at the water's edge were three of the Whipple Wash fairies. Why they were called fairies no one was quite sure. Other than their pointed ears, they looked much like humans and were just as tall, unlike the tiny fairies that roamed the flatlands near the Cliffs of Orhem. Zabethile, the youngest of the Whipple Wash fairies, was trying to complete a task given to her by her mentor, Elder Athia. It wasn't going so well.

"Alright, hold steady now Zee," Enna said. Enna was the middle sibling and was assisting Zabethile or Zee, as she liked to be called, with her task. "That's it, that's it, steady, steady, wait, wait, watch, watch, oh, oh, no, no. There she blows!" A gale of laughter erupted from Enna when Zee toppled off the rocks she was try to balance on and splashed unceremoniously into the water.

"Must you say that every time she topples over?" Mariela, the second eldest, asked indignantly. "And why do you have to say everything twice? It's rather annoying don't you know?" Mariela sat several feet away on a large boulder that jutted out of the water a few feet from shore. She had been dangling her feet in the cool water while she read from a rather thick book that looked very old. She had started reading the book just the day before and she was almost half way through it.

"Well yes, yes I think, I think, I do, if it accomplishes nothing more than to irritate you," Enna said then smirked cheekily at her rhyming. Enna had been spotting for Zee as she tried balancing on the stack of rocks. When Zee came sputtering up for air Enna grabbed for her arm to help her stand.

Mariela clicked her tongue in annoyance and said, "You're such a dung butt," and then promptly turned her back on the pair of them. She went back to her reading and missed the look of false indignation on Enna's face.

"Did…did she just call me the butt of a Dungbar beetle?" Enna asked Zee as she picked a boulder up out of the water and placed it on the two that hadn't tipped over with the others.

She and Enna had been stacking the five large slabs of stone all afternoon. Instead of stacking the stones in the meadow, they had placed them ten feet from shore where the shallow area gradually sloped to deeper water. That way when Zee fell off she could aim for the deep water instead of landing on the hard ground of the meadow. This was now the twenty-fifth time. Zee muttered dishearteningly under her breath as she fished around in the water for one of the other stones, "I'm never going to get this."

When Enna did not reply, Zee looked up and shook her head. Enna had picked up a rather large round rock; big enough to have to be carried with both hands, and was silently wading through the water towards the unsuspecting Mariela. Mariela, immersed in the book again, did not see Enna throw the rock into the air nor did she see the rock land in the water just inches from where she sat. She did however feel the water from the large splash the rock had caused; it soaked her back thoroughly. Mariela shrieked in shock and nearly dropped the book. She scrambled off the rock and frantically dabbed at the pages of the book with the sleeve of her shirt.

"Are you insane?" She yelled rudely back at her sister.

Enna however was doubled over with laughter. Zee stood back on top of the rocks and ignored the outburst. Enna and Mariela were always batting heated words back and forth at each other, which usually resulted in one or both of them apologizing afterward.

"Elder Raylee gave me this book," Mariela said haughtily as she continued to dab hopelessly at the wet pages. Luckily the aged print had not smeared. "Seriously Enna, you are such a child at times."

No longer amused, Enna stopped laughing immediately. She was offended by Mariela's tone. "You called me the butt of a Dungbar beetle!" she yelled as she put her hands on her hips and stamped her foot in the water. Airam Andiela was overseeing the harvest, and looked over at them curiously. Jarrott Jones, the captain of the Eagles, looked over as well. They both however went back to what they were doing, as each had witnessed several arguments between Mariela and Enna before. Like Zee, they chose not to get involved.

"Do you know where the Dungbar beetle lives?" Enna continued to howl at Mariela, not caring if anyone else could hear her.

"Yes...of course I know where the Dungbar beetle lives," Mariela said haughtily again as she walked to the shore. The ends of her long flowing brown skirt were tucked into the waistband. She had done that so that her skirt would not get wet as she waded barefoot into the shallow water to sit on the large rock. Now however, it did not matter as the back of her skirt and most of her beige coloured shirt had been soaked with water.

Not one for giving up on a good argument, Enna continued. "Do you know what a Dungbar beetle eats?" She said in a calmer voice that still held an edge of hostility to it.

"Oh, oh I know the answer to this one!" Zee said excitedly from atop the pile of stones. They had just learned about the Dungbar beetle the other day in their Entomology class that was taught by Professor Kirby. "They feed off the parasites that live in the fecal matter of the flying Rapcicors." She stuck out her tongue, screwed up her face and shook her head as if she had just tasted something awful. Her movements nearly toppled her over again, but she steadied herself by flinging her arms out to the side.

"So," Mariela said as she plopped down beside her shoes. She opened the book to see if any of the pages had been damaged; she tried to ignore her sisters.

"So?!" Enna yelled loudly back at her as she stomped her foot in the water again. The ripples made their way to the stack of stones and Zee rocked precariously back and forth, but did not fall off them.

"Hey! Watch what you are doing. This is harder than it looks," Zee said as she wobbled on the stones.
Enna ignored Zee as she walked around the large boulder Mariela had been sitting on. She stared menacingly at Mariela as she sat on the soft green grass. "You called me the butt of a beetle that eats poop. The butt of the beetle that eats poop!" she said, emphasizing each of the words.

"Parasites actually," Zee said as she continued to balance on the rocks. "Not the poop."

"Oh shut up Zee! You're not helping," Enna shouted. However remembering that she was supposed to be spotting her, Enna quickly added, "Remember if you fall towards the shore tuck and roll, tuck and roll." Hearing Enna repeat her instruction twice, Mariela rolled her eyes and huffed.

Zee nodded a little too enthusiastically and the motion wobbled the first rock just enough that the one beneath it slipped and the rest followed suit. She had just enough time to aim for the deeper part of the pond as she went head first into the water.

Mariela looked up. Seeing the hurt expression on Enna's face she immediately felt bad about her comment. "Oh Enna, I am sorry," she said sincerely. "You are right. That wasn't a very nice thing to call you."

Enna smiled. Her anger deflated as quickly as it had risen and she accepted the apology with a nod. She then quickly walked back through the water to help Zee stack the rocks.

"You don't understand how important this book is though," Mariela said as she looked over at her sisters. "It's the history of the Southern Kingdoms and all that dwell within it. It holds a wealth of knowledge. It is actually an exciting read!"

"Yes, yes, we're sure it is," Enna smirked as she helped Zee place the last rock on the stack. Mariela had read every book in the village library at least a dozen times and often bored her sisters greatly with the details found within them. She only stopped after they begged her to.

"It holds very important information about not only humankind, but the creatures we may encounter on our journey as well. I feel very blessed that Elder Raylee asked me to read it," Mariela said. She looked at the book as if it were made of priceless sparkling gems instead of parchment. In actuality the book was centuries old. Its pages, stained from age, were bound between large thick pieces of dried Lea-Ther leaves. Over time they had curved up at the corners.

"Yes, yes," Enna mimicked her. "You're very important."

Mariela clicked her tongue. "That is not what I said, nor what I meant." She looked over at her sisters again; they were both smirking at her. Mariela sighed and smiled back at them.

She placed the on her lap and watched as Zee walked several feet into the grassy area beyond the pond. Zee then turned and looked at the rocks sternly as if her mental thoughts could persuade the rocks to stay still. She quickly rubbed her hands together and blew into them. She then dropped her hands to her side and relaxed her fingers. Zee emptied her mind of all thoughts and inhaled deeply as Elder Athia had taught her. She then squared her shoulders and ran full tilt towards the stack of rocks and yelled, "Here we go for the twenty-seventh time." Once she reached the edge of the pond, she jumped high into the air, landed lightly onto the stacks of rocks with both feet and flung her arms out for balance.

"At least all you have to do," she said tilting on the rocks, "is read a silly old book. I on the other hand have to balance on…on…on these!"

Enna stood in front of Zee, holding her arms out wide as well. She swayed back and forth like Zee, as if her actions would help Zee to balance better.

Zee looked down and chuckled as Enna concentrated. "You know that doesn't really help me any. Besides you loo…," she started to say as Mariela cleared hear throat. Enna's eyebrows rose in question. "You look….like a lovely graceful bird standing in the water." Zee said brightly instead of what she was going to say which was '*you look like a fool.*'

Mariela chuckled as she opened up the book again. Enna looked back at her sternly. Mariela could feel her intense gaze and she stopped chuckling instantly.

"Well, how about if you do it all on your own then. I don't need to be here you know. I had my task done before you even thought of rising this morning. I just thought you might like my help," Enna said angrily. She stomped out of the water without a backward glance. The water rippled just enough, and all they could hear as the rocks tumbled over was Zee moaning, "Not again," just before she hit the water.

Mariela looked over just as Zee disappeared under the water and whispered, "There she blows."

Zee sputtered for air as she came up out of the water. She hit her fist against the water, stomped her feet and yelled, "This is ridiculous. I am never going to get this!"

Airam looked over at her and frowned. It would seem that

Zee was having trouble with her task, which Airam found concerning. The fairies would soon be leaving on their mission to unite the Southern Kingdoms. She wondered if Zee would be ready for it. Airam gathered up the last of the harvest and with the other Water Lilys, she started to wade through the water towards the drying huts. They were several hundred paces away on a large dock that stood out over the water.

As the Water Lilys left, Zee walked to the shore and plopped down on the ground. "Why couldn't Elder Athia have given me a book to read?" She said exhaustingly as she wrapped her hands around her long dark brown hair and squeezed out the water.

Enna and Mariela looked over at their youngest sister. She had been working very hard on her task all afternoon, but was only able to stand on the rocks for a minute or two at a time before they tumbled over. Mariela placed the book beside her shoes, got up and walked over to Zee. Enna walked back to her as well and they sat down on either side of her.

"It's not for us to question the Elders Zee," Mariela said; even though she often questioned in private the validity of their training for their forthcoming mission. Instead of voicing her thoughts she took Zee's right hand and held it warmly in hers.

Zee looked sadly at her toes as she dug them into the soft dirt in the pond bed and sighed heavily, "I know; but why a stack of rocks? It doesn't make any sense."

Enna put her right arm around Zee's shoulders. "When the time comes, it will all make sense. Do you really think Mariela *needs* to read one more book?"

"No," Zee said shyly as a small smile lit her face. The sisters chuckled lightly.

"How about," Mariela said with an encouraging tone as she looked over at Enna, "if I help too? Perhaps you could start with two stones then work your way up. Elder Athia didn't say you had to start with all five of them at once did she?"

Enna shook her head, as Zee said, "No."

"Well then, why don't we start with two, until you get the hang of it? Then we will do three and so on until you are steady enough to sleep standing all night long on the stack of rocks." Zee and Enna chuckled.

"I don't think there will ever be a need for me to sleep while standing on a stack of rocks, but I get your point," Zee said. The sisters all smiled. Enna and Mariela wrapped their arms around Zee and gave her a big hug.

"Hey! Can anyone get in on this or is it only the three of you," someone called from behind them.

Caught off guard the sisters quickly turned around to see who it was. Shanata, the eldest of the sisters stood several feet behind them with a rather large weaved basket in her right hand and a bottle of sweetened gooseberry juice in the other.

"We thought you might be hungry," she said as she looked over at Ashlina, the second youngest. She was taking a large blue and green tweed blanket out of a sack. She unfolded the blanket, snapped it into the air once and then spread it neatly onto the grass. As Shanata knelt down and placed the basket and juice on the blanket, Ashlina took something else out of the sack and carried it over to Zee.

"We also thought you might need this," Ashlina said as she held open a large fluffy cream coloured towel.

"Oh yes, just what I needed," Zee said thankfully as she stood up. Ashlina wrapped the towel around Zee's shoulders and rubbed her arms briskly with it. Zee sighed. Although the day was warm the water was cool; Zee shivered violently and thanked Ashlina for the towel as she wrapped it around her more snuggly.

The four of them walked to the blanket and plopped down beside Shanata who had already spread out the food and dishes from the basket. She sat properly on the blanket with her legs curled under her to one side. A pale yellow cloth napkin lay neatly on her lap. Shanata was very proper and hated if she got any crumbs of food on the lovely dresses she wore. That day she wore a long pale blue dress that hugged her hips and had long flowing delicate sleeves. She nibbled lightly on a piece of bread.

Zee on the other hand eagerly dug into the food nearest her, not caring if crumbs got on her clothes or not. She promptly filled her mouth with a large chunk of freshly made bimble berry bread. She hadn't realized how hungry she was.

"Zee," Shanata admonished her lightly. "Slow down! You're going to choke on your food."

Zee smiled sheepishly. She took the cup of gooseberry juice that Mariela held out for her and quickly washed down the bread.

"Sorry," she said as a bit of juice dripped from her lips and splashed down the front of her, staining the towel. "I didn't realize how hungry I was. Is that fried bastion you got there?" She asked eagerly as she hungrily looked at the food piled high on Enna's plate.

"Yes," Enna said. "And it's all mine."

"Here," Shanata smiled as she passed a plate of food to Zee. Ashlina smiled as well as she finished filling her plate and sat down between Enna and Zee. She, like Shanata, sat with her legs curled under her, but she was not as particular as Shanata was and did not place a napkin on her lap. Like Enna and Zee, she preferred to wear pants and tops rather than skirts and dresses as the older two sisters did. Today she had on a dark pair of pants and a brightly coloured short sleeved orange top. She also wore several beaded necklaces that dangled down at varying lengths.

The sisters ate their meal in silence, which was unusual for them. Usually the conversations were so animated and lengthy their food often went cold before they finished it. However, each of them was now deep in thought as they reflected on the day's tasks that had been laid out for them by the Elders. Like Zee's, theirs didn't make much sense to them either.

Shanata, seventeen years old, was apprentice to Elder

43

Enyce. Her task was to learn all about the medicinal plants growing outside of the Whipple Wash Valley. She had been in the village library pouring over books all day. She was taller than the rest of her sisters at five feet eight inches. Being the oldest, she naturally took on the responsibility of caring for her sisters. As well, she made sure they completed their studies and the tasks given to them by the Elders.

Shanata had long dark hair that hung down to her waist that she normally wore in a bun at the nape of her neck. Today however, she had weaved her hair into a braid that hung over her right shoulder; a small blue ribbon was tied at the bottom of it. She was lovely, as were all the fairies. They had high cheek bones, dark eyes with dark curved thick lashes, regal noses, and full pink lips, light brown skin and small pointed ears. Unlike the other fairies of the forest however, the sisters had no wings. Why they were called fairies, no one knew for sure, but that is what it was and they did not question or argue the point.

Mariela, the apprentice to Elder Rayley, was sixteen years old. The book she was reading was very thorough, however the only creatures that had little written about them was the Ogres, which was unfortunate as their settlement lay just beyond the borders of the valley. Like her older sister she had dark hair, but preferred to wear it cropped short. It curled under at the nape of her neck. Her ears were just a little bit smaller and so too was her nose.

Enna, at fifteen years old, had already completed her task of learning how to forge steel into a sword. She was the apprentice to Elder Andi. Enna had not been able to sleep the previous night and had sought out Jonas who owned *The Smithery*. He also could not sleep and had been working on something when Enna approached him just before dawn, asking if he would help her with her task. She, like Shanata, had long flowing dark hair that she preferred to let hang loose over her shoulders. The ringlets cascaded down her back. She was a couple of inches shorter than Mariela and stockier in stature. She was often seen digging in the garden along with the Garden Gnomes and chatting excitedly with them.

Ashlina was the apprentice to Elder Phinney. She had the task of starting a journal of all the wildlife in the forest surrounding Elsbrier. She not only had to learn what species there was, but what their tracks looked like as well. Like Mariela, she chose to keep her hair cropped short, but often streaked her hair with different colours. Pink one day, green the next and so on down the line. Today the streaks were a dark orange that matched her shirt. She was the same height as Enna, but her ears were a little bit longer and her nose just a tad bit plumper.

Zee was eleven summers old. She was the apprentice to Elder Athia. Zee looked much like Shanata only she was shorter and her eyes and ears were larger. Her dark brown hair hung in soft ringlets past her waist. She often tied feathers in it; today however she opted not to have feathers as they would only get ruined by her task. Zee collects feathers and when she has enough of them, she weaves them into a headdress and sells it in the gift shop owned by Bethel Radek and her spouse Trebor Radek; the great explorer of the lands beyond the Evergreen Forest.

Time passed as time does and the sisters had come to the end of their meal.

"That was delicious," Zee said as she wiped her mouth with the towel that Ashlina had given her. Her plate sat empty, all but for several leg bones of the fried bastion. Her sisters looked over at her in surprise as she burped loudly and rubbed her stomach. "I think I ate too much," she complained then moaned as she continued to rub her stomach.

"You will feel better on the walk back to the village," Shanata said to her as she started to pack up the rest of the food and dishes. "And if not I will ask Elder Rayley for a tonic that will settle your stomach down. You probably just ate too quickly."

Zee nodded her thank you as she and the others helped to

pack up the rest of the food and dishes. With the repacked basket in Shanata's hand, the empty bottle of gooseberry juice in Enna's and the folded towel in Ashlina's, Zee stooped to pick up the sack that Ashlina had carried the blanket and towel in. Underneath the sack was a large black feather and Zee picked it up. She looked curiously at it before she stuffed it into the sack. As Zee slipped her feet into her shoes, Mariela who had been shaking off the blanket, gasped as she looked down at Zee's feet.

"Oh, I almost forgot," she said and then tapped the palm of her right hand on her forehead. Everyone turned and looked at her curiously wondering what she had forgotten.

"The book," she said. After throwing the folded blanket to Zee, she ran to where her shoes and the book lay in the grass near the pond.

"Oh yes," Enna said sarcastically as she watched Mariela walk back to them with the book clenched to her chest. "Goodness forbid, if you should forget a book." Her words made the other chuckle lightly.

Hearing her sisters' laughter, Mariela could not help but laugh along. She was well aware that everyone knew she preferred to read books and pen parchments than do anything else. Xander was the only other person in the village who loved books as much as she did. He was an elderly man who had escaped from Lord Canvil and made his way to Elsbrier. He was the one who told the Seven Elders about Queen Faywyn's abduction. When he and Mariela were not talking about books she was transcribing Xander's time with Lord Canvil.

As the fairies started to walk back to Elsbrier they heard water splash and whoops of laughter behind them. They turned around quickly and watched as the members of the Hawkeye team jumped into the pond. They had apparently finished their workout and had stripped down to just their underwear. Mariela, Enna and Ashlina gawked at the team's bare chests and legs as they dove into the water. They turned back around and blushed before they giggled. Shanata looked crossly at her sisters for being silly.

"Do you want to have a swim with them," Zee asked innocently.

"No," each of her sisters said in unison as they started walking towards the village. They hadn't gone far before they heard someone calling Shanata's name. They turned around as Rhethea quickly walked towards them. Rhethea Jarrell was Shanata's best friend and the only female on the Hawkeye team. In fact out of all the teams, Rhethea was the only female player. Rhethea was the only sister to the Jarrell brothers who the fairies did combat training with. She was no taller than Enna, but she had a lean muscular build. She was a pretty girl with shoulder length hair the colour of wheat and her eyes were hazel. Like Enna, Rhethea was known for her short temper, which was usually set off by one of her brothers. She was not above delivering a punch, wrestling or kicking her brothers to the ground when they pestered her beyond her tolerance level.

"Do you mind if I walk back with you?" Rhethea asked as she caught up to them.

"No of course not," Shanata said. "We would like the company. "

"Do you not want to swim with the others?" Zee asked innocently again.

"No," Rhethea said. "I have to get back home to help my grandmother with the evening meal. My brothers and their families are coming over for dinner. Afterwards we are going to finish making the 'Welcome to Autumn' gifts. Shanata, would you like to join us? Of course the rest of you are more than welcome to come as well."

"I have made my own gifts this year," Mariela said.

"You have?" Enna asked. The sisters looked quizzically at each other.

"Why yes, I have made bookmarks," She replied.

The fairies looked at each other and smiled. So that is what she has been up to. She had been acting quite secretive about something all summer.

"That is lovely," Rhethea said. "What if we tie the bookmarks to the gifts that we have made? I think they would go nicely with the candles and dried flowers." Mariela nodded and smiled, indicating that she would like that very much. "That settles it then. How about the rest of you?" Rhethea asked.

Before the sisters could answer they heard someone else calling for them; it was Arnack and Zan. Arnack was a handsome, elderly man who had salt and pepper coloured hair. He was neither slim nor stocky, but somewhere in between. He was short by human standards at only five feet tall. He had a jolly laugh and told the most wonderful jokes. Most days he sat at *The Baron's Den*, a very popular Pub in Elsbrier that served a perfect mug of mead. Zan was handsome with dark colouring, but was younger in years than Arnack. He had a muscular build and was taller than Arnack by several inches. He too was a regular customer at *The Den*. He and Arnack often got into trouble with the Elders because of their pranks and mischievous ways.

The fairies and Rhethea were surprised to see them this far from *The Den*. They looked at them quizzically as they approached. They were riding on a small carri-shift that was being pulled along by a larger than normal pokey. Pokeys were small four-legged horse like creatures with thick legs, strong backs, thick, curly short hair, a short nubby tail and a mane that is closely cropped. Their large ears were curled at the ends just like a mountain goat's horns and stuck out straight from the sides of their head. The pokeys were used to pull the carri-shifts; small open carriages with four wheels that are used to transport produce from the growing fields to Elsbrier. Some of the families in Elsbrier also used the carri-shifts to transport their families around the village or when traveling to the other villages in the area.

"What are the two of you up to?" Shanata asked

suspiciously as Zan pulled back on the reins. The pokey stopped just beside Rhethea and the fairies. He nickered softly as Ashlina came forward and stroked his neck.

Enna walked to the carri-shift and pulled back the canvas blanket that covered it. "Firebangers," she said and then looked at Zan who smiled sheepishly back at her.

Firebangers were cylindrical in shape and filled with powder that when ignited lit up the night sky with a multitude of explosive colours. They were used at each of the changing of the season ceremonies. Arnack and Zan were not normally the ones who set them up; that job was left for Osborne and the Jarrell brothers.

"Do the Elders know that you have those?" Shanata questioned them.

"Now Shanata, you know better than to ask us a question that we cannot answer truthfully," Arnack said. He then nodded at Zan who smiled wickedly before he snapped the reins. Ashlina stepped to the side just as the pokey started forward.

"You never saw anything," Arnack said as he winked at the fairies and Rhethea.

"Those two," Rhethea said shaking her head. "Are you going to tell the Elders?"

"I don't know," Shanata said and then chuckled softly. Her reaction surprised her sisters and Rhethea.

Zan and Arnak's antics were for the most part harmless, however Firebangers were another matter altogether. They could do quite a bit of damage if they were set off improperly.

"At least they are taking them away from the village, how bad could it be," she said and then shrugged her shoulders. Rhethea and the fairies smiled and nodded in agreement.

"Are you all excited about tomorrow?" Rhethea asked. "I love the Seasonal Celebrations. They are always so festive."

"We are more excited about our next lesson," Mariela said as she jostled the large book from one arm to the other. All but one of the fairies nodded enthusiastically.

As they walked towards the outcropping of trees that surrounded the meadow, Mariela told Rhethea what the Elders had planned for them. They were learning how to ride the Avidraughts, the flying horses of the Whipple Wash Valley. Zee was the only one who wasn't thrilled about it. As her sisters talked excitedly with Rhethea, she instead wondered how she was going to learn to ride and fly an Avidraught when she couldn't even balance on a stack of boulders.

As the girls walked along the path from the meadow to the village, none of them saw the tall darkly clothed man peering at them with great interest from behind a thick cluster of trees. Nor did they see the expression of anger he had on his passably handsome face as he stared at the book in Mariela's arms. He was so hoping she would have left it behind; the knowledge within the book would have made his job a little easier to do. While keeping to the shadows of the trees he stealthily followed the girls back to the village. All the way he planned and contrived ways to get his hands on that book.

Chapter 5
In the Nick of Time

A week had gone by since Zusie and the Elfkins said their last goodbyes to Willham and Horman. Barton and a few of the other Tara Aquians were able to roll the boulder off of them. They gathered the weathered bones into a pile against the crevice wall and arranged small stones over top of them. Old Barty carved their names into a piece of wood from Lizbeth's trolley and Zusie placed it at the head of the stone graves. As the Caravan of travelers passed, each said a prayer of hope that Willham and Horman were safely placed in a better realm than the one they had left behind.

The sky had grown dark earlier than usual due to a storm that was quickly rolling in. The shelters that everyone called *Bella-huts*, in respect to their inventor, Mirabella, were erected. Everyone settled beneath them and ate a simple meal of dried fruit and bread. No one wanted to take the chance of starting a fire as the wind had picked up considerably and strongly blew against the sides of the shelters.

Most of the men were either already asleep, resting before their turn at guard duty, or already standing guard. Zeander had voiced his opinion that perhaps Willham and Horman's demise had not been by accident and extra guards were posted. This didn't really ease everyone's mind however; how could they protect anyone if rocks fell on top of them?

The journey had become very stressful over the past week as Paramo and her small group of friends had become vocal about having to scale the large boulders and how long the journey was taking. Most everyone ignored them and kept up the stringent pace, knowing what would happen if Lord Canvil caught up to them. However after finding Willham and Horman, Zusie noticed that even the forest creatures nervously looked up at the steep crevice and had become skittish with each sound. Everyone, including the forest creatures, was fearful that loose rocks might tumble down upon them or worse, someone might start a rock slide and everyone would be buried beneath it. And even though they slept in the *Bella-huts*, which were great for sheltering them from the rain, they would not protect them from a downpour of rocks.

Zusie and Chrystalina were in a *Bella-hut* at the end of the caravan. Chrystalina was adding entries to the journal that Lizbeth had started to write before she had fallen ill. It was a field guide of sorts about life in the forest with detailed drawings of the Elfkins, flora and fauna. They had taken the book with them and added to it while they had journeyed through the forest, meadow and over the lake. Although there wasn't a lot to collect or write about in the Hollow of Rock, Chrystalina had kept up with the journal and could often be seen sketching one of the younger ones or asking Janilli and Lindrella to tell her about the Tara Aquians. Chrystalina smiled as she looked down at a drawing of Zeander. He had made such a fuss about having to stay still so that she could sketch him before the day light faded. However upon seeing the finished picture he was quite delighted by it; it was a drawing of him and Paraphin.

Zusie was administering to Lizbeth. Her trolley had been left behind when they encountered the large boulders. It was difficult enough climbing over the boulders let alone trying to pull a trolley over them, so Lizbeth was placed in a sling and carried on Barton's back. The scrolls, medicine and provisions were evenly distributed among everyone, and the statues they had taken from the Crystal Cave had been wrapped in cloth and given to the Tara Aquians to carry. It had been a difficult week having to climb over the boulders with the extra provisions; everyone was quite tired by the end of the day. Zusie and Chrystalina were no exception. Chrystalina stifled a yawn as she passed her mother a lotion they put on Lizbeth's skin to keep it from drying out after they bathed her. Since entering the crevice, bathing for all of them had been limited to wiping with a wet cloth.

Zusie was just about to tell Chrystalina that she could finish up with Lizbeth when the flap of their tent was flipped back roughly; they both jumped in surprise. Saphina stood there with an excited look on her face. Seeing her mother beside Lizbeth she rushed into the tent and nearly tripped on the pile of mats set out for Lizbeth to sleep on.

"What in the name of Zenrah," Zusie said harshly as she and Chrystalina looked crossly at Saphina for frightening them.

Saphina ignored her and said breathlessly, "Here you are! I've been looking for you." Without waiting for either of them to respond she hurriedly said, "They're here."

"What!" Both Zusie and Chrystalina cried out in unison.

"How could they reach us this quickly? A week ago there was no sign of them!" Chrystalina asked nearly in tears.

Saphina looked strangely at her sister for a moment then shook her head violently, "No not them," she said impatiently. She got up, held the flap of the shelter open, pointed upwards and said, "*Them.*"

Zusie and Chrystalina scrambled out of the shelter, looked up and were surprised to see that an army of people surrounded them. They were standing on a ledge that ran the length of the crevice walls. It was difficult to distinguish the ledge from the wall as they blended together. The army was also hard to see as their colouring was similar to the grey rock. Saphina tugged on Zusie's hand.

"Come," she said urgently. "Jasper is talking with one of them." Zusie and Chrystalina looked at her questioningly. Saphina returned their looks with a bright smile.

"Jasper is talking with one of them," Zusie repeated, not sure she had heard correctly.

"Yes," Saphina said as she tugged on her mother's hand for her to follow.

"Stay with Lizbeth," Zusie shouted over her shoulder at Chrystalina as she went with Saphina.

Chrystalina shivered with fright as the people stared unflinchingly down at her. Even though Saphina acted like all was well, Chrystalina had an uneasy feeling that it wasn't. She quickly dashed back inside Lizbeth's shelter, tripped over the pile of mats and nearly fell on Lizbeth. She yelped then moaned as she vigorously rubbed the pain away from her knees.

Zusie and Saphina quickly ran through the caravan making sure not to trip over the lead wires of the shelters. "Saphina, slow down before you trip," Zusie called out after her daughter; worried for the baby that Saphina was carrying. Saphina was too excited to slow down and expertly made her way through the caravan without tripping once. Zusie ignored the calls of the Elfkins and Meadow Imps who had poked their heads out of the shelters to see what the commotion was all about. Luckily, there were no boulders in this stretch of the crevice and the travelers were able to all be in one place. Not like the previous two nights where they had been separated into three large groups. As they neared the head of the caravan Zusie thought fleetingly that perhaps having all of them together wasn't such a good idea after all.

Finally, and breathlessly, they made it to the head of the caravan where they could see a large group of travelers standing not a hundred feet away. They were looking into a clearing that was lit with torches. Zusie and Saphina walked through the crowd; who stepped aside so that they could make their way to the front. Zusie stopped abruptly once she reached the edge of the clearing. Surrounding the clearing were Tara Aquians, Meadow Imps, Elfkins and a large group of the newcomers. Jasper was fluttering in midair in the center of the clearing while one of the boulder people talked animatedly to him; occasionally Jasper nodded in response. Everyone standing around looked relaxed; obviously Jasper had told them that they had nothing to fear.

Zusie cautiously walked forward and stopped when she reached Jasper. Jasper turned and smiled at her. "Oh hello Zusie, this is Bablou, leader of this scouting party." Jasper smiled at Bablou as if he were an old friend. "They are of the Boulder Clan of Mount Alpanatia," he said in a matter of fact way, like their existence was wildly known.

"Mount Alpanatia?" Aldwin inquired.

"Yes this is Mount Alpanatia," Jasper said as he waved his hand towards the wall of the crevice. Aldwin nodded his head. It was as he had expected. What they once called the Mighty Alps was in fact named Mount Alpanatia. *Well*, he thought, *at least the elders got part of the name correct.* Aldwin made a mental note that he needed to let Chrystalina know so that she could change it in Lizbeth's journal.

Jasper turned and looked at Zusie. He was surprised that she had a scowl on her face. "You know these people?" She asked.

"Oh yes, yes," Jasper nodded his head and smiled at Bablou who smiled back at him.

"And when were you going to tell us?" Zusie asked impatiently.

Jasper looked at her strangely at first. Then, as if a light lit, he stammered an apology. "Yes, well I, I am sorry. I didn't think we would come across them. I knew they lived in the Alpanatia Mountains, but I had no idea these were them." As if that made sense, he stopped talking.

"How do you know them Jasper?" Zusie asked impatiently again.

"Oh, well they are craftsmen and they trade with the vendors in my village."

Zusie looked at Bablou just as curiously as he was now looking at her. In the light from the torches, she could see them more clearly. They were taller than the Elfkins but not as tall as the Tara Aquians. Bablou was not as tall as she was, but Zusie could see that some of the others standing behind him were. Their bodies were lean but not as muscular as the Tara

Aquians. They were covered from head to toe in an ashen grey coloured dust; it was difficult to make out their facial features. All she could see were full lips and dark eyes that looked back at her brightly. Their hair was matted down with clumps of what looked like mud. The upper part of their body was bare but their lower half was covered with a ragged length of cloth that wrapped around their waist and hung to their knees. Their feet were also bare. Each of them carried a slender spear that was a few inches taller than they were.

Bablou started to talk excitedly again and urgently pointed up at the sky. He then pointed past the group of Boulder people towards the dark crevice ahead.

Jasper nodded his head and translated, "Bablou has come to warn us."

The hairs on the back of Zusie neck immediately stood up and she looked worriedly from Bablou to Jasper.

"Warn us?" She repeated Jasper words.

"Of the water," Jasper said.

Zusie looked questioningly at the others standing around. They shrugged their shoulders and shook their heads. They didn't understand what he was talking about either.

"What water Jasper?" She asked anxiously as Bablou looked up at the sky nervously.

"From the storm," Jasper said and looked up at the sky too. As if on cue, lightening lit up the dark clouds and thunder roared in the distance. Bablou quickly gestured for them to follow him.

"What of the others and our provisions?" Zusie cried out over the sound of the thunder.

Jasper translated what Zusie had said to Bablou.

"Bring your people," Bablou said, "and what provisions you can carry. But we must hurry."

Zusie and the others looked strangely at Bablou who had spoken clear Elfish. He was now motioning earnestly for them to follow him. The rest of his Clan was already making their way through the crevice. Zusie noticed even the ones standing on the ledge were quickly making their way along it. Zusie looked over at Saphina inquiringly. She shook her head; she could not read Bablou's mind. Janilli came to stand beside Zusie.

"I think we should listen to him. If they wanted to harm us they would have waited until we were asleep to do so," she said. Then they both looked up as the last Boulder Clan member skillfully made his way along the ledge. "Besides," she added, "Jasper knows them."

Lighting lit up the sky again; thunder quickly followed it as a light rain began to fall. The storm was moving fast. Zusie looked at the others standing around "Do as he says!" She yelled. "Tell everyone to grab what provisions they can, but leave the water barrels and shelters; I don't think we will have time to pack them." As if on cue again, the skies opened and the rain pelted down on them, dousing out many of the torches. The light from the others would soon diminish as well. They quickly ran back through the caravan and yelled for everyone to get up and grab what they could. A dozen Tara Aquians led by Barton ran back to Lizbeth's shelter with Zusie.

Zusie quickly explained to Chrystalina what was happening. Chrystalina looked fearfully at her mother, but did not question her. She instead motioned for six of the Tara Aquians to follow her. They went to a shelter that had been erected to house the medicines, scrolls and statues. Each of the Tara Aquians went inside one at a time and picked up as many of the sacks as they could carry, then rushed out of the shelter and started to make their way forward. The rain had started to fall more heavily and they slipped on the wet ground as they ran along.

Chrystalina ran back to Lizbeth's shelter and grabbed the journal. She wrapped it in a thick blanket and crammed it into an empty sack. She ran out of the shelter to where Zusie stood. Lizbeth was already in the sling and on Barton's back; Zusie tucked a blanket around Lizbeth to shelter her from the rain.

In his large hands Barton carried four sacks. Zusie handed Chrystalina two sacks and slung two over her shoulders. The packs thankfully had not been unpacked fully since setting out on the journey through the Hollow of Rock. Each night they took out what they needed instead of unpacking everything just to repack it the next morning.

As they started on their way, the skies broke open and rain plummeted down on them, dousing out the last of the torches. The ground became slick with water and they slipped with each step. Zusie looked down at the ground. The rain was not running off, it was accumulating around their feet. She quickly looked at Chrystalina and Barton who looked back at her nervously. Now they understood why Bablou insisted they leave. This section of the crevice for whatever reason fills up with water instead of draining off. If they didn't leave they would all drown.

They quickly ran forward, but Zusie wanted to make sure no one was left behind and briefly stopped at each shelter. She had urged Barton and Chrystalina to go on ahead without her, but they refused to leave her. As quickly as they could they made their way forward. The water was getting deeper; it was now up to their ankles. They finally reached the head of the caravan. Zusie stopped abruptly for a moment and looked back. Satisfied that no one was left she nodded to the others and they started to make their way down the pathway. It was very dark and with the rain pelting down, they could only see what was directly in front of them. The crevice began to fill with water.

They came to the bend, the one Rangous had told them about; they had no idea what was on the other side. Chrystalina had slipped several times and Barton stopped to make sure she was all right. The water was now up to Chrystalina's hips and it was no longer possible for her or Zusie to go through it quickly as they also struggled to hang on to the sacks.

"Drop da sacks," Barton hollered at them over the noise of

the thunder and rain. Chrystalina cried out as she slipped and went under the water. The sacks that she had put over her shoulders, now soaked with water, weighed her down and she could not get back up. Barton dropped the sacks he was carrying, grabbed the collar of Chrystalina's tunic and roughly pulled her out of the water. He started to tear the sacks off her shoulders and she screamed at him when he got to the one that the journal was in.

"Not this one, not this one," she cried and sputtered as she frantically held on to it. Understanding, Zusie dropped her sacks and grabbed Chrystalina's arm. Together they made their way up the pathway.

Several hundred paces later, the lightening lit up the sky. Just ahead of them they could see Bablou standing in front of a solid wall of rock. Zusie looked frantically about, no one else was around. Where had they all disappeared to? Dumbfounded, she stopped walking and looked at the wall. It was slick like polished stone and spanned the width and height of the crevice. There was no getting around it or climbing up it.

Bablou quickly walked to them, grabbed Zusie's arm, shook it urgently, and then pointed to a spot on the rock face to the left of the wall. He walked towards it. Barton understood and pushed Zusie and Chrystalina forward. At first glance it looked solid but when lightening brightened the sky again they could see that there was a large hole in the rock face. Bablou walked through it. Chrystalina and Zusie quickly followed him in. When Barton came to it he had to duck down as he was at least two feet taller than the hole. Once he stepped through the hole however, he was able to stand upright, as the ceiling was several feet higher. The hole led to a large square landing that had two walls of solid stone; one wall with the hole in it that led back to the Hollow of Rock and one wall with a large opening that led through to a passageway. It looked similar to the passageway that led from the golden archway in Mount Aspentonia to the Crystal Caves where Zusie and her daughters had resided. However, it was not as wide and its walls were just grey rock as was the ceiling. As they looked down the passageway they noticed that it gradually slopped upwards and was periodically lit with a strange crystal. The crystals were set in holders that hung on the wall. Although they were not very bright, they did illuminate the passageway enough so that whoever walked down it did not have to do so in total darkness.

They looked down and noticed that the water was rising in the landing; it would soon be submerged. Bablou quickly made his way along the passageway and the others followed. Without their sacks weighing them down they were able to move with ease. Before long they could hear the others trudging along ahead of them. Zusie sighed heavily with relief. Several minutes passed before they caught up to the back of the caravan. Zusie called out with excitement when she saw who was there; Janilli, Saphina, Jasper and Aldwin. They stopped when they heard her voice and waited for them to catch up. Bablou nodded as he squeezed passed them and continued along without them.

Janilli and Saphina both dropped their packs, grabbed Zusie and Chrystalina and hugged them tightly. "You hadn't followed," Saphina said as relief washed over her and she began to cry. "We thought the worst."

Zusie wiped the tears from Saphina's eyes, hugged her quickly and apologetically said, "I had to make sure everyone was out."

Saphina nodded her understanding then looked at Chrystalina who looked to be more disheveled than the other two. She also noticed that Chrystalina was the only one carrying a sack. "You fell didn't you," Saphina said teasingly.

"I might have," Chrystalina said then smiled sheepishly. She bent down and picked up one of the sacks that Saphina had dropped to give her mother a hug.

Saphina shook her head and smiled. "How is Lizbeth?" she asked; looking up at Barton who towered over all of them.

"Oh my," Zusie cried out. She had forgotten all about Lizbeth.

Barton got down on his knees so that Zusie could see if Lizbeth was alright. She pulled the blanket off her head and was not surprised to see that she had stayed dried and was still sleeping. Zusie had covered her in a blanket that had been covered with tar on one side. She wrinkled her nose at the smell of it. The tar did not smell very good dry, wet it smelled even worse. She folded the blanket and looped it through the straps of one the packs that Janilli had dropped to give Chrystalina a hug. Satisfied that Lizbeth was alright she picked up the pack and with the others started down the passageway again.

The time seemed to pass slowly as the passageway continued to wind its way through the mountain. They were all quite tired and their pace gradually slowed. They occasionally passed by large holes that had been naturally formed in the walls. When they peered into them all they could see was darkness. Aldwin picked up a rock and dropped it through one of the holes. They heard the rock bouncing off the walls as it descended, but never heard it come to an end. An hour and a half into their journey through the mountain they heard cries coming from up ahead. Startled, Zusie and the others abruptly stopped and waited. Their hearts raced; could it have been a trap after all?

The cries came again. However it was not cries of distress, but that of delight. They looked at each other, smiled and quickened their pace. Several moments later, they could see Bablou standing in front of a large archway that led to a brightly lit cavern. They walked up to him. He smiled at them with a wide toothy grin; they could not help but smile back. He was obviously proud to show them what they hoped was his home. They stepped through the archway and onto a large landing one at a time. Their reactions were the same; they looked about with delight and awe.

Bablou's home was a massive circular cave that was

hundreds of feet deep. They seemed to be standing at the top of it, because several feet above their heads yellow crystals jutted down from the ceiling, illuminating the cave in a bright light. On either side of the landing stone stairs led down to the next railed landing and so forth until they came to the cave floor. The landings curved around the circumference of the cave and were several feet apart.

On the other side of the cave a small waterfall about two hundred feet high flowed out from a large hole and cascaded down into a large pool at its base. It then flowed along the bottom in a trench and vanished into a large hole on the other side of the cave. Little wooden bridges spanned the width of the trench. Along the walls of each of the landings were arched holes much like the ones on the walls of the Golden City of Awnmorielle; the Tara Aquians' home. However, these arches were not golden; they were a plain grey colour. Bablou's home was not as stunningly beautiful as Awnmorielle, but it did have its perks.

Various plant life; like trees, small bushes and even brightly coloured flowers were growing in large stone pots on the cave floor or in smaller containers on each of the landings and along the stone rails. Plants with dark green and bright white leaves that were sharply pointed cascaded over the containers and hung down several feet. It was beautiful in a rustic, quaint way. After months of only seeing grey rock from the time they woke to the time they slept the abundance of plant life was a welcome reprieve to the travelers. As Zusie looked around with delight she made a mental note to ask how the plant life survived without the sun's light.

Bablou motioned for them to follow him as he descended the stairs to the left of the landing. Occasionally he stopped to say something to one of the Boulder Clan who came out of the arched doorways. Unlike the Tara Aquians, the Boulder Clan were very curious about the newcomers and were not shy about openly staring at them as they walked by. Zusie and the others followed Bablou all the way down to the bottom where the rest of the caravan, fifteen hundred in total, stood waiting for them.

Bablou walked through the crowd of travelers towards a large archway that led into another cavern. At the entrance to the cavern, he motioned for them to follow. The others turned and looked for guidance from Zusie who was still descending the stairs. Zusie nodded that it would be alright and they turned and followed Bablou into the other cavern. Whatever he had planned for them she knew was better than what they had just come from.

*

A week had passed and the caravan of travelers were on their way again. Zusie and Janilli waved a goodbye to Bablou and the other Bolder Clan who had come to see them off. The rest of the caravan had already started on the next leg of their journey.

The week with the Boulder Clan had been a much needed respite and most of the caravan was sad to leave. Not because they were on their way, but because their new friends would not be traveling with them. Zusie was also sad. She had tried to convince them to follow, but they felt that they were quite protected deep in the mountain as they were. If Lord Canvil was indeed able to make it across Lake Kellowash and past Kerchot and Duntar they would come to a wall of rock. Bablou and several of the Tara Aquians had gone back to the hole that lead to the Hollow of Rock and buried it under a mass of boulders. Zusie had hoped that Canvil and his army would not find a way into the passage that lead to Bablou's home.

She considered how quickly life could change as she and Janilli turned to follow the others down the long underground tunnel that would lead them to the other side of Mount Alpanatia, and the Whipple Wash Valley. The Boulder Clan people had been generous and lively hosts who had treated the travelers to a delicious feast that had been set out waiting for their arrival. To the travelers' surprise there was a buffet waiting for them of fresh pan-fried fish, breads, vegetable stews and fresh fruits.

For the seven days that they were with them they stayed in the large cave that Bablou had taken them to that first night. They ate and slept there. For the rest of the day the Boulder Clan were eager to show them the beehive of caverns that were interconnected with tunnels that ran throughout this side of the mountain. In each cavern a specific task was carried out; laundry and housekeeping, food preparation, weapons and fishing gear. That had been Rangous and Septer's favorite cavern. They made several fishing poles that they took with them. They sorely missed fishing. Bablou also introduced them to the fishing hole where they caught several different species of fish.

Zusie smiled with the thought of her favorite cavern; the bathing chamber. The first night while they ate, Zusie asked Bablou how he was able to find them. He said they had been out scouting the area then chuckled. Even though it was dark out he knew exactly where they were because he could smell them, he wrinkled up his nose for effect.

The others sitting around on the stone floor looked self-consciously at each other, leaned over and took a long sniff. They had gone months without a proper bath and were used to the smell, but they supposed that they probably did smell quite bad. Zusie curious as to why they would be out scouting with an impending storm blowing in asked who or what they were scouting for; Bablou simply shrugged his shoulders. Zusie had a feeling that perhaps someone from the Whipple Wash Valley had asked him to watch out for their arrival. He did not offer the information and so she did not press for it. Instead she asked him if they had a bathing chamber. With a wide toothy grin he nodded excitedly and after they ate he showed them the way to it.

It was a large cavern that had a large pool in the middle of it. A stone stairway led down to the pool. The cavern was lit with the same crystals that lit the passageway to Bablou's home. However, these crystals were much larger and lit the cavern in a soft welcoming glow. The pool was supplied with water that had been diverted from the main branch of the river and flowed from holes on one side of the cavern; constantly filling the pool with water. On the other side of the pool, several holes continuously drained the water out, this way the pool, to everyone's delight, was always filled with fresh cool water.

Another favorite cavern was the one where they grew the fruit and vegetables. Bablou explained that the energy from the crystals overhead, which were in each of the caverns, helped the plants grow. It was an easy enough explanation and the crystals had been similar to the ones in the Crystal Caves of Mount Aspentonia, but with the Greenwood Forest so handy Zusie and her daughters never thought to grow vegetables and fruits under them.

The pebbles, the name given to the younger members of the Boulder Clan, were very excited to see the newcomers. They became quick friends with the younger members of the caravan. Even the standoffish Tara Aquian young ones quickly warmed up to the pebbles; how could they not, they were so animated, full of life and laughed all day long. Each day, all the young ones took off right after the morning meal to explore the caverns and did not come back until the midday meal. After that, they found their way to a cavern that was used as a workshop. That is where the Boulder Clan made their tools and decorative wares like; brightly coloured weaved mats, wooden bowls, drums, flutes and beaded necklaces that they traded with the vendors in the Whipple Wash Valley.

Each of the newcomers, if interested, was taught how to make the wares. The young ones took a special liking to the beaded necklaces which were made from colourful wooden beads, stones, weathered bones and small feathers. As parting gifts, they were each given a necklace.

Zusie ran her fingers over the beads that hung around her neck. They sat alongside the crystal that she had given Willham; she smiled at the memory. Bablou's youngest son Bobbly had given them to her as a parting gift. He had become quite enamored with Zusie and followed her around wherever she went until his ma, Souphey told him to play with the others. He went reluctantly, but found a friendship with Isla. Every night the two of them sought out Zusie and ate their meal with her.

Zusie sighed heavily. Janilli looked at her and seeing the look of concern on her face she took the hand that was holding the bead and told Zusie that all would be well. Zusie smiled back at her. As she walked with her sister, she quickly said a prayer to Zenrah to keep the Boulder Clan safe from the marauding army.

Her thoughts then wandered to the Whipple Wash Valley and the inhabitants living there. What would come of all of them, would they believe Jasper when he told them of the Lord Canvil? Would they welcome, as Jasper was sure they would, the caravan of travelers?

Her thoughts then turned to the prophecy and the fairies. Would they vanquish Lord Canvil and bring peace to the world and all of its inhabitants? The way Jasper talked of them it sounded as if they were still young ones themselves. Would they, she wondered, be up to this incredible challenge? She said another prayer to Zenrah that they were indeed brave and skilled enough to follow through with the prophecy and bring peace to them all.

Chapter 6
The Failed Lesson

Two weeks had passed since the day at the Lily Pond. The fairies began their training with the Nayew and the Avidraughts. Much to the sisters' delight, the whole week's lessons had been taught in the open meadow to the northwest of the village where the Avidraughts roamed freely. Every morning, while the rest of the village children were in the large three story schoolhouse, the fairies were outside in the fresh air; which they were grateful for.

In the prior weeks before this lesson they had been stuck in the library for three hours every morning with Alamat. She was one of the apprentices to Orliff, the village healer. Alamat, a young woman that was not much older than Shanata, had taught the fairies the medicinal properties of the various plant life in the Evergreen Forest and beyond. Most of the three hour lessons were taught in a room on the second floor. It had only two small windows for ventilation. The days were still warm and the heat in the room, on most days, was stifling. If it were not for Elder Rayley's homemade lemon spiced tea they would not have endured the long lessons at all.

For what seemed like hours on end they poured over books day after day for a month; which Mariela did not mind so much. When they weren't reading they learned to make salves and healing potions. Other than the practical lesson which consisted of gathering the plants needed for the day's lesson, they were stuck in the room. They read books on medical terminology, learned about plants that could save a life and those that could take it. They also learned how to mix a Soothe Ease potion that allows a patient in a coma to swallow and take in nourishment.

Ashlina complained to Alamat about having to learn such

mundane things; she preferred to be outside adventuring in the forest. Her argument was; "When will any of us be in a coma." Alamat's retort was to the point. "Do you know that the sting of a Hummingmoth Messenger is poisonous and the victim will fall into a coma-like sleep? The antidote takes over a month to prepare. Without the Soothe Ease potion to keep them alive, until a batch of antidote can be made, the victim will die before it is ready. If you want I can teach you how to insert a feeding tube instead. If done incorrectly you could do more damage than good. The Soothe Ease potion does the same thing only without the tube and all the fuss that goes with it."

Each of the fairies looked at Zee who was looking down at her hands. How often had she carried Jasper in her hands or on her shoulders? They were best friends. They often played hide and seek games among the trees and bushes. She couldn't recall if his snout was ever unfurled when they played, but she did remember that he had narrowly missed flying into her on several occasions as he dashed in and out of the hiding places. Zee looked questioningly at Ashlina who nodded first before she went back to her reading. She never complained again about what Alamat taught them.

Since Queen Faywyn's disappearance the fairies had learned several things that would help them on their mission to unite the Southern Kingdoms. They learned more than the usual academic studies like mathematics, history, philosophy and biology. Alamat had not been their only teacher. They learned how to make fishing poles, bows and arrows, long poles and knives from Obwyn, the master hunter. They learned how to construct makeshift shelters from the Jarrell brothers. The week long lessons were overseen by Osborne Jarrell, the brothers' grandfather who gave the fairies an approving nod after he inspected their shelters for stability. They learned how to scavenge for food on the forest floor from Zila, a Pixie, who also taught them how to make a savory stew from what they gathered. They also learned how to hand sew garments from Mary Kattelley, the village seamstress.

Learning to ride the Avidraughts from Nayew, Keeper of the Avidraughts and mate to Elder Enyce however, had been the most enjoyable of all their lessons. The fairies had not only learned the history of the Avidraughts, but also how to care for them. The theory part of their lessons had been quite easy and all of them had passed with flying colours. The practical part of the lessons however was a little harder to grasp, especially for Zee.

Zee had been paired with Farley; an incredibly large roan with a dark reddish brown coat, four pure white feet and a cropped off mane and tail. His feathered wings were the same hue as his coat and majestically spanned out six feet on either side of him. He stood a staggering 19hands high (hh) to his withers, had a long thick neck, a slightly large head and sharply pointed ears. He had a rather unpleasant disposition and it would seem that he did not like Zee very much.

Farley ordered Zee around with harsh commands. *Don't sit back so far. Hold onto the reins lightly but securely. Don't brush my coat that way.* Nothing she did seemed to please him. He even complained about the way she prepared his food; which she really didn't have to as the Avidraughts fended for themselves quite well. However, Nayew thought it would be good practice for the fairies to learn how to take care of something other than themselves.

Unlike Zee, her sisters' Avidraughts were delightful to work with. Shanata was on Felon, the only female of the group of Avidraughts. Felon was a lovely regal creature with an even temperament and stood 15hh. She was white in colour with several large black spots all over her body. Except for her face and muzzle that is, which had a large brown splotch of colour on it. Her mane was long and flowing like her tail, and her delicate streamlined wings were pure white.

Mariela was on Topez, a sturdy looking Avidraught standing 16hh. He didn't say much and paraded around the others looking bored as if he had better places to be and things to do and wished he was doing them. His coat was a soft muted grey mixed with darker spots of grey. His mane, like Farley's, was cropped short but he preferred his tail to hang long and loose. His wings were a fine mixture of grey and white feathers.

Enna was on Amos, a large stocky Avidraught with thick legs and neck that stood 16.2hh. His coat was the opposite of Topez's; it was dark grey mixed with lighter spots of grey. His feathered wings were dark grey mixed with white. He preferred to wear his tail and mane long. He was a little rough around the edges in his manner and speech, but unlike Topez, he talked nonstop with Enna about everything and anything and they often laughed outwardly at each other's jokes.

Ashlina zoomed around the open meadow on Arturo, the smallest yet fastest of the Avidraughts. He was dainty in stature at only 13hh, but oh could he fly. Ashlina seemed to take to flying like ducks to water. They zoomed expertly in and around the others. Arturo's body was covered in a mixture of large white and black splotches, his legs were pure white and he had a long splotch of white down his otherwise black face. He allowed Ashlina to adorn his mane and tail with colourful wooden beads that he proudly paraded around the other Avidraughts.

The girls continued to fly around the meadow as Nayew called up to them. "Feel the beat of their wings. See how they move with the air currents. Move your bodies with their movements. Lean when they lean. If you want to go faster lie low over the neck and grip them tight with your knees. Relax," he said over and over again. "Enjoy the experience. Become one with your Avidraught."

Ashlina, no longer listening to the instructions, leaned over Arturo and whispered to him to fly higher and faster. Arturo, needing no further encouragement, took off high into the air and Ashlina laughed heartily with the acceleration. Nayew said nothing as he watched them leave; confident that Ashlina could handle herself. He looked at the other girls who had been doing well and nodded at them as they each flew by him. However, when Farley flew past Nayew looked with concern at Zee. She did not look well and he thought she might actually be physically sick. He hoped for her sake she would not be, as it would not bode well with Farley at all; he was quite upset with her as it was.

*

During the previous day's late afternoon lesson Zee had hit Farley with the straps of the saddle several times as she tried to throw the saddle onto his back. She did not even come up to his withers so the task was quite difficult for her to do. The other fairies that had finished their task for the day were waiting patiently for Zee to finish hers. They noticed that unlike their Avidraughts, Farley wasn't giving Zee any help or instructions. Tired of being hit with the straps he instead yelled rudely at her, "If you hit me one more time with those straps I am going to hit *you* with them."

The other fairies looked crossly at Farley but Nayew told them not to interfere. "If she is going to be paired with Farley they will need to find a way to work together without your interference." He then told them to leave. Nayew was a stern teacher and the fairies knew better then to argue with him. They took the saddles off their Avidraught's back, thanked them for the lesson and left without saying goodbye to Zee. Nayew left with them, making sure that they did not return.

He did not worry about Zee as her sisters did. He knew she was strong. Her only problem was that she lacked confidence. He had paired her with Farley for many reasons, but mostly because he knew that Farley would teach her how to be more direct. It wouldn't be easy because Farley was just as bullish and pigheaded as any human Nayew had ever encountered. The paring would be good for both of them as Zee would teach him humility in return.

Hearing Nayew's words Farley decided that perhaps it

71

was time to help her out; as he was quite sure Nayew was not going to change his mind about pairing her with another Avidraught. Seeing a large boulder several feet away, he walked over, stood beside it, and waited for Zee to follow.

When Zee did not follow, he looked back at her with a disgusted look on his face and rudely yelled at her again. "Well come on with it, the day and your lesson is almost done. Your sisters have long since gone and I am getting hungry." Zee looked around; her sisters had indeed left. So caught up with her task she had not even noticed that their Avidraughts and Nayew were gone as well.

Zee was exhausted and hungry. She looked at Farley questioningly, unsure what it was that he wanted her to do. Farley sighed heavily then spoke slowly accentuating every word. "Pick up the saddle Zabethile, bring it over here and stand on this rock while you put the saddle on me. Must I explain everything to you in minute detail?"

Zee sighed again. She walked over to him, dragging the saddle behind her. This was the first time he had explained anything to her, so she was not quite sure what he meant by 'everything.'

"Don't drag the saddle along the ground Zabethile," Farley said angrily. "Dirt will get under it and it will prick at my skin and rub it raw."

Zee huffed loudly as she slung the heavy saddle over her shoulder. She looked crossly at Farley. She had had just about enough of his ill temper and rude comments; she was trying her best. Couldn't he see that?

Fifteen minutes later and the pair of them were cantering around the meadow. Zee securely hung onto the reins while Farley continued to bark out orders at her. The sun had started to set and Farley heard Zee stifle a yawn. *She was a determined little one*, he thought to himself.

"I have business in the village," he said gruffly as he heard her yawn again. "Stay up there and I will give you a ride back to the village." Zee sighed heavily and loosened her grip on the reins. It had been an exhausting day for her and she was quite tired and thankful for the ride back to the village. *Tomorrow* she hoped, as her head lolled sleepily to the side, *would be a better day*. But unfortunately for Zee, Farley's disposition had not changed.

*

"Farley I think you need to land," Zee said as she held on tightly to the reins and pulled back on them roughly. He shook his head violently from side to side as he tried to loosen her grip.

"Zabethile loosen your grip and stop tugging on the reins. You are going to kink my neck." He scolded her loudly; the others flew around and looked over at the pair with concern.

"Oh...oh...I don't think I am ready for this," Zee mumbled. Farley had run around the clearing several times before he lifted off the ground and flew gracefully into the air. The reins, which were attached to his muzzle, were clenched in Zee's tiny fist. She held on to them as if her life depended on it. Her head swam and her vision blurred every time she looked down. The bushes and boulders in the meadow swiftly disappeared from view as they flew past them. She squeezed her eyes shut as her heart pounded in her chest. Her breath caught in her throat and she sat rigid in the soft leather saddle between the base of Farley's neck and where his powerful wings jutted out from his body. All she could hear was the rapid thudding of her heart as the wind rushed by them. She missed what Nayew was yelling up at them.

"No really," Zee said as she moaned pathetically. She quickly put her right hand over her mouth as her stomach rolled violently. "I think I am going to throw up!" She cried out.

"If you throw up all over me I will take you to the Lily Pond and toss you into it," Farley said crossly. He turned his head and looked back at her. He noticed she indeed looked like she was going to lose her breakfast. Her eyes were tightly closed, her mouth was in a deep frown behind her hand and her skin had gone a sickly pale shade of green.

He clicked his tongue and huffed loudly as he landed not too lightly onto the ground. The landing jolted Zee and she burped loudly. Thankful that they were on the ground she quickly slipped out of the saddle. Her foot caught on the reins and she fell with a thump to the ground and landed on her backside. Pushing herself up, she grasped her stomach with one hand and held her mouth with the other. She quickly ran to the rock she had stood on days before and threw up behind it.

Farley shook his head as Nayew made his way over to him. He looked from Zee to Farley. The other fairies seeing their sister in distress quickly asked their Avidraughts to land; they ran over to her.

"Don't be discouraged, Farley," Nayew said confidently as he took the saddle off Farley's back. He could tell that Zee had had enough for the day. "Before you know it she will get the hang of it."

"I don't know Nayew. She was awfully frightened up there. I could feel her little body shaking. I didn't dare go any higher than twenty feet," Farley said. He then slowly moved his head from side to side; trying to ease the kink in his neck. "Are you sure you chose right?" He questioned Nayew once again. He had the night before as well after he carried her to the Whipple Wash Tree.

"Yes my friend," Nayew said as he rubbed Farley's neck for him. "I stand by my decision. If she is strong enough to kink your neck I think she will be strong enough to ride you. Besides she is not one to give up on a task." Farley looked at him doubtfully as he heard Zee belching and moaning loudly behind the rock. Her sisters looked on helplessly with concern. Nayew smirked. "Ah…. so you haven't heard yet." Farley shook his head indicating that he had not heard. "Athia's task for her two weeks ago was to stand on a stack of rocks." Farley did not look impressed.

Nayew continued and chuckled as he recited what he had witnessed. "I, with the help of Jemas..." Nayew stopped talking when he saw the confused look on Farley's face. "Jemas, he's been living in the village for a couple months now. You know that good looking young fellow with dark hair." Farley still looked like he didn't know who Nayew was talking about. "Remember last night when we saw that group of girls walking by *The Baron's Den*, pointing and giggling at someone sitting with Jarrott, Luke and Marcus."

"Yes," Farley said. "Is he going to join the Hawkeye team with Jarrott and the others? Those boys could use another strapping young lad on their team. I've heard rumors that the Boswick Trappers have hired Herb Marrona to play for them. He won the gold three years running at the Nationals."

Nayew smiled. Farley was an avid fan of Hawkeye. He knew all the teams, the players by name, all of the stats and never missed a game.

"I saw him chatting with Osborne's granddaughter Rhethea, the other day," Farley said. "Are they dating?"

"I don't know Farley. He's a nice enough young fellow; always eager to help out. I don't think Osborne would mind if they dated. Do you mind however if I get back to my story," Nayew asked. Farley nodded his head. "Anyway, we stacked the rocks using a four legged wooden ladder that Osborne had provided. We waited half way through the night for her to either fall off or ask for help down. Instead, we noticed as we sat around a fire with the other fairies that she had fallen asleep. She was so soundly asleep that I had to prod her with a long stick to wake her. Instead of using the wooden ladder to get down she jumped into the air, did two summersaults and landed lightly on her feet."

"Not only," he continued to say when Farley hadn't changed his expression, "Did she get up to twenty rocks, she fell asleep standing on them." Nayew looked at Farley whose expression still hadn't changed. Avidraughts often fell asleep

75

while standing. He was not sure why Nayew was making such a big deal out of it until he added, "On one foot."

Farley's eyes brightened in surprise and he looked over with new appreciation at Zee who was still bent over behind the rock. Now however dry heaves racked her small body. Shanata rubbed Zee's back as the other fairies talked to her encouragingly. *Perhaps*, Farley thought to himself, *there was more to this little one than meets the eye. Besides, she hasn't hit me once with the strap all day.* Zee stood up, thanked Shanata for her help, and looked helplessly at the others in embarrassment. Seeing their expressions of empathy made Zee angry.

"A tower of rocks two weeks ago, flying Avidraughts this week; do you think Elder Athia thinks I am afraid of heights or something?" Zee said. "Doesn't she know I live in a ruddy old tree?" Zee was more cross with herself for failing the task then at Athia. Tears quickly welled up in her eyes once she realized what she had said.

Ashlina and Enna laughed at Zee's bizarre outburst. Mariela smiled at her grimly. Shanata looked angrily at her like a mother who was just about to scold her child. Zee knew that look and waited for the words of scorn that would follow for her impertinence.

"First thing; the Whipple Wash Tree is not any old ruddy tree and you are never to call it that again. Secondly," she went on to say; Shanata always scolded her younger sisters in a chronological point-form order, "Elder Athia knows that you live in a tree. But when, can I ask you, was the last time you climbed to the top of it?"

Zee looked up at Shanata with a surprised expression; the scolding was to be a short one as Shanata always finished her scolding with a question. Seeing her sister's stern look however changed Zee's surprised look to one of sadness.

Shanata knew as well as the others did that Zee has never climbed to the top of the tree and has barely made it past the third limb. Her sisters were able to climb the tree before they were six years old and Ashlina had climbed to the very top when she was just three.

The tears in Zee's eyes spilled over and ran down her cheeks; she bowed her head in shame. Shanata put her arms around her little sister and gave her a quick hug. She placed her finger under Zee's chin; lifted it up and looked sympathetically into her eyes. "Zee, you have to trust the Elders and know that the tasks they give us are to better prepare us for the coming war. They would not ask us to do them if they did not think they were important." Zee remembered the words; they were the same ones Mariela used when they were at the Lily Pond. "Somehow Zee, you will have to find the courage to get over your fear of heights and learn to fly." Her sisters smiled kindly and nodded their heads in agreement.

"Besides," Mariela said as she put her arm around Zee's shoulders and turned her to look at Farley, "Farley hasn't given up yet has he? He doesn't have to stay you know. He can leave whenever he chooses. We do not own the Avidraughts. They live on this land and are as free as we are. They have chosen to fight with us, not against us. Besides," she said again but more as an afterthought. "He didn't complain about the way you prepared his oats this morning, did he?" Zee noticed that Mariela conveniently left out that Farley had complained about everything else that she had done.

Zee wiped her eyes with the back of her hand then looked at Farley who returned her look with a compassionate one that he quickly masked. But Zee had seen it and she smiled lightly. "All right," she said. "I will try harder, but perhaps tomorrow. For now I would like to lie down."

"All right," Shanata said. "Would you like us to walk you back to the village?"

"No, no… you go on. I'll make my way there on my own," Zee said then smiled reassuringly at her sisters. "I know you are anxious to get on with your flying lesson."

Her sisters gave her a warm hug before they walked back to their Avidraughts. Zee watched as they mounted them and gleefully took off in flight around the meadow. Her heart sank as she watched Ashlina and Arturo fly faster and higher than the rest of them.

Chapter 7
A Burden too Large to Bear

Zee quickly walked down a path that led to the back of the Whipple Wash Tree. It wasn't a well-used path and she hoped that she would not run into any of the villagers. However, upon hearing voices she dashed behind some bushes and waited for whoever was walking to pass by. It was Rhethea and Jemas. They were on their way to watch the fairies fly their Avidraughts. Although they were friends, the way Rhethea looked and giggled at him suggested there was something more between them; which Zee wouldn't mind at all.

She liked Jemas. He came from a Port that Zee couldn't remember the name of. It was however, she knew, located along the most Northern tip of the Western Sea. Jemas was tall and muscular with dark hair and dark eyes; he had a quick smile and fit right in with everyone else. Zee couldn't understand however why all the girls in Elsbrier looked at him strangely as he walked by or blushed and giggled if he said hello to them. Zee just knew that he was good for a piggyback ride after a day of working in the Gnome Gardens.

Thankful they had not seen her, Zee started on her way again. She didn't want anyone knowing that she had miserably failed her first flying lesson. They would soon know she had, no doubt. News carried quickly around the village, but for now she didn't want to be confronted about her failure.

Over the coming weeks many of the villagers would be paired with an Avidraught and learn how to fly them as well. It was all they talked about day in and day out. She had talked excitedly about it as well but afterwards, when she was alone, she fretted well into the night. Many times she awoke shaken and scared from a nightmare that usually ended in her falling off the back of an Avidraught while flying thousands of miles in the air. She never knew what became of her, as she always woke up before the dream ended.

"How," she muttered to herself, "am I going to fly hundreds of feet off the ground on the back of an Avidraught when I can't even climb a tree?" Zee was just making her way around a bend when she nearly bumped into J. Z. Jones, the director of *The Briers Edge*; the local theatre company. J. Z. was pulling a wagon full of material down the path that led past the Vendor Market and onto the path that led to the theatre. The theatre sat in a large area on the south side of the village. Zee knew that she and Annie Dee, the costume designer, were busy preparing for the Winter Solstice Celebrations. Annie Dee was married to Edward Dee, the owner and head coach of the Elsbrier Eagles Hawkeye Team. Annie had made new uniforms for the team and was now making outfits that the fairies would wear for the celebrations.

"I am sorry dear, did you say something?" J. Z. asked. However she did not wait for Zee to reply as she was absentmindedly talking to herself while she pulled the wagon. It sounded, to Zee, like she was making a list of sorts. "Three curtains, five stages, half-dozen backdrops, must ask Jarrott to assist with the building of the stages, twenty-five carolers, nineteen band members" and so on. Thankful that J.Z. did not stop to chat, Zee quickly went on her way.

Finally Zee stood in front of the Whipple Wash Tree, which she knew wasn't just an ordinary tree. She looked up at its branches sadly. Standing majestically before her she bowed to it in greeting. The Tree bowed back to her. Well not really as after all it was a tree with a very large trunk, but it moved its branches in just such a way that those who knew it well could tell how it was feeling. The Tree sighed and the long flowing, thin, light green leafy limbs parted for Zee. She stepped slowly between them. Other than the fairies, the only ones who the Tree welcomed to the sanctity of its inner core were

Queen Faywyn, the Seven Elders, Obwyn, Orliff, Nayew and the Hummingmoth Messengers. Anyone else who tried to get through the flowing limbs unescorted would be scooped up and thrown hundreds of feet into the air.

Zee sighed heavily in despair as she stood before the massive trunk of the Tree. It was white in colour and the bark lay paper thin against it. Every animal in the Whipple Wash Valley was depicted in carvings all around the trunk and along the thick roots that lay against the ground and gradually sunk into the rich earth. Six feet off the ground, the trunk split into three. From that split, it twisted like a braid, a thousand feet into the air with hundreds of branches growing out of it in all directions. Small steps naturally formed by knots in the Tree spiraled all the way up to the upper branches. All one had to do was literally walk up the steps to reach the top branches.

Zee sighed heavily again. The Tree sensed her pain and reached out a willowy limb, placing it gently under Zee's chin. It lifted her chin up so that Zee would look up into the Tree's branches.

"I'm not ready," she said sadly as she brushed the limb from her chin and walked to the base of the Tree. A hollow in the trunk, six feet high and three feet wide made for a natural doorway that led into a cavern. Zee walked into it and the Tree sighed again, but this time in sadness. The youngest of the fairies would have to learn very quickly that she had no option. To unite the Kingdoms with the little time they had, she would have to conquer her fear of heights. There was not enough time for them to travel to the outer regions by land. They would have to fly. Besides, the only way to make it to the Kingdom of the Mighty Gimble Beings and the Willy Knads that lived south of the Guardian Sea was to fly. No watercraft would get them there and back in time. The fairies had to find a way to fulfill the prophecy, or all would be lost.

Zee stood for a moment on a large landing on the other side of the doorway. Slowly she descended the wooden stairs that were made naturally from the large roots of the Tree to the chamber eighteen feet below. The walls of the cavern were solid packed earth. The chamber, forty-five feet in diameter, was a large Gathering Room that had several groups of comfortable chairs, four to a group. Each had a little side table that had a lantern on them with a crystal shining in each. There was also a large oblong table made from wood that had sixteen wooden chairs placed evenly around it. Nine archways, spaced evenly around the room, led into hallways which led to several other chambers.

Between each of the archways were empty cubbyholes. Above each cubbyhole was a long rectangular lantern with sliding shutters on it. Each lantern held a bright crystal in it. The shutters could be opened or closed depending on how much light was required. They were now three quarters of the way closed and lit the Gathering Room in a low light.

Zee looked around the room; directly across from where she stood was an archway that had a wooden door on it that swung both ways. The door led to the kitchen. Zee looked at it cautiously as she wondered if she should go and fetch herself a drink. Her throat was parched from being ill.

She listened intently for a moment, hoping that the Elders were nowhere around. Not wanting to take the chance of meeting one of them in the kitchen, she instead went through the first hallway to left of the stairs. It led to the fairies' sleeping quarters.

At the end of the hallway was a small sitting chamber. In the center of the room were five wooden chairs with thick cushions on them. Multi-coloured hooked blankets lay over the back of each of the chairs. They were given to them on the day of their birth by Bethel Radek. The chairs were evenly spaced around a low round wooden table. In the middle of the table was a large octagon shaped lantern with the same shutter mechanism as the lanterns in the Gathering Room. The light shining from the crystal lit the chamber in a low light as well.

Evenly spaced on the walls of the small chamber were archways that lead to each of the fairies' sleeping quarters. Each archway had a brightly coloured curtain hanging from a rod. Each curtain was tied back with a brightly coloured braided rope. It was not unusual for the curtains to be tied back, whether the fairies were in the room or not. Zee walked to the archway on the right, which led to her room and untied the rope as she stepped through.

She slowly walked down a small hallway that led to her sleeping chamber and looked about; her chamber was exactly like her sisters. A sleeping cot with a thick mattress, covers and several pillows sat on the left wall; beside it was a small side table with three drawers. A lantern sat on top of it. On the floor of the chamber, beside the cot, was a brightly coloured woven rug made by a member of the Boulder Clan. Zee's had been made by Bablou and like the throws over the chairs in the sitting chamber, it was given to her on the day of her inception from the cocoon. On the right wall stood a large wooden desk and chair given to her by Osborne Jarrell. He was a master woodworker. Beside that were two large open wooden cases with five shelves in each of them. On the shelves, blankets and clothing were neatly stacked. The sparse furniture is where the likeness of each of the fairies' rooms ended, for each of them had put their personal touch to it.

For Shanata her sleeping chamber had been full of things that she had collected from her travels with Trebor and Bethel. In the far corner beside the desk were three elongated fish-shaped statues from the Sapphire Springs. Hanging neatly and in an organized fashion on every wall were framed pictures, woven mats or small wooden masks from every corner of the Whipple Wash Valley. On her wooden shelves was a basket full of shells from the shore of the Guardian Sea; the furthest she had ever traveled.

Each summer, since she was eleven, she and Rhethea had gone with the Radeks on one of their excursions. They usually left the day after Queen Faywyn came back from her sabbatical to the Gilded Hand and returned at the end of the summer. However, last year when the Queen did not return the trips were cancelled, much to Shanata and Rhethea's disappointment. All year long, they looked forward to the coming summer months and their trips with the Radeks. It gave Shanata time away from her responsibility to her sisters, who she loved greatly, but keeping them in line was sometimes trying. It gave Rhethea time away from her five older brothers who she also loved dearly, but they were overly protective of her.

Mariela's room although neat was so full of books there was only enough floor space for her to walk to her cot, the desk and her shelves. Her shelves were full of books and her covers, towels and blankets were neatly stacked on the floor beside it. Mariela loved to read more than anything and whenever anyone left the village for a trip, they always brought her back a book from the land they traveled to. Her desk although neat was full of stacks of parchment, inkwells and quill pens, as she loved to write as well.

Unlike Shanata, Mariela didn't have a best friend. She kept mainly to herself either closeted in the library or sitting beneath a tree, writing or reading. Sometimes she would put music to the words she wrote and after she memorized every word she would perform it for her sisters and the Elders. On occasion, when she really liked a piece, she would go into the village and perform it at *The Baron's Den*. Zan and Arnack would join in, with Zan playing the guitar and Arnack the flute.

Enna's room was messy and disorganized. Half folded clothes lay on her cot, her mat was turned up on one corner, the covers on her cot were not tucked in and her pillows lay both on her bed and the floor. Her wooden shelves were half empty as she never replenished them until Elder Rayley actually brought clothes and blankets to her. She would place them on the end of the cot so that Enna could put them away. It however took her several days to put them away and they usually ended up on the floor. Her desk, like Mariela's, was full of parchment as well but instead of inkwells and quill pens she had a large wooden box that was full of colour sticks. On every wall Enna had hung colourful pictures that she had drawn of Elsbrier, the Whipple Wash Tree, her sisters and the Elders as well as the plant and animal life found in the Evergreen Forest. Just the day before, she had taken down several of the pictures and replaced them with drawings of Amos.

Enna's best friend had been Rine Vaspin until her family moved to Chatham Court, a port along the Western Sea. Occasionally when the Radeks travelled there they would deliver a package of letters and drawings from Enna and return with a package from Rine. However for many years now, her best friend has been Ellda, the youngest member of the Water Lilys. The two were often seen in the village looking in the shops, having lunch at *The Baron's Den* or one of the cafés along the Vendor Market. Ellda could only stay out of the water for brief periods of time, so most of their time was spent around the Lily Pond.

Ashlina's room was neat, tidy, and other than three clear crystal jars of colourful beads on her desk and a ball of bimble yarn, her room was empty of anything extraordinary. Her clothes, blankets and towels were always neatly stacked and her cot was always made. It often looked like she hadn't even slept in it. Ashlina preferred the outdoors and was rarely in her room.

Like Mariela, Ashlina didn't have a best friend. But unlike Mariela, she never kept to herself. Most times she could be found working beside the villagers as they did their chores. She enjoyed learning how to use the various tools. She was the first of the sisters to learn how to fish and shoot a bow and arrow from Obwyn. She also learned from Osborne how to carve and whittle wood into flutes. From Zan and Arnak the jesters of the village, she learned the tricks of magic; like how to make things appear out of thin air and all manner of slights of hand. Much to the Elders and Shanata's disappointment she had become very good at it and often pestered her sisters with making their prize possessions disappear only to show up right where they had left them a day or two later.

As Zee stood at the entrance to her room, she looked at her desk and slowly walked over to it. Sitting beside her collection of masks and feathers sat a plate with herb scones on it. Beside it was a large mug filled with water. She sighed heavily. Under the plate was a piece of parchment. She slid the parchment from under the plate and read the message slowly:

Zee,

I thought you might need these. Don't eat if you can't, but make sure you drink the water. I am sure your throat is parched.

Love R.

P.S. Don't worry about the flying lesson. I am sure tomorrow will be a better day for you.

Zee sighed heavily again as she reread the note. Elder Rayley had somehow found out about her failed attempt at flying. Her cheeks reddened with embarrassment and she whimpered as she laid the note on the table and picked up the cup of water. The thought of eating, as she looked at the scones on the plate, had her stomach rolling. Instead, she took a long drink from the cup. Walking the few steps to her cot, she placed the cup on her side table and plopped down on the cot. As she lay back on her pillows she stared up at the ceiling. Tears formed in her eyes as she thought of the disappointed looks the villagers and Elders would give her once they heard of her failure.

The prophecy was a burden that she was not sure she was up to carrying. Tears dripped down her face the more she thought of the many tasks they had yet to accomplish. She was not sure she was up to the challenge. As tears dripped down her cheeks, Zee placed her arms over her head and cried herself to sleep.

Chapter 8
A Ghostly Visit

Back in the Greenwood Forest Queen Faywyn paced back and forth nervously in front of the fireplace. The dishes from the midday meal sat unclean on the counter. Something was amiss, but Faywyn could not put her finger on it. The more she paced the more nervous she became. Summeria had long but stopped asking her to sit still and talk with her. Summeria picked up a small bag from a pile of bags that sat in front of her. With a quill, she wrote on the bag with a steady hand, *Soothe Ease*. She picked up the next bag and wrote the same thing on it.

Summeria had collected the various herbs that made up the Soothe Ease potion and according to Faywyn's instructions, crushed the herbs and placed them in small bowls. After that, she took a spoonful of each herb and placed it in one of the bags. After she had finished that, she vigorously shook the bag so that all the herbs mixed. She then tied them shut with a piece of bimble yarn and was now writing on them.

With Faywyn's help, they prepared the herbs all week long. Each day they had bagged the herbs that had been hand-picked earlier that month and hung on hooks in a small room off the back door to dry. The person who had lived here, they surmised, must have been the village healer as there had been several telltale signs other than the hooks. There were also several decanters; some full others empty, of medicines and a recipe book of herbs and their healing powers. The hut reminded Faywyn of Orliff's drying hut back in Elsbrier. His drying hut however was much bigger and located behind his house. It had several more hooks and shelves that were filled with woven baskets and clear jars. Even though the herbs were grown in the Gnome Garden and overseen by Elder Andi, Orliff liked to dry the herbs himself making sure it was done correctly.

Summeria picked up the last bag and started to write on it but dropped it when Faywyn grabbed her shoulder. Busy with her task, she did not realize that Faywyn had stopped her pacing and was now looking intently at the bag that Summeria wore around her neck; the bag that held the bones of Baun Berlot.

"What is it Faywyn?" Summeria asked anxiously as Faywyn continued to stare at the bag. Faywyn thought for a moment before she answered her.

"Can you send Baun Berlot to the village?" Faywyn asked as she sat in the chair across from Summeria. Summeria looked anxiously at her. Faywyn did not have to explain what village she spoke of. Summeria sighed heavily. Faywyn had talked lovingly about her home and told her all about the fairies, Elders, merchants and villagers so often she thought she knew them herself. Summeria looked out the window. Their ever-standing guards were just outside, but none looked their way. Summeria hoped that they had not heard Faywyn's words.

Motioning for Faywyn to follow her, she walked to the back of the hut and opened the door to the storage room. Faywyn, hearing one of the guards cough understood and followed Summeria into the room. Even though she had closed the door behind her Faywyn whispered the idea that had formed in her mind as she paced back and forth. "I feel a great unease in the village with one of the fairies; Zabethile."

Summeria nodded her head indicating that she knew whom Faywyn spoke of. Summeria however looked at her quizzically, not sure she understood what Faywyn was asking.

"She is having grave anxiety with her recent task; I have been feeling it for days now. It is very important Summeria that she learns this task. If she doesn't, well I fear all may be lost." She thought for a moment before she asked her question. "Can you ask Baun Berlot to give her a message?"

Summeria thought for a moment. She had never asked Baun Berlot to carry messages before and she was unsure he would agree to it. However she could not turn down Faywyn's request, especially since she was so adamant about it.

"Yes, I can try," she said nodding her head in agreement.

"I'll stand watch," Faywyn said excitedly in a low whisper.

"You mean now?" Summeria asked.

"Yes Summeria, now." Faywyn said gravely. "It is paramount she receive the message today!"

Summeria sighed, "If we get caught Faywyn," but then she stopped as a look of sadness came across Faywyn's face. "Alright then, yes. You stand watch. I will raise the bones here in the storeroom."

Faywyn walked back into the common room of the hut and sat down at the table. She opened the herb book and said loud enough for the guards to hear. "Why don't you rest Summeria while I look through this book for a tonic for your headache?" Faywyn watched from the corner of her eye as she pretended to read from the book. Her words had the desired effect on the guards. Two of them left while two remained. The remaining two relaxed and leaned against the trees that stood beside the hut. None of them feared the 'old woman' as they rudely called Faywyn; however, all of them were very afraid of the witch woman. Faywyn smirked. The Venom Horde were indeed a suspicious lot. They were afraid to call Summeria by her given name; thinking that perhaps it would curse them if they spoke it aloud. She smiled inwardly as she flipped through the pages of the book. She had her own powers and one day they would witness her wrath.

A half hour later Summeria walked out of the storeroom. Hearing her soft footsteps Faywyn turned. Summeria whispered, "It is done," before she walked to her sleeping cot and laid down on it. Raising the bones always made her feel weak afterward and she quite often needed to rest. Just as she closed her eyes, someone knocked loudly on the door. Not waiting for Faywyn to answer it, Lord Canvil pushed opened the door and stepped in. The doorframe was shorter than him and he had to stoop under to get through it. Once he was inside however he was able to stand straight. His massive stature took up a considerable amount of space. Faywyn looked past him to the two guards who had left earlier. One of them had a split lip and a large bruise on his cheek.

"The guards tell me," he said with a sneer, "that Summeria is not well." He looked over at the cot where Summeria lay fast asleep.

"Is that concern I hear in your voice Gregor?" Faywyn asked cheekily. Faywyn and Summeria were the only ones who called Lord Canvil by his given name. Canvil scowled at her. Not waiting for his answer she walked over to the table and picked up one of the Soothe Ease bags.

"What is wrong with her?" He asked gruffly.

"A minor pain in her head is all. I was about to prepare a Soothe Ease tea when you barged in," she said. Faywyn held out her hand to show Canvil the bag. "If that is all you wanted to know, I ask that you leave now so that I might take care of her in peace." Lord Canvil scowled at her again. Faywyn returned his look unflinchingly.

It was unlike Summeria to fall ill. When he heard that two of the guards had left their post he ordered them brought before him. The guard with the split lip and bruised cheek was the one who had answered the question. Canvil did not believe that Summeria was sick. Instead he thought that perhaps it was a trick and he came to find out for himself if the pair of them was up to something. Seeing that she was asleep on her cot and that Faywyn at her with concern, he conceded that Summeria was indeed sick.

"Send word if the Soothe Ease tea and rest does not work. I will have Egreta and Ibisha prepare something for her."

Faywyn flinched inwardly at the mention of their names. She had only seen them once. They had passed by the open window the first day they had arrived in the village. Upon seeing them the hairs on Faywyn's neck stood and a chill ran down her entire body. There was something unholy about them; for hours afterward she shook as chills continued to run up and down her spine.

"That won't be necessary," she said with confidence, masking her feelings for Canvil's servants. "I am sure she will be better, if not by the evening meal then by tomorrow morning." Lord Canvil left the hut without another word to her. From the open window Faywyn could hear him addressing the guards. "If you leave your post again before your relief arrives, you will not see the light of day."

Faywyn walked over to the window and closed the shutters. She sat back down at the table and sighed with relief; that was a close call. If Canvil had entered the hut minutes earlier, he would have seen the glow of Summeria's aura coming from under the door of the storage room. It always shone brightly whenever she spoke with Baun Berlot. Summeria had taken a great risk to raise the bones in the storeroom. If any of the guards had been walking behind the hut they would have seen the glow and alerted Lord Canvil to it. Summeria was not permitted to speak with Baun Berlot unless Canvil had requested it. Faywyn sighed heavily again and shuddered at the thought of the beating that Summeria would have received if Canvil had caught her.

Faywyn looked over at Summeria; she was still asleep and would be for some time. Faywyn decided that she would never ask her to raise the bones again. She then said a quick prayer to the Light of Goodness that Baun Berlot was now visiting with Zee and relaying the message to her.

Zee startled awake and looked frantically around the room. She was sure that someone was with her, watching her sleep. However, there was no one else in the room. She slowly got up and sat on the edge of the cot. Her bare feet brushed against the soft mat on the floor beside the cot and her feet tingled with the sensation. If she could feel the rug then surely she was no longer asleep, she reassured herself. She shook her head. The dream she had seemed so real. She brushed at the long tendrils of hair that had fallen over her left eye as she thought of the dream.

A great white bear had stood in front of her coaxing her to wake. He spoke to her in a grumpy voice saying that he had a message for her from Queen Faywyn. He then said he was asked to help her with her task and that it was paramount that she trusted him. Zee shook her head trying to dispel the dream. She was not known to be fanciful, that was Mariela's trait. Mariela had such fantastical dreams that were as vividly colourful as real life. She quite often entertained her sisters by retelling the dreams over breakfast. They were always full of action and she recited it with great clarity like the dream actually took place.

Zee chuckled. Perhaps she was becoming more like Mariela. She made a mental note to tell her of the dream over their evening meal. She took a sip from the cup of water sitting on the bedside table. She noticed the note that Rayley had written and groaned as she wondered how many people now knew about her riding mishap.

As she put the cup down an eerie feeling overcame her. She was being watched; she knew she was. The hairs on the back of her neck stood up and her breath quickened. She knew that it was quite possible that entities could be present on this plane of existence without being embodied. They could present themselves like Dear Ones did during the Solstice and Equinox celebrations. She also knew that there were both kind and evil entities. Not knowing which one was in her room she stood and walked to the door. As she tied back the curtain she could feel warmth at her back; the entity was following her.

She slowly walked out of her sleeping chamber and the warmth followed her. She walked into the Gathering Room, hoping that one of the Elders would be there. No one was around. She did not want to cry out for fear that the entity would turn ugly and cause her harm. A thought quickly formed; if she went outside the Tree would protect her. For no being or entity could enter the sanctity of the Tree without permission. Yes that is what she would do, go outside and let the Tree dispose of it.

She didn't stop to think about the logic of the situation. The entity would have had to pass by the Tree to enter the sanctity of it first. Zee walked up the stairs to the landing before the door. The entity followed her. When she reached the landing she quickly stepped out and ducked down. She waited for the Tree to scoop up whatever was behind her. Zee waited a bit longer, but nothing happened. She looked curiously up at the limbs; they were swaying gently with the breeze.

"Oh, it's like that is it then," Zee said as she got to her feet. "No help from you, I suppose he is a friend of yours." The warm entity gently pushed her forwards to the first knot in the Tree. Zee sighed heavily as she placed her right foot on the first step. Her hand automatically grabbed the Tree. She ran her hand across the rough bark; surely, she was not asleep if she could feel the bark against her skin.

Resigning to the fact that the entity was indeed real and he was sent by Queen Faywyn to help her conquer her fear of heights, Zee took another step up. The warm entity was still behind her, pushing lightly on her back. She went up another step, then another and another. All the while, the entity was behind her following her up the Tree. She was comforted by its presence. Higher and higher, she went; afraid to look down she only looked upwards. Soon she was well past the third branch and still she climbed slowly higher and higher with the strange entity forever at her back.

She gradually felt calmed by its warmth and the higher she climbed the less afraid she became. Another half hour passed and she came to the part of the Tree where the steps ended. If she wanted to go to the very top, she would have to actually climb up onto the branches. She hesitated. The entity pushed at her back; she climbed onto the first branch, then the second and so on.

Another half hour later and she was as far up as she could safely go. Here the branches were too tiny for her to stand on and too far apart for her to reach. The entity did not push her to go any further. She settled her back against the trunk of the Tree and peered through the thinning branches. She could clearly see the countryside far below. She shivered in fright but the entity once again warmed her and her shaky nerves immediately calmed.

"Will you stay with me?" She whispered shyly. The spirit of Baun Berlot smiled as he wrapped its mighty arms around her. A calming strength like nothing she had ever felt before came over Zee and she sighed happily. She settled down on the crook of the branch she was standing on and leaned against the trunk of the Tree.

Looking behind her she could see Elsbrier; the breadth of it amazed her. The Vendor Market was quite large with its many shops and eateries. Zee could see the rooming houses, the school, the library and the theatre. The Grandiflora River wound its way through the square. Stone and wooden bridges connected the two sides. Zee had learned to fish off the bridges. Past the Vendor Market several roads and pathways interconnected the village with the Gnome Garden that she could barely see in the distance, the Lily Pond, *The Flour Mill* and *The Smithery*. She had walked most of those roads and pathways, never realizing how many there were or how far they went.

Just to the right of the village she could see the grassy

plains that went for miles until they reached the Firelog Forest, home of the Rapcicors. To the left of the village she could see past the Lily Pond and the grazing area; home to the Avidraughts. She could just make out her sisters flying around the open field; they looked like tiny specks. Surrounding all of this except for the north was the Evergreen Forest that spanned as far as she could see. She looked north. Being this high in the air, she could almost see over the foothills that lead to Mount Alpanatia. Zee wondered if she waited long enough if she would be able to see Jasper coming home. She chuckled lightly and thought, *well perhaps not him, as he was so small, but the caravan for sure.* Elder Jolise had told them that Jasper was leading a caravan of travelers from the valley on the other side of Mount Alpanatia; that is why it was taking him so long to come home.

Zee sighed contently as the limbs of the Tree swayed with the breeze. Tired from her climb, she leaned over the branch she was sitting on folded her arms and rested her head on them. Before she closed her eyes, she wondered; if upon waking would she still be in the upper branches of the Tree or on her cot. Did she finally conquer her fear of heights or was she still dreaming? Closing her eyes, she promptly fell asleep.

*

Night was falling over the Whipple Wash Valley. The villagers who had been frantically looking around Elsbrier stopped to light torches and lanterns before they continued with their search. Shanata had come home after her flying lesson to check in on Zee. Seeing that her cot was empty, she went in search of her in all the usual places- the kitchen, the bathing chamber and the workshop. Not finding her, she sent her sisters out to look for her in the village and at the Lily Pond. They came back without Zee and Shanata immediately went to the Elders.

None of the Elders had seen her or could sense Zee's

presence. She was either unconscious somewhere or too far away for them to pick up her presence. No one wanted to think that perhaps she was no longer with them. Raylee sent out an alarm and every villager took up the hunt to find Zee. Nayew had asked the Avidraughts to fly beyond the village in case she had run away. Every stranger in the village was questioned. Every building in the village had been searched several times and every tree, bush and boulder had been looked behind.

The fairies were getting anxious as the night sky grew darker fearing that Zee, instead of facing her fear of heights, decided that it would be better for all of them if she was no longer with them. None of them suspected that she might be fast asleep in the upper branches of the Whipple Wash Tree. If they had stood still for a minute they would have realized that that was the case.

"Zee," a gruff voice yelled, waking Zee from her sleep.

Startled she sat up quickly and hit the back of her head on the trunk of the Tree. Seeing where she was, almost a thousand feet in the air, she grasped tightly onto the thick branch she had fallen asleep on. Her nerves quickly calmed as a surge of excitement took over. She shouted out with glee and threw her arms up into the air, "It wasn't a dream!" She had actually climbed to the upper branches of the Whipple Wash Tree. Zee giggled with pure delight.

"Zee," the voice called roughly to her again. She looked about thinking that it was the entity that was calling to her. A cold breeze touched her skin and goose bumps immediately formed on her bare arms. Zee knew that Baun Berlot was no longer with her and she frowned.

"Zabethile!" The voice, now angry, called to her again. This time she peered through the branches of the Tree; she knew that voice.

"Farley!" She exclaimed in delight and smiled broadly. "Look, I conquered my fear of heights." Farley couldn't help by smile as well.

"Yes, yes I can see that." Although still upset his voice was not quite as gruff. He thought her disappearance had something to do with the way he had been treating her and he was relieved to see that she was alright. "Come out as far as you can on that branch and jump to me. Don't be afraid, I will catch you."

Without hesitation, Zee walked slowly to the very tip of the branch, jumped high into the air and landed squarely on Farley's back. Farley was impressed, but did not say so.

"Oh Farley, I had the most wonderful dream," Zee said wistfully.

"Did it have anything to do with a white bear?" He asked in his usual gruff voice as he descended to the ground.

"Well… yes it did," she said brightly. "Do you know him?"

"No," Farley said as he shook his head. "But he came to me when I was almost to the foothills and told me where I could find you."

"Oh," is all Zee said as Farley landed with a gentle thud onto the ground just on the other side of the Tree.

Zee heard shouts of excitement coming from the pathway that lead to Elsbrier and she quickly dismounted. Running excitedly towards her were several of the villagers and her sisters. Shanata yelled out to her, "Where have you been!?"

Mariela added, "We have been so worried!"

Before she could answer their questions, she heard a rustling behind her and then heard Athia's stern voice. "You have much to explain little one." Turning Zee saw Athia and the Elders coming out from behind the branches of the Whipple Wash Tree. All of them were wearing the same expression on their face, a deep frown of disappointment.

Zee however did not worry at their expressions or that they and her sisters might be angry with her. When she finished telling them her dream of Baun Berlot and that he was sent to her by Queen Faywyn, she knew that they would no longer be disappointed with her. Their Queen was alive and had found a way to communicate with them.

Elder Enyce dismissed the villagers who had gathered, then nodded at Zee to explain where she had been and what she had been doing. Zee quickly explained what had happened. Everyone looked at her as if they did not quite believe her. Farley however confirmed her story when he told them that Baun Berlot had told him where he could find Zee.

The Elders immediately called for a Council Meeting. Orliff, Nayew and Obwyn were summoned to the Tree. Zee explained to all of them the message from Baun Berlot. Jasper was safe and on his way home with a caravan of travelers from NeDe-- the valley that time forgot. Queen Faywyn was also safe and was living comfortably in one of the Elfkins' huts with Summeria. So far Lord Canvil had not done her any harm. Of course, the Elders were elated about the news. No harm could befall Faywyn as long as the carved statues remained in the Crystal Cave. None of them realized that if Canvil and his army were in the valley that the statues were already gone and on their way to the Whipple Wash Valley.

They talked for quite some time about how they were going to save Queen Faywyn from Canvil. Several scenarios were discussed with the answer always being, 'We will have to wait for Jasper.' Baun Berlot's message had been quite vague about Canvil and his army.

The conversation turned to Zee's disappearance and she was scolded for not leaving a note. She explained that she was as sincerely surprised as they were because she thought she was still sleeping. Elder Enyce looked doubtfully at her and suggested that Zee should leave a note, as should her sisters, stating where they were going any time they left the Tree. The fairies began to immediately argue the point.

"I am not a child," Shanata said. "And I will not be treated like one. Every summer since I was eleven I have gone on trips with the Radeks and I have never given you reason to be concerned about me or my actions."

"Nor have I," Mariela said.

"Well neither have I," said Enna indignantly. She crossed

her arms and huffed loudly in annoyance. Ashlina sat suspiciously quiet.

"Perhaps," Phinney said as she looked at the other Elders, "That we should discuss this further…"

Before she could finish Elder Athia spoke up. "But until we have come to a decision we will need to know where you are at all times."

Shanata huffed in disapproval. Mariela agreed with just a nod. Enna looked crossly at Zee who bowed her head. Ashlina got up from the table and did not stop when Elder Enyce called out to her. She briskly walked down the hallway that led to the fairies sleeping chamber. A minute or two had passed before she came back into the room, carrying two metal whistles, strung on yarn, and a note. She handed the note and one of the whistles to Phinney and the other whistle she hung around her neck. Phinney read the note and smirked before she read it aloud to the rest of the room:

To whom it may concern,

Blow on this whistle three times. If I do not answer with a whistle, expect the worse. Come looking for me. I will be somewhere outside.

Big hugs and kisses,

Ashlina

Everyone broke out laughing; even Andi who was the most serious of them all. The note had the desired effect and the Elders, as promised, talked about it after the fairies had gone to sleep.

Chapter 9
A Cloud of Despair

The next morning Zee rose before anyone else and was in fine spirits. So fine, in fact she was almost giddy and could not stop smiling. Everyone was genuinely pleased that Zee had finally conquered her fear of heights even if it was in such an unorthodox way. No one however was more pleased then Zee herself. It was as if her fear of heights had weighed her down and now, without the burden, she felt light and airy. Her last thought before waking was that if she were to run very fast, spread out her arms and jump high into the air she could fly. Silly yes, because she had no wings to catch the wind, but that is how she felt all the same. Zee stretched before she sat up. A note lay on the bedside table; she read it quickly:

Zabethile

We have decided that you are to leave a note on the stone table as to your whereabouts when you leave the Tree. Your sisters however at this time can come and go as they please. Parchment, a quill and an ink well have been set on the sideboard for your convenience.

Love Athia

Zee was too happy and excited to be offended. Before the others woke she decided to walk to the village to see the Radeks. Zee was anxious to see if any of her masks had sold the day before. A caravan of traders had arrived in the village. They were traveling to Kitcherloo and Bridgecam, fishing ports on Lake Purieors. It was a large lake located on the other side of the Firelog Forest. The traders had stopped in Elsbrier to replenish their supplies and rest as there was no outpost between Elsbrier and the Firelog Forest. Zee hoped they had bought some of her masks to sell or barter with on their travels.

Zee and her sisters wanted for nothing. All their needs were taken care of. To them it was the principal of the thing. To make something that someone else wanted and was willing to pay for, it was very satisfying. She quickly dressed in a pair of dark brown pants and a fawn coloured shirt that hung almost to her knees. She tied a large belt around her waist and slipped on her shoes. She plaited her long hair into a single braid and tied a bow around the end of it. Before she left her room, she grabbed a couple of coins out of a pouch in the top drawer of her nightstand and put them in her pant pocket. She walked into the sitting room quietly so that she would not wake her sisters.

When she entered the large Gathering Room she spied the parchment and ink. With them she quickly wrote a note stating that she was going to the Radeks. As she placed the note on the table she looked at the kitchen door and wondered if she should get something to eat before leaving. She decided that she had enough coins in her pocket to purchase breakfast from one of the shops in the Vendor Market.

Zee stepped out of the hollow in the Tree, breathed in deeply and sighed heavily. The air was crisp and cool but the sky was clear. The day promised to be a beautiful one with the sun already lighting the sky with a warm glow. She stepped away from the tree and for no reason at all twirled quickly around several times and laughed with glee as the movement tickled her stomach. She stopped suddenly and wobbled on unsteady legs as her head continued to spin from dizziness. The Whipple Wash Tree had never seen any of the other fairies do this before and looked down at Zee with concern. Before Zee fell to the ground, the Tree reached out with a couple of thin limbs, wrapped them gently around Zee's forearms and steadied her. She looked up into the branches and smiled brightly.

"Well thank you Tree, that was very kind of you," she said.

The Tree bowed in greeting and Zee replied, "And good morning to you."

It was truly pleased that Zee had conquered her fear of heights even if it did mean letting a stranger pass through its branches. Baun Berlot had arrived just after Zee had come from her failed riding lesson. Before the Tree could swat him away, Baun Berlot declared that Queen Faywyn sent him. The Tree looked deep into Baun Berlot, stripping away everything but the purity of his soul and found his words to be truth; so it let him pass through.

Now looking down at Zee the Tree sighed. Zee had come up to it and gave it a big hug with her tiny arms. The Tree reached out a wispy limb and patted her on the back. Zee giggled.

"So you are a tree hugger now are you?" Someone behind Zee asked in mild amusement. Zee spun around. Obwyn was standing just ten feet from her his hands on his hips with a slight smile on his face.

"Yes Obwyn, I am now a tree hugger," Zee said with a smile. She then looked up at the Tree and whispered, "You could have warned me that someone was coming."

"Where are you off to this early in the morning?" Obwyn questioned her with a raised eyebrow. Zee's smile widened as she stepped away from the Tree. Obwyn always looked comical when he looked at her that way. His eyebrows were quite bushy and when he raised one, they looked like small caterpillars moving across his forehead in single file. Zee and Ashlina often laughed about it after their lessons with Obwyn. Enna and Mariela only smirked and Shanata would scowl at them until they stopped laughing.

"No worries Obwyn," Zee chuckled, "I left a note on the table in the Gathering Room." She said lightly as if she didn't have a care in the world and wasn't speaking with one of the elders of the village.

"I didn't ask you about a note did I Zee," he said, no longer smiling. Obwyn's moods could change as quickly as Enna's.

Obwyn had expressed how worried he had been for her the night before and suggested that she always carry a bow and arrow or at least a knife in her belt or boots. He looked at her sternly noticing she had neither.

Zee stopped smiling and looked at him timidly as her cheeks reddened. "I am going to the Radeks and then on to Rishley's to see Jackson. I heard from Shanata who was speaking with Rhethea that Rishley was watching him as Yan and Awna both had to work today."

Obwyn only nodded in reply. He walked up to her, took a knife sheaved in a Lea-Ther pouch from his belt and tied it onto the belt around Zee's waist. "I want you to carry this with you always and practice with it every day." He said in a stern voice.

"Thank you Obwyn I will," Zee said as she ran her hand down the soft pouch and wondered how sharp the blade was.

"Think of everyone as a foe Zee, until you know them well enough to call them friend."

"All right, I will" Zee said somberly.

"Now be on your way and make sure you are back before nightfall. If not make sure one of the Jarrell brothers walks you home."

"Yes Obwyn," Zee said then walked out of the sanctity of the Tree. Obwyn looked up into the Tree as he felt it scowling down at him.

"What?" He said crossly. "She needs to be on her guard at all times, they all do. We all do," he corrected himself. The Tree reached out with its branches as if to give him a hug.

"None of that now. I am not in the mood for a hug," he said then smiled lightly before he stepped into the hollow at the base of the Tree's trunk. It was time the rest of them were up. There were things to discuss.

Zee's mood of delight diminished slightly as she ran her hand down the length of the pouch again and she thought of Obwyn's warning. Then she looked down at Elsbrier. The ever expanding village was beautiful at any time of the day, but especially so when the sun rose on a clear day. You could see for miles from this advantage point, atop the hill, where the Whipple Wash Tree sat, as if it were a lone sentinel keeping watch over Elsbrier and the Whipple Wash Valley. Zee's mood lightened and Obwyn's words pushed to the back of her mind as she looked at the village.

It was quaint even though it was one of the largest settlements around. The streets were hard padded earth that was lined on either side with tall maple trees that had large full canopies. Every fifteen feet along the main pathways, leading through the Vendor Market where all the shops were located, were twelve-foot tall metal lampposts. Atop the posts were shuttered lanterns with large crystals in them. Large hanging baskets filled with brightly coloured flowers hung from metal bars with large hooks at the end of them, on either side of the posts.

The posts had been handmade in *The Smithery*; a large forging shop located just outside of the village. Jonas Plerzany a strapping young man with dark hair and handsome features owned *The Smithery* with his father who everyone called Papa Plerzany. Papa Plerzany was a rather tall robust man who always had a quick smile and a joke to tell for everyone. His wife, who everyone called Mama, was a small woman not more than four and half feet tall who loved to cook. You couldn't walk pass their house without her inviting you in for something to eat. When Papa started with his jokes she would say, 'Oh Papa no one wants to hear those tired old jokes.' Papa would look at her and smile, then tell his jokes anyway and Mama would laugh at them even though she had heard the jokes a hundred times before.

Atop the hill Zee could see the smoke rising from *The Smithery*; Jonas was probably already hard at work. Although he owned the shop with his father, Papa stayed home most days and Jonas ran the shop on his own. At the beginning of last summer, however, and on advice from the Elders he hired an apprentice, Jopha Qwyn. Jopha was a tall strapping young

Pixie and Zila's brother. He had been Queen Faywyn's traveling assistant. Whenever she traveled outside of the village, he would drive the carriage.

Jopha had blamed himself for allowing Queen Faywyn to travel on her own to the Gilded Hand of the Hawthorn Springs, even though she always made the trip on her own. So caught up in his guilt he gradually took up a permanent seat alongside Zan and Arnack in *The Baron's Den* and drank himself into a stupor most nights. Hamy, the owner of *The Baron's Den*, was so concerned for Jopha that he sought council with the Elders. The Elders had concluded that Jopha needed something to keep himself busy so that he wouldn't have the time nor the energy to think of Queen Faywyn. So now he not only worked at *The Smithery* with Jonas, but also worked on whatever building projects the Jarrell brothers had going on. Zee wondered whether or not Jonas had heard about Baun Berlot and the message from Queen Faywyn. She would take a special sidestep to *The Smithery* on her way to Rishley's and if Jopha was not there, she would leave the message with Jonas.

Zee walked down the hill and onto the path that led into the village. Elsbrier on any given day was abuzz with commotion, but as Zee drew nearer to it the village seemed like it was alive with more commotion than usual. If Zee had the gift of foresight, she would have waited to visit the Radeks and call on Rishley, but she didn't and her mood of delight once again changed. This time however it was as if a cloud of despair followed her, the further she made her way through the village.

Word that Queen Faywyn had contacted the Elders through Zee by way of a bear named Baun Berlot had everyone talking over their breakfast. You couldn't go anywhere in Elsbrier without someone saying, 'Did you hear about last night and what happened to Zee.' The villagers asked the question even though most of them had been out looking for Zee and knew what had happened. Word, whether good or bad, tended to travel through Elsbrier like bees through a mystic meadow in springtime.

Every shopkeeper had already opened their shop for the day and was either placing their wares on the wooden tables under the awnings in front of their shops or standing around talking with each other. Their topic of conversation was the previous night's events as they speculated on what it meant. As Zee approached, they each called her over and said exactly the same thing to her. 'Glad to see that you are safe.' 'Next time, leave a note.' and 'What was the white bear like?" Zee would never say anything to offend anyone so she answered their questions politely. However, after the twentieth time and only part way through the village she was getting tired of it and wished she had slept in or taken the long way round to the Radeks. Their shop was the very last one on the west side of the Vendor Market.

Zee was about to turn around and go home when Ira and Awna came out of their bakeshop and handed her a small basket filled with freshly made bimble berry biscuits. Zee smiled slightly. She liked Ira and Awna. They were always kind to her and were the best bakers in the village. Ira and Awna were Pixies. They were married to two of the Jarrell brothers. Ira was married to Aro and Awna to Yan. Ira was a little bit taller than Zee but not by much and looked like most of the Pixies did; long red hair, slightly pointed face, small nose, large green eyes, medium sized pointed ears, clear complexions and slim bodies. Awna almost looked the same however she had long dark hair, blue eyes and her body was slightly plump, but only because she had just had Jackson, their first child, a few months before. Ira could tell that Zee was upset.

"Don't worry Zee," she said kindly. "Everyone else should just mind their own business and go back to their work," she said loud enough for the nearest shopkeepers to hear. Most of the shopkeepers went inside their stores while others fiddled with their wares on the wooden tables and pretended not to listen in on the conversation.

"Thank you," Zee said shyly as she reached inside her pocket and pulled out a couple of coins. "How much do you want for the biscuits?"

Most of the villagers gave the fairies things without asking for payment. As they were all well aware of the sacrifices the fairies were making to keep them safe. The fairies however always asked what they wanted in return.

Ira could see that it would mean a lot to Zee if she paid for the biscuits. "How about if we barter instead?" she asked.

Bartering often happened between the villagers, rather than purchasing what they needed with Noolies, which were small silver coins, or Nooties, which were large gold coins. Ten Noolies made one Nootie. If you didn't quite have enough the shopkeepers would barter for the rest of it. Usually they asked the purchaser to split wood out back, carry product in from a trolley, sweep out the front of the shops, or ask what they might be carrying to make up the difference.

The Vendor Market was always an interesting place to be, especially so when traders or travelers came in on their way through the valley. Families as far away as the Guardian Sea had come to see the fabled Whipple Wash Tree, meet the fairies and the Elders who walked among them like they were normal people rather than who they were. Elsbrier also held the largest festivals for the Solstice and Equinox celebrations, which drew all walks of life to join in on the fun. Zee looked at Ira in surprise as no one had ever asked her to barter before.

"I have always admired the masks you make. How about the biscuits for a mask?" Ira suggested. Zee smiled; the cloud overhead started to diminish.

"Oh," Awna said excitedly. "I love your masks as well." She put a couple of cream filled pastries in with the basket of biscuits. "I would love one for Jackson's room. I think it would look lovely hanging on the wall over the bookcase that Osborne made for him."

Zee now smiled broadly and said excitedly, "Alright then, thank you. Thank you. I am going to the Radeks. I will bring the masks back with me." She thought for a moment, "As long as they didn't sell out of them yesterday." Then she thought for another moment, "If they did, I will make some up for you today."

"There is no hurry Zee, whenever you have the time," Awna said chuckling lightly.

"Oh no, I have the time," Zee said eagerly. "The Elders gave us a day off, so I have all day to make them if need be." Zee paused. "Oh no I forgot, I was going to call on Rishley today. You don't mind if I spend a little time with Jackson do you?" Zee asked inquiringly of Awna.

"I would be honoured if you spent time with him Zee," Awna smiled as placed a couple more of the cream filled pastries in the basket.

"All right then," Zee said excitedly as she skipped away. Awna and Ira smiled broadly as they watched her go.

A little further down the path the Ronans were busy setting out their wares. They were the shopkeepers of *The Fishing Hut*. Zee was so excited about selling her masks she didn't even care if they asked her about last night or chastised her for not leaving a note.

Ronan Black, the taller of the two, plopped a large thick-scaled fish down on a bed of lettuce that sat on the framed table. They always fished very early in the morning, before the sun rose, so that the fish would be fresh for the day's sale. "Good morning Zee," Ronan said.

"Good morning," she said. Zee looked at him and waited for him to make mention of last night, but he didn't say anything else. Instead he went into the shop whistling a merry tune.

Ronan Brown came out of the shop with a handful of lemons and a sharp knife. "Good morning Zee. How are you this fine morning?" He asked as he sliced the lemons in half.

"Good morning," Zee said and then waited for this Ronan to say something about last night. He however didn't say anything either. He placed the lemon slices on either side of the large fish. The yellow of the lemon and the dark green of the lettuce leaves made the rainbow speckled fish look very appetizing, even though its large mouth was agape and its eyes were wide open.

The other Ronan came back out of the shop with a large bowl lined with green leafy lettuce. It was full of small fish. He placed it on the table beside the large one. Ronan Brown quickly sliced up some lemons and placed them along the edge of the bowl.

Zee looked at the fish then at the Ronans, "You had a great catch today."

"Hmm…yes indeed," Ronan Black said with a wide toothy grin before he went back into the shop, whistling.

Zee liked the Ronans even though they were half Ogre. Ogres were fierce creatures that lived in the marshes and woodlands to the south of the Evergreen Forest. They were very territorial and didn't like anyone trespassing on their land. They lived in Clans of fifty or more and often fought among themselves for food and clothing with tragic results. Most of the traders steered clear of them. However, on occasion while hunting, they would come across a Clan of them. They would then come to Elsbrier telling horrific stories about their encounters with the Ogres, which made everyone listening cringe with fear. Zee was not looking forward to visiting them. The thought actually scared her more than flying did, even though she often heard Obwyn or Nayew say to the traders 'and yet you survived the attack to tell this tall tale.'

The Ronans, as the villagers called them, were nothing like Ogres, although they looked a little bit like them. Ogres were tall and thick set with large bellies, thick legs, large heads, hands and feet and large wide mouths with little or no teeth.

They also had a large bulbous nose, squinty dark eyes and big flabby ears. The Ronans were tall, taller than most of the villagers at almost seven feet and a little bit stockier. While they had wide set mouths and large flabby ears like an Ogre's, their facial features looked mostly human.

Although they looked human, no one knew for sure what the other half of the Ronans was. The Ronans themselves didn't even know. They had been in the village ever since they were young. They used to belong to the fur trader John Blackthorn. He was a tall burly fellow with a mean streak and nasty disposition. The shopkeepers tolerated him because he always paid for his purchases with coin. He was known for his cruelty to animals and half-beings, which he called anything that wasn't human. He knew when he traded in Elsbrier he had to mind his "P's and Q's" so to speak, as Elsbrier was full of "half-beings" that lived in harmony with the humans. Therefore, no one in Elsbrier actually saw his cruelty firsthand and you couldn't condemn a man on hearsay.

One day however, Osborne, Obwyn, Nayew and Orliff, who were young men at the time, were in the Evergreen Forest a couple miles from the village. Osborne was teaching them how to cut wood properly for carving purposes. They had been chopping up trees that had not made it through the winter. Halfway through the day while they sat quietly eating their lunch, they heard a horrible heart-wrenching scream coming not two hundred feet from where they were. The four of them went rushing through the forest and came upon a clearing to find a horrendous scene playing out before them.

On the other side of the clearing a young boy stood in front of another who was unconscious on the ground, covered in blood. Blackthorn was drunk and holding a bow whip high in the air, yelling at the boy to get out of the way as he accused the other of stealing. The boy that was standing, was growling angrily back at Blackthorn. From what they could surmise, the one standing was trying to protect the other as he had several whip marks across his chest, but he was not moving out of the way. Orliff was kindhearted and soft spoken with a gentle touch. He always helped whenever it was needed. In that moment however he ran towards Blackthorn with a furious rage. Before Blackthorn knew what was happening he was picked up into the air and body slammed onto the ground so hard that it knocked him unconscious.

The others rushed forward and clapped Orliff on the back saying, 'We didn't know you had it in you, old chap.' Orliff laughed nervously and said, 'I did.' Then he smiled sheepishly. Seeing that Blackthorn wasn't getting up they walked slowly over to the boys. The one standing was barring his teeth and growling lowly. He was not about to step away from the one on the ground. Obwyn, Nayew and Osborne had quite the time trying to convince him that they were friend. Orliff, who was apprenticing to be the village healer, needed to attend to the one who lay unconscious. Finally, they had to drag the one who stood away. Orliff immediately started to attend to the other. He took salves and bandages out of the medicine bag he always carried over his left shoulder and applied them liberally to the cuts and gashes.

While Nayew and Obwyn packed up everything Blackthorn owned into two carri-shifts that were standing half full at the edge of the clearing, Osborne tried to talk to the young boy. He was only able to understand clearly that their names were Ronan Black and Ronan Brown, as he could not speak more than just a few words. Osborne who had seen much and met many kinds of people realized that the two young boys were part Ogre. He was able to piece together that although the boys were already four feet tall and burly they were only about five or six summers old. When he asked how they came to be with Blackthorn and where the rest of their Clan was the young Ronan Black became agitated and Osborne could not get anything more out of him.

Osborne told the others what he was able to find out. Obwyn and Nayew looked wearily at him. Obwyn said he did not think it was wise to take them back to Elsbrier and Nayew agreed, saying that if their Clan was looking for them there would be trouble. Orliff heard their conversation stood and walked over to them. 'I will take them in,' the others looked surprisingly at him and Osborne asked if he was sure. Orliff looked over at the boys. Emotion had caught in his throat as he watched the one called Ronan Black kneel beside the other. He looked worriedly over the now cleaned and bandaged injuries. Tears dripped from his eyes as he tenderly wiped blood soaked hair away from the large bandage covering Ronan Brown's right eye. The whip had almost taken the eye out of the socket. Orliff was able to save it but he doubted that Ronan Brown would be able to see from it. Ronan Brown moaned as Ronan Black whispered soothing incoherent words to him. He settled down quickly. Ronan Black looked over at Orliff and smiled a thank you to him. Orliff nodded and smiled back. 'Yes, I am sure,' he said to the others.

When it was time to go, Nayew and Obwyn looked around for the pokeys that would pull the carri-shifts. They were now full of everything Blackthorn owned; including several bags of coins that they found hidden in a hollowed out log. While they searched Osborne helped Orliff to place Ronan Brown in one of the carri-shifts that was full of furs. Nayew came back saying that the pokeys were nowhere around. He surmised that perhaps they had run off when Blackthorn had started to whip the boys. They were about to go look for them when they heard Orliff gasp in disbelief. They both turned around quickly thinking that Blackthorn was awake. They stared unbelievingly however at Ronan Black. He had walked up to the carri-shift that they had just laid Ronan Brown in and put the harness around his shoulders. Hatred deeper than any of them had ever known took over them as they looked disgustingly at Blackthorn. He had used the boys to pull the carri-shifts.

Orliff screamed in outrage as he went after Blackthorn, but Nayew and Obwyn held him back before he could reach

Blackthorn. "Fate has sealed his future Orliff," Osborne said sternly. "We all know what he is now. If he should wake from the thumping you gave him he will know that he will never be able to travel through this valley again."

It took a considerable amount of effort for Orliff to calm down, but he eventually nodded. Nayew and Obwyn let go of his arms. Orliff walked over to Ronan Black, took the harness from him and put it around his own shoulders. Tears welled up in Ronan Black's eyes as Nayew and Obwyn started to pull the other carri-shift across the clearing. Orliff not able to say anything waited as Osborne gently guided Ronan Black to the back of the carri-shift and motioned that he was to sit down. Ronan Black looked up at him disbelievingly as Osborne smiled encouragingly down at him. He settled himself down beside the other Ronan. The carri-shift jolted as Osborne and Orliff started to pull it along. Ronan Black held onto the wooden side with one hand as large fat tears dripped down from his face. He looked to where Blackthorn lay and smiled. He would never be allowed to hurt them again.

Once they arrived in the village, they immediately went to Queen Faywyn and explained what had happened. Furious, she decreed that Blackthorn would never be allowed in the Whipple Wash Valley again. If he ever set foot there, he would be put to death. It was the one and only time she ever had to take that stand with anyone. Osborne and several of the villagers had gone back to the clearing to escort Blackthorn out of the valley but he had already disappeared. Queen Faywyn kept all of his belongings and sacks of coins in trust for the Ronans until they were old enough to take care of themselves.

They had come a long way since their youth. When they first arrived in Elsbrier they could barely speak and only knew that their names were both Ronan. They had no manners for polite civilization. Queen Faywyn and the Elders accepted them into the village however. After hearing the story, many of the villagers stepped in to help Orliff raise the boys. They stayed with Orliff who had a large cottage in the village. He taught them at home until they learned enough and were gentle enough to go to school with the rest of the children. To everyone's surprise, they had learned quickly and were quiet, polite boys.

When they reached their eighteenth birthdays Queen Faywyn was so impressed with their accomplishments she declared them mature enough to be on their own. All the villagers chipped in to build them a home just down the road from Orliff's. When they were twenty-one Queen Faywyn gave them the sacks of coins. They used the money to build *The Fishing Hut*, which they have run successfully for ten years. On occasion when the village is busy with traders and travelers, they work behind the bar at *The Baron's Den*. If you ask them, they don't remember the time they spent with Blackthorn, how they came to be with him or where they are from. No family member came searching for them. They will tell you though that Orliff is their father, the villagers are their family and Elsbrier is their home.

The Ronans smiled down at Zee, she smiled back at them. She was about to leave when Ronan Brown stopped her gently with a beefy hand on her shoulder. "Zee," he said kindly. *Ah,* she thought, *here it comes.* She looked up at him. His left eye sparkled with life while his right eye looked blankly at her. He had lost sight in that eye from the beating with the bow whip. Everyone and gotten used to it, but it was a constant reminder of the cruelty of some men. "Can you let Ashlina know that we have new lures and hooks in? She came by last night asking for them."

Zee was at first surprised then she smiled brightly and offered them both a biscuit. They each took one and said thank you. Zee nodded in return. Either the Ronans didn't know about last night or they didn't care, which was just fine with her. *Perhaps,* she thought, *the day was not going to be so bad after all.*

Zee continued to skip along the path, passing *Jarrell's*

Woodworking Shop; Osborne was inside. Several customers were already in line waiting to either purchase goods or barter with him. Osborne was a skilled woodworker and everyone came from all around to buy furniture from him. Seeing Zee, he waved, but was too busy to stop and talk with her. Thinking that she would see him later, she waved back at him.

Zee had only taken a couple of steps before she heard someone calling out her name. She looked around and across the river, motioning to her was Mary Kattelley. She was standing several feet from her shop talking with Zila. They smiled as Zee crossed the nearest bridge. Zila, like Ira, had red hair but she chose to wear it cut short just below her ears. She had a slim body as well, but was taller than Ira and Awna. Where they chose to wear clothes similar to the women in town, Zila wore what most of the female Pixies wore- green or brown tight fitting tunics and long thin-legged pants. They lived mainly in the forest in tree houses and liked to blend in with their surroundings. Zila always carried a quiver of arrows on her back, a bow around her left shoulder and a knife in a pouch similar to the one Zee now wore in the belt around her waist.

"Good morning Zee," Mary said cheerily in a whispery voice. Mary was human, like most of the Whipple Wash villagers. She was tall and slender with long flowing blond hair and was quite pretty. Being a seamstress, she always wore lovely clothes made from the finest materials. That day she had on a pale blue floral dress that came down to just above her knees. It had short puffy sleeves and a scooped neckline. She wore a matching head band. Zee thought she looked very feminine. Once Shanata and Mariela saw the dress they would want one for themselves.

"Good morning," Zee said to them as she stepped off the bridge. As she walked over to them she looked at them keenly and waited for them to ask her about what had happened. However they didn't say anything. Zee sighed with relief.

"That is a lovely dress you are wearing Mary," Zee said.

"Thank you Zee," Mary smiled prettily. "I bought the material from Lenny Millstone, the fabric trader, just yesterday. I loved the print so much I was up all night making this dress." And then she swung her hips back and forth; the soft material brushed against her knees.

"It is lovely. I am sure Shanata would like it. Do you have more material?" Zee asked.

"Oh yes," Mary grinned brightly. "The print comes in all different colours as well and they are just as lovely as this one."

Zee smiled. "I will let Shanata know."

She was about to leave when Mary spoke. "I see you are wearing your new top." It was one of Mary's creations. "It looks lovely on you," she said as she walked around Zee. She moved Zee's long braid to the side, and pulled and tugged on the fabric, making sure that it fit Zee properly across the shoulders.

"Yes I like it very much," Zee said. "I think Enna said she wanted one just like it, but perhaps in blue."

"Oh good; I have an order to make for Elder Enyce. She has a couple of new Wood Spirits that need clothing. I will get started on Enna's top as soon as I am finished with her Elder Enyce's orders."

While Zee and Mary talked, Zila was looking at the basket on Zee's arm. The aroma of the still warm biscuits wafted in the air. Zee noticed this and held up the basket for each of them to take one, which they did and then nodded their heads in thanks.

"There are new Wood Spirits?" Zila asked, just realizing what Mary has said. She popped a piece of biscuit into her mouth and chewed thoughtfully before she said, "I didn't know."

"Yes," Mary nodded, "Just the other day." She too popped a piece into her mouth and moaned with delight as the light and fluffy biscuit melted in her mouth.

"Isn't it a little late in the season for them?" Zila said with a worried frown on her face as she continued to eat the biscuit. Mary just shrugged her shoulders as she popped another chunk of biscuit in her mouth. Zee didn't understand why Zila looked worried and made a mental note to ask Elder Enyce about it later.

The fairies had learned about the Wood Spirits in one of their lessons given by Elder Enyce. Zee did not fully understand the lesson. The Wood Spirits were born of a tree. Not like Zee and her sisters, who came from cocoons as infants and would age into adulthood. Wood Spirits walked right out of a tree fully grown. They looked like Pixies in stature and facial features, but had long flowing pale hair and luminescent skin. Unlike the Pixies who were either male or female and had parents, the Wood Spirits were only female. They helped Elder Enyce with the animals and plant life living in the Evergreen Forest. They were quiet creatures that chose not to socialize with the villagers. Other than knowing they existed, no one ever saw them except for the Elders. They normally lived for a season from early spring just as the trees started to come into bloom to late fall after the trees lay barren of leaves. When it was their time to leave they walked right back into a tree; and not the tree they were born from, just any old tree.

Zila's concerns jogged Zee's memory about something that she had overheard. Late one night last winter, she couldn't sleep and after going to the bathing chamber she came around the back way to the kitchen to get something to eat. Before she entered the room, she overheard the Elders talk as they sat around the counter drinking tea. Instead of announcing herself, she stayed hidden in the dark passageway. Elder Enyce spoke with concern as she said, 'The Wood Spirits from last season have not left.' The other Elders looked at her in surprise. 'When I asked them why, all they could say was, it is not time.' Zee watched as each of the Elders looked at Enyce with concern. Elder Jolise asked, 'Do you think it has anything to do with Queen Faywyn's disappearance?' Enyce shook her

118

head and said, 'I don't know.' Zee left quietly back down the dark passageway and told no one of the conversation she had overheard.

Zee looked at Zila and Mary as they continued to talk about the Wood Spirits and wondered if she should say something to them. She decided instead that she would talk with her sisters about it first. Just as she was about to say goodbye she noticed that the shop next to Mary's was not open.

"Have you seen Homsa?" She asked Mary. Mary looked over at Homsa's shop and just realized that he had not opened it yet.

"No I haven't," she said looking strangely at the other two. "He's usually here before I am."

"Maybe he is not feeling well today," Zila said plainly. She was obviously not concerned.

Homsa owned *The Whistler*; it was a music shop. The shop had all kinds of musical instruments in it and Homsa could play all of them quite well. There were Boofa Hoots that were made from the horns of six different kinds of animals that Zee had never seen; they lived in the grasslands passed the Guardian Sea. Depending on the animal the horns came from, determined the sound it made. The notes ranged from very low to a medium pitch, but only one note could be played on them.

There were flutes in several sizes and colours made from thick hollow reeds with several holes in them. If you were good at it, like Homsa, you could play several notes from low to very high. Tumble Drums lined one wall and were made from different size tree trunks that were hollowed out and had thick pieces of Lea-Ther stretched over them. There were several smaller metal instruments like whistles, harmonicas and Bristle Reeds. The Bristle Reeds were made from hollow metal tubes in varying lengths that were strapped to a slab of wood. To play it, all one had to do was strike the metal tubes with a stick that had a metal ball attached to the end of it.

There were several different sized acoustic instruments as well like mandolins and a seven-string guitar.

Zee's favorite instrument however was the Pinano; a large upright, wooden, instrument with several white and black keys that stretched the length of it. Because it was so big, you actually had to play it by sitting on a bench. Homsa said it was from a time long ago and he had the only one that he knew of in existence. The pinano was the instrument that Homsa liked to play the best. During the season celebrations, he, with the help of some of the villagers would roll the pinano out of the music shop to the Vendor Market. Homsa had formed what he called a *Band of Players*. Each member of the band knew how to play several instruments and some of them even sang. Whenever they played the villagers, young and old, would dance along with the music.

Zee walked over to the shop and peered in the window. It was dark inside and she could not see Homsa. She cautiously turned the handle. The door was unlocked. Zee opened it and poked her head around the door as she called out Homsa's name. He didn't answer. She looked back at the others with concern. "Something doesn't feel right," she said. "I'm going to his house to see if he is alright."

"Do you want me to come with you?" Mary asked. She was getting worried as well.

"I think you two are overreacting, he is old after all. Perhaps he just slept in," Zila said as she popped the last bit of biscuit in her mouth. Then she asked flippantly, "How old is he anyway hundred, hundred and fifty, two hundred." Mary and Zee looked at her disbelievingly. "What!?" She said indignantly then chuckled nervously.

"Perhaps that's the reason why we should check in on him, because he's old," Mary said. "It's not like him not to open his shop," she said thoughtfully. "He is usually here before I am and already sitting outside playing one of the instruments."

"Well I can't," Zila said taking offense to the tone in Mary's voice. "I have a meeting with Elder Phinney."

Just as Mary was about to say that she would go with Zee, several women from the outer communities walked into the dress shop. Zee recognized them. They usually only came into the village once a month, to pick up supplies. Occasionally they shopped for clothes and had lunch in one of the little cafés. Once the shop, they immediately started to coo over the clothes hanging neatly from racks. Mary looked apologetically at Zee as she started to walk towards her shop.

"Don't worry," Zee said. "I will check in on him. I am sure there is nothing wrong with him. He probably slept in like Zila suggested."

Zila nodded her head and looked at Mary as if to say, 'See.'

"All right then," Mary said cheerily. "Let me know what you find out."

"All right I will," Zee said to Mary, but she was already in her shop talking with the women and didn't hear what Zee said.

Zee and Zila stared at Mary who had just pulled a dress off the rack and was explaining to the women about the fabric and the coloured dyes that had been used to create the intricate design. All worried thoughts of Homsa were now far from her mind.

"So much for being worried about a friend when there is a coin to be made, eh," Zila said cheekily.

Zee hunched her shoulders. For a moment, they just looked at each other. Zee lifted up the basket offering Zila another biscuit. Zila took one of the cream filled pastries thanked Zee with a nod then walked with purpose to the bridge that Zee had crossed over. Zee turned and left as well, but not in the direction of the Radeks. Homsa's place was in the other direction on the other side of the village. Just as she stepped her foot onto the path between Homsa's music shop and Mary's dress shop, she remembered something and called out to Zila. She was just stepping onto the bridge. Zila turned when Zee called her name.

"Can you let Elder Phinney know that I am not going to

the Radeks and will be going to Homsa's instead," Zee asked hopefully. She didn't want to have to run back to the Whipple Wash Tree to leave a note just to run back to Homsa's. This having to leave a note was going to be more of a nuisance then she had first thought. Since Zila was meeting up with Elder Phinney, perhaps that would be good enough.

Zila looked at Zee wondering why Zee needed to tell the Elders where she was going. She didn't think long however as she realized that Zee must have got into trouble for not telling anyone where she had gone the night before. Zila nodded her reply then left without a word. Zee also turned and shuddered, the cloud of despair was back again. *Perhaps,* she thought, *she should have stayed in bed after all.*

Chapter 10
A Voice From Out of Nowhere

Zee quickly walked down the path while she tried to dispel the feeling of despair. Homsa's place was the last cottage on this path and she would have to pass several homes to get to it. She hoped no one would stop her as the fear that something terrible had happened to Homsa nagged at her. A queasy feeling started to churn in the pit of her stomach. The further she walked down the path the worse it got. Zee's heart started to race and sweat formed on her brow; something was indeed wrong. She could feel it in her bones. She dropped the basket of biscuits and took off running, ignoring the worried calls from the villagers as she speedily ran past them.

About a half hour later Zee stood on Homsa's front porch. Her heart beat rapidly as she tried to catch her breath. Looking nervously at the door she wondered whether she should knock. The thought that he had been in danger sped her along the pathway but now, facing his door, a worse thought came to mind: What if he had died through the night? After all, he was quite old. Was she prepared to see that?

Zee knocked lightly on the door anyway and waited for Homsa to answer. When he didn't she looked anxiously at the door and wished that Mary or Zila had come with her. Cautiously, she knocked louder; there was no answer. Turning the handle, she opened the door and called out his name. Again, Homsa did not answer. The queasy feeling in her stomach grew painful.

Zee stepped into the small dark cottage and noticed that all the curtains were drawn closed. She waited for her eyes to adjust to the dim light. She slowly looked about the gathering room; everything was out of place and covered in a thick layer of dust, which wasn't odd as Homsa was not a very good housekeeper. Stacks of books and parchment were placed haphazardly on every flat surface- the settee, the four chairs around the kitchen table, the table itself and the countertops that lined the far wall in the small kitchen. The curtains on the windows were tattered and the settee had several large patches on it. Homsa was frugal and did not like to spend the extra money that would make his home more comfortable. Plenty of people in the village offered to keep house for him but he always argued that he liked things just the way there were. The only things in the large room that were dusted, and recently, were the musical instruments that hung on the walls, sat on the floor or rested on the tattered settee.

Homsa's cottage was like most of the smaller cottages in this area of the village. It was an area that was designated for the older citizens of Elsbrier. The cottage had a large front porch with two steps leading up to it. Inside, a large two-sided stone fireplace that was used for cooking and heating separated the kitchen from the gathering room. The kitchen had an "L" shaped bank of cupboards along the back and sidewalls. A double sink and hand pump sat under a small window located on the sidewall. The hand pump was used to draw water up from an underground well.

There was a center island between the cupboards and fireplace and a table with four chairs usually sat under the window at the front of the room beside the front door. The gathering room usually had a settee, chair, side tables and bookshelves on either side of another window on the right side wall. A fourth window was located at the front of the room on the other side of the front door. The quaint cottages had high peaked ceilings with open rafters, a bathing chamber and one large quarter or two smaller ones. Zee did not see Homsa and immediately started to look around.

Several cups that had the remains of dried up liquid in them lay about. Homsa was absentminded. Zee knew he often forgot that he had already made himself a drink only to make another before he finished the one he just made. Although this was her first time to Homsa's home, the office in his music shop looked very much the same way- disorganized and messy.

As Zee continued to walk about the room, she noticed that the embers in the fireplace were cold. Homsa hadn't cooked breakfast nor would it seem supper from the night before. The queasy feeling in her stomach grew heavy. Zee walked cautiously to the back of the room towards two doors. One was to the bathing chamber and the other led to the bedroom. She knocked lightly on the door to the left and called out Homsa's name. When he did not answer, she opened the door and looked warily about. The bathing chamber was smaller than she expected it to be, but she then remembered that behind the bathing chamber was a small porch that had a staircase. It led to a cold cellar located under the bathing chamber. Zee looked into the tub against the opposite wall to the door, hoping he had not fallen asleep and drowned while taking a bath. The bathtub was empty.

A washbasin on a wooden stand under the small window on the left wall looked like it had not been used that morning either. A thud sounded behind her and she quickly turned around, but it was only the door hitting the shelf on the wall. Relieved that she did not find him in the room, Zee sighed as she walked out and closed the door behind her.

She then knocked on the door to the sleeping quarter and called out his name. When he did not answer, she opened the door and peered tentatively around it hoping she would not find that he had died in his sleep. Finding nothing Zee exhaled the breath she didn't realize she was holding. The large canopy bed on the right side of the room stood empty. The blankets and pillows were askew. Zee could not tell if Homsa had slept in it or not. As she looked around she was surprised at how big the room was. On either side of the bed were two small three-drawer dressers that had a shuttered lantern on each that sat on a stack of books. Against the far wall and under the only window in the room was a long dresser that had several drawers. Clothes hung out of some of the drawers while others were stacked on top. Zee was surprised to see that the curtains on the window had been drawn open and they were not tattered like the ones in the gathering room.

On the left wall and on either side of the door were heavily laden bookshelves. Zee walked to the other side of the room and looked beside the bed. She sighed heavily once again; Homsa was not lying on the floor. Although relieved that she had not found him, the churning in her stomach started to burn.

As Zee passed by the window, she looked outside. In the back of the lot just before the cropping of trees that surrounded the house on three sides, Zee could see the outhouse on the left and the bastion coop on the right. Homsa, like many of the villagers, kept bastions in their backyards. Some raised laying hens while other raised roasters. Homsa had one of the largest lots and the largest coop Zee had ever seen.

A bastion coop normally consisted of a four by four foot shed six feet high with a peaked roof. The bastions could wonder in and out of the shed by way of a wooden ramp and a small cutout in the door of the coop. A fence made from several tall posts and weaved wire screened in a grassy area surrounding the shed. There was no need for the wire mesh to incase the top as bastions, although birds, could only fly about five feet off the ground. Along one side of the fence would be a water trough. A hand pump could be found at one end or the other. There was also access to the coop by way of a door in the fence.

Homsa's bastion coop however, was impressive to say the least. The peaked roof building was twenty feet long, twenty feet wide and at least twenty-five feet high at its peak. The fenced grass area surrounded it by another twenty feet in four directions. It was divided into two parts with a tall fence separating the laying hens from the roasters.

As Zee looked out the window she noticed that the laying hens were quite agitated. They squawked loudly as they ran around the grassy area. The fat roasters just ambled about giving no mind to the laying hens. Zee wondered if one of the wild dogees that ran freely around the countryside had found its way into the coop. She quickly ran out the front door and around the cottage to check. The dogees were friendly, but skittish animals. All one had to do was yell at them and they would run away. Unlatching the gate to the coop, she ran through the pack of bastion who squawked even louder as they scattered in every direction to get out of her way. Zee ran up the large planked ramp and threw open the door. She waited until her eyes adjusted to the darkness before she started to look around for the dogee.

The front half of this side of the coop had five long wooden shelves stacked two feet apart lining each wall. Steps led up to each of the shelves. Large straw nests sat evenly apart on each of the shelves and were separated by a wire screen. The bastions would walk up the steps to their nesting bed. Each of them had their own bed and would squawk loudly if one of them took the wrong bed. On rare occasions fights would break out over the beds.

The back half of the room was used for storage of grain and bales of straw. It was separated from the front half with a wall that spanned from floor to ceiling. The nests lining the walls were empty and there didn't seem to be a dogee anywhere or at least not in that half of the building. Zee walked to the door that led into the other half and opened it. She was surprised to find that that half of the building was bathed in sunlight. A large pyramid of hay bales sat toward the back of the room and almost reached the overhead rafters. Zee looked up. There was a large gaping hole in the roof just above the bale of hay.

Zee wondered what could have made such a large hole. She started for the door; the mystery of the hole in the roof and why the laying hens were in such a tizzy would have to

127

wait until she found Homsa. She walked out of the door making sure to shut it tightly behind her. She was almost to the other side of the building when she abruptly stopped. An eerie feeling took over her; her brow began to sweat again. Her heart started to race and she tingled from head to toe. The churning feeling in her stomach now flip-flopped in her belly.

She walked back into the storeroom and carefully climbed to the top of the stack of straw. Zee gasped. Homsa lay motionless on the floor on the other side. Smashed bales of hay lay all around him. Zee now knew what had made the hole in the roof.

She carefully climbed down then ran over to him and frantically called out his name. Thankfully, he moaned weakly in response. Zee pushed away the bales of hay and knelt down beside him. Homsa was in an awful state. He lay on his right side. She could see that his right leg was broken as his foot and leg from the knee down stuck out at an odd angle. His face, hands and chest were caked with dry blood and his complexion was deathly white.

Homsa was a handsome man that stood no taller than five feet. Although he was old his hair was still dark brown. He had a tanned complexion, always dressed nicely and was fit for his age. Zee often witnessed the older women in the village, human and otherwise, batting their eyes at Homsa as he walked by. He however was a surely fellow that rarely acknowledged that they existed, which of course made them like him even more. They liked him so much they would often leave fresh baked pies on his front porch for when he got home from work. Once the ladies in town find out that he has been hurt, he will never have to cook again.

"Oh Homsa what have you gone and done to yourself!" Zee cried. Not wanting to move him for fear that she may injure him more she quickly looked him over. Other than the broken leg and the blood she could not see what else might be wrong with him. His breathing, although shallow, was steady. Zee leaned in close, kissed him on the forehead and told him that she was going for help. Homsa moaned weakly in reply. His eyelids fluttered but did not open.

Zee ran out of the coop to the front of the cottage. She looked frantically around. The path to the village square was void of travelers. She ran to the closest cottage and frantically knocked on the door. No one answered. She quickly moved on to the next house, but no one was their either. Zee started to panic. What if she couldn't get help to Homsa in time? Tears filled her eyes. Then quite un-expectantly, a voice filled her head. All she could hear was, "Run Zee. Run as fast as you can to the end of the path. There you will find help."

Without hesitation Zee ran as fast as her feet could take her, faster than she had ever run before. So fast, she felt like she was flying. As she neared the end of the path she heard the familiar thud, thud, thud of hammers hitting nails. *Yes*, she thought gleefully. The Jarrell brothers and several villagers were building the Mediplace at the end of the pathway. It would be finished soon and would be a place where the injured and sick would come so that they would have around-the-clock care.

Zee ran towards the first person she saw after clearing the trees. Reg Jarrell was walking towards a group of men. Reg turned and seeing the panic look on Zee's face he motioned for his brothers to follow him as he ran to her.

Even though her heart was racing, something took over Zee. She spoke calmly and assuredly, telling the brothers what had happened to Homsa. The brothers immediately jumped into action. Mitch ran into the Mediplace to fetch Orliff who was organizing the storeroom. Reg and Yan ran to harness a pokey to a carri-shift, Aro jumped onto the back of an Avidraught and held onto the reins of two others for Orliff and Mitch who mounted them quickly and took off at a full gallop towards Homsa's place. Reg and Yan followed with the pokey and carri-shift. Ody, the youngest of the Jarrell brothers and only a few summers older than Shanata, stayed with Zee.

Zee started to shake like a leaf, all the colour drained from her face. She looked like she was about to faint. Ody put his arm around Zee's waist and walked her towards the Mediplace. All the while he assured her that she had done well. As they walked up the stone path that led to the Mediplace, Rhethea and Jemas came out the door smiling at each other. They however abruptly stopped when they saw that Zee was half walking half being carried by Ody. Jemas quickly ran to them. He scooped Zee up in his arms and carried her into the Mediplace while Rhethea held the door open. Just inside the main entrance was a waiting area with several benches. Jemas sat Zee down on the nearest one.

Rhethea looked anxiously at her, "What happened Zee? Are you alright?" Zee looked around. She felt disorientated.

Ody quickly explained what had happened. Jemas immediately left to see if he could help with Homsa. Rhethea made sure Zee was alright and left to tell the Elders and Zee's sisters what had happened.

"Zee," Ody said gently after Rhethea left. "I am going to look for Alamat or Niella." Zee looked at him blankly. "You know them Zee- Orliff's assistants."

Zee took a moment to clear her mind. "Yes, yes of course I do," Zee said.

"Will you be alright then… if I leave you just for a moment? I won't be long. They are probably just in the storage room." Ody looked at her. Zee seemed a million miles away and he wasn't sure she had heard everything he had said or truly understood where she was.

"Yes," she said. Then she smiled slightly as her head began to clear. The queasy feeling in her stomach had started to subside.

Not quite reassured, Ody went in search of Alamat and Niella anyway. Before he left he told Zee to remain sitting on the bench. Zee nodded that she understood then leaned her head against the wall and closed her eyes. Her heart and nerves quieted; colour came back into her face, her breathing calmed.

Zee thought over what had happened. Every moment from the time she realized that Homsa might be in trouble played through her mind. The recollection of it seemed surreal; yet there she was in the newly built Mediplace waiting for Orliff and the others to bring Homsa back with them.

Zee, tired from her ordeal, started to drift off until she remembered something; a voice spoke to her. She wondered who it had been. *One of the Elders* she thought. No the voice did not sound like any of them. She quickly ruled out her sisters as well. Zee thought harder. She remembered that a quick vision popped into her head just as the voice told her to run. It was a vision of a Tree. Zee's eyes shot open when she realized that it was the Whipple Wash Tree that had spoken to her. It entered her mind, read her thoughts, knew her feelings and actually *spoke* to her.

Shocked by the revelation Zee abruptly stood. As far as she knew the Tree had never actually spoke to anyone. Zee's head immediately began to reel with this newfound knowledge and she quickly became lightheaded again. She should have stayed seated. The colour drained out of her face, leaving her as deathly white as Homsa's had been. Zee felt woozy as she stared blankly ahead. Alamat and Ody were quickly running towards her. Zee's head lolled to the side. Through a haze she heard Alamat yell, "Catch her Ody before she falls and bumps her head!" In Zee's ears, Alamat's voice sounded as if she was miles away rather than just on the other side of the large room. Zee looked puzzled. She didn't understand what was happening to her. Then out of nowhere a loud buzz filled Zee's ears. Her legs could no longer support her weight and she crumpled downwards. As the haze turned to black, Zee felt Ody's arms catch her just before she hit the floor.

Chapter 11
Homsa And The Seven Elders

Time speeds by quickly when your days are full. Two weeks had passed since Homsa's accident. After explaining that she felt like he was in trouble, Zee was immediately put into lessons with Elder Andi. Up until Zee's hunch about Homsa, the fairies, while intelligent, had shown no signs of extraordinary skills or powers. Zee was taught how to harness her skills of premonition, connect with her life-force, quiet her thinking and of course, breathe correctly. Never before had anyone told her she was not breathing properly. But according to Andi she had been doing it wrong her whole life.

Zee went to sleep every night exhausted. Along with the lessons with Elder Andi she also had to keep up with her academic studies and combat training. Needless to say Zee wasn't very happy about her "special powers" and the extra lessons that ensued because of it. She had no time to make her masks or visit any of her friends in the village. As it was she had only visited with Homsa once since his accident. She often wondered if she should tell the Elders that it wasn't actually a premonition, but rather that the Whipple Wash Tree had warned her about Homsa.

She had told no one that the Tree had spoken to her. Everything had happened so fast she wasn't sure it had actually taken place. The Tree had not spoken to her since nor showed outwardly as she came and went that it had indeed spoken to her. So, she decided to keep the information to herself. Besides, she was afraid that if the Elders knew she could speak with the Whipple Wash Tree they would give her even more lessons and then she would definitely never see Homsa or anyone again.

Homsa, much to his displeasure, was still in the Mediplace

mending slowly. He had not only broken his right leg but his right arm as well. He also had a nasty bump on his head; thankfully he had not suffered a concussion. The scratches on his face and chest were healed over, but because of his age, his arm and leg would take much longer than the usual two months to heal.

For the most part he had slept the first week away. At the beginning of the second week, he was alert enough to remember what had happened. He told Orliff and the Elders that he had climbed up onto the roof by way of a ladder to fix a hole. The Elders and Orliff looked at him disbelievingly while several of them caught their breath.

"What?" He asked crossly.

"Homsa," Elder Sianna said. She paused as she tried to find the words to mention the subject of his age without offending him. However, there was no other way around it so she said it plainly, "You are one hundred and seventy eight years old. Why didn't you ask one of the Jarrell brothers to fix the hole for you?"

Homsa immediately took offense, "Now you listen hear Miss Sianna." Homsa was the only villager who used Miss before any of the Elders' names. "I may be one hundred and seventy eight years old, but I can still move quite fine, thank you very much." Homsa was staring at Sianna and missed the exchanged look of skepticism between Phinney and Athia. After all his argument was not very sound; he was laid up in bed with a broken leg and arm.

"I didn't mean to offend you Homsa," Sianna went on to say with a gentle voice. "But you are human after all and do not mend like we do."

Homsa scowled at her then raised his voice, "Huh. You're just as human as I am. What's this, 'like we do' stuff?"

"Yes.....we are...sort of," Sianna stammered then looked at her sisters for help. The Seven Elders and Queen Faywyn were human in every aspect but age and healing. While humans live to be three hundred, the Elders and Faywyn were thousands of years old. Each had their own special power or gift, as they called them, which made them unlike the other humans in Elsbrier and the rest of the Whipple Wash Valley.

Enyce, the first born, was Elder of the Wood Spirits and Keeper of the Evergreen Forest. She had the gift of healing. She stood five feet tall, had a slim build, short white hair that curled up at the nape of her neck, bright blue eyes and a small pointed nose. She was able to speak with the Wood Spirits because they were healers as well. After many centuries of looking for a human healer Orliff was the only one capable of learning the fine art of healing and Enyce had apprenticed him since the time he was able to walk.

Enyce was the only Elder that had an animal friend; it was a dogee. Dogees were large dog-like animals that had short curly black hair. They roamed the land freely in large packs. She had rescued him from a trap long ago and had nursed him back to health. When he healed he chose to stay rather than go back to his pack. She learned that his name was Datoka. He was larger than most dogees. Whenever she entered the forest, Datoka always went with her.

Rayley, the second born, was Elder of the Dear Ones and Keeper of the Forest of Glen. She was a conduit for the spiritual realm and oversaw the *Day of Remembrance* celebrations. Standing not much taller than Enyce, Rayley had a lean stature. Her white hair hung to her shoulders. She had dark blue eyes and a pointed nose. Along with Queen Faywyn she kept care of the Whipple Wash Tree. They made sure that its limbs were trimmed, its bark was kept clean and the walls of the rooms and interconnecting tunnels were stable. The Whipple Wash Tree, unlike other willow trees, never lost its leaves. They paled in the winter to almost white, but in the spring they always brightened to a light green.

Andi, the third born, was Elder of the Gnomes and Keeper of the Gnome Gardens. She had the gift of forethought. She was five feet eight inches tall, had a slim build, curly, white shoulder length hair, light green eyes and a regal nose. She was able to see things before they happened and was the one who told the other Elders and Faywyn that the fairies would be born one year a part during each of the season's celebrations. She however had not seen that a fifth fairy would be born, three years after the last one.

Andi, along with several Clans of Gnomes, took care of the Gnome Gardens located in fields several miles from the village. The Gnomes were hard working creatures that stood no taller than three feet and looked like miniature Ogres, only their features were finer and their dispositions were friendlier. They had dark hair that the women wore long and the men wore short. Rarely did you see either without a kerchief or a weaved straw hat on their heads. They sowed, weeded and harvested the vegetable and herb gardens and took care of the fruit orchards. The harvest was stockpiled into a large underground chamber that kept cool all year long.

The Gnomes preferred to live in a miniature version of Elsbrier called Little Springs. It was located several miles away on the other side of the gardens. They lived in rows of small bunkhouses that were set in small rounded grass hills. Little Springs, like Elsbrier, had walkways, shops, a school, and a meeting place where they held council meetings and large celebrations. The Gnomes were friendly, well liked and could have lived in Elsbrier, but chose to live a quieter life in the countryside.

The only Gnomes who came to Elsbrier were the O'Grady sisters- Jenni, Anni and Dani. They ran the *Gnome Garden Stand* located next to the Radeks. This is where most of the villagers purchased their fruits and vegetables, rather than taking the half-day trip out to the gardens and warehouse. The sisters came to Elsbrier at the beginning of the week, stayed in a small cottage in the village, and then went back to Little Springs for more supplies on the weekend. Mitch's wife Lashia watched the stand on the weekends. Through the week when she wasn't busy caring for Lewis and Chella, their son and daughter, she made beautiful patchwork blankets and pillows that she sold at the Gnome Garden Stand and several other shops in the surrounding communities.

Sianna, the fourth born, was Elder of the Mountain Hermits and Keeper of the Quill Pen. She had no extraordinary talent, but was able to recall past events and write them down with divine clarity. She was the tallest of Elders at almost six feet, had long flowing white hair that she normally kept up in a bun at the nape of her neck or under a hat. She had dark black eyes and a small pointed nose. She had written the history of the Whipple Wash Valley and several other books in the Village library.

As the Elder of the Mountain Hermits, there really wasn't very much for her to do. They were hermits after all and preferred to keep to themselves. They didn't like company nor did they attend any of the seasonal celebrations. The Mountain Hermits lived in well-hidden caves throughout Mount Hillside, which was not really a mountain rather a very large rocky escarpment located on the other side of the Lily Pond. The Lily Pond wasn't really a pond either. It was a small lake that was connected to five larger lakes on the other side of the escarpment by way of the Grandiflora River that ran through the center of Elsbrier.

On occasion Sianna would attend a wedding, birthing or a Ritual of Passover for the Hermits, but she was the only one of the Elders who did. As the Keeper of the Quill Pen Sianna kept detailed accounts of everyone who lived in the Whipple Wash Valley and their lineage. The books were located in the library so that everyone had access to them. A copy of them was also located in a safe room below the Whipple Wash Tree. Sianna was often away from Elsbrier gathering the information from the bookkeeper of each community who kept accounts of everyone who was born, married or passed over throughout the year since her last visit.

Usually she traveled alone, but since Queen Faywyn's abduction, a band of armed villagers now traveled with her. Instead of her usual mode of transportation which was a large canopied carri-shift that was pulled by four pokeys; she and the armed guards traveled to the outer communities on the backs of Avidraughts.

Phinney, the fifth born, was Elder of the Pixies and Keeper of Elsbrier. She had the gift of reading minds. She was almost as tall as Andi, but had a slight figure, closely cropped white hair, grey eyes and a medium sized pointed nose. Her gift was a little harder to define. Beings whether human or not often had ill thoughts, but rarely acted upon them. So she needed to determine which thoughts was truth and which were not. For example, she had sensed something about John Blackthorn the fur trader who had brutally beat Ronan Brown, but he was very good at masking his true thoughts when he visited Elsbrier. She had felt quite guilty about it until Andi told her that something evil was at play and one day it would all make sense as to why she could not read Blackthorn's thoughts.

As Keeper of Elsbrier it was her job to plan the different communities within the village and oversee the various builds. The Pixies helped her with this even though most of them lived in the Evergreen Forest. Several of the Pixies were trusted with keeping up the many flowerbeds in the Vendor Market and along the pathways that lead from the Square. They also ensured that the streets of Elsbrier were clean and the Grandiflora River was kept safe from refuse. Zila was the Pixie in charge of making sure that Elsbrier ran smoothly. Elsbrier, on any given day, was a hub of activity with several visitors coming and going at all hours. Zila had a small office just outside the Vendor Market that was attached to a large barn. The barn housed all the gardening tools like hoes, rakes, shovels and wheelbarrows. On the other side of the barn was a large field where the Pixies grew flowers and ornamental trees to plant in the flowerbeds. The villagers also came there to buy flowers for their gardens and hanging baskets. The money earned paid the wages for the workers.

Athia, the sixth born, was Elder of the Water Lilys and Keeper of the Lea-Ther plant. Her special gift was speech. As tall as Rayley, she had white shoulder length hair that curled up at the ends, a slightly plump stature, dark green eyes and medium sized pointed nose like Phinney. She knew several languages and each of their dialects and was known as the interpreter. When there were land disputes in the outer communities Athia would go and settle the disputes as she could communicate effectively with both sides who often did not speak the same language. As Elder of the Water Lilys she over saw their development and the upkeep of the Lily Pond.

Jolise, the seventh born, was Elder of the Hummingmoth Messengers and their Keeper. Her special gift was Astro-Telepathy. She was as tall as Phinney, had a slim build, long white hair, like Sianna, but she preferred to wear hers loose. She had dark blue eyes and a small pointed nose. Jolise trained the Hummingmoth Messengers who in bands of five delivered messages from the Elders to the outlying communities. She was able to converse with the Hummingmoth Messengers over long distances through dream sequences, which was very convenient as many of the communities were hundreds of miles away.

The Elders and Faywyn ruled over the Whipple Wash Valley and all that lived within it with kind and fair hearts. However if confronted they were a force to be reckoned with. Most beings would have been intimidated if the seven of them stood at the foot of their bed scowling done at them. However, Homsa just scowled back. He had lived his life the way he pleased and did not take kindly to anyone telling him what he could or could not do, even if they were the Seven Elders or Orliff, whom he respected greatly.

When Orliff told him that he was to stay in bed for at least another month he argued loudly and got quite agitated the more he yelled. "Who is going to run my shop, take care of my cottage, the bastions and fix the hole in the roof of the coop while I lay in bed all day?"

"That is all taken care of," Orliff said as he tried to ease him back down on the pillow. But Homsa struggled so much that Orliff let him sit up before he could hurt himself any further. Orliff then stepped back behind the Elders, hoping they could talk some sense into Homsa. He however huffed indignantly as he swung his legs over the side of the bed. His legs hadn't even touched the floor when streaks of severe pain traveled up his broken leg. He grasped the mattress of the bed with his left hand and leaned backwards; pain shot up his broken arm and his chest began to burn. As he stretched back the scabbed over cuts did not stretch like the surrounding skin, causing pain. He stopped himself from rubbing them.

"Perhaps you should lie back down and stop being so stubborn!" Elder Enyce said quite sternly. Homsa looked at her through squinted eyes. Although Enyce's words were harsh her expression showed that she was quite concerned for him, so too, he could see, were the others. Without having been told, Homsa knew that if he did not comply with their orders, they were not beyond giving Orliff the permission to strap him to the bed. He sighed heavily and slowly brought his legs back up onto the bed, but instead of lying down, he sat up against his pillows. The Elders sighed and looked pleased with his decision.

"Casey Farriva had heard about your predicament and immediately printed a leaflet that was distributed throughout the village the day after Zee found you," Sianna said. Casey was the owner and editor of *The Village Voice*; Elsbrier's periodical. "By the end of the day she had a line of villagers standing at her door who were offering to help."

"Shanata has offered to run the shop for you..." Orliff started to say, but stopped when Homsa opened his mouth to argue. He however closed his mouth quickly when Phinney picked up the straps at the end of the bed. "During the times that she has lessons, Rhethea will run it for you." Homsa thought reflectively for a moment. He liked both girls and knew that they would do a good job.

"Zee and Ashlina said that they would take care of the cottage," Sianna said.

"Ody and Kale, offered to take care of the bastions," Rayley said. Kale, who was brother to Zila had helped Homsa with the bastions in the past; so had Ody. When he heard their names the frown on his face lessened. At least he didn't have to worry about his birds.

"The rest of the Jarrell brothers along with Jopha, Jarrott, Luke and Marcus offered to fix the roof," Enyce said. Homsa contemplated for a moment.

"I can't afford to pay all of them," He whined. "All those wages would cost me my house and shop, if I am here for a month or more." The Elders and Orliff did not miss the emphasis he had put on "if."

"The Jarrell brothers," Andi said curtly, "have offered to do the work in exchange for a couple of laying hens and half dozen roasters; each." Homsa quickly tallied up the numbers in his head and nodded that it would be a fair barter.

"And what of the rest?" He said looking straight at Enyce. His handsome bruised features were in a scowl. "Surely they don't expect to work for free."

"Jopha is working off his punishment," Athia said. "When I spoke with Jarrott he said Luke and Marcus were interested in learning how to play a guitar, and would take lessons in exchange for their services." Homsa again contemplated over that. The boys were handsome lads. If they learned to play well he would enlist them for his *Band of Players*. So he nodded his head that he would comply.

"And of the fairies?" Homsa asked.

"It is the fairies duty to their people to help out, they expect no payment," Enyce looked sternly at Homsa, daring him to counter the point. She had grown tired of his arguing. There were things to do; she could not stand around all day debating with him, no matter how ill he was or how much she liked him.

He opened his mouth to ask about the others, but Raylee offered the answer before he could ask it. "The others said they would take as many singing lessons from you as you thought were fair, in exchange for payment." Homsa thought this over for a moment; handsome members for his band and now singers; he should have hurt himself months ago. He wondered fleetingly if they would be ready for the Winter Solstice celebration. He would have to get started soon.

Homsa smiled up at them and nodded his head indicating that he was pleased with the arrangements and would stop giving Orliff grief. The Elders smiled back at him.

Homsa considered something for a minute. Before they could rush off he said, "Make sure you tell Zee and Ashlina to change nothing in my cottage. I like it just the way it is. They can dust if they like, but that is all!" The Elders smirked inwardly.

"I like things just the way they are," he repeated. The medicine that Orliff had given him just before the Elders had arrived had made him quite tired. He yawned loudly and mumbled, "I like things just the way they are."

The Elders smiled warmly at him as they watched his eyes close. Homsa was a cantankerous old fart, but each of them liked him very much and couldn't bring themselves to tell him that more than dusting was going to take place.

Everyone who had offered to help had already made plans as to how they were going to improve Homsa's life and the Elders had agreed. Mariela and Enna had offered to help organize Homsa's book collection in the cottage and the musical instruments in the store. Annie Dee offered to make new curtains for his windows. Osborne offered to give him a new table and chair set that he had made himself. Hamy had a settee and a set of dishes to give him. Zan and Arnack offered to pick up everything that was being donated and deliver it to Homsa's cottage. And several of the single older ladies offered to bake and cook for him until he was able to do it on his own.

Homsa began to snore and the Elders looked at him and smiled.

"Perhaps he will like the changes," Sianna said. Her sisters looked over at her and chuckled. Once he saw the changes that had been made there would be hell to pay. However, that was a month or more away. Perhaps they could ease him into it before he was well enough to go home. They highly doubted however that he was going to be happy about any of it.

The Elders left Homsa in Orliff's capable hands. They had more important things to worry about then trying to keep an old man in his bed. The fairies were receiving their powers. Zee had shown hers; the gift of foresight and speed. Even though she was a day late in sensing that something had happened to Homsa, she had still sensed it when Andi had not. They questioned the reason why, but none of them could come up with an immediate answer and felt frustrated by it. So they discussed several scenarios over the last week; two seemed more likely than all the rest.

The first explanation offered by Enyce none of them liked very much. She suggested that perhaps they were losing their powers as the fairies grew older and stronger. The second reason, offered by Jolise, they favored more. Perhaps their powers were being blocked so that the fairies' powers could come to light. By whom or what, they did not know. Whatever the reason, they watched each of the fairies closely and wondered who would show their powers next and what it be.

Chapter 12
Ashlina and the Mysterious Foot Prints

Ashlina was in a thicket of trees and bushes. Arturo stood behind her. She was peering into a clearing with interest. Several fallen logs were placed into a circle around a rather large tree. It was not as wide as the Whipple Wash Tree but quite large all the same. Creatures, that were light, like wisps of smoke, were placing flowers around the base of the tree. Once the flowers were placed they floated over to one of the logs and sat on it.

"What are they?" Ashlina whispered.

"Wood Spirits," Arturo said with little emotion.

Ashlina caught her breath. She had seen drawings of them in the village library, but had never seen any this close. There were so many of them. They were beautiful creatures with long flowing silvery white hair and fine features. They wore hooded gowns made from lightly weaved material in the palest of colours. The sleeves of the gown were long and flowing and reached to the ends of their fingertips. The gown had a scooped neckline and flowed loosely over their slim bodies, brushing the tops of their feet. Ashlina knew that Mary had been commissioned to make the dresses for them.

The Wood Spirits looked unearthly as they glided across the forest floor towards the large tree trunk. Ashlina had recognized the flowers they placed at the base. They were peppermint blossoms from Mount Hillside; The Wood Spirits had traveled a great distance to retrieve them.

The tree trunk was ancient and she could tell, even though it no longer had its full trunk and canopy of leaves, that it was a ginkgo- A rare species of tree. She and her sisters had learned about the tree at the beginning of summer. It was over ten thousand years old and had lost its battle to age and decay last winter during a terrible storm. Ashlina wondered why the Wood Spirits were paying homage to it.

"I have never seen one up this close before, let alone this many," Ashlina said in awe. Ashlina spent most of her time outdoors. Much of that time was spent exploring this section of the Evergreen Forest south of Elsbrier. Once or twice, she had seen a Wood Spirit or she thought she had. However, by the time she got to the spot where she thought she had seen one it had disappeared. So she could never really be sure that she had actually seen one.

"There's so many of them," she said knitting her brow. "Why are there so many of them?" Arturo shook his head. Ashlina then remembered something that Zee had told them one night shortly after she had found Homsa. It was something about a conversation she had overheard the Elders having about Wood Spirits and why they were still with them.

"We should leave," Arturo said. Ashlina gave him a sideways glance.

"Do they frighten you?" She asked then smirked at the astonished look on his face before he answered her.

"Hardly," was his reply. Arturo then slowly and as quietly as he could, made his way back through the forest in the direction of the Lily Pond. He would never admit, especially to the other Avidraughts that the Wood Spirits freaked him out, just a little. Ashlina caught up to him quickly and walked beside him. She was still smirking. Arturo gave her a sideways glance and asked gruffly, "What is so funny?"

"Oh nothing," she said lightly. She then patted his neck as they walked on and thought perhaps her Avidraught was afraid of wisps of smoke. Usually Ashlina explored the forest on her own as her sisters were busy doing their own things. However, since the episode with Zee and Homsa, the Avidraughts accompanied the fairies wherever they went, especially if they went into the forest. The fairies wondered if the Elders had suggested it.

Whatever the reason Ashlina was glad to have him with

144

her. Arturo was as inquisitive as she was and knew much about tracking; something she favored to do the most. They had decided to explore the forest on the other side of the pond. Trebor had told Elder Phinney that he had heard an odd sound coming from it just yesterday when he was making his way to the Lily Pond to fetch a bale of dry Lea-Ther leaves from the Water Lilys. Ashlina decided to investigate it.

As they walked Ashlina looked up at the kaleidoscope of colour over their heads and sighed. The forest canopy was bright with leaves coloured in pumpkin orange, fire reds, bright yellows and splashes of green. Ashlina was born in the summer season when life in the Whipple Wash Valley was in full bloom. It was nearing the end of the fall season and she normally felt a little melancholy at this time of year. However, this year was different. She was actually excited for the winter season to begin because they would be leaving on their journey. She was looking forward to it even though Zee was the only one who had shown her special powers thus far.

Ashlina frowned. She so wanted to know what her special powers were. The fairies knew that not everyone or every creature they came across was going to be kind and helpful. It was foretold that the special powers were to help them on their journey. One afternoon while they sat with Phinney who was teaching them how to braid vines into a thick rope and tie knots that would hold even the heaviest of the Avidraughts, they asked her why only Zee had received her powers. All Phinney could say was that perhaps they would show when they were in great distress, or like Zee, when someone dear to them was in need.

The sisters looked at each other and wondered who would be next and what would bring it forward. They each knew their mission was going to be a dangerous one, but like Ashlina, they were looking forward to it. They had been training very hard for it too and each of them knew how to wield a sword and shoot arrows with deadly accuracy. Soon they would learn how to shoot arrows from the backs of their

Avidraughts. If it came down to hand combat with a knife they could hold their own.

"Ashlina," Arturo said to her while he nudged her shoulder with his snout. She looked at him blankly for a minute.

"I called you several times where did your mind wonder off to?"

"I'm sorry Arturo what were you saying?"

"We're here. Are you sure you want to go in or have you had enough for today?" Ashlina looked up at the sky; there was still a couple of hours before nightfall.

"No let's go on, if we travel too far in to walk back before the evening meal you can fly me back," she said smiling at him.

Arturo nodded. He was not wearing a saddle, but that did not matter she often rode him bareback. They continued on their way crossing into the forest that surrounded the clearing before the Lily Pond. They traveled through the dark forest for about an hour but hadn't seen anything out of the ordinary when Ashlina stopped abruptly and knelt down on one knee. She lightly brushed away a pile of leaves. Under them was a footprint, a strange one; one she had never seen before.

"What is it?" Arturo asked as he peered over her shoulder at it. He obviously had never seen one like it before either.

"I can't be sure. It's three-toed like a bird's, however it is so large." She bit her bottom lip as she thought for a moment. "I think it might belong to a Flying Rapcicor. They are the only birds I know whose footprint would be this large," Ashlina said quietly. "And look, it's a fresh one," she added. She had only seen a picture of a Rapcicor in a book from the library.

The Rapcicors were quite large, red-feathered birds with long black thick legs and large heads with spiky rigid feathers that stuck out at odd angles from the top. Their tiny black eyes sat in a yellow mask of fine tiny feathers. Their black beak was quite large and unlike the other birds in the Whipple Wash Valley, they had large jagged teeth protruding down from their upper beak. Their teeth could rip open prey with ease.

They were fierce predators, but they lived in the Firelog Forest that was located hundreds of miles east of Elsbrier.

"Should we follow it?" Arturo asked. He was curious to know if it was a Rapcicor; Ashlina nodded. She knew the Elders would want to know as well and what it was doing so far from home. Perhaps, she thought, it was injured and disorientated, however she didn't see any blood. Ashlina motioned for Arturo to cease all conversation as they slowly moved forward. Rapcicors were not the friendliest of creatures. She had never heard of them attacking anyone outside of the Firelog Forest before. But then she had never heard of them leaving the Firelog Forest either. If the creature was injured she would need to take it to Enyce. If it were near death's door, with no hope of surviving, she would do the humane thing and put it to rest.

They followed the three-toed footprints through the forest. She occasionally stopped and brushed aside leaves that had obscured the prints. Arturo thought it looked like the bird had been trying to cover his tracks with leaves to mask the direction it went in. If that were the case, they may come across a very uncomfortable situation. He however did not want to voice his concerns. He already felt that Ashlina knew he was wary of the Wood Spirits and he did not want her to think he was afraid of a bird too.

They continued through the forest for another half hour. The deeper they traveled the darker the forest became. Even though the sun was shining, this side of the forest was thick with trees and the canopy almost blocked out the sun entirely. Ashlina had keen eyesight and was able to follow the prints without difficulty. She abruptly came to another stop however about fifteen minutes later. Arturo was looking around and did not see her stop until he bumped into her; he started to apologize.

"Shh," she said as she looked back at Arturo. The singular footprint they had been following had branched off into two different directions. They looked at each other and then down at the prints questioningly. They thought they were following one bird when in fact they could have been following two or more.

"Do they travel in single file like that?" Arturo asked quietly. Ashlina shrugged her shoulders. That had not been mentioned in the book she had read. She wondered how many birds they were actually following.

"Perhaps we should leave." Arturo said as an uneasy feeling came over him. One bird they could handle, even two or three, but if they were following a whole band of them they might have more difficulty getting away. He looked calculatingly about. With the thickness of the trees he would not be able to fly them out of the forest. If it came down to it, he would stay and fight while Ashlina ran for help. He wasn't afraid of fighting but if he could avoid it, he did.

"Ashlina its time to go," he spoke in a harsh whisper.

Ashlina however did not answer him; instead she squatted low to the ground and was peering into the dark forest. Arturo nudged her shoulder. Ashlina aggressively put up her hand for him to stop moving. Arturo caught his breath as he looked down at Ashlina. An unnerving feeling came over him as he watched her persona change right before his eyes.

For Ashlina, every one of her senses intensified a hundred fold. Her nostrils flared as she caught a faint animal scent that was not Arturo or any other animal that inhabited the forest. Her ears tingled as a muffled sound gradually became louder the more she concentrated on it. She motioned for Arturo to stay put. He watched as she quickly made her way through the forest as light and sure footed as any animal that was hunting its prey. She stopped about hundred feet away and squatted on the ground next to a large oak tree. Arturo could barely see her through the undergrowth. She looked up from what she was looking at on the ground- Avidraught footprints. She could tell by the prints that it was a large one and that it was carrying a rider. Ashlina peered curiously into the woods for several more minutes. She then looked over at

Arturo and motioned for him to come forward. He made his way to her as quietly as he could.

The Elders had warned the Avidraughts that the fairies might receive their special powers at any time and at the oddest of moments. Arturo had never seen Ashlina move quite that way before, so stealthily and with cat-like reflexes. The gleam in her eyes as he reached her was unsettling. They had turned a golden brown and looked like the eyes of a Splinx- a mountain cat that was both cunning and intelligent. They were fierce creatures that had two long eye teeth that perturbed out of their mouths past their lower lip. They could rip an Avidraught to shreds.

He looked cautiously at Ashlina. It was as if a surge of unearthly power had taken over her body and every movement she made was done with calculated, methodical precision. Without being told, he knew that she had received her special powers and would be the tracker of the group.

Ashlina stood, climbed onto Arturo's back with a quick and fluid movement, then jumped high into the air and caught the first limb of the oak tree. Quickly and effortlessly, she made her way up to the top branches of the tree. For several minutes she looked through the leaves and caught a movement several hundred yards away. A stranger dressed in a black hooded cape riding on the back of a massive black Avidraught, at least three or four hands taller than Farley, was making his way south through the forest.

They stopped in a small clearing and looked around. A few minutes went by before a band of Rapcicors, three dozen in total, gradually came out of the forest from all directions and surrounded the stranger and his Avidraught. The birds were quite large and looked fierce. The Avidraught however stood steadfast as the stranger casually swung his leg over the flank of the horse and landed on the ground with a light thud. He hitched his cloak behind the hilt of a massive sword hanging on the left side of his hip. Ashlina had never seen the likes of the sword before. Every one of her senses prickled with electric energy. If need be she would come to the stranger's aid, but for now she would wait and watch the scene play out before her.

The stranger had not drawn his weapon; he was expecting the Rapcicors to be there. A large Rapcicor five and half feet tall with a bright crop of orange and yellow feathers atop his head came forward. The stranger looked down at the bird and spoke. Ashlina careened to hear them. This far away and even though her senses were heightened, she could barely make out what they were saying. She did however catch bits and pieces of their conversation. She leaned forward to better hear what they were saying and froze when the stranger raised his voice.

"It's not time yet. If you come across them leave them for me," the stranger said in a cold menacing voice that sent shivers up Ashlina's spine. Whom he spoke of she could not be sure, but she had a strange feeling that he was talking about her and her sisters. Nervous, her foot slipped on the branch of the tree and she caught her breath. The stranger hearing the noise turned in her direction. Ashlina lay flat against the trunk of the tree, closed her eyes and didn't move nor breathe for several seconds. She was wearing a dark brown tunic with long sleeves and matching pants. She often wore clothing of this colour so that she blended into the forest surroundings. Finally, she heard the stranger speak again and she gradually relaxed her hold on the tree. The rough bark left imprints on her face and hands.

"Until we know for sure that he has not made it back to this valley you are not to make a move. If you move too quickly you will foil all the work I've done."

Ashlina could not see the strangers face, but his heavily accented voice sounded familiar. The Rapcicor, not happy with the strangers words, grunted his disapproval. Without warning, the stranger grabbed the Rapcicor by the throat, pulled it up off its feet, and looked at it square in the face. Ashlina, thinking that she and Arturo would now have to intercept, looked strangely at the other Rapcicors. Not one of them came to their comrade's aid. Instead, they watched curiously from the sidelines. "Make a move before I give the okay and you will be the first to die," the stranger said menacingly.

Ashlina shivered at the words, but could not help but watch as the stranger threw the bird down on the ground. He then mounted his Avidraught in one fluid movement. The bird feebly stood and ruffled its feathers before it nodded its head in agreement. Not saying another word the stranger left the clearing and went in a southern direction. The Rapcicors filed one behind the other and left in a south easterly direction. Ashlina sighed. They had not seen her nor were they coming in her direction. She waited several more minutes then quickly made her way down the tree and jumped onto Arturo's back. He looked back at her expectantly waiting for her to tell him what she had overheard.

"We need to get back to the village I have to speak with the elders immediately," Ashlina said with a command and urgency that made Arturo's mane prickle.

He watched as her persona and eyes changed back to normal. Unlike Zee, Ashlina did not faint after receiving her powers, but she was weak. Arturo's heart lurched with concern for his charge. Questioning her would have to wait; he needed to get her safely back to the village. Arturo picked his way through the forest as quickly as he could. All the while Ashlina kept looking nervously behind them, making sure that they were not being followed.

Chapter 13
Dressed To Kill

Arturo and Ashlina had made it safely back to the Whipple Wash Tree. They bowed to the Tree and it quickly let them pass through. Ashlina was just dismounting when Andi and Rayley came through the long curtain of limbs. Rayley had been in the village fetching a crumble apple pie from Ira and Awna's bakery. She had decided the pie would be a nice compliment to their meal of pan-fried fish, a mixed vegetable salad and seasoned mashed potatoes. She had met Andi along the way. She was just getting back from a long day of work in the Gnome Gardens. Hanging over her left arm was a basket full of fresh vegetables that Rayley had asked her to bring back for the salad.

Seeing them Arturo called out for them to help Ashlina down from his back. Ashlina was weakened from her ordeal. Seeing that she was having trouble dismounting Andi and Rayley ran up to her. As she slipped off of Arturo's back they each grabbed an arm to hold her steady. Arturo quickly told them what had happened. Rayley told him to find Obwyn, Orliff and Nayew and instruct them to come to the Tree as soon as they could.

Ashlina insisted that she could walk on her own so Rayley ran ahead with the pie and basket of vegetables while Andi walked beside Ashlina to the hollow in the Tree. She held onto Ashlina's arm as they descended the steps.

The rest of the Elders were already sitting with the fairies. They were waiting for Andi, Rayley and Ashlina to arrive so they could eat their evening meal together. They looked curiously at Ashlina as she slowly made her way down the steps and to the table. When Rayley entered the common room, she quickly told them that Ashlina had received her special powers and then went into the kitchen to make the salad. Andi pulled out a chair for Ashlina; who plopped down on it with a dull thud, then looked wearily about her. Her sisters looked back at her with excitement. They were eager to ask what her power was and how it came to her.

But before the fairies could ask their questions, Elder Enyce saw the concerned expression on Ashlina's face and spoke first, "I know you are anxious to hear Ashlina's tale but it can wait." The fairies moaned their displeasure. "She looks famished," Enyce said. "And besides, we have invited Obwyn, Nayew and Orliff to hear the tale too." She nodded to Sianna, Athia and Shanata who got up from the table and went into the kitchen to help Rayley with the food. Enna and Mariela stood and fetched three more chairs and placed them around the table; Zee grabbed the plates and cutlery from the sideboard.

Ashlina looked at Enyce and smiled. She was thankful that the questions could wait; she was quite hungry, which she found surprising. When Zee received her powers, she couldn't keep anything down for a day afterward. However, here she was hungry as a bear. Her throat was parched as well. It felt like she hadn't had anything to drink for days. She grabbed for the glass of water in front of her plate and drank it down quickly. She immediately started to feel better. Jolise sat next to her and filled her cup with water from the glass pitcher that in the middle of the table. Ashlina thanked her before she gulped down that glass of water as well. The others looked curiously at her as Jolise filled her cup again. This time Ashlina only sipped the water before placing it back down on the table.

Just as Rayley, Sianna and Athia came out of the kitchen with a large platter of fish and the rest of the food, Obwyn and the others entered the hollow. They quickly made their way down the steps and to the table. Orliff immediately went to examine Ashlina. He looked into her eyes and checked her pulse. After asking her a couple of questions about how she felt he announced to the room that she was fine.

"Good," Enyce said. "We have decided to eat our meal before Ashlina tells us of her adventure in the forest." Nayew went to argue. Arturo had told Nayew what happened from the moment they had entered the forest up until she climbed the oak tree. He however was not able to tell him what Ashlina had seen or heard as she had not told him. Enyce looked at Nayew sternly. "It can wait until she has eaten." She looked at Orliff who nodded his approval.

"Alright then, let's get this over with," Nayew said and sat down on a chair next to Andi.

Obwyn sat on a chair next to Ashlina and immediately took two large pieces of fish off the platter. He placed one on Ashlina's plate and the other on his plate. He then passed the platter to Mariela who sat next to him.

He and Jopha had caught the fish earlier that day and he was looking forward to having some of it. No one could cook up pan-fried fish like Rayley. She always had just the right amount of spices and never allowed the fish to cook too long; which dried it out. He picked up the bowl of mashed potatoes and scooped a large spoonful onto Ashlina's plate then he gave himself two large scoops. Passing that bowl along he picked up the bowl of salad and gave Ashlina two helpings of it and himself one. As he passed that bowl along, Phinney, who sat on the other side of Ashlina, buttered them both a large slice of hunkyberry spiced bread and placed it on the small plate in front of their dinner plates. Obwyn thanked her. He chose not to wait for the others to finish dishing out their food and immediately dug in. Ashlina watched him with an amused look on her face until he nudged her elbow and told her to eat.

Enyce and Rayley were looking expectantly at Orliff who was still standing behind Ashlina. He looked down at Obwyn with an amused look on his face. He was remembering the time at the winter celebrations a couple of years before when Obwyn stole Nayew's plate of food. Nayew had put it down while he went to get them both a drink and asked Obwyn to watch the plate of food for him. By the time Nayew got back Obwyn had devoured half of Nayew's dinner.

Orliff couldn't help but chuckle at the memory and the excuse Obwyn gave Nayew for eating his food. 'Well you told me to watch it, so I have been watching it as I put it on the fork and brought it to my mouth.' Everyone around them chuckled, but since then no one left their plate of food unattended when Obwyn was near.

"What is so funny Orliff?" Rayley asked with a twinkle in her eye. She smiled at him warmly. Everyone knew that the two liked each other, but Orliff had yet to proclaim his interest for her. He looked warmly back at her.

"I was just remembering the day Obwyn stole..." The room erupted into chuckles before Orliff could finish his sentence. Everyone knew what day he spoke of. Even Nayew laughed.

"Yes I learned a valuable lesson that day; never to trust you when food is involved," Nayew said as he looked at Obwyn. Obwyn smiled. "Did you know I stood in line at the banquet tables for another forty-five minutes? Thankfully, there was still food left, slim pickings, but there was still food."

With a mouth full of food, Obwyn smiled again. He shrugged his shoulders as he swallowed and looked sheepishly at Nayew. "Why do you think I ate your plate of food?" Nayew looked at him with a confused expression. "I took one look at that line up and thought there had to be a better way. I saw an empty chair beside you and noticed that your plate had everything on it that I liked. So I limped over pretending I was hurt and asked if you wouldn't mind getting me a drink."

Everyone looked at Nayew as he processed the new information. "You faked being hurt so you could steal my food?" Nayew asked.

"Well ya, I was hungry and didn't want to wait," Obwyn

said as if it made perfect sense. He took a big bite out of the slice of bread, licked his lips and smiled self-assuredly at Nayew. Nayew's look of disbelief had Enna, who was sitting next to him, break out in laughter. Her mouth was full of water. She laughed so hard it squirted out her nose, which in turn made everyone else laugh as well. The tension of the moment eased and the conversation flowed lightly around the table as they continued to eat their meal.

Ashlina was glad that she did not have to tell her tale right away. Her special powers had drained her energy. It was not as bad as Zee's experience, but then Ashlina was older. What she saw and heard frightened her. She was not sure she wanted to relive it openly. While the food made her feel better, being around loved ones lifted her spirit.

As she finished her meal, she could not help but think of the dark stranger. His words left a chill down her spine that she could not suppress. An evil presence had made its way to the Valley and had settled in Elsbrier. And if her assumption was right, the Rapcicors had picked a side to fight on. She knew that what she had overheard was going to drastically change things for the fairies, the Elders and the villagers. *But who was the stranger*, she thought. He was very cunning. Up until that day no one had seen him. His words, '*if you move too quickly you will foil all the work I've done*', surely meant that he had been living amongst them. She knew the Elders would agree. She sighed heavily. Orliff, who had not moved from the back of her chair, put a hand on her shoulder; Ashlina looked back and smiled at him.

"Are you not joining us for dinner?" She asked.

"No," Orliff said as he smiled down at her. He moved to the sideboard where a large pot of tea stood and poured a cup. As he leaned his back against the sideboard, he blew the steam off the tea and took a sip.

"I was talking with Hamy at *The Baron's Den*. He had just invited me in for a drink when Arturo found me. I already ate supper with my sons." The others sitting around the table smiled and nodded as they continued to eat. Everyone knew how close Orliff was to the Ronans.

"Will you be joining us for dessert then?" Rayley asked him.

"Oh I couldn't pass up dessert, especially if you made it," he said and walked to the empty chair beside her.

"I didn't make it," she said apologetically as he sat down. "Ira and Awna did."

"Ah, well it's not yours, but I am sure it will taste good all the same," Orliff smiled at her and Rayley's cheeks deepened with a blush. She quickly stood up, picked up her plate and said to no one in particular that she was going to get the pie. Orliff stood as well and followed her into the kitchen. Everyone sitting around the table smiled at the exchange and wondered why it was taking him so long to declare, what was obvious to everyone else, his love for Rayley.

While they ate dessert, Ashlina told her tale of what she saw and heard in the forest. The room had gone very still and no one spoke. They did however look about with worried frowns on their faces. When she finished, Elder Enyce stood and told the fairies that it was time for them to retire to their chambers. Shanata and Mariela immediately argued with her, declaring once again that they were not children. The other Elders stood and looked at the fairies with stern expressions. Shanata and Mariela resolved to the fact that they would not win this argument and left in a huff; their younger sisters followed behind them.

Back in their Sitting Room, the fairies talked well into the night about Ashlina's powers, what the stranger's words meant and who he was talking about. They knew for sure he had referred to them, but were uncertain about the other person he spoke of. They pondered it over for only a minute or two when Zee said with conviction that the stranger had been talking about Jasper as well. Her sisters readily agreed.

The rest of their conversation was of Jasper and the others that he was bringing home with him. They wondered what they were like and how many there were. Their conversation gradually lulled. Sleepy eyed and yawning, the fairies said goodnight to each other and went to their beds. Ashlina was the only one of them that slept soundly and dreamlessly.

The Elders, Nayew, Obwyn and Orliff settled into the Gathering Room and talked well into the night. They came to many of the same conclusions that the fairies had, but their concern was much deeper. Someone living amongst them was spying on them. It would be near impossible to narrow it down and seek out the spy however, as Elsbrier had opened its doors to several newcomers since Faywyn's disappearance. They settled right in; some opened shops, others worked in the crystal mines and there were some who brought their whole family- including their extended families. They talked for hours about what their options were and planned what they would do next. No one discussed what the next steps were for the fairies, until Obwyn broached the subject.

"We will have to upgrade their training," Obwyn said somberly. He poured himself a cup of tea and took the last two cookies off the plate that Rayley had brought out. He walked back to the table and sat down. The Elders nodded their heads in agreement. "Perfect," Obwyn said as he finished the first cookie and picked up the next. "Nayew and I will get started on it in the morning." Nayew only nodded. Before Obwyn could take a bite of the last cookie Nayew snatched it out of his hand and shoved it in his own mouth, whole; smiling triumphantly. Neither were known for their playfulness so their unexpected actions had the rest of the room chuckling. Once again, the seriousness of the moment passed.

*

While the fairies ate breakfast the following day, they learned that their academic lessons had been canceled until further notice. All but Mariela smiled. Their smiles quickly faded however when Elder Rayley told them that their combat training would be intensified. The only one of them that was genuinely pleased about it was Enna.

The training started right after their breakfast. They were told to meet Nayew and Obwyn in the small room on the second floor of the library. The sisters did not argue, but as they made their way to the village they talked about what kind of combat training they would learn in the library. Everyone, but Mariela, hoped that their first lesson would not be from a book.

As they entered Elsbrier they noticed that many of the villagers were openly staring at them, which wasn't unusual. What was unusual, however, was that no one approached them or said as much as a 'good morning'. "They must have heard that you received your special powers," Shanata said.

"Yes, but that doesn't explain why they are not approaching us," Ashlina replied. "When Zee got her powers, we couldn't go anywhere without someone stopping us to congratulate her. It was kind of annoying actually." Zee frowned and bowed her head when she heard Ashlina's comment. None of her sisters had mentioned before that they had been annoyed at all the attention she had received.

Enna roughly elbowed Ashlina in the arm and cocked her head in Zee's direction. "Oh Zee, I didn't mean that truly," Ashlina said then put her arm around Zee's shoulder. "Their staring is freaking me out a bit. It is as if they are afraid of me," Ashlina whispered.

Zee heard the anguish in her voice and looked up at her. "I am not afraid of you Ashlina," she said with a bright smile.

"Perhaps it's not you but the circumstance in which you received your powers that has them frightened," Shanata said wisely. The sisters nodded their heads in agreement. It was obvious from everyone's reaction that the news a spy may be living among them had traveled very quickly through the village. This made Ashlina feel somewhat better.

The sisters continued down the path until they heard

someone calling Ashlina's name. They looked behind them to see Miss Casey Farriva briskly walk towards them. They stopped walking and waited for her to catch up.

"Oh, I am so glad I saw you," she said breathlessly. "As soon as I heard the news I wanted to come straight away to chat with you about your powers and what you saw. I think it would make a wonderful story for the *Village Voice*, don't you?" Miss Casey said.

She was very bubbly this morning and talked just as quickly as she walked. The fairies smiled at her. Normally she was never seen without a parchment and pen in hand. That day however she was carried a basket of cookies with bright yellow suns in the center of them. The fairies looked inquiringly at the basket. Miss Casey looked down at the basket as well.

"Ah yes, well this is the reason why I didn't come and see you earlier. I was making cookies for Homsa. Ahh, the poor dear; it is tragic what happened to him. My heart pounded so hard when I heard, I thought it was going to jump right out of my chest, which would be a messy business indeed. It is a good thing you received your special powers when you did Zee otherwise this basket of cookies might be a basket of flowers and I would be walking to Cross Over Point rather than to the Mediplace," Miss Casey breathed in deeply then chuckled lightly.

"So then, do you and Zee have time to come for tea later today so that we might talk about it?" Ashlina and Zee looked to Shanata for guidance. "And yes of course you other girls can come with them, even though you don't have your special powers yet. I am sure you have something interesting to say," she smiled broadly as she looked at each of the girls in turn.

Shanata, Mariela and Enna took no offense to her words. No one had any idea of when the special powers would appear or who would receive it next. It looked like they were appearing in a sequence, starting with the youngest and working its way to the oldest. But no one could be certain that Enna was next.

"I am sorry," Shanata said. "I am not sure we will have time today. We are on our way to the library to study with Obwyn and Nayew." Miss Casey looked at her suspiciously.

"In the library with Obwyn and Nayew," Miss Casey repeated. "What will they be teaching you in the Library?"

"Oh, well we are not sure," Shanata said convincingly. Her sisters did not correct her. "We were just told that we were to meet up with them this morning."

"Do you think it has something to do with the spy," Miss Casey asked in a hushed whisper.

Shanata shook her head. "I am sorry Miss Casey, but I am not sure what we are doing in the library."

Just as Miss Casey opened her mouth to ask another question J.Z. Jones called out to them. She was standing with Hamy at *The Baron's Den*. They were in earshot of them and Shanata wondered if perhaps they had overheard the conversation with Miss Casey. She was a delightful woman, but if she sensed there was news to be made she didn't stop until she uncovered the story. Shanata wasn't sure that the Elders would approve of them talking about what Ashlina saw and overheard. Although they never told the girls not to talk about it, Shanata felt it more prudent to wait until they were given permission.

"Miss Casey," J.Z. said brightly as she and Hamy walked over to them. "I was wondering if I could enlist your help with designing the brochures and flyers for our next play, *A Stab in the Park*". We are going to present it during the Winter Solstice Celebrations. I am very excited; the play is an adaptation of the book written by the famous author Thurston Field. I want them to be exceptional."

"Yes, and I was wondering if you have the new menus ready for *The Den*," Hamy added. As soon as they reached the group they stepped right between Casey and the fairies, blocking her view of them. As they waited for her reply,

Hamy put his hand behind him and waved it at the girls, indicating that they should be on their way.

Shanata and her sisters quickly said goodbye and walked briskly towards the library. Casey was so busy talking to J.Z. about the design of the brochures and flyers she didn't see the girls leave.

When they walked through the door of the small room in the library they were met by Obwyn and Nayew; both scowled at them. They were fifteen minutes late. All Shanata did was mention Miss Casey's name, and Obwyn and Nayew instantly forgave them for their tardiness. They knew how tenacious she could be at times. She had cornered both of them the day after Zee received her powers and neither of them could get away from her for close to an hour.

The sisters looked surprisingly around the room. The long wooden tables that were usually bare were blanketed with charts, maps, measuring tools, little solider figurines and a pile of books. All but seven of the chairs were stacked neatly beside the door. When Obwyn announced that they would be learning battle strategies the fairies groaned. All but Enna, that is. She was very keen to learn.

The morning dragged on as they read books and poured over the maps and charts. After they ate the light lunch that Elder Rayley brought them, the afternoon had gone much quicker. Nayew presented the girls with a series of battle scenarios while Obwyn helped them form a strategy that would conquer each scenario. Before they knew it, lanterns were being lit so that they could see properly. Each of the girls then had to strategize a battle scenario on their own. They were not allowed to give each other assistance, Obwyn did not help either. By the end of the lesson Enna was the only one that passed with flying colours.

As they got ready to leave, Nayew announced that they were to return for another day of lessons. The day after that they would train with the Jarrell brothers. They had trained with the brothers before and learned swords play, hand to hand combat and archery. While they had occasionally received welts or large bruises they never walked away with serious injuries. The sisters smiled. They wouldn't have to train in the stuffy room and would get to play war with the brothers outside, whom they liked very much. The look of firmness on Obwyn and Nayew's faces however made their insides cringe. They had a feeling that the combat training was about to become very serious. As they looked warily at Obwyn and Nayew they feared that one or all of them might be coming home with more than just a couple of bruises and blisters.

*

The second day's lesson had gone by far too quickly and it was now the morning of the third day. It was early, the sun had just risen. The fairies ate a quick breakfast and made their way down the path which led through the right side of the village towards the Lily Pond. As they walked along they noticed that a number of the shops were closed, which was unusual. The shopkeepers often opened their shops early for the traders who left at first light on their cross-country trips. The fairies noticed many of the shop owners stood in a group just outside *The Baron's Den*. When the fairies passed they said a quick hello to them. The shopkeepers nodded curtly back to them. Hamy was the only one who smiled. The smile, Mariela noticed, did not quite meet his eyes and was quickly replaced with a worried frown.

Obviously word that they would be combating the Jarrell brothers had made its way around the village. Seeing Hamy's worried expression, Mariela immediately felt an uneasy sensation in the pit of her stomach. Had he heard something more about what would be taking place? Obwyn and Nayew had been vague about what they could expect, and when she asked Elder Andi at breakfast, they too had been vague.

Mariela, along with her sisters, carried on down the path even though the unease in her stomach had increased.

When they came to the outcropping of trees that separated Elsbrier from the meadow they heard several voices up ahead. After walking around the trees they came to an abrupt stop and looked in surprise at the clearing. Several hundred villagers had formed a large circle in the clearing. They were sitting on chairs or blankets and were facing inwards. They had even brought some of their children; the ones that were old enough to wield a sword and train in combat. Upon seeing the fairies the crowd immediately erupted into cheers and applause.

The fairies walked to the circle. As they passed through it they were clapped encouragingly on the back. They noticed that the Jarrell brothers were standing at the opposite end and dressed in full body armour. Metal plates covered their arms, chest and legs. They had metal helmets on as well. Each carried a sword and shield. The fairies looked cautiously at them, but then smiled. The brothers did not return their smiles; they scowled at them instead as they slapped their swords against their shields. Mariela looked at her arms; she was wearing a long sleeved shirt and pants just like her sisters. She looked at the brothers again. The unease she felt earlier turned into anger.

"So that's how it's going to be is it then?" Mariela said as she looked at her sisters.

"I believe so," Shanata said.

"I don't know about this," Ashlina said.

Zee only whimpered as she looked over at the brothers. She liked each of them and did not want to hurt any of them or be hurt by any of them. She looked at Enna who was smiling ruthlessly at the brothers.

"No mercy," Enna said.

"This is ridiculous," Mariela said with disgust, letting her anger take over.

"You will fight as if your lives depend on it," Nayew said

as he walked up to them. Following him was each of the fairies' Avidraughts. They had been dressed for battle as well. Armour plates covered the sides of their head, neck and on each of their legs. The saddles they wore were larger than usual. They had plated armour hanging down from the leather saddle covering their sides and flanks. The Avidraughts looked fit for battle.

"Well this is interesting isn't it," Mariela said with scorn as she looked about her. "We've come to battle with cotton on and our Avidraughts and the Jarrell brothers have come with metal armour. How do you expect us to fight them with no protection? Today's training will be over with before it begins." The fairies looked astonishingly at Mariela's outburst. She was normally the calm one. Shanata put her hand on her shoulder; Mariela shrugged it off and looked with contempt at Obwyn and Nayew.

They looked sternly back at her. Mariela had made no bones that she hated to fight. He motioned for someone to come out of the crowd of villagers who had formed around the fairies. Mary Kattelley walked towards the girls, smiling brightly.

"Take the girls to their tent and outfit them with their armour," Nayew said.

The girls looked around and noticed that two large tents had been set up several feet away. Mary walked to the nearest one and held the flap open for the girls. Mariela looked apologetically at Nayew and followed her sisters to the tent. Mary entered after them and closed the flap behind her.

Five cots were set up evenly around the room. At the end of each was a suit of armour. However, it looked nothing like the bulky armour that the Jarrell brothers and the Avidraughts wore. The fairies cooed as they ran their hands over it. Instead of the colour of steel, the fairies' armour was a golden white that shimmered in the light. Instead of plates that were fastened together, their armour was a suit of pants and a long sleeved tunic.

"What are they made of?" Shanata asked as she picked hers up off the bed and held it against her. It was not much heavier than the clothes she was wearing. Her sisters picked theirs up as well and furrowed their brows.

"Jonas helped me make them. We found a way to melt the crystals together with the finest of steel. We have been working on them in secret for months," Mary said with pride.

"But they are so light Mary. How are they to protect us?" Enna asked as she started to undress.

"No wait. Here, put these on first then the armour," Mary said as she picked up a stack of light cotton skin-tight pants and a sleeveless vest from a table by the door. She handed a set to each of the fairies.

"The armour is indestructible. Trust me. We tried it out several times with mallets, swords and knives." Mary said then looked at the girls sheepishly. "I made a set for myself and Jonas. We tried it out."

She smiled with pride as the fairies got dressed in their new armour. "The first couple we made were not very good. Mallets did nothing to them, but swords and knives went right through." The girls looked over at her in fright, thinking that she had been cut. "Oh no!" Mary said, seeing the concern on their faces. "We dressed up a stuffed scarecraw first. When the mixture was right, we tried it out with me wearing the armour and Jonas wielding the sword."

The girls smiled. Jonas and Mary had been best of friends since they were school children. They were thick as thieves back then. It made sense that they would work on the same project together.

"Walk around. See how they move. Let me know how they feel," Mary said. The fairies walked around the tent; waving their arms, bending their knees and twisting their torsos. Zee did a couple of summersaults and Enna flipped Ashlina over her back. The fairies laughed; the armour moved fluently with each of their movements. It was as light as clothing and did not weigh them down.

"They are wonderful Mary," Shanata said.

"And pretty too," Mariela said. "It is a shame to dirty them." The other fairies nodded.

Mary smiled, "Yes, well I am sure by the end of today they will not look quite so pretty. But we didn't make them with pretty in mind; that was just an added bonus."

"Thank you," Shanata said. "I guess we will see what they look like after today's battle. The Jarrell brothers look fierce and ready to shed some fairy blood," she chuckled nervously.

"Oh, I almost forgot," Mary said as she ran to three wooden chests sitting on the ground at the end of the tent. "We have a set for each of you." From one chest she pulled out a sword, from another a shield and the last, a helmet. All three were shiny silver in colour. Mary passed a set to each of them. They noticed that they were a little heavier than the armour was, but not as heavy as the wooden swords and shields they normally practiced with.

"Yours and Jonas's creations again?" Enna asked as she swung her sword in a large arc then thrust it towards Shanata who raised her shield to block it. A light ping reverberated around the tent when the sword made contact with the shield.

"No, Jonas's creations this time, but the paintings on the shields are mine," Mary said modestly. The girls turned their shields around. Depicted on the shield in pale green was a stylistic likeness of the Whipple Wash Tree. Five white stars were placed in an arc above it. Written on a purple banner beneath the tree in white lettering were the words: *May the Light of Goodness Prevail.*

"It's beautiful," the girls all chimed together as they looked through teary eyes at their shield.

"Don't forget your helmets," Mary said with rising emotion. She was as close to the fairies as any family member would be. She feared for their safety, hence the reason for taking so much care in designing their armour. The sisters picked up their helmets and placed them on their heads. They fit snugly against their scalp. The face guard was set on hinges. It could either be brought down to cover their face entirely or put up to sit on the top of their head. There were two oblong shaped holes for their eyes. A contoured piece was formed to fit over their nose and had slits so that they could breathe through them. The section that fit over their mouth also had a contoured mouth with a slit in it so they could breathe. The sisters looked at each other through the holes in their face plates. Until that moment, the reality of their mission and what they were brought into this world to do had not seemed real.

Even though they had been born from a tree, their lives had been like any other child's growing up. They each thought that the Elder they had been paired with was like their mother, the rest were like aunts. They thought of Obwyn, Nayew and Orliff as their uncles. They saw Queen Faywyn as their grandmother. They went to school with the village children and were not treated any differently than their classmates. They played catch and tag with them, hopped rocks and fished off the bridges with them. They had friends they cared very deeply for. However, seeing each other dressed as they were, brandishing swords and carrying shields, made them all wonder what the future would hold for them.

Enna stepped forward and raised her sword in the air. She looked at each of her sisters in turn and said commandingly, "For the Light of Goodness may we prevail."

Each of the fairies came forward and raised their swords to touch the tip of Enna's. They recited her words, but without conviction. Enna looked at her sisters crossly. "I can't hear you," she snarled at them.

"For the Light of Goodness," she triumphantly yelled. Her sisters joined in. They loudly cheered 'For the Light of Goodness' three times in unison as they ran out of the tent.

Chapter 14
The Ominous Warning

One by one the fairies exited the tent. They abruptly stopped several feet from the entrance and looked around in astonishment. Some of the villagers lined the pathway from the tents into the circle. Upon seeing the fairies in their armour, they started to cheer them on. The fairies giggled nervously. The seriousness of the previous moment subsided as they looked at all the smiling faces. The training session with the Jarrell brothers had turned into a festive event.

Ashlina and Zee looked at each other warily. Not sure what to do they turned to Shanata for guidance. She looked about her and smiled. Memories of an event she had attended with the Radeks in Boswick, the largest settlement on Lake Periours, came forward. The event had been housed in a large arena which normally hosted the annual year-end Hawkeye Games. It was summer then, however, so several different sports went on all at once. A number of contestants from various regions of the Southern Kingdoms were there to compete. Shanata smiled again at the memory. She had enormous fun as she cheered on her favourite competitors. Before the award ceremonies and closing celebrations, she visited the many vendors who had come from great distances to sell their goods. She had sampled dozens of exotic food and was given scarves and flowers that she could pin on her clothing. During the ceremonies she cheered on the winners of the games as they received their prizes. The prizes varied in worth from livestock, to coins, jewels and even plots of land. Later they danced into the wee hours of the morning while a *Band of Players* played lively tunes.

Shanata giggled as she remembered a group of lively contestants from Orhem, a small Kingdom on the cliffs along the Guardian Sea. The contestants were short, burly and had bright red shoulder length hair that they wore in ponytails while they competed. She remembered how they riled the crowd into frenzy by waving their hands in the air then slapping the hands of the crowd as they ran by them. She looked cheekily at her sisters as she slowly raised her right hand and waved back at the crowd. The crowd cheered. In turn each of her sisters followed suit; the crowd cheered even louder. As the fairies ran down the long pathway to the circle they slapped the hands of the villagers as they passed by.

Once they entered the circle they heard Rhethea calling out to them. She was stood by a carri-shift several paces away. The pokey that had pulled the carri-shift to the field moved nervously back and forth. The noise from the crowd made it skittish. Jemas quieted it with a gentle hand. The fairies walked over to them and spied the contents in the carri-shift. It was full with normal weapons like arrows, bows and long-poles, which were made from hardwood. The tips of the long-poles were sharpened to a point and dipped in liquid metal. There were also several sizes of knives and metal studded clubs. Sitting open beside the clubs were two wooden crates. The sisters cautiously looked at their contents.

The first crate had spice balls in them. They were the size of a large nut. They didn't look very threatening, but when cracked open they released a nerve toxin that would immobilize the victim for several minutes; giving the person who threw the ball time to either kill their opponent or capture them. Hanging on hooks on the lid of the crate were five slingshots made from the Lea-Ther plant; one for each of the fairies. In the next crate were thin metal plates with razor sharp jagged edges. They were called tarjas and were the size of a small plate. When thrown with speed and accuracy, they could cut off the limb of a tree with one clean slice. Hanging on hooks were five pairs of gloves made out of the same material as the fairies' armour.

"We're not actually going to use those today... are we?"

Mariela asked. "I won't use those against your brothers." The fairies looked at each other nodding their heads. Rhethea smiled at them.

"No, you won't use them against my brothers," she said. In a whisper she added "although on occasion I have thought of using the spice balls on them, if only to shut them up for a minute." Shanata smiled. She knew better than anyone how protective Rhethea's brothers were and how bossy they could be towards her. Being her friend, Shanata often had to talk Rhethea out of doing something drastic against her brothers. Rhethea loved her brothers dearly but they teased her until her temper came to a boiling point. When that happened she wasn't beyond violence. Rishley was the only other one who could talk Rhethea out of doing something drastic.

"You will practice with those today," Rhethea said and pointed to several stuffed scarecraws that were erected on poles about fifty paces away. The scarecraws were made from overalls that were stuffed with straw. The villagers used them in their gardens to scare away the craws, which were small birds with purple tipped wings. The birds flew in pods of thirty or more and when your back was turned they could strip a garden of its vegetables in no time flat. The craws rarely bothered the Gnome gardens however. The Gnomes armed themselves with slingshots and pattipods. Pattipods were large oblong pods filled with water. When shot up into the air they would explode open with a loud bang and drench the birds in water. The craws, afraid of the noise, would fly away. It was more humane than picking them off with stones, which is what the Gnomes used to do until Elder Andi stopped them.

The scarecraws looked quite comical; each had a large pumpkin for a head and straw stuck out where their feet and hands should be. Each of them also wore a plaid shirt that looked similar to the ones the Jarrell brothers wore when working.

"Are those your brothers' shirts?" Enna asked with a smirk. Rhethea smiled.

"You will practice on the scarecraws, but will also do hand to hand combat using the rest of these weapons. Hence the reason for the armour. No mercy," she said, repeating the words that Enna had used. She winked at the fairies.

"Zee, Ashlina. Girls here, over here!" Familiar voices called out to them. The fairies turned to see the Ronans waving excitedly at them just outside of the circle. A large woven basket and a neatly folded blanket were set on the ground beside them. The Ronans had also closed their shop. It looked as though there were going to stay for the duration of the training session. The fairies waved back at them.

The sisters looked around the circle as the villagers smiled and waved at them. They smiled and waved back. Their smiles abruptly faded however when they came to Orliff. He looked at them with a deep scowl on his face. Alamat and Niella stood beside him; they looked calmly at the sisters. Each of them carried a medicine bag over their shoulder. The fairies noticed that behind them were pole-shifts; two poles with a piece of canvas stretched between them. No one had to tell them what the pole-shifts were for. If one of them were too injured to walk off the field they would be carried off. Now they understood why the tents had been erected and cots set up inside for each of them. In case of serious injuries, Orliff could tend to their wounds inside the tent rather than take them back to the Mediplace.

Upon seeing the pole-shifts, nervous energy began to rumble in Zee and Ashlina's stomachs. They looked nervously at Orliff who hadn't changed his expression. Orliff was a healer not a fighter. He understood the reasoning for this event- it was to increase their training. However, he was reminded of the time he saved the Ronans from Blackwood. The boys had been so little and so young. To be treated as badly as they had been was unforgivable. Even though they were strangers to him, it was difficult to work on them and help them heal. But it was different with the fairies. They were like his family. He was at each of their births and helped care for them in their early years. If one of them were to be injured now… he was not sure how he would handle it. Would he, in a rage, pick up one of the Jarrell brothers as he did Blackwood and slam them to the ground? The rage that took over him that day had never reared its ugly head again, but there had been no cause for it. Until that moment he did not understand what had possessed him to react that way.

Shanata, seeing the look on Orliff's face, instinctively understood his fear. She smiled warmly at him. His features lightened and he smiled back. She then turned to Ashlina and Zee. "All will be well. We have the Light of Goodness on our side," she said confidently.

Enna looked at her oddly. "Shanata, we are not fighting a foe. These are the Jarrell brothers. The Light of Goodness is on their side as well," Enna said. The sisters looked at Shanata.

"Well yes…," then she thought for a second. "Then I suppose that means that the Light of Goodness will take care of all of us and none of us will be… too badly injured," she said cheerily.

"Humph," Enna said with a scowl and walked towards the center of the circle where Obwyn and Nayew stood. Her sisters followed her. The Jarrell brothers were already there. They looked menacingly at the fairies. Mitch snarled and banged his sword against his shield for effect. Enna, not one to be intimidated easily, growled back at Mitch and stepped forward.

"Now," Nayew said as he stepped between Mitch and Enna, "you are to treat this as if you are in battle. The Jarrell brothers have been given clear instructions not to give into your girly tears or pleas to take it easy on you." Shanata and Enna looked with shock at Nayew. None of them, other than Zee, had any difficulty with their training. Nor did any of them ever cry or beg. Perhaps, Shanata thought, that Nayew was just trying to goad them on. Nayew ignored the look of scorn on Enna's face.

"There are five stations," Nayew continued. "You are to go from station to station and battle against the Jarrell brother who is posted there." He pointed to each of the stations. The sisters followed where he pointed.

Five stations had indeed been set up. The first one was a square enclosure with a pole in each corner. Two ropes were strung between the poles; the sisters recognized it as a boxing ring. The scarecraws had been set up at the second station. The fairies noticed that Rhethea and Jemas had already set the two crates down about ten paces from them. Just to the left of that the third station was positioned at a large outcropping of rocks, several hundred paces away from the Ronans. Rhethea and Jemas were making their way to them. The fairies remembered a similar scenario in their lessons and smiled inwardly. Nayew then pointed to the fourth and fifth spot. The fairies looked at empty spots, nothing was there. They turned to Nayew, but it was Obwyn who spoke.

"Long poles in one," he said then added, "and over there, you will fight while riding your Avidraughts." The fairies saw their Avidraughts make their way to the clearing. Zee turned back and noticed that the armoured roans that Yan would be using also made their way to the clearing.

Upon Nayew's prompt each of the Jarrell brothers started to walk to one of the fighting stations. After receiving their instructions, each of the fairies left for their first station as well. Shanata was to start with the long poles where she would fight with Yan. Mariela was sent to the Cropping of Rocks where she would fight with bows and arrows, against Reg. Enna was sent to the scarecraws where she would go against Ody; skill against skill. Ody was an accomplished marksman and had won many competitions. Ashlina was sent to start with Aro and the Avidraughts where they would combat with swords. Zee was sent to the boxing ring where she would fight hand to hand combat and with knives against

174

Mitch. When everyone reached their station, a horn blared across the open field and the matches began. They were to fight at each station until one of them declared defeat.

*

The autumn sun was starting its decent and the battle field would soon be blanketed in darkness. The night air was starting to grow cool, which was refreshing for the competitors. Many of the bystanders had gone back to the village throughout the day to grab blankets and sweaters. The tournament had been very exciting and they wanted to watch it until the end.

The fairies had fared well against the Jarrell brothers. There had been plenty of cuts and bruises on both sides, but no major injuries. However, that was not to last as they battled it out at their last station.

The scarecraws had taken a beating and Mariela was doing her best against Ody; who was indeed an excellent marksmen. None of the sisters had actually outmatched his skill. The sun had been hot and the day, long. Mariela was on her last thread of patience. Her disposition became worse when Ody began goading her after she missed the first scarecraw, by several feet.

"You throw like a girl," Ody teased as he expertly threw a tarjas at one of the scarecraws; severing the last of the pumpkin heads clear off. The crowd behind them clapped and cheered heartily.

"I am a girl, you idiot!" Mariela shouted angrily at him as the tarjas she threw veered to the left and landed a few feet away from the Ronans. They were sitting on the blanket eating what looked like large slices of apple pie. They looked up at her in surprise; she looked apologetically back at them. Her stomach grumbled as she watched Ronan Black bite into his slice of pie. She had eaten at the noon day break with her sisters, but the time for the evening meal was fast approaching

175

and all of the physical exertion was making her hungry.

She picked up another tarjas and threw it. Again it missed the target, but this time it landed five feet away from the nearest scarecraw. Ody laughed, heartily. Mariela looked furiously at him. Ody laughed even harder. She could hear snickers from the crowd behind her. The anger that she normally kept in check bubbled to the surface as she picked up the last tarjas. She tried her best to throw it straight but her right arm cramped and the tarjas skimmed across the grass and landed at the base of a scarecraw she wasn't aiming for. Mariela sighed heavily.

It wasn't really that she was that bad at throwing; her right arm ached something fierce from the bruise that Mitch gave her in the boxing ring. Her armour had stood up against the knife but it was not protected from the thumping of Mitch's beefy hands. Orliff had looked at her arm after she complained that she had trouble lifting it and she was given a twenty minute reprieve to rest it. However now she was throwing tarjas at the scarecraws that had already been mutilated by her sisters. There was not much more of them left to sever off. The sun had beat mercilessly down on them all day and the armour, although light, was chafing her inner thighs and scraping her neck. Ody had teased her constantly and now the crowd around them had started to snicker at her as well.

Without thinking, Mariela ran over to the crate that held the spice balls, picked one up and whipped it at Ody. It exploded on his chest and he instantly fell to the ground, unconscious. Alamat and Rhethea were standing nearby and quickly ran over to Ody. While Alamat examined Ody, Rhethea smiled broadly down at his prone figure. Shamefaced, Mariela went over as well and started to apologize profusely. Rhethea started to laugh outright and gave Mariela a one arm hug. Mariela cringed when Rhethea's hand grabbed the spot where the bruise was.

"I can't tell you how many times I wanted to do that...shut

him up good didn't it?" Rhethea chuckled then released Mariela's arm. Mariela instantly grabbed her arm and moaned. "Oh sorry," Rhethea said. "I forgot about your arm."

"That's okay," Mariela replied. They watched as Alamat ran aromatic salts under Ody's nose. He sputtered and coughed before he slowly opened his eyes.

"Do you concede brother?" Rhethea asked triumphantly as she stood over him. Ody nodded his head and Rhethea whooped with laughter as she raised Mariela's left arm in the air. The crowd cheered with delight. Mariela however felt awful. She let her anger get the better of her. She couldn't enjoy the win against Ody.

She cautiously sat down on the grass next to him. Alamat handed her a decanter of water. After a long drink Mariela looked apologetically at Ody. She handed him the decanter. Ody took it graciously and drank deeply from it. We wiped his mouth with the back of his hand and set the decanter down between them. "That was a good throw. You should get angry more often," Ody said and bumped Mariela playfully with his shoulder. His show of kindness however did not make Mariela feel any better. Her anger simmered under the surface and she abruptly got up from the ground and stomped away.

"It was a compliment you know," Ody called after her. Mariela however did not stop. She left in search of Obwyn and Nayew; she had a thing or two to say to them about today's events.

Obwyn stood with Elder Enyce and Andi fifty feet from the Cropping of Rocks where Ashlina and Reg were having a mighty go at it. Both had used all their arrows and refused to admit defeat. Instead of confronting her with hand to hand combat, Reg wanted to see how clever Ashlina was with tracking. He had obviously heard she had received her powers and decided to hide on her. She was now tracking him. What she would do once she found him, with no weapon to use other than her shield, no one was quite sure.

The Cropping of Rocks was a perfect place to play a game of hide-n-go-seek. The villagers had often played there when they were younger, including the Jarrell brothers and the fairies. It was eight hundred feet wide and over one thousand feet long. The boulders ranged in size from two feet to three times the size of a man and spread out in all directions on a sandy bed. Parts of the area also had large deep crevasses. Reg was hiding in one of the crevasses smack dab in the middle of the cropping. Ashlina sensed that he was not hiding somewhere along the outer edge and started to make her way inwards. She stealthily moved from rock to rock. She occasionally stopped, listened and took a sniff of the air before continuing on her way.

Time lapsed and the sky steadily grew darker as she looked for him. There were so many places he could be hiding. She finally picked up the footprints he had left when he climbed atop the boulder that stood just before the crevasse he was hiding in. She peered down and her eyes adjusted to the dim lighting. Spying just the top of his head, she smiled as she quietly positioned herself just above where he sat behind a large boulder; he was looking in the opposite direction. She silently lowered her shield and tapped him on the head with it. Reg jumped up in surprise and bumped against the boulder next to him. The sand under his feet gave way and the boulder rolled forward. He quickly tried to jump out of the way but his left leg and hip were caught between the two boulders. Reg screamed out in agony.

"Reg, Reg. Oh my goodness!" Ashlina cried out. "Are you alright?"

"My leg is caught between the boulders!" He cried. He pushed at the boulder but the sand underneath gave way more and the boulder rolled tighter against his leg. He cried out again. Ashlina was about to jump down to help move the boulder when he warned her not to.

"No," he yelled. "Don't come down the sand is giving way…go for help will you!" Reg said frantically. He cringed as pain shot up his leg and into his back. Thankfully the boulder was not as tall as he or else his arm and chest would have been caught as well. He winced from pain again as he waited for Ashlina to return.

Ashlina quickly jumped from rock to rock and climbed to the top of the tallest boulder. Seeing the Elders and Obwyn, she frantically waved her hands and called out to them. The spectators saw her but did not understand her gestures. They began to cheer. Obwyn however had keen eyesight and upon seeing the anguished look on her face rushed forward; Enyce and Andi followed him. As soon as Ashlina told them what had happened Obwyn and Enyce followed her to the spot where Reg was. Elder Andi made her way back to the outer edge and hopped onto the back of Arturo who had been watching anxiously from the sidelines. Andi explained to him what happened and they raced off in search of Orliff.

They found Orliff sitting with the Ronans. Andi quickly told Orliff what had happened and that he was needed. The Ronans didn't wait to hear more. They took off running towards the Cropping of Rocks. Orliff took Andi's place on Arturo's back; they quickly flew over to the Cropping of Rocks. The Ronans were just a few paces away. Andi asked Alamat to ready a cot. Seeing Jopha and Zan standing nearby, she instructed them to harness a pokey to a carri-shift and take it to the Cropping of Rocks. Zan was about to retort with a cheeky quip, but upon seeing the seriousness in Andi's face he quickly did as he was asked.

Meanwhile, oblivious to what was going on at the rocks, Shanata was deep in concentration as she dueled with Aro. The clinking of their swords could be heard over the hushed whispers of the crowd as they looked frightfully on. Shanata was a strong fighter and Felon was light on her feet; Aro however was stronger and the roan he was riding was a brute named Burch. He had no problem charging at Felon or kicking out at her. Even though Aro had been fighting all day his jabs and parries were precise. With each passing moment

Shanata's breathing became laboured. Aro was relentless and he started to gain the upper hand. Just at the moment when Aro was about to deliver the final blow that would have knocked Shanata off of Felon's back, Mariela yelled from the sidelines.

"Shanata stop toying with Aro and do him in already, I have something of great importance to talk with you about," Mariela said with scorn. Aro, distracted by Mariela's choice of words, was caught off guard as he looked over at her. The slight distraction was all Shanata needed. Without waiting she threw down her sword and launched herself from Felon's back and body slammed Aro off Burch. Instinctively Aro clutched the reins as he toppled off. Burch was caught off guard and lost his footing. With a pull on the reins he fell over, right onto Aro's legs. Shanata had summersaulted away after hitting Aro but had landed on her back, hard. The air was knocked out of her. Nayew and Elder Phinney, who were watching from the sidelines, instantly came to both their aids.

Nayew grabbed the reins out of Aro's hand and helped Burch to his feet. Nayew quickly asked if he was okay. Embarrassed, Burch grunted his reply and walked off no worse for wear. That was not the case for Aro however. His right leg stuck out at an odd angle and the tibia poked through his pant leg. Blood began to stain the trampled grass beneath him. Aro rolled in agony as he tried not to call out, but the pain was incredible. A nervous energy erupted in the crowd until Phinney called out for everyone to settle down. She looked angrily at Mariela, "Take Amos and find Orliff. Felon you go with them and bring him back here immediately." Mariela, with a dejected look on her face, jumped on Amos' back and rode off without knowing if Felon followed or not. She however followed right behind them.

"Aro, look at me, look at me," Nayew demanded as he leaned over and held Aro down with a heavy hand on his chest. "You are going to get dirt into the wound and make it ten times worse than it is. Settle down."

"Easy for you to say," Aro said through clenched teeth as he continued to moan in agony.

"Aro you have had broken bones before," Nayew said as he applied pressure to the wound while holding Aro still. Aro moaned loudly.

"Yes, but none of them have actually been poking through my skin!" Aro yelled back. Nayew looked over at Phinney for suggestions.

"Here, wrap this around his thigh. It will slow down the bleeding," Phinney said as she threw Nayew the sash that she wore around her waist.

Phinney searched the crowd for someone. Spotting who she was looking for, she called out to them. "Arnak, do you have your flask of whiskey with you?" Arnak's first reaction was that of insult; a look that quickly turned to one of suspicion. Everyone in the village knew that Arnak carried a flask of whiskey wherever he went.

"Yes, of course I do. Why?" Arnak asked as he held his hand protectively over the pocket of his jacket. Hamy, who stood beside him, chuckled at Arnak's instant reaction to the question.

"Bring it here you fool and quickly!" Phinney yelled.

Arnak took the large silver coloured flask out of his pocket, walked over and held it out for Shanata. "Not for Shanata. She'll be fine. Give it to Nayew!" Phinney said with disgust. Misunderstanding, Arnak instantly became defensive.

"What? You want to pour one hundred year old whiskey onto his leg? That's blasphemy that is and I will have none of it!" Arnak said. He held the flask tightly against his chest as if it was worth its weight in gold. Phinney reached up, grabbed the flask from Arnak and threw it over to Nayew who promptly uncorked it and held it to Aro's lips. Aro took a long drink from it. The effect was instant. He calmly laid his head back; the warmth from the whiskey settled him down.

"Where did you get one hundred year old whiskey from?"

Hamy asked Arnak suspiciously. "I don't serve that at *The Baron's Den*."

"Eh," Arnak said as he looked confusedly from Hamy to Nayew, who held up Aro's head so he could have another sip. "Oh ya, well I bartered for it from Trebor Radek, didn't I. He brought it back for me the last time they went to Periours."

"You bartered. What did you have to barter with?" Hamy asked a little suspiciously. Everyone in the village knew that Arnak lived on meager means and had very little; nothing of worth to barter with that was for certain.

"Oh ya, well my services right!?" Arnak's retorted as he looked worriedly at Nayew who was taking a sip of the whiskey himself.

"Services," Hamy said incredulously. "You...work?"

"Well of course I work!" Arnak said. Deeply insulted, he continued. "I can't be sitting keeping you company all day can I? I do yard work for several of the older villagers. And how do you think Homsa takes care of all those bastions? He is too old to do the work by himself, so on occasion I help him out I do." Guilt flooded Arnak's senses at the memory of the day Homsa had been hurt. Arnak had not been there all week and he kicked himself for that. He became angry however when he saw the look of doubt on Hamy's face. "Where do you think the money comes from when I pay my bar bill," Arnak said leaning towards Hamy.

"Pay for your bar bill... now that's funny," Hamy said heartily. "And work; I can't even get you to mop out the men's washrooms..." he started to say but was interrupted by Arnak.

"What do you mean that's funny, I pay my way..." he started to say but was interrupted with a loud gahuff from Hamy. The two started to bicker and the crowd standing around snickered. Having enough of their nonsense, Elder Phinney stood, placed her hands on her hips and scolded them as if they were young children.

"Are you two serious?!" She said. "You're going to do this right now. Right now!?" She said pointedly then continued, "While we have injured about? Do something useful and find a pokey and a carri-shift. We will need to transport Aro back to the tent when Orliff gets here." Arnak and Hamy looked at her dejectedly.

"Can I have my flask back?" Arnak asked.

"Can you have your flask back?" Phinney said. Her voice rose with her anger. "Are you insane? No you can't have your flask back! Go, be useful!" She said as she waved her hands dismissing them. Turning her back she mumbled under her breath, "Can I have my flask back." She then clicked her tongue loudly in disgust as she looked down at Shanata. Arnak looked pitifully at the flask before he and Hamy quickly walked away.

A commotion from the crowd caused everyone to look in the opposite direction. Mariela had arrived with Niella, who promptly slipped off Felon's back and made her way through the crowd. She immediately assessed the situation and went straight to Nayew and Aro.

"Where's Orliff?" Nayew asked.

"He is tending Reg," Niella retorted curtly. "Aro, we will have to set your leg back in place and then I'll wrap it for you; are you okay with that," Niella asked. She looked with concern at Aro who was smiling goofily back at her and nodded his head. She looked questioningly at Nayew.

"One hundred year old whiskey," Nayew said.

"Ah yes, well that should deaden the pain a bit," Niella said. "Hold him still will you." Phinney came over. With the help of Nayew and two other villagers they held Aro down. Niella placed her hands above and below the break. Shanata turned her head and cringed as did many of the villagers. A loud pop echoed around the clearing as Niella snapped the bone back into place. Excruciating pain erupted in Aro's leg, a heart-wrenching cry quickly followed; Aro fell unconscious.

"Oh good that will make this next bit a little easier," Niella said. She quickly sterilized the wound with a potion from her medicine bag. The green liquid, made primarily from the bristle herb, instantly stopped the bleeding. She then ripped open his pant leg all the way up to his thigh. She placed a thick patch over the wound then started to bark out orders.

"Hand me those two sticks from behind Felon's saddle," Niella said to Phinney who quickly got up and did her bidding. Taking the two large sticks from Phinney, Niella placed them on either side of Aro's leg. "Nayew, hold his leg straight and Phinney you hold the splints in place so that I can wrap them to his leg." The three of them worked quickly and not before long Aro's leg was wrapped tightly with a filmy gauze. "He'll be wearing a cast for quite some time but I am sure he will walk fine when it is healed. Reg was not so lucky." Niella said absent mindedly. Hearing this Nayew dismissed the villagers as he and Phinney looked questioningly at Niella.

"His leg and hip were crushed between two boulders," Niella started to explain. "He was in one of the crevasses and the sand at his feet gave way. One large rock pinned him against another. The ground was so unstable they did not want to take the chance of more of the rocks rolling on top of the rescue team. So Ronan Black held the boulder to the side while Ronan Brown pulled Reg straight up. Orliff rushed him to the tent but it doesn't look good. We're not sure if he is going to be able to walk again." Nayew and Phinney looked uneasily at each other.

"The odd thing is...," Niella said quietly, "when they pulled him up the sand gave way completely and the boulder rolled away. Behind it," she said lowering her voice, "is an entrance to a cave." Nayew and Phinney looked at her in surprise. Without saying more, Niella rose and walked over to Shanata, who had been listening intently to what she was saying but missed the last part of it. Phinney followed and when Shanata started to ask about Reg and if Ashlina was hurt, Phinney told her that all would be explained later.

Together Phinney and Niella helped Shanata take off her armour. Niella gently lifted up the sleeveless vest and examined Shanata quickly. A large dark bruise started to form. When Niella poked at it Shanata winced in pain and caught her breath.

"Yes, yes, it hurts I am sure," Niella said curtly. She looked in her medicine bag for something. "Here take one of these now and one later tonight," she said as she handed Shanata two purple lizben berries and a decanter of water. "I am sure the pain is going to be worse in the morning so make sure you see Orliff as soon as you can." Shanata nodded as she swallowed the berry and drank from the decanter. Phinney and Niella helped her to her feet. Phinney picked up the armour, "You won't need this for the rest of the day. I will take it to the tent for you." Shanata nodded her reply.

Arnak and Hamy had arrived with a pokey and carri-shift. Together, with Nayew's help, they placed Aro in the back of it. Phinney and Niella joined Aro and asked Shanata if she would like to join them. Shanata declined stating that she would ride Felon over to where Zee was dueling with Yan at the long poles. Mariela helped her sister onto Felon's back and opted to walk beside them.

Hamy jumped onto the bench of the carri-shift and whipped the pokey into action. The pokey was slight in stature but strong and quick on its feet, which was unusual for a pokey. Phinney and Niella held onto the side of the carri-shift as the pokey sped off into the direction of the tents. Everyone else made their way over to the long poles. Everyone else that is, but Arnak. He bent down and picked up the discarded empty flask. It was caked with blood and dirt. Arnak wiped it off lovingly with a hanky that he pulled out of his pant pocket. He was hurt about the things that his good friend Hamy said about him and walked dejectedly backed to the village alone.

Shanata and Mariela watched with pride as their little sister dodged strike after strike of Yan's metal tipped long pole. They hadn't seen Zee since the noon day break; her once lovely armour was now covered with dirt and grass. The sisters and the large crowd that watched safely from a distance chuckled as Zee cheekily goaded Yan on.

"I think having a baby has made you an old man Yan," Zee quipped playfully as she dodged another strike. Yan grunted. "What? That's all you got Yan? Come on old man. You can do better than that!" Zee said as she summersaulted away.

Yan's long pole thudded on the ground where Zee should have been. The vibrations raced up his right arm and he clenched his fist in reaction. She was fast and flitted around the clearing like a butterfly. Although she had not struck him once with her long pole he was feeling pain. He had dueled with Enna an hour before. She was not as fast as Zee but she was as strong as an ox. Enna had landed several well placed blows that had knocked him to the ground. He was aching from head to toe and Zee flitting about was making him dizzy.

"Zee," Farley called out from the sideline. "To win you actually have to strike him or knock him off his feet, you know that right?"

"Shut up Farley! No help from the sidelines," Yan growled. "You won't always be there you know. She will have to figure stuff out on her own." Yan said as he jabbed angrily at Zee. She again however was not there. This time she jumped up into the air, rolled over his head and just before she landed she struck him across the head with the butt end of her long pole. The crowd cheered as she landed lightly on her feet. Yan's ear rang and he fell to the ground on one knee. He shook his head while he tried to stand.

"Now Zee, take your chance and knock him out!" Farley called out. Zee looked from Farley to Yan who struggled to stand. Nayew stood on the other side of the circle and warned Farley to keep quiet.

Zee looked pitifully at Yan. She couldn't take advantage of him while he was down like that. It wasn't in her nature.

While she struggled with indecision, Yan was back up on his feet. The crowd booed. Several of them yelled out that Zee had bested him and he should stay down. Yan scowled at them in response. Anger and self-preservation kicked in. He couldn't let another fairy best him again. Yan came at Zee with fury. She dodged strike after strike but his brute force and erratic motions were wearing her down. Zee became slower and the tip of the long pole grazed her armour. Zee thought, as she looked at the anger on Yan's face, *if I don't find a way to knock him off his feet he will surely try to run me through.*

Zee decided she had no choice; she would have to strike back. Except for the hit across the head Zee hadn't actually hit Yan with her long pole. Her strategy was to wear him down with her agility. It had worked on his brothers, except for Ody of course, who they didn't actually physically fight against. When Yan came at her, instead of dodging away she stood her ground and swung the long pole as hard as she could. The poles clashed against each other and the vibrations ran up Zee's arm. She cried out in pain and shock and dropped the pole. Yan, seeing an opening, took the long pole and hit the back of Zee's leg with it. She instantly fell to the ground and cried out.

As Yan rose his pole to strike her, several things happened in succession. Shanata and Mariela cried out and started to run forward. Nayew however stepped in their way and held them back. Farley however did not heed Nayew's earlier warning and galloped into the clearing. He was bent on knocking Yan off his feet and trampling him if he didn't stay down. Yan looked in shock as Farley came barreling down on him, giving Zee the perfect opportunity to raise her pole. Without thinking she struck at the pole in his hand with all her strength, hoping to knock it from him. However she missed and hit a kink in his armour. The armour split open and the metal tip of the pole pierced Yan's arm. He cried out in pain and dropped the pole.

Everyone looked on in shock as Yan fell to the ground.

Even Yan looked with shock at the pole that stuck out of his arm. Farley skidded to a halt just before them. Zee looked up at him with worry as Yan began to moan in pain. Shanata, Mariela and Nayew ran forward as the crowd began to chant Zee's name. Zee however looked over at Yan; blood trickled from the wound. She covered her face and began to sob greatly.

Farley tried to console her as did Shanata and Mariela, but Zee continued to cry. Nayew talked quietly with Yan as he took off the broken armour. He quickly looked over the wound. The spear head had gone right through Yan's arm but had not hit any major artery that he could see. Yan sighed in relief when Nayew told him.

"I'm going to break the pole off just in case I am wrong," Nayew said. "We need to get you to Orliff." Nayew looked over at the fairies. "Shanata, Mariela leave your sister and come here," he ordered. "Zee," he continued to say. "Man up. You did what you were supposed to; fight or be killed." Nayew ignored the look of scorn from Mariela as she continued to console her sister. Shanata however walked over to help hold Yan's arm still as Nayew broke the pole in two. Yan cried out in pain as Shanata consoled him. Yan looked up at her as Nayew wrapped his arm with a piece of cloth that he tore off his shirt.

"You know, I wouldn't have really struck her," Yan said weakly.

"I know you wouldn't have." Shanata said.

The reality of the moment washed over her. The day's events and the reasons why they were fighting against the Jarrell brothers in the first place brought tears to Shanata eyes. Yan, understanding, reassured her. "You will be okay you know. All of you will," Yan said.

"Don't lie to her Yan," Nayew said as he tied off the makeshift bandage. Yan winced. "Their task is a daunting one; their foe is formidable, if any of the rumors of Canvil are true. None of us knows what the outcome will be. The fairies will have to fight to save their lives," Nayew said. He then looked out at the crowd who had been listening closely. "We all will," Nayew added.

Shanata looked over at her sisters. Zee had stopped crying and was wiping her face dry. Shanata smiled encouragingly at her. When she looked at Mariela however she became concerned. Mariela's look towards Nayew was troublesome. Shanata could tell that Mariela was just about to lose her self-control. Nayew however spoke and everyone started to react.

"Farley, take Yan to Orliff. I will follow beside you on Felon. I think flying will be easier. It won't jostle his arm as much. Shanata, you and Mariela can walk Zee over to the tent to get looked at," Nayew said, still ignoring the look of scorn on Mariela's face.

"I am okay," Zee said as she stood up.

"Are you sure?" Nayew asked. Zee nodded her reply. "All right then," he said and called over the two villagers that had helped with Aro earlier. Together they picked up Yan and placed him on Farley's back. Nayew jumped on Felon's back and they flew off towards the tents.

Shanata looked over at Mariela. Her look of scorn was deflated and was replaced with a pouty lip. She so wanted to have it out with Nayew about how ridiculous it was to fight with the Jarrell brothers. All it was accomplishing was injury and some of them severe. What lessons were the Elders really trying to teach them? She didn't understand and wanted answers. Shanata put her arm around Mariela's shoulders and squeezed lightly. She did not see the deep look of confusion on Zee's face until Zee blurted out, 'What?'

"We didn't say anything," Shanata said as she and Mariela looked at Zee.

"Shhhh....not you," Zee said angrily as she waved her hands at them. She then turned her head to the side and listened intently. She could hear a voice urgently whispering to her and she concentrated on what it was saying. Shanata and Mariela looked at her with concern. Finally Zee looked at them in shock. "Did you hear that?" she asked.

"Hear what Zee?" Mariela and Shanata said in unison.

"The voice, the voice, did you not hear that voice?" Zee yelled angrily. The crowd standing around them started to murmur.

"Zee there was no voice," Mariela said calmly as she looked at the crowd. Zee became agitated as she too looked at the crowd. Many of them turned their faces as she looked at them.

"Yes, yes there was a voice. It was the same one that spoke to me the day I found Homsa!" Zee said.

"Zee, you never told us you heard a voice that day," Mariela said accusingly.

"Shh, Mariela," Shanata said harshly. She looked encouragingly at Zee. Shanata knew of things her sisters didn't. She had overheard many tales on her travels with the Radeks. Tales that were so frightening she couldn't sleep for days afterwards, nor share them with her sisters. She knew that spirits, good or evil, could talk to the living and in rare cases they could control their actions.

"Zee, what is the voice telling you?" Shanata asked calmly. Encouraged by Shanata's response Zee listened intently to the voice.

"It's warning me," she whispered.

"Warning you about what?" Mariela enquired.

"Warning me about, about…. Enna," Zee looked frantically at her sisters. A vision of Enna and a large silver blade flashed before her eyes.

"*Run Zee, run,*" the voice demanded of Zee.

Without waiting to explain to her sisters, Zee took off as fast as her legs could carry her in the direction of the boxing ring and Enna.

Chapter 15
Enna the Warrior

The large crowd that gathered around the boxing ring looked on with worry as Enna circled around Mitch like a Rapcicor circles its prey before devouring it. He had been knocked to the ground several times and was now half sitting and half lying on the ground, holding his right arm. Blood trickled from a long gash under his hand; he applied pressure to it in hopes the bleeding would stop. Enna's knife had found a kink in the armour and split it open.

Mitch couldn't stand. His right foot, if not broken or fractured, was badly bruised. After Enna knocked him to the ground she purposely stumped on it, twice. He was sure however that at least one of his toes was broken. He could feel the pressure building under his boot. He was not looking forward to taking the boot off for fear that his foot would blow up like a bubble fish. His face was bruised from the punch she had delivered, which is why he was presently on the ground. That one punch to the face had knocked him off his feet. A large bruise rapidly spread from under his left eye, over his cheek bone and towards his chin. He could feel the split where her knuckles hit the delicate skin under his eye. It wasn't bleeding however. For that he was thankful.

Mitch squinted up at Enna. The look on her face actually worried him. They had been fighting for well over an hour. Mitch had got in a few well-placed blows earlier on, but he had yet to knock her to the ground. Enna was strong; stronger than her sisters. She could take a hit as good as, if not better than most of his brothers. She was also, he thought with mixed emotions, methodical with each of her attacks. It was as if each blow was timed and placed to deliver the next one. It had been like that right from the moment she entered the ring.

She had not spoken to anyone after her bout with Yan. She walked straight to the ring and entered it. Mitch had started to throw verbal jabs at her as soon as her foot hit the mat, but Enna did not respond to them. Instead she picked up the knife that lay on a wooden stool in a corner of the ring and walked the outer circle. All the while she made sure that her back was to the ropes and she was far enough away to dodge any blows from him, but close enough that if she had an opportunity to strike she could do so with accuracy. He had watched with pride as she assessed each of his moves and countered them with a precise and disciplined action. Now however he was getting wary; something about her had changed since their last scrimmage just the week before.

Enna was fearless and looked forward to training with the young men of the village. Most of the time the young men limped or were carried away with their clothes in tatters after a bout with her. Enna wielded her knife as well as Obwyn did. Her skill was so great that her knife never pierced the skin. She blushed whenever anyone commented on how well she was doing and giggled girlishly.

Mitch looked down at the blood pooling on the ground beneath him, then looked back up at Enna. She was not blushing or giggling. Something had definitely changed about her. He could see it in her eyes. It was as if someone else stood before him. A thought came to him as Enna stared down at him with a menacing sneer. He knew without a doubt that she had received her powers. The Elders had warned Mitch and his brothers that there were still three fairies who had not received their powers. The training session might bring them forth and if they thought that any of them had received it, they were to contact the Elders immediately. The powers could be all-consuming and the fairies, they had quickly learned, could not control their actions when the powers were presented.

Mitch remembered reading a passage in *The Book of Warfare* from the library. The passage described *blood-thirst*; how it consumes the warrior's every thought, every movement. Without conscious, without regret, they carry out the deed at hand with deadly accuracy. Mitch looked with fright at the knife in Enna's hand. The blade glinted as his blood dripped from the tip.

"Enna I concede," Mitch said and laughed lightly. Enna however continued to circle him. "I concede Enna, see," he said and threw his knife away. Enna however was deep in the *blood-thirst* and did not hear his words. She stopped in front of him, glared down at him and growled. The crowd began to call out to her. Enna however did not hear them and several of them screamed as Enna raised her knife. Just then several burly villagers entered the ring and surrounded Enna and Mitch.

"Someone get the Elders before she kills me!" Mitch yelled out. Several of the villagers ran to look for the Elders.

"Put the knife down Enna," the villagers in the ring warned her one after another. Enna looked at them each in turn with a calculating assessment. Robart, with his hands held up in front of him, was the first to approach her. He was a burly villager, about six feet tall, had a large belly, thick legs and large muscular arms. He was a jolly fellow on any given day and had a deep chuckle that made other people laugh along with him. He worked in the Gnome Garden warehouse. Enna knew him well and they had, on occasion, ate meals together with the other workers. Their conversations were always light and comical and usually centered around what had happened that day in the gardens with the Gnomes, who were quite amusing creatures.

"Enna," he called her name softly, but that is a far as he got. Enna grabbed his right arm, twisted it behind his back and placed her foot against his backside. With a mighty push he flew across the ring and landed hard against one of the corner posts. The crowd gasped and many of them backed away from the ring. Robart's head hit the post so hard that it split open, as did his forehead. He crumbled to the ground.

Blood began to ooze from the cut and dripped into his eyes. He wiped his forehead with the palm of his hand. Seeing the blood he looked up in shock at Enna. How could someone so small have the strength to accomplish such a feat?

Enna returned his look with a blank stare. She started to advance on Mitch and the other five villagers instantly went into action. While one dragged Mitch to the side the other four advanced on Enna. Enna however calculated each of their moves and before they could even wrestle her to the ground she had disposed of each of them. One, slighter in stature than Robart, lay flat on his back next to Robart. She had literally swung him over her head and threw him across the ring. The next one she dispatched by stomping down on his left knee, breaking it. She then boxed his ears and punched him across his jaw; he too crumbled to the ground. The third was a little harder to deal with as he was quite quick, but she saw her opening and jumped up into the air as he came forward. She kicked him with both feet square in his chest. He too fell instantly.

The fourth and fifth came at her from different directions; Enna however was merciless in her delivery. She pummeled the first with rapid shots to his abdomen and an upper cut to the jaw; he fell hard. The second, who was not much taller than she, but was muscular, she kneed in the groin. While he was bent over she picked him up and body slammed him onto the mat. The crowd standing around were not sure if they should cheer her on or try and stop her. Too scared to enter the ring they moved further away.

Enna looked over at Mitch who lay propped up against a post in the opposite corner of Robart. As she started to advance on him, Enyce, Rayley, Obwyn and Nayew quickly made their way to the boxing ring. They called out to her to stop; unfortunately Enna did not hear them. The *blood thirst* pumped rapidly through her veins and a loud hum rang in her ears. Enna picked up the knife she dropped and advanced towards Mitch; Mitch cowered against the post. As she raised her knife in the air, he hid his head behind his arms. The crowd cried out, begging Enna to stop. They all knew without a doubt that she was going to kill Mitch. Just as she was about to bring down a deadly blow a vision blurred her view. The image was Zee. She had thrown herself in front of Mitch and laid protectively across his chest.

The crowd cried out as the blade came down. Zee looked lovingly into Enna's eyes and softly called her name. Like a light turning on in her brain the *blood thirst* lost its hold on Enna's senses and receded to her subconscious. Her ears cleared. Zee spoke her name again. The Elders gasped in horror as the knife came down; however it stopped less than an inch from Zee's face.

Enna looked at Zee who smiled calmly back at her and sighed with relief. Enna did not return her sister's smile. Instead she backed away from Zee and Mitch and walked to the middle of the ring. Her hand shook slightly as she placed the knife in the sheath at her waist. She looked around calmly at what she had done. The six villagers still lay on the ground groaning in pain. Elder Enyce and Rayley entered the ring and quickly made their way to her. Obwyn and Nayew had also entered, however they started to bark out orders as they tended to the men on the ground.

"Jopha," Nayew called out. Jopha had just arrived with Rhethea and Jemas. The news of Enna receiving her powers had spread like wild fire throughout the clearing. "You and Jemas take some of the villagers and find a half-dozen carri-shifts and pokeys." Jopha nodded, but Jemas stared at the carnage on the ground and did not move until Rhethea elbowed him in the ribs. Nayew looked at him with scorn. "Be quick about it will you. We need to get these men to Orliff!" They hurriedly left with five of the other villagers.

"Mary," Obwyn called out. Mary and Zila had also made their way to the ring. "Find the other Elders and bring them here. I think they may be at the Cropping of Rocks."

"Yes Obwyn," Mary said and started to run toward the Cropping of Rocks.

"Zila find the other fairies," he said then added. "Enna is in need of her sisters." Zila nodded her head and left in the opposite direction of Mary. She had seen Mariela and Shanata making their way across the field to the boxing ring.

"Enna dear would you like to sit down?" Rayley asked with motherly concern.

"No, I'm fine," Enna said.

"Perhaps you should sit down and have a drink of water," Enyce said as she put her arm around her waist.

"I'm fine," Enna said with authority and walked away from the Elders to the opposite side of the ring. She leaned her back against the ropes, crossed her arms in front of her chest and stared at them. Enyce and Rayley exchanged worried glances with Nayew and Obwyn.

"Enna bring that water and stool over here," Obwyn demanded as he pointed to her corner of the ring where the wooden stool and decanter of water sat. She had not used either of them the whole time she was in the ring. Enna did as she was told.

Until her sisters arrived that is how Enna's time was spent. The Elders gave her orders and she carried them out methodically. Even though the men were wary of her they allowed her to tend to them. The Elders were never far from her. Zee came forward and worked beside her, but neither of them spoke.

Mariela and Shanata hurriedly entered the ring and made their way to Enna and Zee who were tending to Robart. Shanata laid her hand on Enna's shoulder. Enna looked up. Her bottom lip immediately started to quiver. A single tear ran down her cheek as she stood up.

"Let us go to the tent shall we?" Shanata said.

"There is still work to be done," Enna said as she wiped the tear away with the back of her hand. Just then Jopha and Jemas returned with six pokeys and carri-shifts.

"Look, the pokeys are here, they will carry these men to Orliff. There is nothing more we can do here," Shanata said calmly. Enna nodded and the fairies started to turn; all of them that is but Mariela. Seeing the carnage around her, the stress on her sisters' faces and the dirt and blood on their armour, she was now ready to have her say.

Chapter 16
A Valuable Lesson

Obwyn and Nayew were securing Mitch onto a pole-shift when Mariela yelled at them. "What were you trying to accomplish today?" She demanded of them. Upon hearing her heated words, Nayew called over to Hamy, Zan, Jopha and two of the villagers to help. After they maneuvered Mitch through the ropes safely, he ordered them to take the injured to Orliff.

They were joined by the Elders and walked purposefully across the mat to the fairies. Mariela stood defiantly in front of her sisters with her hands on her hips. They knew Mariela detested fighting; she had made it quite apparent over the last two weeks. She hadn't always however; she had enjoyed the times they trained on sword play and was quite skilled at it. Her thrusts were commanding and accurate, the parries were timed to perfection and her footwork was poetic. Losing interest for it happened quite by accident. She had been dueling with Jopha and had knocked the sword from his hand. They both bent down at the same time to pick up the sword and she accidentally stabbed his hand with her sword. Jopha screamed out in pain as the blood immediately oozed out the wound. Mariela shrieked in horror at what she had done and apologized profusely.

After Alamat and Niella, who were always on hand for those "just in case moments" dressed the wound, Obwyn gave the okay for the dueling to continue. Mariela had refused however, stating that she would not fight someone who had been injured. When Obwyn insisted that she continue, Mariela threw down her sword and stomped off. Shanata and Rayley tried to reason with her but she refused to return.

Since that day she started to arrive too late to practice

combat training. When asked what kept her she made up one lie after another. When she ran out of plausible lies she became defensive to point of being argumentative. On advice from Rayley, Nayew and Obwyn allowed Mariela the time to come to terms with what she and her sisters were destined to accomplish. The combat training was paramount to their success.

They looked at the anger on her face and the resolve in her stance. This confrontation had been building rapidly since that day and now was as good a time as any to confront it and put it to rest.

"Mariela stop," Shanata said as she placed her hand on Mariela's arm. Mariela pulled her arm roughly from her sister's grasp and confronted the Elders.

"Look at us," Mariela said earnestly. "We are caked with sweat, dirt and our armour is stained with the blood of our friends."

"Mariela, there will come a time when each of you may have to take a life to save another or even your own, I might add," Rayley said. "We have talked of this." Mariela huffed with annoyance. As her guide and confident, Rayley and Mariela often had lengthy discussions about the beings and creatures they would meet on their mission. At the time, Mariela had enjoyed her newfound knowledge of the inhabitants living just outside of the Whipple Wash Valley and in the nether regions of the Southern Kingdoms. She poured over several books in the library until the wee hours of the morning, learning all she could about them. The languages they spoke and their customs intrigued her. She was looking forward to meeting each of them. In her fanciful imagination she only envisioned them welcoming the fairies with open arms and warm hearts. To think that she may have to take up arms against them was in stark contrast to what she had envisioned. Coming to terms with that fact had become problematic. So when Nayew began to speak again, Mariela's anger boiled over.

"The Jarrell brothers are strong young bucks. Their injuries will heal, as will the villagers. Besides," Nayew said, "they knew what they were signing up for. You are training to become warriors."

"Warriors," Mariela interrupted him rudely with a sarcastic laugh. "Is this journey not one of peace Nayew?" Her words dripped with scorn as she looked up at him. He returned her stare with a raised eyebrow and an angry frown. All those who stood around gasped at her contempt. Nayew was a no nonsense kind of man. Many of the villagers preferred to stay away from him and would never confront him in such a defiant manner.

"Mariela!" Shanata whispered harshly as Zee, Ashlina and Enna looked on with concern. Mariela refused to heed the warning; instead she stared rudely at Nayew.

"Are we not supposed to be uniting the Southern Kingdoms," she said. "What kind of intentions will we present if we show up dressed in armour, no matter how lovely they are, and with swords and shields in hand?"

"Mariela!" Shanata warned again. Mariela ignored her once again. She was long past listening to reasoning.

"No seriously," Mariela said as she returned the look of scorn towards the Elders. "What message is that conveying? Accept our terms or we will have Enna beat you into submission." Enna's cheeks reddened as she looked away with embarrassment. The essence of the warrior was now gone and the young girl had returned.

"How would you rather present yourself, with flowing dresses and flowers in your hair, spouting sonnets while tinkling on a mandolin?" Obwyn asked with disgust.

"Yes," Mariela said brazenly. "It would be more cordial than what the lot of you have planned," she said with loathing.

Rayley's cheeks also reddened, however it was from anger and embarrassment. Enyce's eyebrows knit together in anger as she fumed at Mariela's outburst. In all their years no one had ever spoke to them with such distain or loathing. Mariela however did not pick up the warning signs and continued with her tirade.

"If that is what you and that bloody tree are rearing us for, then you are no better than Canvil." At that precise moment Mariela knew that she had crossed a line and there would be no turning back. Without a doubt, a great punishment was forthcoming. To talk with contempt towards the Elders, Nayew and Obwyn was one thing, but to slew insults towards the Whipple Wash Tree was quite another.

Enyce, who was normally composed and gentle by nature bellowed, "Enough" so loud that some of the onlookers cried out in surprise. The Ronans were shocked. They had never heard any of the Elders raise their voice in anger. They both dropped the large glass mugs they had just filled with ale. The mugs shattered on contact with the hard ground. The warm liquid and shards of glass splattered all over the shoes and pant legs of everyone standing nearby. Rhethea, Mary and Zila looked at each other with disbelief at Mariela's audacity, then with pity. Many of the villagers instantly turned their backs, indicating their disapproval.

The anger Mariela had felt quickly deflated as she slumped her shoulders. She looked forlornly back at her sisters who started to move towards her. However, Rayley and Obwyn immediately stepped in front of them. All the fairies could do was look with pity at their sister. Nayew ordered all the villagers to leave. They obliged without a word of concern for Mariela. Mariela could hear their urgent whispers and feel their glances of scorn as they walked by the ring. She knew that soon all of Elsbrier would know about how she insulted the Whipple Wash Tree and her shoulders slumped even more. Whatever punishment the Elders would give would be nothing compared to the looks of distain she would receive from the villagers. Tears welled up in her eyes as she thought of the reception she would receive from the Tree. She wondered fleetingly if it would allow her to pass through the curtain of limbs or if it would toss her away as if she was an enemy.

In the absence of Queen Faywyn, Elder Enyce was head of the family. Although she and her sisters ruled the land jointly, Enyce's word would be final until Queen Faywyn's return. So when Enyce told Rayley to take the fairies back to the village, Rayley complied. The fairies instantly became defensive and started to argue as they tried to move closer to their sister.

"It is okay," Mariela said as she raised her hand. "I will endure whatever punishment the Elders bestow upon me. My words were disrespectful and unforgiving." Enna and Zee looked at her with empathy before they reluctantly left the ring. It was the look on Shanata's face however that gave Mariela the strength to square her shoulders and straighten her back.

Shanata and Mariela did not always get along nor did they see eye to eye on many things, so the look of pride on her sister's face gave Mariela hope that all would be fine. Enyce and Rayley looked with surprise at the exchange. They had often witnessed arguments between them. Shanata, being the eldest, had naturally adopted a motherly relationship with her sisters and often reprimanded Mariela for not taking on more of a leadership role. Mariela however, the most passive of the girls, preferred to believe that the world was an artistic garden of wonderment and she the peaceful flower dwelling within it instead of see it for the hostile world it was becoming.

The Elders understood her trepidation. The fairies were to unite the lands but that did not mean that the people and creatures they encountered would agree. No one knew for sure how far Lord Canvil's influence had reached. Perhaps many of the Kingdoms had already chosen to fight on his side. The Elders were positive that the combat training would be useful on the fairies' journey. Obwyn looked at Enyce. He did not need to voice his thoughts; she knew it was time to teach Mariela a valuable lesson and one she would not soon forget. Enyce nodded her compliance. Before she left the ring she stopped beside Mariela and laid her hand on her shoulder, "I will see you in the morning." Mariela nodded, but could not speak as she looked nervously at Obwyn and Nayew.

Nayew waited until the last villager left the clearing before he addressed Mariela. "Take off your armour," Nayew said. Mariela did as he asked without question. Her hands however shook as she started to pull the armour over her head. When finished, she placed the armour on a stool in the corner of the ring. Sweat marks stained the cotton pants and the sleeveless vest. For the most part however the undergarment had stayed clean.

"Pick up the knife," Obwyn said as he unsheathed the knife at his waist. Mariela hesitated.

"Do as you are told!" Nayew commanded before he walked to the side of the ring and ducked under the ropes.

Mariela's hands shook even more as she picked up the knife. She looked with worry at Obwyn as Nayew lit large oil lamps hanging from poles all around the ring. As the light fought off the darkening sky, Mariela watched Nayew take two sets of long poles and swords from a carri-shift. He leaned them against a corner post of the ring.

A movement caught the corner of her eye and she looked over again at Obwyn; her heart sank as he raised his knife in the air, indicating that he was challenging her to a duel. Mariela knew what was to come next. Once she raised her knife in the air, the duel would begin. There would be no talking her way out of it- her arguments would fall on deafened ears. A shiver of fear ran up her spine; her punishment was to fight Obwyn the Great Hunter and that was that. The outcome she knew, without a doubt, would not end in her favour. Regardless of that fact, Mariela timidly raised her knife in the air.

*

Mariela returned home well after midnight. The Tree had
let her pass without issue. With assistance from Rayley and
Jolise she made it down the stairs and into the fairies' sitting
room. The other fairies were sitting around the light in the
middle of the room. They were washed, their injuries had
been tended to and they had eaten a large meal. While they
waited anxiously for her return they discussed what Ashlina
and Elder Andi and Athia had discovered earlier that day in
the hidden cave in the Cropping of Rocks. Upon seeing their
sister however they immediately jumped up and quickly
assaulted her with questions.

"Girls, girls can't you see she is hurting and exhausted,"
Rayley scolded them. From the light in the room they could
see that Mariela was covered in dark bruises that spanned the
length of her arms. She limped slightly. Her cotton pants were
cut open and they saw that several long gashes had been
tended to with a clear glistening ointment. A black eye and a
bruised, cut lip marred her pretty face. Her lovely hair was a
mess and looked like she had teased it relentlessly with a
comb. Dry blood stained her clothing. They would be
surprised to find that it was not all hers.

"Oh Mariela!" Zee cried out as tears instantly welled up in
her eyes.

"Mariela," Shanata whispered and frowned deeply.

"What have they done to you?" Enna asked wishing she
had stayed.

Too upset to speak, Ashlina said nothing. As she went to
give her sister a hug, Jolise held up her hand to stop her.
"Whatever you have to say to her can wait till the morning,"
Jolise said sternly.

Together she and Rayley walked Mariela to her sleeping
quarters. To make sure she was not disturbed Niella had been
sent along with a sleeping cot so she could tend to her needs.
The sisters watched Jopha and Niella walk pass them with the

cot and a medicine bag, quilt and pillow. It was the first time either of them had been in the inner sanctum of the Tree and they looked apprehensive at the fairies as they walked by. Just a few minutes passed before Jopha came back out, followed by Rayley and Jolise.

"Time for bed," Rayley said curtly as she closed the curtains to Mariela's room.

"Thank you Jopha," Jolise said amusedly. Jopha had been looking curiously around the room with large eyes and his mouth was agape. "I will show you out. Good night girls," she said as she and Jopha left the room.

"Girls, I know you are worried about Mariela, however there is nothing you can do for her tonight. I am sure she will be well enough to talk with you tomorrow." Rayley said.

"Yes Rayley," the girls said unison. They went immediately to their rooms. After Rayley left, Shanata came out of her room and dragged a chair over to Mariela's door. She sat there all night standing vigil and wondered curiously about what Mariela would tell them in the morning.

Mariela however had not spoken about the things Nayew and Obwyn did to her, the things they said or the training they gave her. All she said was that she learned a valuable lesson; one she hoped her sisters would never have to.

The fairies had been taken by surprise when Elder Enyce showed up just after breakfast carrying a stack of ancient looking books and ordered everyone out of the Gathering Room, even Niella. The fairies were told not to return until after lunch. When they did, the books were gone and Mariela refused to talk about what she had read. The girls could see that a different light shone from her eyes. Three days later Mariela was well enough to join them for combat training. She showed up on time and participated with enthusiastic brutality; especially when she was paired with Nayew or Obwyn.

Chapter 17
The Battle with the Rapcicors

Three weeks after their combat training with the Jarrell brothers Zee was in the meadow at first light putting a saddle expertly on Farley's back. She still needed to stand on a boulder to do it, but Farley no longer minded. Instead he quietly waited for her to finish. Zee jumped down from the rock and walked several paces away from him. She then turned slowly and faced him. She looked keenly at the saddle as if she could will herself onto it. However, she instead took a deep breath and ran as fast as she could towards him. Farley did not flinch when she got nine feet from him, jumped high into the air, did a summersault and a twist then landed with a soft thud onto the saddle. Farley smiled broadly as Zee placed her feet in the stirrups and held onto the reins the way he taught her to.

"Well done little one, you are getting better every time you do that. I hardly felt it that time," his voice was still gruff, but it now had an edge of warmth to it that made Zee smile. "You do know that you can stand on the rock and jump up as well don't you?" He questioned her teasingly as he looked back at her. She leaned over and patted him warmly on his neck.

"Thank you Farley for the compliment and yes, I know, but then how much fun would that be? Besides," she said with a cheeky smile, "there won't always be a boulder for me to stand on."

Farley nodded his head in understanding, but decided not to ask what she would use to assist her with the saddle if there was no boulder. Some conclusions she was going to have to learn on her own. Instead, he took off galloping around the meadow before he spread his wings and jumped effortlessly into the air. Zee laughed with exhilaration as the wind caught

Farley's wings raising them higher and higher off the ground. They had decided to leave at first light without the others and explore the countryside from an Avidraught's eye view, as Farley would say.

Zee left a note for the Elders explaining where she had gone and who she was with. Even though she had proven during the combat training that she was quite capable of taking care of herself, the Elders insisted that she leave a note. They had not found the spy yet and he very well could still be among them. Her sisters did not have to leave a note, but they did have to check in with the Elders throughout the day. They were also not allowed in the forest without their Avidraughts and one or two of the villagers who had been asked to escort the fairies if needed.

Zee had packed a sack of food that she had tied to her waist; it sat behind her between Farley's wings. She chose to wear tight fitting black pants, a crisp white long sleeved tunic with a thick belt at her waist and black soft leather boots that came up to her knees.

Normally Zee wore her hair loose or in a long braid, but Farley had complained that it snapped at his wings whenever the wind caught it, so she always made sure to put it into a bun at the nape of her neck. She brought a quiver of arrows and a bow with her, which she made herself. Through their training with Obwyn, they learned what tree limbs were best for bows, arrows, and fishing poles. They had to make each of them from his precise instructions. The fishing poles were easy enough, but the bows and arrows had been difficult to make. Finally after a week of trying, they each received a favorable comment from Obwyn.

Zee was out with Farley to practice shooting the arrows while in flight. She had done well, as her sisters had, while they galloped around the open meadow and shot arrows at stationery targets. However, shooting from the back of an Avidraught while its wings flapped was going to be more challenging. They would also be at the mercy of the wind. It was a testament to how well Farley and Zee were getting along that he would even allow her to attempt it without further instruction from Nayew or Obwyn.

Their friendship had steadily grown since the day he found her sleeping in the Tree. Many things about Zee had changed that day. It was as if conquering that single fear had had given her the confidence to do more. She had certainly proved herself on the battle field. Since that day she had matured considerably. She took on each new task with enthusiasm and no longer complained about them. Normally she completed the task in the time given and on occasion finished it well before her sisters. The other fairies not wanting to be "shown up" by their little sister stepped up their game as well. All in all the combat training, although it had been fierce with dire consequences, was the precise element needed to push them forward.

Over the weeks the three younger sisters worked on controlling their powers and the effects it had on them. They gradually began using them without it draining their energy. Shanata and Mariela's powers had not arrived as of yet, but something had changed between them; they had become closer and no longer argued. Instead they worked compatibly together, especially while training. It was as if their thoughts were connected and they knew precisely what the other was going to do next; which was unfortunate for their dueling partners who they defeated mercilessly.

Obwyn, Nayew and the Elders had noticed and although pleased about it, they did not want to bring attention to it. They had hoped they would work it out eventually for themselves. The combat training had been proceeding well, however none of them uttered the concerns that plagued their minds. The fairies did extremely well against the village men, but death was not on the line. What would happen in hand-to-hand combat against a real enemy when taking a life to save their own was their only option?

The cool breeze stung at Zee's eyes as Farley flew

northward towards the foothills of Mount Alpanatia. The sun rising behind her would soon warm the air and chase away the early morning chills. They decided to go north because Jasper and the caravan of travelers would be coming over the foothills. Zee was very anxious to see her little friend again; it had been too long. They were confidants. She had often voiced her fears to him and he in turn voiced his. They had also talked lengthy about what life outside of the valley was like. Before the Hummingmoth's mission, the furthest Jasper had ever been was to Little Springs. He took several messages back and forth from Elder Andi to Hobart- the head council member of the small village.

The night before Jasper left on his mission they had spent the evening together. She had voiced her fears to him about how far away he was going and that she worried that he would not return. He had assured her that he would be back before she knew it. Time however slipped by his scheduled return. Zee remembered the day when Elder Jolise had told them that she was no longer in contact with him and that she expected the worse. Zee's sisters looked sadly at her, but were surprised at her response to the information. 'He will be home. He promised that he would. He has just been delayed that is all; I can feel it in my bones.' Even though she spoke confidently that night she prayed desperately to the Light of Goodness that he would shine down upon Jasper and bring him home safely; even if it meant that he should find a new best friend to help him along the way. Little did Zee know that the Light of Goodness had heard her and did just that.

Zee soared a hundred or so feet in the air and sighed lightly. The sky was clear; she and Farley would be able to see for miles and miles in front of them. Hopefully, she wished that they would catch sight of the caravan coming over one of the foothills. The foothills before Mount Alpanatia were tall rolling hills covered in a thick carpet of low growing grass. It was dotted here and there with large boulders and a variety of trees that were usually grouped together. In some of the valleys, small rivers carved their way through them.

Even though the nights had grown steadily colder, once the sun had risen the days were still warm. But it would not last. Winter was on its way and according to Elder Enyce and the information she received from the Wood Spirits, a record snowfall would hit the valley and stay well passed the Spring Equinox.

Each of the fairies groaned deeply when they heard this; they were to leave after the Hawkeye tournament ended. The journey would be difficult enough without adding record snowfalls to the mix. Their saving grace however was that they were traveling south and the weather would gradually get warmer with no chance of snow impeding their journey. There were other natural elements that could though. Those they would deal with as they arose.

Today however, was not a day for forlorn thoughts. Farley dipped with the air currents and Zee laughed. Leaning forward she whispered in Farley's ear, "Faster."

"Faster, is it, you say," Farley said. "All right then, grip harder me with your knees." Zee brought her knees tighter against his sides. "That's it. Now lean low over my neck." Zee did as she was instructed. "Good, now hold on tight to the reins, but not so tight that I can't move my head. Good, now hold on Zee." Before she could say anything Farley tucked his wings in and dove straight towards the ground. Zee's stomach rolled as they descended and she screamed. Spreading his wings out well before they came in contact with the ground the air currents lifted them swiftly upwards again. Once he got to a certain height, he tucked his wings in and they plummeted back down towards the ground. Zee's stomach continued to roll, but not from sickness; the motion made her laugh with glee. Over and over Farley dove and rose, dove and rose. Zee laughed and laughed until she begged him to stop; so, on the last dive instead of ascending upwards he leveled out and flew just a couple feet off the ground.

Seeing this Zee started to sit up straight just as they were approaching the top of the first foothill. Her hair had come undone from its bun during the last dive and got caught in the reins which prevented her from sitting up. This had been a good thing however. As they got to the top of the foothill, something whizzed by; just narrowly missing Farley's head. Farley cursed and Zee gasped. They both turned their heads sharply to see what had flown by them in such a great hurry. As they did, the thing that had whizzed by them stopped as well and fluttered in midair. It looked strangely at them; not sure it was seeing what it was seeing.

Zee however immediately recognized who it was and whopped with glee before she shouted with delight, "Jasper!"

Jasper seeing that it was Zee immediately broke down and started to cry; his little wings faltered as he did. Farley quickly turned and Zee caught Jasper just as his wings stopped beating.

"Jasper!" Zee said is name urgently. His whole body shook from fright. "What's wrong?" She asked. Jasper tried to calm his nerves but his breath came in big gulps and tears blurred his vision. Just as Zee was about to ask him again what was wrong she heard someone call her name from overhead. She looked up; flying towards them were her sisters on the backs of their Avidraughts. Farley flew to them and they all landed at the base of the foothill.

Seeing Jasper in Zee's hands, they all smiled with delight and called out his name until Zee violently shook her head. "No. No. Shh, can't you see, something is wrong with him?"

Shanata looked sternly down at Jasper who was trying desperately to compose himself. "Jasper," She said firmly. It took him a second to realize she was speaking to him. "Jasper," she said firmly again. "What has happened? Where are the others?" Everyone then looked in the direction that Jasper had come from and saw no one.

A chill shot up Shanata's spine as she looked down at Jasper who had stopped crying and was now composing himself. Seeing Zee had shocked him and his first reaction was one of great relief, which resulted in him crying for joy. He wiped the tears from his eyes as Shanata spoke to him again.

"Jasper where are the others?" She said slowly, emphasizing each word. Jasper looked up at her. His eyes were large, his bottom lip quivered as he tried to control his emotions.

"The Rapcicors, they attacked us," he said in disbelief.

Enna was the first of them to jump into action. "Ashlina you and Arturo take Jasper back to the village. At all cost keep him safe. Tell Orliff to expect injured and make sure that they bring plenty of carri-shifts with them." Her voice was commanding and had everyone listening to her. Arturo nodded his head and walked over to Farley. Ashlina held out her hands and Jasper stepped shakily off Zee's hands into Ashlina's. He still looked terrified, but his crying had stopped and his breathing was steadier.

"Jasper, do you mind curling up your snout please," Ashlina said. Jasper looked down at his snout, understanding, he curled it up. Before leaving, Ashlina looked compassionately at her sisters, "May the Light of Goodness prevail." They nodded as she added, "I will be back as soon as I can." Arturo lifted off the ground and they quickly made their way towards Elsbrier.

"What next?" Shanata and Mariela both said in calm, controlled voices as they looked at Enna.

Of all the fairies, Shanata understood best what they might be up against. She had seen much in her travels with the Radeks. The places they traveled to were lovely and their people had been friendly and open to strangers. However, on her last trip they had traveled to Boswick. The large Kingdom sat nestled in a valley at the base of the Cork Mountains which along with the Alpanatia Mountains separated the Southern Kingdoms from the Northern Kingdoms. Shanata had been there once before with the Radeks and had a wonderful time, however during their last visit she noticed that the openness and friendliness of before had declined rapidly. The people had become cautious and suspicious of strangers. When she returned home she retold only the good parts of her trip to her sisters; after her sisters went to their beds she met with the Elders and told them that a feeling of ill-will had descended upon Boswick and shadowed its people.

Mariela however also understood what they were up against. The books that Elder Enyce had given her the day after the combat training were an account of what the Elders had witnessed over their time on this plane of existence. The first book started with the telling of the two Supreme Beings that warred for dominance over this world; the Light of Goodness she knew of, Chaos however she had learned very little of. By the end of the last book she had read the history of man and the brutality of their actions that had been orchestrated by Chaos over the course of time. She looked at Enna with the same expression of determination that Shanata had.

"Ready yourself sisters. I am not sure what we will be up against. The battle might already be over with, but if not, well, we know what must be done," Enna said.

Shanata and Mariela nodded their heads; this is what they had been training for. Yes, they had only shot arrows at targets and fought hand-to-hand combat with the village boys and men, but they were ready.

Farley looked with concern at Zee. He could feel her body shake with fear. She looked down at him with a grim expression. She then looked up at her sisters and nodded that she was ready. Farley sighed heavily. His young rider's courage would be tested today as would her sisters'. He worried that Zee was not ready. If Farley however had thought longer on it, he would have realized his worry had more to do with his own fear; fear of losing Zee. He had become quite fond of her.

They all flew high in the air and traveled north. Although the Rapcicors could fly, they rarely did so as they preferred to walk. Enna thought that perhaps they could assess the situation better if they were above the action. As they started for the next hill, they could hear the sounds of a battle coming from the other side of it. With quick hand signals Enna motioned for her sisters to spread out. Zee and Mariela flew east while she and Shanata flew west. They circled around the hill and flew over the peak of it.

Upon seeing the battle before them the fairies gasped. Several dark skinned travelers efficiently fought off a large group of Rapcicors who attacked from the east. On the other side of the valley a smaller group of travelers fought off a group that attacked from the west. Between them women, children and elders from three different Clans huddled together on the ground. Their injured lay off to the side; a handful of travelers tended to their wounds. A small band of travelers surrounded the unarmed group. They shot arrows over the heads of their comrades, taking out many of the Rapcicors as they advanced from the east and west. This battle strategy seemed to be working in their favor as more Rapcicors fell injured or dead than the caravan of travelers.

Three large Rapcicors- Batice, Fabet and Cahn- stood on an incline looking down onto the battlefield. They were the leaders of the three bands of Rapcicors that live in the Firelog Forest. A small regiment surrounded them, standing guard. The fairies were not surprised to see that they had not joined in the fight. It was rare that the leader of a band would engage in battle. Enna and her sisters had learned that Rapcicors were cunning ferocious creatures who did not give up easily and would battle as long as they thought they could win. Seeing that they were not giving in, Enna searched the ground to the north. Behind a large cropping of trees she spied a band of Rapcicors as they made their way to the top of the hill. They were flying.

"There," Enna yelled, "to the north."

Zee looked up as did Mariela and Shanata. The Rapcicors had crested the top of the hill and were making their way down. The travelers on the ground were too busy defending their stance to look upwards. The band of Rapcicors, too intent on taking the travelers by surprise, did not see the Avidraughts and their riders flying high above the battle field.

Amos looked back at Enna. He did not have to speak for Enna to know that he was asking if she was ready for battle. Enna smiled down at him, let go of the reins and confidently notched an arrow in the bow. Farley looked back at Zee. She nodded her head nervously as she squeezed her legs together to hold onto him. She wrapped the reins loosely around the horn of the saddle and notched an arrow in her bow. Mariela and Shanata did the same and urged their Avidraughts to follow Amos' lead. They swiftly flew north.

Zee looked down at the dark skinned travelers. As she did a female with braided hair and a red flowing skirt looked up. She was armed with a long spear. As if she read Zee's mind the woman looked north. Seeing the band of Rapcicors barreling down on them, she quickly spoke to a rather tall broad shouldered male who stood beside her. She pointed at the oncoming band. The man did not hesitate and quickly ran towards them; a small group of men followed. The woman looked up at Zee as she flew overhead and nodded. Zee nodded back. Raising her bow, she pulled back on the taut string, ready to shoot the arrow.

"Not yet Zee, we are too far away. As of yet they have not seen us. Wait until we are almost on top of them. I will tell you when," Farley said. Zee nodded as they drew nearer. The bow slightly shook in her hand. She jumped with fright as Farley yelled, "NOW!" and dove down towards the enemy.

Zee took a deep breath to try and control her fear. She closed her eyes as she drew back on the bow and let the arrow go. She was too frightened to open her eyes to see if she hit her mark. She was startled when she heard Mariela yelling at her, "Zee, open your eyes. You almost shot Farley's ear off!"

Hearing this, Farley clicked his tongue in disgust. He flew upwards, banked sharply and started to head back from where they came. Zee looked back and saw that her sisters did not join her. They shot their arrows carefully from the back of their Avidraughts, as Obwyn had taught them. They picked their targets and made sure every shot counted.

"Farley what are you doing? Turn around. My sisters need me!" Zee pleaded as she just now realized that Farley was taking her away from the battle. She picked up the reins and pulled back on them.

Farley snorted and shook his head, "You are not ready for this Zee. I am going to drop you off over the hill. You can wait for the others to arrive."

"Farley no!" Zee cried as he landed on the soft plush green grass with a hard thud that jarred her bones.

"Get off Zee," Farley said in a voice that was unlike any he had used when speaking to her before. Zee quickly slid off and looked sadly at Farley. "Wait here for the others. See they are coming now." Zee looked up and there indeed in the distance, high in the air, Ashlina and Arturo were coming towards them. Three dozen villagers on Avidraughts were flying in a "V" formation behind her.

When Zee turned back around to plead with Farley, he had already taken off and was returning to the battle. As fast as she could, Zee ran up the side of the foothill to the crest. She may not be able to shoot arrows from Farley's back but she could from the ground. Upon reaching the top of the hill, she sank to her knees and notched an arrow in the bow. The band of Rapcicors who had come over the hill to the north had been effectively stopped in their tracks, but that left the east side vulnerable.

Zee heard a scream coming from a young woman who stood guard over the injured travelers. The woman called out someone's name and started to run towards them before a man came from behind her and grabbed her arm. Zee noticed that the woman was pregnant. "Janilli," the woman called out the name again as she struggled to free her arm from the man's grasp. Zee looked at the scene before her and noticed that the woman in the long red skirt had been knocked to the ground. She was trying to fight off a Rapcicor that stood over her.

No one saw what was happening and without thinking Zee drew back an arrow. Something then took over her, a strange and unexplainable feeling. The cries of battle silenced, the wind ceased to blow. Time crawled at a snail's pace. Zee's senses increased a hundred fold; she could hear each beat of her heart, feel the sweat on her brow and each blade of grass under her knees. Her toes scrunched up in her boots as if she was drawing strength from the ground itself. Her shoulders squared as her back straightened. Her eyes, as if telescopic, zeroed in on the target several hundred feet away. With firm concentration and a steady hand, she let the arrow go.

The arrow sped past several of the dark skinned travelers and found its mark just as the gaping beak of the bird was about to strike the woman's face. Zee watched as the large bird toppled over and fell to the ground with a heavy thud. The head of the arrow stuck out of its neck on the other side. The big bird's legs kicked out involuntarily as it gasped for its last breath. Zee's heart lurched in her chest and her senses returned to normal. The woman in red scrambled up and quickly picked up the spear that had been knocked out of her hand when the Rapcicor jumped on top of her. She looked down at the bird; its mouth was agape and its long red tongue hung over its lower jaw. It was no longer moving. She looked around for the person who had saved her life. She then looked up at Zee. The woman nodded to her again. Zee slowly nodded back. She was thankful that the woman was too far away and could not see the tears that instantly welled up in her eyes. She had taken a life to save a life.

Zee did not have time to ponder the fine differences between killing fish with a hook and killing with a bow and arrow as she heard a cry coming from the other side of the valley. Three Rapcicors had made their way through the ranks and were running towards the woman standing guard over the injured. Zee quickly ran along the top of the hill and dropped to her knees when she was close enough to take an accurate shot. The woman had thrown her spear with deadly accuracy and now only had a knife in her hand. The Rapcicors however had not gotten any closer to her. Zee let two arrows fly in succession and the Rapcicors toppled over each other as they skidded across the grass. The arrows had found their mark as fat tears dripped from Zee's eyes. The woman looked up at her and nodded as the woman in red had. Zee nodded back before she wiped the tears from her eyes with the back of her hand.

Hearing a battle cry overhead, she looked up. Ashlina and the villagers had arrived. Ashlina, her face alight with the thrill of battle, smiled down at Zee as they flew by. Notching an arrow in her bow she let it go. The arrow found its mark and Ashlina whooped out another battle cry. Enna met up with her and ordered them into action. They divided in three groups and went east, west and north. Enna and Ashlina landed next to the woman in red and helped to defend the east side. Farley had joined them and they effectively kept the Rapcicors from reaching the inner circle.

Zee continued to shoot arrows from the hill top, each found their mark. From her vantage point she could see that the Rapcicors began to falter in their attack, some looked towards the incline where their leaders stood. Zee looked over to the leaders as well. The largest of them opened his mouth and an awful honking noise pierced the air. Every man and beast stopped what they were doing as the honking noise erupted over the small valley again. Hearing the honk, the Rapcicors took flight, flying eastward to the Firelog Forest. Zee stood up and watched them go.

As they passed their leaders, Zee saw something quite odd. A tall figure dressed in dark clothes and a long dark cape walked out from a grove of trees. The figure noticed that Zee was staring at them and glared back at her. A violent chill ran up her spine and she shivered. Even though she could not see who or what was under the long cape, she knew it was the stranger Ashlina had seen in the forest. She had a sense that he was not pleased with the outcome of the battle.

Zee watched as the man said something to the three Rapcicor leaders then turned and jumped onto the back of a large black Avidraught. Zee did not recognize the Avidraught; it was not one from the valley. As her sisters and their Avidraughts landed on the ground near her, the stranger and his Avidraught took off flying in a northeastern direction. Zee watched as one of the elder Rapcicors flew off in the same direction as the stranger; three Rapcicors flew behind him. The other two leaders flew off in the direction of the Firelog Forest; the remainder of the guards followed them.

Zee made a mental note to make sure to tell the others of the stranger dressed in black, but for now she looked at each of her sisters in turn with a worried expression, hoping none of them had been injured in the battle. She quickly looked over at Farley and the woman in red as they made their way up the hill. The woman spoke urgently with Farley about what had transpired prior to the fairies' arrival.

Chapter 18
The Healing Circle

The majority of the caravan of travelers from the Valley Time Forgot left for Elsbrier. Orliff, Obwyn, the Jarrell brothers and three dozen villagers had arrived with several large carri-shifts and several dozen pokeys to help pull them home. It would take four to five hours to get to Elsbrier, but at least they would not have to walk. Those who stayed made quick introductions then set to work cleaning up the valley. It took them an hour to pick up the carcasses of the Rapcicors. The bodies were put into a pile and set on fire. The smoke that billowed hundreds of feet into the air blackened the late afternoon sky.

The mood of the onlookers, who had formed a circle around the fire, was mournful. Barton, Lindrella, the woman in red named Janilli, Zeander, Bauthal the badger, the mighty snake Paraphin, Aldwin, Saphina, Zusie, Chrystalina and the villagers from Elsbrier who had come with Ashlina held hands. Shanata and her sisters joined them. Their Avidraughts stood a few paces behind them. There they stood in the *Healing Circle,* as Janilli called it, and paid homage to the lives of the Rapcicors that were lost. Two dozen Tara Aquian warriors stood guard around them.

As the onlookers bowed their heads they stood on grass that was now stained crimson red. Luckily the rains would wash away the blood and the grass would grow lush again, but the lives taken needlessly would haunt the fairies' dreams for days to come.

Barton, one of the Tara Aquians, started to sing a mournful chant. His deep melodic voice echoed around the small valley. The fairies, startled by the timber in his voice, could not help but look at him. The chant was picked up by the other Tara

Aquians and Janilli. The sound of their voices filled the fairies with remorse. The song pulled at everyone's heartstrings; even the Avidraughts had a hard time keeping their composure. Restless, they raised their feet and bayed lightly until Farley looked at them and they settled back down. Zee, tired from the battle, broke down and openly wept. She made to let go of the hands she was holding, but Lindrella, who stood on her left, held firm. Her sisters and Farley stepped closer to comfort her but stopped as Lindrella spoke over the song.

"Do not break the *Healing Circle*," she warned them in broken speech. She looked at them sternly then looked back at the fire. She had learned to speak the Elfkin language during the long journey but her words were still heavily accented. "It is not a sign of weakness to cry Zee, but one of great strength that is matched by your compassion."

Zee looked up at her and stopped crying as she listened intently to Lindrella's words. Somehow she knew that they would be the most important words she would ever hear. Without taking her eyes off the fire, Lindrella continued, "Stand tall little one and wail to the four winds of your sadness. The winds will hear you and respect you for it. Out of that same respect they will carry your cries around this valley so that all can hear the depth of your sorrow and compassion for your enemy, and know you to be a great leader."

Zee was confused and did not understand. How could killing your enemy make someone a better leader? How could crying, which she had always thought was a sign of weakness, make her a better leader?

Lindrella continued, "Then the winds will carry back to you the thoughts and prayers of those who heard your cry. They will understand that you did what needed to be done to protect what is yours from an enemy that shows no compassion or remorse for their actions."

Zee looked oddly at Lindrella. How could she know

whether or not the Rapcicors felt compassion or remorse when she was new to this valley? Lindrella saw the puzzled look on Zee's face and her sisters', who were listening just as intently. She realized that they questioned what she was saying so she looked at Janilli for assistance.

"If they had compassion, they would not have left their dead. They would have taken them with them or prepared them for the crossover," Janilli said. She looked with pride at the Tara Aquians. They were a noble race who did not evoke war but did not stand down from one either. "The battle had stopped. We had lowered our weapons."

Zee thought for a moment as did her sisters trying to remember what happened after they heard the loud honking noise. A vision of the Tara Aquians lowering their weapons and walking slowly away from the battleground popped into Zee's head. She looked at each of her sisters who remembered seeing the same thing and they nodded at her. Zee then looked around the circle at the others. Zusie's face was wet with tears as was her daughters standing on either side of her. They, who had endured so much to get to the Whipple Wash Valley, had compassion for their enemy.

Emotion caught in Zee's throat as her eyes were drawn to Barton; the tallest scariest man she had ever met. He was not just tall but muscular with a barrel shaped chest and powerful arms that could crush her with one squeeze. If not knowing that he was on their side, just the sight of him would have made her cry out in fear. She was shocked to see tears flowing from his eyes as well. Unashamed, he cried while he sang his song. At seeing him, the tears welled up in her eyes again and the emotion in her throat grew painful. She looked at her sisters who could no longer hold back the tears and openly cried as they looked at the fire.

Lindrella, seeing that Zee was coming to an understanding, spoke once again to her, "For the good of your people you made a stand this day and the winds out of respect will carry back to you their love and you will be comforted by it." She smiled slightly at Zee before rejoining the chant.

Farley stepped closer to Zee and nuzzled her back; she did not need to look back at him to know that he too was affected by what he was seeing. This was their first contact since he had left her in the heat of the battle. He had come with Janilli when she walked up the hill to thank Zee for saving her life. But neither spoke to each other as Zee shook Janilli's hand. Her sisters had quickly made their way to Zee as well and crowded around her. As the girls talked rapidly, making sure none of them were hurt, Farley and Janilli had walked away.

Zee's chest started to heave uncontrollably from Farley's comforting touch and tears spilled from her eyes. A raw emotion like nothing she had ever felt before consumed her. She stood tall before the fire, threw back her head and wailed her pain and shame to the four winds. Lindrella squeezed her hand, as did Shanata who stood on her other side. The winds, as Lindrella said, caught Zee's cries and carried them around the valley and over the foothills.

The song gradually quieted. The words were reduced to a deep humming that played on in the same melodic tune. The *Healing Circle* slowly broke apart as each member had resolved his or her remorse for taking a life. The five fairies, Lindrella, Janilli and Barton were the last standing around the circle. Barton looked over at Zee. She was staring blankly at the embers and her stance faltered once Lindrella and Shanata let go of her hands. He walked over and before anyone knew what he was doing, he scooped her up. Drained of all emotion and energy she was not afraid; instead she snuggled closer to him. His strength was a comfort to her.

Barton walked her over to Farley and hugged Zee gently before he softly placed her on Farley's back. Zee thanked him as she wrapped her arms around Farley's neck and rested her head. Farley's cropped main felt rough under her cheek but she was too exhausted to care. She looked down at the grass and allowed her mind to go blank.

Shanata looked sadly at Zee. The battle had been so

unexpected and caught each of them off guard. Yet without hesitation, they went into battle as if it had not been their first time. Mariela, Ashlina and Enna walked up to her; their expressions were the same. They looked at Zee with worry. Someone standing to the side of them cleared their throat. The sisters looked over at Janilli who was standing a few paces away. She looked at them fondly as if she had known them their whole lives instead of for just a few short hours. In a kind voice, she said, "It's time to go."

The fairies looked around in surprise. Everyone else, except for a half dozen Tara Aquian warriors had already started to walk up the hill. Many of them were almost to the top. The fairies nodded and quietly picked up their weapons. Farley, with Zee on his back, walked with Barton up the hill. Lindrella, Janilli and the other fairies followed them. The other Avidraughts walked behind them and the Tara Aquian warriors brought up the rear.

None of them seemed too eager to reach the village as they caught up with Zusie, Saphina, Chrystalina, Aldwin, Zeander, Bauthal and Paraphin. Seeing the fairies just a few paces behind them they quieted. They had been discussing their apprehensions. They had traveled so far, telling everyone that they would be safe in their new home; Jasper's home. A half day away and they were brutally attacked, by birds none the less. Zusie took a sideways glance at the fairies. They were so young. Although they had proved themselves against the Rapcicors, even the youngest who had saved Janilli's life, they were still so young. Zusie admonished herself; she had led the caravan to a brutal land, to saviors that were underlings. She shuttered at the thought; *what if the fairies had not arrived when they did, would they have won the battle.* The Tara Aquians were strong, but the journey had taken its toll on them as well. Zusie sighed heavily. Chrystalina and Saphina looped their arms through the crook of their mother's arms.

"It will be better," Saphina whispered. All Zusie could do was nod as she swallowed a lump of emotion and smiled at her. Perhaps Elsbrier would be better, she thought as they continued to walk on and listened to the conversation Lindrella was having with the fairies.

"She is strong," Lindrella said as she and Janilli walked beside the fairies. They had each been caught up in their own thoughts, so when she spoke they looked mechanically at their little sister, asleep on Farley's back. Not knowing what to say they nodded in response. "She will be a great leader to her people," Lindrella said then looked at each of the fairies in turn and added, "As will all of you."

Shanata sighed heavily and smiled, "Thank you Lindrella."

The simple reply seemed to wake her sisters out of their thoughts. Each had been reliving the battle, going over the impromptu battle strategies. They wondered if there was something better they could have done and worried what would have happened if they had not followed Zee. She and Farley would have been caught in the battle by themselves. In the end she had proven herself and Lindrella's words eased their minds. The fairies smiled and looked eagerly at each other. They didn't need to read each other's thoughts to know that each of them was just a curious as the next to learn more about their companions, so they began to ask Lindrella questions.

"Why did you burn the dead of our enemy?" Ashlina asked. Prior to this day the fairies had never thought of the Rapcicors as enemies; just creatures that they needed to be cautious of. But since Ashlina's encounter with them and now battling against them to protect the travelers, they knew which side of the war the Rapcicors had chosen to fight on. No longer would they just be cautious of them but on guard and would not approach them again without sword in hand.

"It is said in our *Tollismayn* that after great battles our ancestors would burn their dead with the dead of their enemies in hopes that they would find peace in their resting place. Luckily, we had no dead to burn with the Rapcicors and sang the Healing song to clench our spiritual wounds and send the souls of the Rapcicors to their resting place." The fairies nodded thoughtfully. Barton's song and the tears they shed did make them feel better.

"What is a *Tollismayn*," Mariela asked quickly; she was very interested now in all things Tara Aquian.

"The *Tollismayn* is a set of stone books that Awnmorielle, our foremother and reverend Goddess, wrote to guide our people spiritually throughout our lives." She looked at Mariela's curious expression knowing that she questioned the stone books.

"The books are stone tablets made from thin sheets of rock that the words of Awnmorielle were etched on. The stone tablets are secured together with thick pieces of rawhide from an ancient animal that once roamed freely in Lake Kellowash but is now long past extinct." Mariela nodded her head. She had read of such books in the Library. Many Kingdoms had their own set of books similar to the Tara Aquians'.

Before she could ask if they brought the books with them, Enna piped up, "Why do you dress as warriors? Were you expecting there to be a battle?"

Lindrella looked at Janilli. She was unsure of what Enna meant. Janilli explained to her in Tara Aquian. Lindrella looked puzzled for a brief minute then said plainly, "This is how we have always dressed. We know of no other way. And yes, thanks to Desamiha we were prepared for battle."

The fairies nodded their heads as if they understood and looked about for the one they called Desamiha. Perhaps she had gone on with the others to Elsbrier. As Enna made a mental note to seek her out and find out how she knew that there was going to be an attack. Janilli smiled; the telling of her powers would keep for another day. She looked over at Zee. She had a sneaky suspicion that Zee had powers similar to hers.

Enna opened her mouth to ask another question, but Shanata was eager to ask her own question and interrupted her. "Janilli had quickly told us about you....the Tara Aquians

I mean as we cleaned up," she said looking over at Barton who was speaking quietly with Farley. "I am curious to know how you can breathe under water without assistance." Ashlina's shoulders slumped. That was her question as well. She quickly thought of another question and was just as eager to ask it.

Lindrella pulled her long braided hair away from her left ear and bent down so that the fairies could see. Behind her ear was a series of flaps. They were layered one on top of the other and ran down the length of her neck. The fairies could see that they were now tightly closed. Lindrella explained that when they are under water the flaps open, filtering the water through them, which their bodies in turn take out the oxygen in the water so that they can breathe.

Janilli explained further that Tara Aquians babes are birthed in water from Lake Kellowash. They live in the birthing pool with their mother and father for several days before they are brought out. It is important for the Tara Aquians to pay respect to Lake Kellowash and learn to become one with it. If it were done the other way, land before water, Lake Kellowash may be insulted and reject the babe and they would not be able to swim in it without breathing assistance.

The fairies, even more intrigued after hearing this, looked at each other with delight. The newcomers were very interesting. Even Shanata, who had met many people during her trips with the Radeks, found them intriguing. They could hardly wait to learn more about all of them. The sisters spread out; Ashlina and Shanata stayed with Lindrella and Janilli, Mariela sought out Zusie, her daughters and Aldwin, while Enna found Bauthal, Zeander and Paraphin. For a moment, the fairies forgot all about the battle while they eagerly asked their questions. Later, while resting in their Sitting Room, they would relive the battle with the Rapcicors. For now the sisters were content to learn about the newcomers. Especially the one they called Lizbeth who had slept through the whole journey.

Chapter 19
An Untimely Demise

Far off in the Greenwood Forest Lord Canvil paced back and forth in front of the fireplace. His hands were clasped behind his back and his brow was furled in a deep scowl as he pondered his next move. The Tara Aquians had indeed proved to be worthy adversaries. They were intelligent and quick; he had yet to capture one and find their weakness. They were also as merciless as he and had foiled every attempt he made to cross the lake. Four dozen of his men had lost their lives, another dozen were badly injured and six watercrafts lay at the bottom of the bay.

A commotion at the door made him scowl even deeper. He had left strict instruction with the guards that he did not want to be disturbed. So when he pulled open the door he was surprised to see Egreta and Ibisha standing there. They held onto a large mug that had a plate over it. Large smiles lit their faces. Rishtoph and the guards stood behind them. The scowl on his son's face was as deep as Canvil's had been a minute ago. However upon seeing the elderly maidens, Canvil suppressed his anger.

"My Lord," Rishtoph said. "Ibisha and Egreta have caught something for you and wanted to deliver it to you in person." Canvil could tell by his son's tone that he was not pleased by it. He looked quizzically at the elderly maidens who had been the closest thing to a mother he had ever had. Seeing the delight on their faces he smiled back at them and gestured for them to come in. Rishtoph followed, and then closed the door behind him.

"What is it that you have for me?" Canvil asked. Ibisha who was holding the cup stretched out her arms then lifted the plate off partially. It was just enough for whatever was inside to fly out, but before it could fly into the rafters Canvil snatched it out of the air. It squirmed then yelped when he began to squeeze his fingers closed. He looked curiously at the creature; it was a relatively large bug with red dots on its wings; he hadn't seen one like it before. He looked questioningly at the maidens wondering why they brought him a bug and was so pleased about it. He never knew them to have flights of fancy, so it must have been important.

"Spy," Egreta said. Ibisha nodded her head.

"Spy?" Canvil said looking at his son.

"I don't know my Lord," Rishtoph said coldly. He was not pleased that his father always gave into the elderly women. It irked Rishtoph that his father seemingly cared more for the two of them than he did for his own sons.

Canvil walked over to the table and sat down, he motioned that the others should as well. Ibisha and Egreta sat. Rishtoph chose to stand behind them. Canvil looked down at the bug who returned his look thoughtfully. The bug was scared, but not as frightened as he should be.

"Do you understand me?" Canvil asked. The bug nodded its head. Canvil pulled the small knife out of his boot with his other hand. He flipped the small knife over and held the blade between his fingers. "See that candle on the mantel." The bug looked over; seeing the lit candle it nodded its head again. Canvil raised his arm. With a quick flick of his wrist the small knife flew across the room and sliced the wick of the candle in half before it imbedded into the wall behind it. The bug looked with alarm at the knife. "If you try to fly away again that is what will happen to you. Do you understand?" The bug nodded. "Do you have a name?" Canvil asked as Rishtoph handed the knife back to his father. Canvil placed it on the table and then stood the bug beside it.

"My name is Monto," the bug said and then bowed. Before rising he took a sideways glance at the knife.

"Are you a spy for the Tara Aquians?" Canvil asked. "Do not lie to me."

"No my Lord," Monto said. His voice shook slightly which made Canvil raise one of his eyebrows in doubt. "Honest my Lord," Monto said sincerely. Canvil relaxed. Seeing this, so did Monto.

"How did you come to be here then Monto?" Lord Canvil looked at him appraisingly.

"I live here." Monto had been living undetected in the house that the village carpenters had built for Jasper. They had fastened it to the tree beside the hut that Lizbeth had lived in. Jasper had only two days to use it before he and the others fled south. Lizbeth's hut now housed Egreta and Ibisha. When Rishtoph and the scouting party had ransacked the village no one had looked in the small house that sat in the tree. Throughout the day Monto stayed hidden in the house. At night when the village had calmed, he scavenged for food and eavesdropped outside of doors and windows.

The village had quieted down for the night and he thought it was safe to come out. He had flown down to the window of Lizbeth's old hut and was peering through the crack when Egreta had come around the corner; she had been gathering wood for the fireplace. Monto had not heard her until she was right behind him. With quick agility she dropped the wood, cupped her hands around him and took him into the hut. He had struggled to get loose but Egreta held on tight. Ibisha had been sitting in a rocking chair. Upon hearing her sister and seeing that she was holding something in her hands, she quickly got a mug and plate. Egreta dropped Monto into the cup and Ibisha quickly placed the plate over top it. He struggled but could not force the plate up.

"I was told all but the fish had left the forest," Canvil said as he looked over at his son who was again standing behind Ibisha and Egreta.

"I stayed my Lord," Monto replied.

"Why?" Lord Canvil looked at him curiously.

"I have no allegiance to the Elfkins or the forest creatures or any other creature that lives in this valley," Monto said with contempt. He remembered vividly the day Camcor had swatted him to the ground just after he had confronted Aldwin and Zusie while they told the Elfkins of the invading army. He thought they had been friends, but Camcor turned out to be no friend. He had flown off into the forest. It hurt him that no one came for him or asked if he wanted to leave with them. He waited until Zusie and the others had left before he returned and made a home in the Jasper's wood house. He was there when Rishtoph and the others had invaded the village. He watched Rishtoph kill Camcor. It made him feel good. He then watched as they killed everyone who remained, piled them into a large heap and set them on fire. It had not disturbed him as much as he thought it would. Seeing how strong and ruthless the enemy was, he picked a side. Monto flew off the next evening, deciding that he would go in search of Zusie and the others and spy on them. Perhaps what he gathered would one day be to his benefit.

"I see," Canvil said. "Why should I keep you alive?"

"Because I know the Tara Aquians' weakness," Monto said with confidence. Canvil's eyebrow rose in question again as he looked from Monto to his son. This bug had indeed been spying on them for some time. "And," he added for effect. "I have very important information to share with you that no one else in the valley knows about." Canvil looked back at Monto questioningly. Monto was ready to tell them about the crystal lined boxes that held the ancient scrolls hidden in a cave behind the waterfall and the information he had of Zusie and Janilli.

"Well then Monto, you have a reprieve. I will not kill you...yet. What is their weakness?" Canvil asked smugly.

"Kindness," Monto said. Canvil looked blankly down at him. He had never shown kindness to anyone other than to the two maidens that had raised him from infancy. He did not understand how warriors as fierce as the Tara Aquians could be brought down by kindness. But this small bug had been living in the valley. Perhaps he was right.

"Explain," Canvil was intrigued.

"Although the Tara Aquians are fierce they are also very kind and will not hurt the innocent." Monto knew this because he had been spying on the Elfkins for several days while they stayed in the Meadow Imps' village waiting for Zusie, her daughters and Jasper to return from their visit with the Tara Aquians. He had been in the meadow, when he witnessed Duntar carrying Lizbeth to the beach. He was there when Rangous and Duntar had found Paraphin severely injured. Duntar had carried the great snake in his arms like he was a small underling and took great care not to cause him any further injury. He had also watched from the tall grasses when Duntar taught Rangous how to use a summoning whistle.

"What do you mean the Tara Aquians will not hurt the innocent?" Canvil said as he looked at Monto thoughtfully.

"You have two prisoners. One is from Jasper's home. The Tara Aquians know all about Jasper and that you kidnapped his Queen. What they don't know is that you brought her with you," Monto finished saying with a smug expression.

Canvil pondered thoughtfully for a moment as a gleam lit up his eyes. He had not thought of that. Canvil looked at his son. Rishtoph also had the same expression on his face. Finally they may have a way across the lake. "You know what to do," Canvil said. "And don't wait until the morning, begin tonight."

Rishtoph smiled. The men would not be pleased as they were going to have to pack everything up and travel back through the forest to the meadow. There they would cut down several trees and move then across the meadow on the large trolleys they had built. They would once again build watercrafts but his time the majority of them would stand guard. Lord Canvil would place Queen Faywyn and the witch woman on the first craft and a hold a knife to Queen Faywyn's throat. One false move by the Tara Aquians and she would be food for the fish.

"And what of him?" Rishtoph asked before he left. Canvil looked down at the bug. Something about Monto bothered him; he couldn't quite figure out what it was. He had proven useful with his knowledge of the Tara Aquians, but something about him irked his senses. The bug was of no further use to him.

"Kill him," Canvil said and turned his back.

Rishtoph immediately picked up his knife. Stunned Monto couldn't move or say anything until he saw the flash of the knife blade coming towards him.

"You have daughters," was the only thing he could think of saying that would stop the knife. Canvil whirled around and caught Rishtoph's arm just before it skewered Monto.

A memory came to Canvil. He had been sitting with Theodoric when he was still but a young man. Theodoric had been reading the tea leaves left from Canvil's cup when the orb that was sitting on the table next to him began to glow brightly. The smoky fog within it swirled violently. He finished reading the leaves and then gazed into the orb. Never before had he used both to predict the future for Canvil who often sought out the Oracle before he invaded a Kingdom. But that day had been different; everything about the ritual was different.

Theodoric had been dressed in his usual long dark purple hooded robe that he wore over his clothing. But something was amiss about him. Normally he was fastidious about his appearance, but that day his pointed, purple and gold embroidered cap was askew on his head. His long white beard looked matted, like he had been twirling it between his fingers. His complexion was ashen and he had large puffy bags under his eyes. His thick eyebrows were knitted together and his mouth was turned down in a deep frown.

When Canvil entered the room Theodoric restlessly motioned for him to sit at the table next to the fireplace. The tea had already been poured so he began to drink it. Theodoric walked restlessly in front of the fireplace. When he heard the distinctive clink of the cup hitting the saucer he immediately sat down opposite of Canvil and grabbed the cup. He swirled the remains of the leaves in a counterclockwise direction three times while he muttered the truth incantation under his breath. Just as the leaves stopped swirling the orb began to glow. Theodoric looked at it quickly with a stunned expression, but then he read the leaves. A visible calmness came over him as he finished reading. He then gazed into the orb and a vision appeared; it was of two infant females. When he looked at Canvil his expression was composed, but serious. Canvil would remember the ominous words that came next for the rest of his life. The words now came to him as if he had just heard them moments ago:

Death has stalked my dreams for seven nights long and has settled here at the nape of my neck throughout the day. Theodoric had pointed to the back of his neck. *When death foreshadows a reading you must take heed to the words I will speak. Your life will most certainly depend upon it.*

Canvil remembered nodding his head that he understood. Theodoric continued:

The leaves speak of children that will be born of your seed. Sons strong and healthy, but death augurs their lives and out of two hundred and fifty, two will remain. One fair-haired with ambitious goals that cannot be trusted; the other, darkness shadows his footsteps and his certainty has not yet been set in stone. The orb also speaks of children born of your seed, daughters, sisters, one older, one younger that has the gift of the Gods. A messenger will bring them together and if they are allowed to mature to adulthood and have daughters of their own, one day they will become your demise.

Canvil shook the thoughts from his head. He looked at Rishtoph who was wincing from pain. Canvil loosened the hold he had on his son's arm, the knife slipped from his hand

and landed on the table beside Monto. Rishtoph rubbed his arm before picking up the knife and sheathing it at his waist. He stepped away from his father and stood once again behind Ibisha and Egreta.

"Leave," Canvil said as he looked at his son. "Take Ibisha and Egreta back to their hut."

"And of the men," Rishtoph said sensing that their earlier plans had changed.

"Leave it till the morning," Canvil snarled.

Without a word Ibisha and Egreta stood up and walked to the door. Rishtoph opened it for them and closed it behind him. He walked several paces away and spoke with the guards. The guards escorted the elderly maidens back to their hut. Rishtoph waited until they were out of view before he walked around the building to the back door and let himself in quietly. He needed to hear what Monto was to tell his father of the daughters he never knew he had.

"Explain," is all Canvil said after he sat in the chair at the head of the table.

"Will you spare my life my Lord?" Monto asked uneasily. Canvil looked menacingly at him, but nodded his head in agreement.

"Their names are Zusie and Janilli," Monto started to say. "Zusie is the older of the two; she lived in the Crystal Cave up in the mountain." Monto knew that Canvil had known about the cave. He had spied on a group of the Venom Horde who were examining crystals they had taken from it. They had stripped the cave of everything; only the walls remained. "The younger one lived with the Tara Aquians and was their truth sayer." Monto did not have to explain, Canvil knew of another who had the gift of divination.

"How do you know they are sisters and my daughters?" Canvil spoke calmly as he looked steadfastly at Monto. Monto could see however that a tick had started to twitch at the corner of Canvil's left eye.

"I heard them talking one night while they sat in the

meadow," Monto continued. "Through a reading they learned they were sisters and that you are their father."

"Is that all?" Canvil asked. The muscles in his jaw clenched in anger. Theodoric's prediction was coming true.

He had been so careful, making sure none of the female children he sired lived. But somehow two had. Visions of two women instantly came to the forefront of his mind, Lilabeth, a tall and full-bodied woman with long flowing white hair and light blue eyes. She was a member of the Mackenzie Clan; a Clan whose roots run deep in the villages of the Brierwood Valley located west of Erebos. The other was Annalina, a woman who looked much like Lilabeth had, but had darker skin. She was from the Sharmtics Kingdom, a grouping of villages along the Agarian Waterfalls southwest of Erebos. Both women he was told had died giving birth and so too had the children. When he heard that both children had been female he never gave it another thought nor regretted the loss.

"No my Lord," Monto said uneasily. "Zusie has two daughters, twins. The younger has the gift of the Gods." Canvil looked at him oddly. Was it just by mere coincidence that Monto had used the same terminology that Theodoric had used all those years ago? Thinking that Canvil did not understand he explained, "She can read minds; like the Tara Aquians can."

Canvil's first reaction to this information was of disbelief until it took hold. That is why they could not catch the Tara Aquians- they could converse without speaking. "She was very close to Jasper. They all doted over him like he was a precious gift. If it hadn't been for him they never would have known the other existed," Monto finished saying with a sneer. Oh how he hated Jasper.

Hearing Jasper's name and that he was the one responsible for uniting his daughters Canvil's emotions that he had tried to keep in check exploded into a great rage. Senseless with anger, he pounded his fist on the table. Monto was not quick enough and screamed out in horror just before the large hand pounded down on top of him and crushed him beneath its weight. Realizing what he did, Lord Canvil picked up his hand. Monto's hard shelled red spotted wings stuck to his skin, and the rest of his broken body lay on the table. Monto's legs kicked out involuntarily as he took his last breath.

Canvil sighed, if the bug had more information he would never know. Indifferently he picked up the plate next to the cup and scrapped his hand along the edge of it. The wings came off and slid across the plate. He brushed the rest of Monto onto the plate and carried it to the fireplace. Tilting the plate down, Monto's lifeless body fell into the roaring flames.

"Burial fit for a king," Canvil said with little emotion. He then looked towards the back of the room to the partially opened door that led to the bathing chamber. "Rishtoph, bring me Theodoric and Padmoor, I wish to speak with them. And be quick about it."

Rishtoph sighed. His father had known that he had overheard everything. As he silently left, he wondered what his punishment would be when he returned with the Oracle and the Alchemist. Rishtoph would soon find out that there would be no punishment. Canvil had expected his son to sneak around the back and listen. He would have been very disappointed in him if he hadn't.

Canvil walked back to the table with a smile on his face. The knowledge that he had daughters and granddaughters was disturbing; he would deal with them when the time came. For now, with renewed purpose he would plan his attack on the Tara Aquians and finally make his way across the lake before winter set in.

Chapter 20
Home at Last

Back in Elsbrier another fire blazed. However, it was contained within in a large stone pit in the grassy knoll on the northeast side of the village. Even though the hour was late Elsbrier was alert and in a state of controlled chaos. The newcomers' camp had been set up around the stone fire pit and the citizens of Elsbrier were traveling back and forth between the camp and the village carrying supplies like blankets, pillows and food.

By the time the travelers had arrived in the village it had been too late to prepare a proper meal. Wooden tables and benches however were set up and the newcomers feasted on loaves of bread supplied by the various bakers as well as fruits and vegetables from the Gnome Gardens. The various cheeses on the platters had been left untouched because they didn't know what it was. Large pitchers of gooseberry juice had been provided for the children and bottles of elderberry wine and honey mead were shared among the adults.

Most of them were very thankful, as they had not eaten well since leaving the Boulder Clan all those weeks ago. The provisions that Bablou had given them had not lasted long. For the rest of their journey they relied mainly on wild berries, mushrooms that they found in small wooded and fish from the streams.

The journey to Jasper's home had been physically demanding and mentally taxing. So many things had changed, especially so for the Elfkins. Most of the forest creatures chose to make the small forests that they had come upon their home and by the time they reached the valley where the battle with the Rapcicor took place, only Bauthal and Paraphin remained.

The elders and many of the underlings were near to exhaustion from the constant walking up and down the rounded top hills. They had to rest more often than they did going through the Greenwood Forest and the Outer Bound Meadow. Several of the men took turns pulling Lizbeth's trolley. It was much like the one she had from the Greenwood Forest. Many of the Elfkins took turns carrying the youngest of the Meadow Imps in backpacks while many of the Tara Aquians took turns carrying the youngest of the Elfkins in similar style backpacks. The strongest of them piggy backed the elders when they were too tired to walk.

Now safe and sound in Elsbrier, the Meadow Imps and Elfkins were given tents to sleep in. The Tara Aquians were escorted to the Lily Pond where the Water Lilys greeted them warmly. The injured were taken to the Mediplace where Orliff, Niella and Alamat tended to them with help from several of the villagers.

The fairies and the rest of the travelers, who had stayed to clean up the valley, were just arriving. They were surprised to see that large torches lit their way to a group of villagers. They stood just before the cropping of trees that separated Elsbrier from the grassy meadow before the Lily Pond. In behind they could see that Elsbrier stood in darkness. Upon seeing them Obwyn walked sternly towards them and greeted them rudely, "It's about time you showed up. We were just discussing whether or not to send out a search party for you." Several dozen armed villagers walked up and stood behind him. Without waiting for anyone to explain why they were so late, he started to bark out orders and completely ignored the confused looks on their faces.

"You," he said looking at the fairies, "are to go home immediately, and your Avidraughts can go home to their families as well." Six villagers stepped forward to escort the fairies home. They were too tired to question him about the torches or why they needed to be escorted. After bowing to Zusie and the others they left with the escorts. Obwyn told the villagers that had arrived with them that they could go home to their families but should expect to be called upon to attend a meeting in the Great Hall the following afternoon.

He looked at the Tara Aquians. Seeing Lindrella he addressed her, "You will be escorted to the Lily Pond, where the rest of your people are. The Water Lilys are excellent hosts and will take care of all your needs." Obwyn looked over his shoulder; Airam Andiela stepped forward with six escorts. She smiled warmly at Lindrella as she clasped her hands together and bowed her head in greeting. Lindrella returned her greeting and they went on their way.

He then looked down at Bauthal and Zeander who stood next to Paraphin. If surprised about either of their sizes he did not say anything. "You will be escorted to the encampment on the other side of the village." From the group of remaining villagers two stepped forward; Zan and Jopha. "All your people are there except for those who were injured. They were taken to the Mediplace," Obwyn said.

Zeander looked up at Zan, "You look like a fellow who might know where I can get a wee bit of ale." Zan looked down at the little man and chuckled.

"That I do my good man," Zan replied. "I am sure we can convince Hamy to leave *The Baron's Den* open for a wee bit longer."

"Will the snake be wanting one as well," Zan said cheekily, which made Jopha laugh heartily. He quickly stopped laughing however when Paraphin answered.

"I think I jussst might," he said as he slithered past the group of villagers who looked cautiously at him as he went by them. The only creatures they knew of that could speak were the Avidraughts.

"And what of you?" Obwyn said as he looked at Bauthal who stood off to the side.

"Yes, I will be going with them. As for the drink I just might indulge in more than a wee bit. It's been a long journey," Bauthal said as he walked past Zan and Jopha who dropped their jaws open in surprise. A badger and giant snake that could talk; if he didn't know better he would think he had already been drinking. A cheeky smile lit Zan's face and he rubbed his hands together.

"Well then," Zan said "I can't wait to see the look on Hamy's face when you order a drink!" He and Jopha lead the small group to *The Den* while Obwyn faced the remaining five; Zusie, her daughters, Aldwin and Janilli.

"You," he said looking at Zusie and the others, "will follow me. Orliff, our village healer is expecting you." He turned abruptly and took a pathway that lead to the center of the village. Zusie and the others followed him, the remaining armed escorts walked behind them. Upon entering the village they passed several buildings until they came to a fork in the pathway. Obwyn took the one that led to the left and they continued to follow him. The path curved around a thicket of tall trees. Zusie and the others were startled when a large building came into view. It was the largest building any of them had ever seen.

"This is the Mediplace," Obwyn said. He then stepped on the cobblestone path that led to it. Zusie and the others walked warily behind him.

The building was a massive peaked wooden structure twenty times the size of the Gathering Hall in the Elfkin village. Zusie and the others were to learn that it had taken longer to build then was expected because the Jarrell brothers had needed time to recover from the injuries they sustained during their battle with the fairies. Other than the slight limp that Reg had, all of them had healed nicely.

The Mediplace was Yan's designs and the brothers had worked diligently on it for several months; it was their pride and joy. It had three floors that were accessed by several staircases, one off the front foyer, one off the kitchen and one between the rooms that Orliff used as a study and conducted business in. A triple wide staircase located at the back of the building led from the upper floors to the ground and was to be used in case of a fire. There were several pulley-lifts throughout the building that were used to transport food, medicine and linens to the upper floors.

The main part of the building was a large room that housed a hundred beds, fifty to each side of a long aisle. Each bed had a side table. Just above each side table, a shuttered lantern hung on the wall. Lanterns hung down from the rafters on long pieces of rope down the middle aisle. Thick-corded lines also hung from the rafters. The cords held up thick tubes that had curtains hanging from them. The curtains if need be could be drawn around each bed. There were several outer rooms for Orliff and his assistants, three surgical rooms, a large kitchen with a walk-in pantry the size of a small cottage as well as several bathing chambers.

The most impressive room in the Mediplace however was the storeroom. Rectangular in shape, the room had two large doors at one end that lead into a hallway that connected the storeroom with the kitchen and the main sleeping quarters. Twenty six tiered wooden shelving units that were fifteen feet long stood seven feet apart in the center of the room. Long wooden shelves lined the three remaining walls. It looked like a library, however instead of books these shelves were laden with all manner of things. Clear bottles filled with colourful liquid medicines were lined three rows deep along one of the long walls. The bottles, varying in sizes from small to large, were all labeled.

The other long wall was filled with cloth bags that also varied in size. The bags were full of herbs and other dried plants that Orliff and his assistants used for their medicinal teas, salves and lotions. The end wall had several weaved baskets; most were empty but some were filled with warming stones, several different kinds of bark, needles and mushrooms that dried in the open air. The shelves in the center of the room held robes, blankets, pillows, bandages, towels, soaps, washbasins and all manner of surgical tools. Several villagers had traveled all over the countryside to the outlying ports buying up whatever supplies they could. The room had been continuously stocked over the summer months in preparation for the coming war. Everything had been meticulously counted and clearly labeled by Xander and Mariela who had offered to help. Orliff had readily accepted their help with the Elder's approval.

As they reached the building someone stepped out of the door. Upon seeing them they yelped for joy. "Oh thank Zenrah!" Marla cried out. "We were so worried that another attack had happened."

Zusie was the first to reach her and hugged her quickly. "How are they?" Zusie asked anxiously as the others hugged Marla in turn.

Marla, knowing that Zusie was afraid that they had lost someone, eased her conscious. "No, we did not lose anyone, they are all mending well. Orliff is a wondrously, amazing, brilliant healer," she said in awe then looked apologetically at Aldwin. Aldwin did not take offense.

"How is Lizbeth? Has she been given the antidote?" Zusie asked. Marla looked sad for a moment until she heard Zusie's sharp intake of breath.

"No, she is fine," Marla said as she reached out and held Zusie's hand. "She was the first that Orliff treated once they made it back to the village. The others he had treated as we walked here. Come, see for yourself!" Marla said excitedly. Before they left Obwyn said his goodbyes. After thanking him and their escort in return they followed Marla to the door.

They entered the large building and were instantly impressed by the breadth and cleanliness of it. They slowly walked past the injured that were all sleeping soundly. A curtain was drawn around one of the beds. They approached Lizbeth's bed with caution. Marla drew back the curtain slowly and they were surprised to see a man sitting on a chair next to Lizbeth. He was holding her hand and chatting away to her as if they were old friends.

Upon hearing the curtain draw back he looked up and

smiled. "Now see Lizbeth I told you there was nothing to fear. Your friends have made it home safely." Everyone looked anxiously at Lizbeth hoping that the antidote had worked, but she was still in the coma. Orliff placed Lizbeth's hand back down on the cot and stood. To no one in particular he said, "It helps to talk with them when they are in this state. It gives them something to live for knowing there is someone who cares for them, waiting for them to recover. But you already know that don't you." Orliff turned and looked straight at Zusie.

"How, how did you know?" Zusie stumbled over her words. She was taken aback by his keen insight.

"She is still with us," Orliff said in a matter of fact way. He had a quick warm smile for them that they couldn't help but return. Orliff was wearing what he normally wore while attending to his patients, a long white sleeved tunic that came to his knees and was unbuttoned to the middle of his chest. Underneath he wore a dark blue shirt and matching dark blue loose fitting pants. Around his neck, he wore a strange silver object that Aldwin looked at curiously.

"Now," he said looking at all their exhausted faces. "You can say a quick hello to Lizbeth, to ease her mind. Then I want each of you to get something to eat...," he wrinkled his nose, "wash up and get some rest."

Zusie went to comment but he raised his hand. "Your people are fine. Morning will be here soon enough and you will need your strength. I am sure the Elders will want to meet you first thing and there will be plenty of work for all of you to do tomorrow."

Zusie and the others looked at Orliff. His voice was kind but they knew that there would be no arguing with him.

"My assistants, Alamat and Niella," as if on cue his assistants peered around the curtain and smiled at the newcomers. "They will show you to the kitchen and bathing chambers."

"And," he said as an afterthought, "you will sleep here."

Zusie went to argue once again and this time the others chimed in as well. They did not want special treatment and would sleep outside with the others. Orliff clicked his tongue, raised his hand and said, "Now, now, I will have no argument on this. You are to stay here tonight. If you want to sleep outside tomorrow, you are more than welcome to. But for tonight, you will each take a bed. And you," he said looking at Saphina, "I will examine as soon as you have eaten and washed."

Saphina automatically touched her round belly; Aldwin stood beside her stiffened in defense. He had been taking very good care of Saphina. He made sure that she rested, had enough to eat and drink. When the pickings were slim he gave her his share.

"Do not take offense Aldwin," Orliff said. Surprised Aldwin looked at Orliff, "Yes.... you and I have much to talk about. I daresay sweet dear Lizbeth would not be with us if it had not been for your Soothe Ease potion." Aldwin looked at Marla who obviously had told Orliff all about him.
Marla looked at Aldwin with pride, "You are a great healer." Slightly embarrassed, Aldwin shuffled from foot to foot. Not knowing how to respond he looked at Lizbeth.

Saphina reached out and clasped Aldwin's hand. "Thank you Orliff," she said looking at Orliff. "I will quickly do as you have asked and come for you when I am finished."

"Take your time dear girl. There is no hurry. I need to speak with the Elders first and then will come and find you." He paused, put his hand in his pocket and pulled out a shiny object. It was on a long chain that was hooked to one of the buttons on his overcoat. "In about...an hours' time," he said as he looked at the object. Everyone but Marla looked at it strangely.

"It's a time piece," she said. They looked at the time piece with strange expressions as if they did not understand. "It tells the time." Marla said again with a broad smile. She chuckled lightly as their expressions changed from bewildered to awe. Each of them now looked very curious at the watch as Orliff put it back into his pocket. He looked at them with a kind, patient expression.

"All will be explained in the morning. From what I hear," he said smiling at Marla, "you all have a lot of catching up to do." He kept his next thought to himself; he worried that once the light of day lit the sky the travelers from the valley that time forgot would be in for a very rude awakening. From what he learned from Marla time had truly left them behind. He wanted to speak with the Elders and voice his fears that once the newcomers saw all the changes and advances that had been made they would not handle it well.

"Until later then," he said nodding his head curtly to them. He left them in the capable hands of Alamat and Niella who would see to their needs. He slowly made his way down the center aisle looking at each of his patients as he passed by who thankfully were still sleeping restfully. Just outside the building Orliff stopped and nodded as Jemas and Rhethea walked by; each of them were carrying a stack of blankets. Rhethea was laughing lightly at something Jemas had said.

"More blankets?" Orliff questioned as he looked from Rhethea to Jemas who smiled broadly back at him. Jemas, Orliff was glad to see, had made a home here in Elsbrier. He was a likeable, kind, young man who was always eager to learn new things and help out whenever it was asked of him. He got along well with Osborne's grandsons, which was good for him as Rhethea was their only sister and their baby sister at that. Many times the villagers would comment, before Jemas came to the village, that they pitied the young man who won Rhethea's heart, as he would have to win over her brothers first. But now here they were, walking in the moonlight without one of her brothers as an escort.

The Jarrell story was one of tragedy. Osborne's only son and his wife died in a tragic accident shortly after Rhethea was born. Osborne and Rishley took the six children in and raised them to adulthood. Rhethea was the only left at home.

Her brothers lived just outside of the main village, in a small clearing surrounded by trees. Each built a house one beside the other in a semi-circle. They were interconnected with cobble stone walkways. The center of the circle was a play area that had a small grouping of trees. Each tree had a small house built securely onto the limbs. Each treehouse was connected with a wooden swing bridge. The children had been too young to play in the house but Ody the youngest of the brothers who had yet to take a wife had been anxious and built the play area as a surprise for Lewis; the eldest of the grandchildren. The brothers had jokingly called their little clearing Jarrellville. Plans were being made to build Rhethea a home as well. The brothers liked Jemas and hoped that he and Rhethea would marry.

Mitch tried to convince his grandparents to move out of the ever-growing and busy village to the clearing. However, Osborne refused saying that he and Rishley needed to be near the shop.

"Yes," Rhethea said smiling. "There is an Elfkin named Paramo who says the ground here is too hard to sleep on." Rhethea shook her head.

"Ah," is all Orliff said.

"She is the same one who complained to Ira and Awna that the bread they brought was stale. She refused to believe when they told her that they had made it fresh that day in their shop." Rhethea scoffed.

"Yes, I do remember her," Orliff said. "I believe her mate Martan was injured in the attack."

"Oh," Rhethea said sadly, "perhaps she is not handling it very well."

"Perhaps," is all Orliff said in return.

"Tomorrow I will offer to watch her children while she visits with her mate," Rhethea said as she looked up at Jemas.

"Oh no," Jemas replied. "The build of the newcomers' homes starts tomorrow once they have picked out their plot of land. You my lovely are on your own."

Rhethea balanced the stack of blankets with one arm and playfully punched Jemas' shoulder. He feigned injury then smiled warmly at her. She returned his smile. *Yes,* Orliff thought to himself. *They would make a fine couple.*

"I should be going, the Elders are waiting," Orliff said as he smiled at the pair of them.

"Yes," Jemas said, "we should be on our way as well."

They parted; Orliff walked towards the Whipple Wash Tree; Rhethea and Jemas walked towards the newcomers' encampment. He turned and watched Orliff walk away. Rhethea looked up to see a scowl on Jemas's face.

"What is it?" She said turning her head to look back at what he was looking at. She saw Orliff disappear behind a building.

Jemas did not answer right away and she looked up at him. He seemed to be deep in thought. "Jemas, what is it?" She said again.

"Um, nothing," he said shaking off the uneasy feeling. "We should be on our way," he said smiling at her. Before she had a chance to ask him again what was wrong Lashia called out to them.

"Ah, there you are," she said walking briskly towards them. They could tell she was upset. Before they had a chance to ask her what was wrong she said disgustedly, "That Paramo woman is impossible. Her complaints have been none stop."

"Yes we know," Rhethea and Jemas said in unison as they looked down at the stack of blankets in their hands. Rhethea told Lashia about the conversation they just had with Orliff.

"Well that is all good and perhaps she is not faring well," Lashia stated, "but before you offer to watch her children, she did call you a lazy sod and complained about how long it was taking you to bring blankets."

"Really," Rhethea said. She looked purposefully in the direction of the newcomers' encampment. For the most part Rhethea was kind, but she had a short fuse and a quick tongue that could cut someone down to size with just a few well-chosen words. The villagers stayed clear of her when she was in a temper. As the only girl with five older brothers she could fight with the best of them and out wrestle even Aro who was the tallest of the brothers. She had felt badly for them after their battle with the fairies. She loved them dearly but they did vex her so. She couldn't help but tell them afterward that they got what they deserved.

Knowing Rhethea's temper, Lashia said calmly, "Don't worry yourself about it. I am going to get her a sleeping tonic."

"She asked for a sleeping tonic?" Rhethea asked.

"No," Lashia chuckled lightly. "Have you met Zeander yet? The little fellow that rides on the back of that large snake... Paraphin I think his name is."

"Yes," Rhethea said smiling lightly. "Jemas and I saw him just before we asked Hamy if he had extra blankets. He is quite commanding for such a short little fellow."

"Yes, well he wasn't too pleased that he had been called from *The Baron's Den* to help out with her. After seeing him she quieted down, but he suggested I put a sleeping tonic in the tea she asked me to fetch for her. I am actually on my way to talk with Orliff about it."

"Oh, we just saw Orliff. He went to speak with the Elders. I believe Alamat and Niella are at the Mediplace," Rhethea said

"Ah, that is good I will ask Alamat then." Lashia said with a nod.

Rhethea leaned closer to Lashia, "Perhaps you should ask for a weeks' worth." Lashia and Jemas smiled broadly as the three of them chuckled loudly.

Rhethea then asked seriously. "Have you seen Jasper yet?"

"No," Lashia said shaking her head. "I heard he was summoned to the meet with the Elders as soon as he got home."

"Ah, the poor dear," Rhethea said. "He has been through so much. No Hummingmoth should ever have to endure what he has let alone the youngest of them; so sad."

"Yes, yes indeed," Lashia said. "It wasn't the home coming we were all expecting to give him was it?"

"No it wasn't," Rhethea said shaking her head. "Tomorrow," she said cheerily, "will be a better day and we will give him a proper welcome home party; complete with song, dance and even Firebangers if my brothers have any left."

Rhethea and Lashia looked up at Jemas who stood quietly behind Rhethea. Their smiles faded as they saw the stone cold expression on his face. "Jemas what is it?" Rhethea asked softly. Jemas was so caught up in his thoughts and did not answer her. She looked worriedly at Lashia.

"Jemas is everything all right?" Lashia said softly, touching his arm. Her touch brought him out of his thoughts.

Seeing their concerned expressions, he quickly said, "Yes, yes of course. I was just thinking of the Rapcicors and how vile they can be. Thankfully the fairies were not hurt in the attack." Jemas clenched his hands into fists. "I'm sorry I just remembered that there was something I needed to do. Do you mind helping Rhethea with these?" He said as he put the stack of blankets in Lashia's arms.

"Jemas," Rhethea said sadly. They had planned to go for a night ride in the moonlight. Remembering, Jemas looked at her and smiled.

"Don't worry dear, this is important," he said softly. "If I don't catch up with you later I will see you in the morning for breakfast. We will spend the rest of the day together."

Rhethea went to argue that he offered to help her brothers with the build when he bent down and kissed her passionately. Rhethea had difficulty holding onto the blankets as she tried to compose herself. Her cheeks reddened with embarrassment by the show of affection in front of her sister-in-law.

"Tomorrow then," he said and before she could reply he turned and walked into the night.

Rhethea stared after him for a minute then looked at Lashia who was smiling broadly at her, "Sorry about that Lashia."

"Oh don't apologize to me. He is quite handsome and if I wasn't already married to your brother..." She stopped as she heard Rhethea's sharp intake of breath.

Lashia smiled reassuringly, "You have nothing to worry about and neither does your brother Mitch. I am madly in love with him and couldn't imagine my life without him. However I don't think he has quite kissed me like that."

Rhethea sighed and her cheeks warmed again as she turned her head to see if she could still see Jemas. He had disappeared and she smiled girlishly as she remembered his kiss.

"Come on, he is long gone," Lashia chuckled. "If he is anything like your brothers, once they have their minds set on something not much can deter them from it." She started to walk towards the newcomers' encampment. "Let's drop these off and then you can come with me to ask Alamat for the sleeping tonic."

Rhethea chuckled, "All right then. Afterward do you think it will be all right to come back to your place?" Lashia looked at her questioningly. "So we can plan a proper homecoming for Jasper."

"Ahh," Lashia said smiling broadly. "Going to have trouble sleeping are you?"

"Oh hush up you," Rhethea said and then laughed embarrassingly.

Lashia chuckled as well. Their light laughter carried over the night breeze. Neither of them noticed the stranger watching them from the shadow of the trees. He waited until they were gone then walked straight to the forest on the other side of the meadow before the Lily Pond. There was so much commotion going on and so many new faces that no one would notice his arrival to the village or see him slip into the shadows of the trees.

Jasper looked at the kind faces staring back at him. Except for Queen Faywyn all those he loved were in the Gathering Room beneath the Whipple Wash Tree. This was the first time he had been there without his brothers and he had mixed emotions. He sat at the end of the stone table which was much like the one he seen in the Crystal Cave of Mount Aspentonia all those months ago. So much time had passed, so many memories; the good and the bad.

Zee sat behind him; her presence was comforting. They had been best friends before he left on his mission, he was happy that that had not changed. She had grown taller and lean though. Her cheeks were no longer plump and she walked with a warrior's gait. He could tell by the expression on her lovely face and the lines at the corner of her eyes that she was wiser as well; as were her sisters.

He was there for a "debriefing" as Elder Jolise called it. He had heard of the term before from his brothers, but as this was his first mission he had never been to one; it had been different then what he expected. Because he was the only remaining messenger it was up to him to report the results of their mission. Jolise had instructed him on the procedure; he had followed it exactly and had not cried once; Joffro, the leader of the Hummingmoth Messengers, would have been proud of him.

As he spoke Elder Sienna transcribed his message in a Lea-Ther bound book. When he came to the part of his brothers' demise her quill pen halted for a moment as she comforted Jolise who wept openly beside her. The others, he could tell were quite disturbed by his recalling of it. Even the hardened and seasoned Obwyn, looked fit to be tied. Frowns darkened the faces of Nayew and Orliff as they tried to keep their anger at bay. When Jasper had finished, the room remained silent as everyone tried to process what they had heard. Finally Elder Enyce spoke.

"Jasper I wish this could have been a better homecoming for you. Regardless you are home at last and that is all that matters," Enyce sighed. "You have been very courageous throughout this ordeal and we are very proud of you." Jasper's bottom lip trembled. Zee moved closer to him. He could feel her breath moving the hair on the back of his head. Everyone nodded their heads in agreement.

"Ladies," Enyce addressed the fairies. "You have had quite the ordeal yourself today and have proved your worth." Zee sighed; obviously no one had told them that she almost shot off Farley's ear. She chose not to tell them at that moment. She looked cautiously at her sisters; they were not going to tell them either.

"Your first battle was successful, your training has come in handy," she said pointedly and looked at Mariela who blushed. "I think it is time for you to rest."

The fairies instantly started to argue, with Mariela and Shanata once again being the loudest. Enyce rose and looked sternly at them. The fairies knew that look, there would be no persuading her or the other Elders, they were being dismissed and that was that. Frustrated with the Elders' decision, they went back to their room and stayed up for several hours talking about what had happened and the dark stranger that Zee had seen with the Rapcicors. They speculated who it was, whether or not it was Canvil or a member of the Venom Horde and what purpose he had with the Rapcicors. Speculation after speculation was addressed, argued and readdressed until their heads became full with conspiracy theories. Finally, drained of all energy, they went to their beds. But none slept well as the day's events played over and over in their sleep.

In the Gathering Room Orliff had explained his fears about the Elfkins' mental state and whether or not they could handle how advanced Elsbrier was. He then made his apologies and left to care for the injured. Obwyn and Nayew had stayed well into the night talking with the Elders about the Elfkins and how they were going to introduce them to Elsbrier. They did not worry about the Meadow Imps or the Tara Aquians; they seemed to be further advanced then the Elfkins. If Orliff's assumption was right, the Elfkins were going to be in for quite a shock.

It had been easy enough to mask Elsbrier in the dark, but once daylight came it would not be so easy. It was a bustling village on any given day with all the comings and goings. But now, people from all over had started to arrive for the Hawkeye tournament. Elsbrier was going to be chaotic to say the least.

Chapter 21
A Surprise Encounter

The morning came with a sharp coolness that froze exhaled breaths in midair. They quickly dissipated though, indicating that the day would eventually warm. When the fairies, with Jasper on Zee's shoulder, and the Elders stepped out from the hollow in the Tree they greeted it with a dull 'Good morning'; they had all stayed up way past the time to greet it any other way.

The Tree looked at their attire questioningly; all wore a simple dress except for Rayley, Zee and Enna; they chose to wear shirts and long pants. Nothing adorned their hair nor did any of them wear jewelry, except for the ever-present medallions that the Elders wore around their necks. Rayley and Enna already had the sleeves of their shirts rolled up to their elbows; ready to work. The Tree bowed to them in return and opened its leafy vines, allowing them to pass through. They all mumbled a thank you.

They woke early so they could make it to the newcomers' encampment before any of them rose and ventured out of the meadow. The trek to the meadow wouldn't be long if they took the shortcut through the village and down the path that led to the Mediplace and beyond. There they would be joined by Zusie, her daughters, Janilli and Aldwin, who would walk them to the encampment. Mariela and Shanata were looking forward to talking with Saphina and Chrystalina, whom they had formed an instant kinship with.

A thick layer of dew covered the ground and they slipped on the wet grass as they descended the hill. As they approached Elsbrier, they could hear that it was already awake with motion as the vendors prepared their shops for the day's sales. Their senses began to wake the nearer they got. It was as if Elsbrier lay cocooned in an electric energy field. One could not help but feel rejuvenated when the sights and sounds met them at the entrance to the village.

"Good morning ladies," Miss Casey said cheerfully as they passed the open door of the *Village Voice*. They returned the greeting. Miss Casey stood in the doorway and rubbed her hands together to warm them. "It's a bit chilly this morning isn't?" They nodded in response.

Miss Casey looked lovely; like a bit of sunshine to brighten the day. Her dark golden hair was neatly plaited into a single braid which hung over her shoulder. She always wore a floral print blouse in lively hues, and a pair of crisp white pants. She wore a thick butcher's apron over her clothes. They could tell that she had already been hard at work as the apron had blotches of dark ink splattered on it.

"You're up early," Sianna said as the group stopped to greet her.

"Yes, well there is a lot of exciting news to report on isn't there," she said. "The Boswick Trappers will be here today and I hear Lord Warden is traveling with them." Involuntarily her cheeks reddened as a pretty smile lit her face at the mention of his name. Not noticing she had done it she continued naming off what she thought was news worthy. "The newcomers have arrived, Jasper is home; which will be on the front page by the way. Happy to see you home Jasper!" Miss Casey added. Jasper nodded a hello from Zee's shoulder. "And if you have time I would like to interview you later today." Jasper, unsure of what to say, looked over at Elder Jolise. Jopha had always spoken for the Hummingmoth Messengers; Jasper became nervous just thinking about it. The Elders looked at Jasper. He immediately frowned.

"I think perhaps we will wait on that if you don't mind, Miss Casey," Jolise said. "There are still things we need to discuss about the mission. We will however send you something by the end of the week," Jolise looked over at Jasper and winked. Jasper smiled a thank you to her.

"That will be lovely then," Miss Casey said. "Good day to you." They all returned her sentiments and continued down the path.

As they made their way onto the path between Homsa's music store and Mary's dress shop they were halted by someone who called out for them to stop. They turned to see J. Z. Jones skip down the path to the left of them.

"Well, now you are all up early and look to be in a hurry. What has gotten you in such a rush so early in the morning?" Miss J said; everyone called her Miss J. She then stopped and gasped, "Oh my, Jasper I didn't see you there son." She called every male under the age of thirty, son. "Oh, oh it is so good to see you home." She immediately picked Jasper off Zee's shoulder and kissed him on the cheek. Jasper blushed and returned the greeting with a quick kiss on hers.

"It is good to be home!" He said.

"Well now," Miss J said excitedly as she sat Jasper back down on Zee's shoulder. "You and your brothers must stop by later for tea and tell me all about your adventures." She continued to talk and did not immediately notice the frowns on everyone's faces. "I daresay I see a play in the making." Noticing the frowns she stopped talking. "Oh dear," she said as she looked apologetically at Sianna. "Have I gone and said something wrong?"

"Don't worry dear, I will come by later and explain things to you," Sianna said. Sianna and Miss J were close friends. Sianna had penned several plays that Miss J had produced and directed. Each year they were showcased at the *Midsummer's Playwright Festival* during the month of August. Playwrights from across the country and as far away as the coast of the Guardian Sea entered the festival. Those that had been picked to compete brought their own troupe of players and musicians with them. Elsbrier was always a little livelier then as all the musicians and actors would engage in impromptu performances at every open café or park bench.

"Oh yes, right then," Miss J said. "I do have to be going; I hear Lord Warden is coming with the Boswick Players this year". Her cheeks reddened and a girly smile lit her face. "I also heard he enjoys avant-garde theatre. I have just the play for him: *A Stab in the Park* based on the novel by Thurston Field. The players and I have been rehearsing it for weeks now. But of course you all know that. I'm rambling. Enjoy the day!" Miss J said embarrassingly as she quickly turned. Her lovely green floral dress twirled around her ankles and her hair bobbed on her shoulders. As she quickly skipped down the path that would take her to the theatre, she broke out into song. Everyone smiled.

The small entourage started down the path again only to stop a few seconds later as they heard someone call for them from Mary's dress shop.

"Zee, girls," Annie Dee called from the doorway. She absentmindedly walked up to Zee and started to measure her without asking. "You have grown taller dear," she tsked. "I will have to lengthen your outfit for the Winter Solstice Celebrations." Annoyed, Annie moved to Zee's shoulder and brushed Jasper off, not realizing that it was he who sat there. Jasper flew up in the air and hovered beside them. He folded his arms across his chest and huffed indignantly. As she measured Zee from the top of her shoulder to her wrist, she tsked again. Ashlina snickered behind her hand and her sisters smiled. The Elders however looked at Annie with impatient frowns. Annie had tunnel vision when it came to her work and was unaware of everything and everyone around her. She was the epitome of a highly creative person and was terribly talented. And not just as a costume designer, but as a painter as well. Several of her paintings hung in many of the Manor houses across the Kingdom.

"Oh my," she said as she took a small book from her pocket and flipped through it till she came to the page she was looking for. She tsked again as she took the pencil from behind her ear and started to scribble in the book. "You will have to come by the shop dear and have another measurement done." She then looked at the other fairies. She mentally measured them from head to toe. "I daresay you will all have to. It seems you have all grown like bad weeds this past month. And look how lean you all are. Oh I hope I won't have to start your costumes from scratch." She then scowled at the Elders as if it was their fault that the fairies had changed so much. "Make sure you come by the shop today so that I can take your measurements. The celebration is only a month away and I still have the costumes for the play to finish."

She then looked up just above Zee's shoulder and noticed Jasper fluttering in midair, "Oh my, Jasper, is that you dear?" Jasper smiled at her and said a good morning to her. "Well dear it is good to have you home. You must stop by as well. I would love to hear all about your adventures. Zee dear make sure you bring him with you." As an afterthought she added, "And do stop by Ira and Awna's bake shop and pick up a few of those berry tarts that I like so well. You know the ones," she said then winked. "We will have them with our tea." She then turned abruptly and waved a goodbye over her shoulder as she went on her way. She flipped through her book and tsked loudly as she scribbled a note.

The fairies giggled as the Elders looked strangely from one to the other. Annie had not only forgotten her wagon of material but she also neglected to give Zee the coin to purchase the tarts. Rayley handed Zee several coins from her pocket. "Bring back a basket of them for us as well," she said with a smile.

As Zee put the money in her pocket, Shanata pulled the wagon back into Mary's shop and told her that they would return for it later. After Jasper sat back down on Zee's shoulder, they started on their way again. They had only walked a few paces however before they were once again halted as someone called out to them. "It would have been quicker if we had gone the long way around," Andi said with exasperation.

They all turned and were surprised as Hamy and Zan

259

quickly made their way to them from across the bridge. Just behind them were Paraphin, Zeander and Bauthal, who the Elders had yet to meet. They looked curiously at the five of them who seemed to have become fast friends. Zeander said something to the others that made them chuckle. Enyce furrowed her brow as she wondered what he said.

"Do you mind if we come with you?" Hamy called out to them.

As they approached, the Elders noticed that they looked like they hadn't slept all night. They were still wearing clothes from the previous day, were unshaven and their hair was tussled. They however smiled as they quickly caught up to them and looked eager to begin the day.

"Have you been up all night?" Phinney asked.

Zan smiled sheepishly as Hamy answered. "Yes we have actually," he said with a smile. He then introduced Zeander, Bauthal and Paraphin to the Elders who greeted them kindly.

"Ah, I be glad to meet ya," Zeander said enthusiastically with a thick accent as he heartily shook each of the Elders hands. "Tis a glorious morning isn't it?" He didn't wait for the Elders to agree or disagree. "And look how lovely you all are. I be having no idea you would be so lovely!" His eyes shone brightly as he smiled broadly at them. The Elders wondered if he was perhaps still under the influence of Hamy's beverages, however he looked to be quite sober. Zee snickered at the lively look on Zeander's face.

The Elders were suspicious that he had ulterior motives for being so jolly and exchanged curious looks. The fairies however were caught up in his enthusiasm and smiled at his animated expressions. They all had an opportunity to chat with him on the long walk back to Elsbrier the day before and found him to be quite an interesting fellow, even if they did have difficulty understanding everything he said.

"Who will watch over *The Baron's Den* for you if you join us?" Enyce asked. "The Boswick Trappers are scheduled to arrive today. Do they not normally stay with you when they visit?"

The Boswick Trappers were a lively bunch of fellows. Hamy was from Boswick and grew up with the team's captain, Herb Marrona. The team always stayed at *The Baron's Den* and often came early so that they could get in extra practices, giving Herb and Hamy time to also catch up. Hamy's family still lived in Boswick and always sent a package of gifts with Herb to give to him. The Lord of Boswick, Mikale Warden, lavished the players with all that they would need on the four week travel to Elsbrier and paid for their lodgings a year in advance. This year, the Elders had heard that Lord Boswick would be traveling with them. He normally came a week before the competition started and with just two armed guards. This year however they heard that he would be traveling with a troupe of armed guards, leaving no room for anyone else at *The Baron's Den*. The Elders had heard several complaints from neighbouring noblemen who normally stayed at *The Baron's Den* during the tournament. However there was nothing the Elders could do about it. Lord Warden had paid well in advance.

The Elders tried to cancel the games when they heard of Queen Faywyn's disappearance. None of the other Kingdoms who had qualified for the *9 Games in 9 Days* event would hear of it however. It was too late to change the location, build a new arena and get news to every competing Kingdom. For the last two hundred years Elsbrier had hosted the games, which took place every four years. It would be impossible to set it up anywhere else.

When the games first started they took place outside but an open-roofed arena was built one hundred years ago. It was located in a meadow on the other side of the Dark Forest. A wide pathway joined Elsbrier with the area. It was perfect for visiting vendors. They came two weeks early to set up their tents along the path. The Grandiflora River also wound behind the Arena. An elaborate pumping station was installed so that there would be a constant supply of fresh running water for the vendors to access. The area that surrounded the arena was flat. Visitors who hadn't book a room at one of the inns or boarding houses set up tents.

Normally the games were not governed by anyone in particular however with Queen Faywyn's disappearance and the impending war with Lord Canvil, this year they would be. A team of armed men had been handpicked by Nayew and Obwyn to patrol the area. The men had come from several of the outlying townships in the valley and had been in training for several weeks.

"Ah yes, well I have left it in the capable hands of Jopha and Arnack," Hamy said.

The Elders smiled. Arnack had changed dramatically since his altercation with Hamy during the combat training. After the match with Shanata and Aro, he made his way to his small cottage located just outside of the village. He had not come back into the village for several days. When he finally made an appearance he was quite sober, clean shaven, his hair was neatly trimmed and his clothes were washed and pressed.

Each day since, he worked from early morning till night. He helped Ody and Jopha take care of Homsa's bastions. And also helped several of the older villagers prepare their gardens for the winter season. Each night he worked in *The Baron's Den*- cleaning out the bathrooms and working in the kitchen. He had not only refused payment from Hamy but had not a drop of mead, wine or spirits. The Elders noticed with concern that not only had his appearance and work ethics changed but so too had the redeeming aspects of his personality; gone were the wise cracks, embellished stories that everyone loved to listen to and the magic tricks. He was now all about working and accomplishing all that he could before the sun set.

One day Ashlina and Zee sought him out and asked him about the transformation. He simply shrugged his shoulders and walked away. Zee noticed however that he looked up at the Whipple Wash Tree as he walked away. At the time she wondered if the Tree had spoken to him as well.

"Well then, you are welcome to join us," Enyce said. A lively conversation ensued as they walked down the path that led to the Mediplace. Luckily, no one else had stopped them. Anyone who they did come across was too shocked to see Zeander, Paraphin and Bauthal. The three of them ignored the open stares that were immediately replaced with urgent whispers as they passed by. One couldn't really blame them; it wasn't every day that they saw a gigantic snake with a little man riding on its back or a badger that was walking upright and talking.

As they neared Homsa's house the fairies and Elders waved at him and greeted him with a smile. He was sitting in a rocking chair in the corner of the large porch, drinking his morning coffee. Upon seeing them he stood and leaned on a cane as he walked to the steps and greeted them. Homsa had healed nicely from his fall through the roof. And although he huffed in annoyance and scowled when he saw all the changes that had been made, he rather enjoyed the attention he had received and was thankful for the help.

"You are all up early. Where are you off to this morning?" Homsa asked.

"We are off to greet the newcomers," Jolise said

"The newcomers? Does that mean then that Jasper is...," he started to say then smiled broadly as he saw Jasper sitting on Zee's shoulder.

"Ah Jasper, it is good to see you home!" Homsa said.

"Thank you Homsa! It is good to be home!" Jasper said.

"Will you need any eggs or roasters for the newcomers?" He asked, looking at Andi.

"We are not sure yet," she said. "But if we do I will send someone to fetch them."

"Well, enjoy your day then and Jasper, stop by as soon as you can. I would very much like to hear about your adventures." Jasper nodded and waved goodbye as they started on their way again. Homsa smiled broadly and waved back until he saw Zeander, Paraphin and Bauthal. His smile then turned to a questioning frown and his hand stopped mid wave. The three of them however didn't notice as they continued to walk beside Hamy, who only waved a quick hello to Homsa. He was in a lively conversation with Bauthal.

Finally, they turned the last corner on the path and were not surprised to see that Zusie and the others were awake and sat on the benches in front of the Mediplace. Orliff stood beside the bench that Zusie and Janilli were sitting on. Upon seeing the Elders and the fairies he waved to them; Zusie and the others stood.

"Good morning," Aldwin said.

"Good morning," the Elders and fairies said in unison. The Elders were introduced to Zusie and the others. Zeander, Paraphin and Bauthal said a quick hello as well. Without hesitation Zeander jumped down from the saddle and started to make his way to the door of the Mediplace; Bauthal followed behind him. They were concerned about the villagers who had been hurt and wanted to see for themselves that they were doing well. They also wanted to stop by and say a quick hello to Lizbeth to let her know that all was well.

"Gentlemen," Orliff said just as Bauthal went to open the door. "Everyone is still sleeping. Your visit can wait till later." Zeander and Bauthal looked crossly at Orliff but it was Paraphin who spoke.

"Orliff isss right, the morning hasss jussst risssen. There will be time for a visssit later today." If shocked to hear the big snake talk Orliff did not let on. He instead smiled at Paraphin. Zusie and Janilli nodded in agreement. Zeander agreed and climbed up into the saddle again. They started down the path that would take them to the meadow where the encampment had been set up, but paused when the others did not follow.

"How are the patients doing?" Enyce asked.

"They are all mending well," Orliff said. "In fact, many of

them will be able to leave later today. One however will need to stay a few more days."

"Is it the one they call Lizbeth?" Andi asked. She had been intrigued when she heard of Lizbeth's story from Jasper.

"Ah, yes dear Lizbeth will be staying, but no it is not her," Orliff said. "It is Martan."

"What be wrong with Martan?" Zeander immediately asked with concern.

Over the journey, he and Martan had become close despite Paramo's disapproval. She still disliked Zeander, however she never said anything out of turn against him since the day he and Barty had shown them the watercrafts that would take them across Lake Kellowash.

"Nothing to worry about," Orliff said. "I have just requested that he get a couple of extra days rest." Orliff looked at Zusie who smiled a thank you to him.

Paramo would not like it, but after talking with Orliff about it, they decided that it would be better that he rest. The injury to his leg would heal quickly, but not if any of the stories of Paramo were true. Zeander noticed the smile on Zusie's face and knew that she had asked if Martan could stay a couple of extra days. They asked a couple of the younger villagers to help Paramo with her children while Martan rested in the Mediplace.

"Zusie," Enyce said. "After we are finished at the encampment we would like you, Janilli, Aldwin and your daughters to join us for dinner." She then looked at Zeander, Paraphin and Bauthal and asked them to join them as well.

"Ah yes," Zeander began. "But we have already made plans for dinner. We would be glad to drop by afterward for a nightcap and perhaps my mate Lillian could join us?" Enyce looked at her sisters who all nodded in agreement.

"Yes that will be fine," Enyce said. They continued to walk down the path talking lightly about what the Elders would say to the Elfkins. As they came to the end of the encampment they saw the Jarrell brothers and several men coming towards them from the direction of the saw mill. Several pokeys pulled wagons full of planks of wood and supplies.

"Good morning!" Mitch said cheerily. He looked like he hadn't slept all night either.

"Good morning," everyone said in turn.

"Getting an early start are you?" Phinney questioned.

"Yes," Mitch said. "There is a lot to do. Aro and I were up all night with Hamy and Zeander plotting out the land on the east side of the meadow for the build. It has several wooded areas that we can build around. After learning more about the Elfkins we thought they might appreciate the gesture. We also devised a quick plan that will give them access to shared wells. For now we will pump water to several holding tanks for them to use over the winter. Next spring we will build their drying and pottery huts. Zeander told us that the Elfkins are quite accomplished potters and farmers. Next year we will clear a portion of the meadow so that they can have a communal garden if they do not want to purchase their food from the Gnome Garden."

"Sounds as if you thought of most everything," Phinney said. Mitch looked at her and she smiled at him. It was Phinney's duty to plan out the different communities in Elsbrier. She had suggested they use the east side of the meadow for the build and was pleased that Mitch and his brothers had done an excellent job in the planning stages. It seems as if they had thought of everything.

"But they came with nothing. What of their clothes and housewares?" Jolise asked.

"Ah well yes," Aro said. "We hadn't quite got that far yet. We were just discussing where to get the brick from for their fireplaces; we don't have enough in our stores to furnish everyone with one. It will be a mighty cold winter if we don't find a supply of them."

"Andi and I were in Warfdorte just last week," Athia said.

"They have a surplus. Perhaps you could send a couple of your brothers to fetch some."

"I will write up a draft note that should cover the cost," Enyce said.

"You also might try the neighbouring villages of Scotcoe and Simland. We have a standing order with them," Athia said.

Aro and Mitch nodded. They had gone to those communities before when they built their homes. Scotcoe and Simland were located along the base of the Dunaster Bluffs. It was a rocky landscape. The clay ground was poor for growing vegetables or fruit. For this reason, the stonemasons often bartered for fresh fruit and vegetables from the Gnome Gardens in return for stone and brick. They were a day and a half ride away from Elsbrier and each other. They could have the brick and stone back by the time it was ready to do the interior of the buildings.

"And what of the other things they will need?" Jolise asked again.

"Athia and I wondered about that some time ago," Andi said. "We sent out a letter of request to the Ladies of Harmony. They have community halls from Dunaster straight through to Mountoak and as far south as Pleasantland. We received a message from them just the other day. They have amassed a large collection of clothing, dishes and bed linens. They are ready for pick up as soon as we can send someone to fetch them."

Dunaster was three days' ride from Elsbrier. If they sent someone today they could be back within a week. If all went well a great majority of the houses would be ready to live in. Knowing this, Enyce looked at Andi and Athia who nodded.

"We will need to take a handful of villagers with us is there anyone you might suggest?" Andi said as she looked at Zan.

"Ah yes of course, I would like to come along," Zan said.

"I would like to come with you," Zeander said, "if you don't mind?"

"Me too," Bauthal and Paraphin said in unison.

"Well now that is the making of a rather nice entourage. We will ask another six villagers and a set of guards to accompany us," Athia said.

The others had stayed quiet for the duration of the conversation between the Elders and the Jarrell brothers. Upon hearing that they needed armed guards, Saphina stepped forward. "I would like to offer my services as guard," she said. Everyone could not help but look at her in surprise then down at her rounded belly.

"Saphina, do you think that wise?" Aldwin asked with concern as he reached out for her hand.

"Yes of course it is wise. I am still able to carry a bow and arrow and shoot them with accuracy," Saphina said. Annoyed by his response, she snatched her hand away from his.

"Saphina you are very courageous dear, but I don't think that will be necessary," Enyce said kindly. Everyone who knew Saphina instantly saw that she was insulted by the way Enyce spoke to her. Neither had the long journey or her pregnancy softened her quick temper. She was about to retort crossly when her mother interjected.

"Saphina, we will need you here. The Elfkins will not take this new land well and we will need your leadership....skills to keep them calm," Zusie said tactfully.

"You mean you will need me to put them in their place," Saphina retorted.

"Yes that as well," Zusie said and smiled. Aldwin sighed in relief when Saphina nodded.

Everyone turned sharply as a high pitched scream came from the encampment. Zusie and the others cringed; they knew that scream well. They had heard it several times over the journey. Paramo was awake. They hurriedly made their way to the encampment.

Just as they entered the outer circle, Rhethea came rushing towards them. "Ah, thank the Light of Goodness you are here," she panted. "Paramo hasn't stopped arguing with me since she got up this morning. I was just going for spice balls to shut her up until you got here." Rhethea looked exasperated. The Elders and fairies knew she was not past using the spice balls on Paramo.

"That won't be necessary!" Enyce said.

"You should have given her a double dose of that sleeping tonic!" Zeander said. The Elders and Orliff looked at him in shock, then questioningly at Rhethea. She ignored their looks.

"She has been demanding to see her mate Martan," Rhethea said with irritation. "I have tried to reason with her, but the more I said no the shriller her voice became. She has awoken most of the encampment."

"Ah yes," Saphina said as she rolled up her sleeves. "I will handle this." And she promptly stomped off towards the screaming.

"Chrystalina and Janilli do you mind going with her?" Zusie asked. They both nodded and quickly followed after Saphina. Aldwin, Zeander, Paraphin and Bauthal followed her as well.

"Zeander," Andi called after them. "We are leaving at noon. I will send Zan to find you." Zeander waved his hand in agreement.

"It has been a long journey," Zusie said apologetically towards Rhethea. Rhethea's anger subsided slightly. She understood that their journey had been a difficult one, however no one else was screaming.

"Yes I can imagine it has been," Rhethea said. Zusie understood her subtle meaning and smiled warmly at her.

"Rhethea," Mitch called from one of the wagons. "Have you seen Jemas yet today? He was supposed to meet us at the saw mill first thing this morning."

"No," she replied, shaking her head.

"Well if you do, tell him we are starting in the east field," Mitch said.

"Yes I will," Rhethea said.

She bade the others a good day, saying that she would be

back after she found Jemas. She quickly walked towards the path that led into the village. It wasn't like Jemas to be late for anything. He had acted strange the night before; she hoped he was not ill. The Elders smiled as Rhethea hurriedly walked away. They too, like Orliff, felt that the pairing of the two was an ideal one.

"Enyce," Jolise said questioningly. "Do you think we could ask Miss Casey to print a bulletin that we can post around the village asking for donations of clothing for the Elfkins and Meadow Imps? I know the clothing will have to be altered but that will keep most of them busy while their new homes are being built."

"That is an excellent idea," Enyce said as her sisters nodded in agreement.

"Zee dear, do you and Jasper mind going back and asking Miss Casey to make the bulletin before she starts to print the *Village Voice*? She will know how to word it." Zee and Jasper both nodded and started back down the path to the village. The Elders turned quickly as a high-pitched squeal followed by a heated argument erupted from a group of Elfkins who had gathered around Saphina and the others. All of them sighed heavily. Talking with the Elfkins and what they could expect when they visited Elsbrier was not going to be an easy one.

*

Zee and Jasper were quickly making their way to the center of Elsbrier when they came across a gaggle of bastions blocking the path.

"Oh no," Zee said. "It looks like Homsa has left the door to the coop open again." Just as the words left her mouth Homsa came around the corner of his cottage carrying a small basket of feed and broom in one hand and a rather plump bastion in the other.

"Ah Zee, good, good, you are just in time to help," Homsa said exhaustedly.

"Ah Homsa, you left the gate open again didn't you?" Zee said. Homsa nodded sheepishly. Zee shook her head as she took the broom and a handful of feed from the basket. This had not been the first time since he came home from the Mediplace that she had helped corral the bastions back into their pen. They were quick and whenever he leaned his cane on the fence the birds would run out before he had a chance to latch the gate shut.

"Jasper, go onto Miss Casey's without me. I will catch up later," she said. Without waiting for his reply, Zee started to make a trail of seed that most of the bastions would follow. The broom was for the stubborn ones who often played peek-n-boo from behind the large gooseberry bushes beside Homsa's cottage.

Jasper quickly made his way to the *Village Voice*, only to find out from Marcus that his mother and Luke had gone to the Cropping of Rocks. Farley had reported that he saw a strange light near the hidden tunnel they found on the day the fairies fought the Jarrell brothers. Miss Casey and Luke had gone to see if it was newsworthy.

Jasper quickly made his way through the village. Instead of going down the path that led to the meadow, he chose to fly through the outcropping of trees that divided Elsbrier from the meadow. His stomach began to churn and an uneasy feeling came over him as he got deeper into the dark woods. He looked about nervously. The forest never made him weary of the shadows before. He saw the light of day up ahead and quickly darted around a large oak tree, but then came to a dead stop and fluttered in midair. Just fifty feet from the meadow two shadows appeared as if from thin air. One was of a person clothed in a dark hooded cloak. The other was of a roan with dark wings. They had been secretly watching the group of people who had gathered around the rocks.

As Nayew and Obwyn barked out orders, Jasper heard the stranger curse harshly as he stood and jumped onto the roan's back. As he did, the hood of his cloak fell. Jasper could clearly see the man's face. He looked familiar. Jasper's mind raced to think of where he knew him from. He then gasped loudly.
Jasper remembered seeing that man on the north side of Mount Aspentonia the night he fled from the Venom Horde. Jasper could not help himself and cried out the stranger's name. Jaja abruptly turned towards Jasper.

"You!" Jaja cried out. The rims of Jaja's eyes burned red as his anger boiled to the surface. Without thinking, he ordered the roan to take flight after Jasper. The roan did not hesitate and neither did Jasper. He took off darting upwards into the thick canopy of the trees. The roan could not keep up and Jasper was the first to clear the upper branches. He raced towards Obwyn and Nayew, all the while screaming Jaja's name.

Upon hearing Jasper, the group of villagers turned just as Jaja and the dark roan cleared the trees. Everyone saw his face, as the hood of the cloak still lay on his back. Jaja saw the shocked expressions of the villagers; people he had come to know; people who had trusted him. In an irrational moment of anger he had blown his cover. There would be no turning back. Jasper would tell them who he was and he would not be able to deny the allegations. Jaja cursed loudly and urged the roan to take flight from the meadow. They swiftly flew south. When they were sure they had not been followed, they banked left and flew towards the Firelog Forest.

Chapter 22
The Last Journey

Jasper quickly flew over to Nayew, while everyone else watched the large dark roan and the rider fly off in the distance. Some of them naively waved at the rider and wondered where the roan had come from, as it was not one of the Avidraughts. Nayew and Miss Casey were the only ones who didn't watch. She was busy writing while Nayew tried to calm Jasper down. He had heard of Jaja the night before while Jasper reported about his mission. If what he thought was indeed true, the spy who had infiltrated the village was Canvil's own son.

"Calm yourself Jasper," Nayew said. "Tell us what you are talking about." Jasper calmed his nerves. Before he started to talk he quickly looked behind him, making sure that Jaja had not followed him.

"That was Jaja, Canvil's son," Jasper said; the others standing near looked suspiciously around them.

"Are you sure Jasper? You have to be sure because we know him by another name," Nayew said. Jasper looked at him with astonishment, but then nodded his head. He would never forget that face or his brother Rishtoph's. They were imprinted in his memory and had haunted his dreams until the day he landed on Lizbeth's doorstep.

"You know him?" Jasper asked as a confused look lit his face. "Who is he to you?" Obwyn and Nayew looked at each other grimly.

"He is Jemas," Obwyn said.

"He has been living in the village for some time now," Nayew added.

Jasper gasped in shock. "So the rumours are true then. The Shadow of Erebos lives," Jasper said shakily. Nayew and

Obwyn looked at him curiously. This was not something they had discussed the previous night.

"How do you spell Erebos?" Missy Casey asked as she moved closer. "And what do you mean by, the shadow lives?"

"Casey, please!" Obwyn said.

Miss Casey looked up from her pad of paper. Seeing the concerned look on his face she looked around her. She was the only one not concerned with Jasper's news. When she looked at Luke and saw a worried frown knitting his brow, she comforted him with a hand on his arm.

"Go on Jasper, what is a Shadow of Erebos?" Nayew asked.

"Not what, but who," Jasper said. "The Shadow of Erebos is a member of the Spiedrux. They are men who are trained in the fine art of disguise, war tactics and can wield every weapon known to man. They infiltrate Kingdoms and become one of its citizens. They are told all there is to know about the land, its people and their spiritual artifacts. Sometimes they live for years within the Kingdoms. When they have all the information they need, they report back to Canvil. With the information gathered, they plan their attack. The Shadow is the most cunning of them all. He can change his look at will and has been known to lead double lives within the same Kingdom. He takes up residence in several of the surrounding villages too. He has been known to take lives as well. Silently, breathlessly, he moves about in broad daylight, none the wiser of who he is or his mission."

"How do you know he's the Shadow and not just a Spiedrux," Miss Casey asked shakily.

"I know!" Is all Jasper said.

Nayew did not doubt Jasper and addressed everyone in the clearing, "I would like everyone to leave," Nayew said. The villagers immediately left without question, except for Miss Casey and Luke.

"You can leave as well," Nayew said. "We will report...." He began to say but Miss Casey interrupted him.

"We are staying. We have news to report here," she looked up from the paper she was furiously writing on. Seeing the look of resolve on her face Obwyn and Nayew agreed that she and Luke could remain.

"Make sure you stay out of our way!" Obwyn warned. "Find the guards...," he said to Farley. "I want to take a closer look at this cave we found. Perhaps it will lead us to Jemas'...," he paused for a moment then continued, "Jaja's lair."

"No," Nayew said. "If what Jasper says is true he might be posing as one of those guards. We need to find people we are sure we can trust." Just then, Zee came running forward.

"I heard what happened. Are the rumours true?" Zee asked anxiously. Obwyn nodded his head. It did not take the villagers long to spread the news that Jemas had been the spy; soon the whole village would know.

"What can I do?" She asked without hesitation.

Obwyn and Nayew nodded. They were glad to see that yesterday's battle had not dissuaded her from her mission.

"Find your sisters and the Elders. Let them know what happened. Take Jasper with you and bring back a half dozen Elfkins and the Jarrell brothers too," Nayew said. Obwyn looked at him curiously. "We can be sure," Nayew said, "That he will not be one of them nor one of the Tara Aquians." Obwyn nodded and immediately left for the Lily Pond to speak with Lindrella and Barton.

"Zee," Nayew said as Zee jumped on Farley's back, "make sure Rhethea comes with you. I don't want her hearing the rumours about Jemas before we have a chance to talk with her." Zee nodded and they were off. Miss Casey and Luke looked at Nayew.

"That was kind of you Nayew," Miss Casey said, "to worry about Rhethea that way."

"I am not worried about Rhethea," Nayew said. "I want to make sure she doesn't track down Jemas and dispose of him before we have a chance to talk with him."

Miss Casey looked over at her son as Nayew jumped onto the rocks. Luke was absentmindedly rubbing his chin. Rhethea had hit him hard in the jaw during tryouts for the Hawkeye team earlier that year. She had knocked him flat on his backside after he teased her about being a girl and that Hawkeye was a man's game. She showed him that she could play just as well as any man and made three goals, one right after the other, earning a spot on the team. No one ever teased her again and she quickly became a valuable player on the team.

"Luke, go to the village and bring back half a dozen lanterns and three coils of rope," Nayew ordered. Luke nodded.

Casey stayed him with her hand on his arm. "Ask Marcus to bring a blanket, a basket of food and my bonnet too. I have a feeling we are going to be here most of the day," Miss Casey said. Luke nodded and smiled at his mother. She couldn't pass up a good story and could find news in the weirdest of circumstances.

As Luke left for the village, Nayew quickly made his way to the crevice where they had found the entrance to the cave. The day after the tournament he and Obwyn had explored it. All they found however was a small, empty cave. If Jaja had been hiding in it he had emptied it before the tournament with the Jarrell brothers. Jaja was indeed clever. While he waited for the others, Nayew wondered whether or not there was perhaps a hidden passageway that led to a larger cave or a series of tunnels. Ashlina had been in the dark forest when she had seen the spy. He had appeared as if by magic. Perhaps tunnels led from the forest to the Cropping of Rocks. The more he thought about it the more he knew it was true. He wanted to start exploring but knew it was best to wait until everyone was there. Again, if Jasper's tale was true, they would need to explore the cave with caution and be on their guard for traps.

Before long a large crowd of people stood in front of the

Cropping of Rocks. Nayew and Obwyn grouped the volunteers together; one Jarrell brother to two Tara Aquians and two Elfkins. Each group would be led by an Elder or Nayew. The fairies and Jasper were to stay behind with Obwyn, Miss Casey, Rhethea, Marcus and Luke. Zeander and Paraphin had also volunteered and had already started to creep along the crevice to the where the entrance of the cave lay hidden behind the boulder.

"Sssomething doesssn't quite ssseem right," Paraphin said. The slits of his nose flared as he breathed in deeply. "There isss a sssmell here. I don't quite know what it isss." Zeander breathed in deeply, but could not smell anything. As the first group led by Nayew approached, Zeander raised his hand for them to stop.

"What is it?" Nayew asked as he jumped down from the rock and started to walk briskly towards them. Rangous, Septer, Barton and Lindrella also jumped down and started to follow.

"Paraphin smells something. Perhaps we should not proceed," Zeander said.

Nayew raised his hand for the others to stop. He took a small step forward before stopping as well. The bottom of his shoe caught on something buried under the sand. He watched as the twig that he stepped on broke in half. In astonishment they all looked at the fine silken thread that ran along the sand and under the boulder. Nayew's slight movement had pulled the thread taut. Nayew looked with concern at Zeander and Paraphin who stood beside the boulder.

"Move away from the boulder," Nayew said cautiously. Just as the words left his mouth however, a loud hissing noise came from behind the boulder. The sand under the boulder gave way. As the boulder rolled forward they heard a series of clicking sounds. In a panic Nayew, Zeander and Paraphin scrambled away from the boulder. They yelled at the rest of the group to get clear of the rocks. With Barton's help they quickly jumped onto the surrounding boulders. As they made their way across them Nayew yelled for everyone to get back. At first people looked curiously at them. Obwyn, realizing that something had gone wrong, frantically ordered everyone to run. Anyone standing around scrambled away from the area as fast as they could.

Nayew, Lindrella, Septer and Rangous were the first of the group to jump off the rocks. Because Zeander was so small, it took him longer to jump from rock to rock. Seeing this Paraphin picked him up with his tail. He quickly slithered across the last couple of rocks towards the clearing. Barton followed closely behind them. But they had not been quick enough. An ear-piercing explosion erupted, causing people and rocks to fly in every direction. Those who had made it away safely were knocked to the ground by the force of the explosion. Barton took the full force of the blast and was thrown fifty feet in the air. He landed on the ground with a heavy thud.

A moment of confused silence was quickly followed by wails of pain as a large cloud of black smoke rose in the air. All around bodies lay on the ground; some were knocked unconscious while others rolled in pain, holding the part of their body that was injured. Those not hurt in the blast immediately went to aid the injured. Orliff started to yell out directions to the fairies, whom had not been hurt. They however were already on their Avidraughts and making their way to the village to get help. He didn't have to tell them what they would need. They had all been trained in the art of healing. They would know whom and what to bring back.

Marcus and Luke helped Miss Casey stand. Upon releasing her however, she cried out and immediately fell back down. She grabbed at her hip as tears started to drip from her eyes. Marcus and Luke immediately called out for Orliff to come and help. Orliff quickly came over and examined her.

"She has dislocated her hip. There is nothing I can do for her right now," Orliff started to say.

"What do you mean there is nothing you can do for her?!" Luke cried.

"Look around you Luke," Orliff yelled. "There are those who are worse off than your mother. Get a grip!" Luke looked stunned. He had never heard Orliff raise his voice let alone yell at someone.

Miss Casey looked up at her son's distraught face. He had been the stronger of the two sons, taking care of her after their father passed away. She laid a gentle hand on his leg. Marcus looked at his brother, making sure he was okay before he addressed Orliff.

"What can we do to help?" Marcus asked somberly.

"Give her these for the pain, for now," Orliff said. His anger had subsided as he handed them a couple of pills from his medicine bag. "When the fairies return with the pokey and carri-shifts, take your mother to the Mediplace. Alamat and Niella will know what to do. And then return. I am sure we will need help!" Marcus and Luke nodded.

A cry rang out and was quickly followed by another one. Orliff looked over at the Jarrell brothers who were attending Rangous and Septer. Each looked to have broken their arms. Mitch and Aro were setting the breaks while Reg and Yan held the two Elkins down. Aro had broken enough bones over the years; he knew how to set them straight. As Orliff approached, he looked disbelievingly at Rangous as he made a joke.

"And I was so looking forward to fishing,' Rangous said as Orliff knelt down beside him.

"Perhaps we can fish with our toes," Septer joked. He grimaced as pain ran up his arm and into his shoulder.

Orliff gave them both a couple of pills for the pain and a flask of water to wash them down. "Make your way to the Mediplace as soon as you can, Niella and Alamat will put casts on those for you." Septer and Rangous looked strangely at each other. Neither knew what a cast was, but they nodded their heads anyway. Orliff looked at the Jarrell brothers and counted them; one was missing.

"Where is Ody…?" Orliff asked with concern as he looked around at the bodies lying on the ground. "And your sister?"

The brothers started to look around. They had seen both Ody and Rhethea get knocked to the ground, but knew they had been unharmed. While searching for their missing siblings they heard Ody's voice frantically calling for them. Looking towards the village, they saw him bolt towards them.

"I couldn't stop her!" Ody said breathlessly as he ran up to them. His brothers looked at the large bruise on Ody's chin, knowing instinctively that their sister had given it to him. They looked fearfully from one to the other. In the confusion, Rhethea had slipped away. No one needed to tell them where she went. She was shocked and heartbroken at first to hear that Jemas was Jaja. Her brothers watched, however, as a silent rage replaced the tears as she wiped them from her eyes. They hadn't seen her so angry since their parents had died.

They had warned her not to follow Jemas. She had obviously not heeded their warnings. Orliff saw the concerned looks on their faces. He had been witness to many arguments between the siblings. He had even tended to the brothers' wounds after they had vexed their sister to the point where she harmed them. Even though they had often complained about her, Orliff knew that they loved her dearly.

"Go," Orliff said. "Before she finds him and kills him. We need to question him."

The brothers needed no more encouragement than that. Ody stopped them before they could leave. "She took your Avidraught," Ody said looking at Mitch. Mitch grimaced as he looked around. It would be quite difficult to follow her without an Avidraught.

The fairies had just dismounted their Avidraughts and had overheard the last bit of their conversation. No one needed to tell them who 'she' was. Shanata instantly gave her reins to

Yan, her sisters followed suit. Mitch took the reins from Zee. She whispered, "Be careful," to Farley as she hugged his neck.

"Don't worry little one," Farley said. "We want to know who this Avidraught is that rides with Jaja. He is not known to us. We have our own questions to ask!" Zee saw the anger in Farley's eyes and knew that it would be more than just questions that were asked.

She gave his neck an extra squeeze and whispered, "I love you," before she let him go.

The fairies and Orliff said goodbye to the Avidraughts and the Jarrell brothers. They watched for a moment while the group of them flew towards Elsbrier. They were startled when the Elders approached.

"Orliff," Rayley said. "We need you over here!" Orliff looked at them with a worried expression.

"It's Barton. It doesn't look good," Enyce said.

The fairies immediately ran over to Barton; Jasper and the others followed. He was lying face up on the ground. Lindrella sat beside him. The force of the blast had ripped open his back, breaking his spine and damaging several of his organs. A thick puddle of blood had pooled under him. Lindrella's mother, Aldus, stood behind her. Her hand rested on her daughter's shoulder. Her father Gando knelt beside Barton and placed his hands on Barton's head. His fingers were splayed open and he whispered urgent words that no one other than Lindrella and Aldus could understand. It was the language of Awnmorielle.

"Give us peace," Lindrella said calmly without looking up at the others.

Orliff knew there was nothing that could be done for Barton and started to walk away. The others quietly followed him as the Tara Aquians who had walked over from the Lily Pond formed a circle around Barton. Zee, realizing what was happening immediately broke out crying and wanted to go back, but her sisters held onto her. They walked her several paces away, hushing her as they did. There was nothing that could be done. Orliff started to delegate a number of tasks. The Elders and fairies did his bidding without question. They were to assess the others and report back as to who was the worse off. He noted that Aldwin was standing unsteadily on his feet and looked to be in a daze. Orliff noticed that he gripped his left arm; blood dripped from a wound.

"Here," Orliff said as he quickly walked over to him. "You will be no use to me if you faint from loss of blood." Hearing his stern voiced seemed to awaken Aldwin from his daze. He allowed Orliff to dress his wound. As soon as he was finished, he thanked Orliff and went in search of someone to help.

Aldwin heard a cry for help coming from behind several large boulders and immediately went to them. Zeander was yelling for someone to assist him. Aldwin ran around the boulder and stopped suddenly; Paraphin lay under the boulder. Zeander was leaning his back against the other side of it and was furiously pushing against it. Paraphin's eyes were open but Aldwin could see that no light of life shone from them. The great Abo snake, the last of his kind, was gone to them.

"Zeander," Aldwin said as he reached for the little man. "There is nothing we can do for him now," Aldwin said as he tried to pull him away from the boulder.

"I can see that ya big dolt," Zeander yelled as he pulled his arm from Aldwin's grasp and wiped his eyes with the back of his hand. "But I can't be leaving him like this can I. He saved me ya know," Zeander sniffed loudly. "Just as the rocks started to rain down on us, he flung me from harm's way. I can't leave him like this!!" Zeander cried as he looked beseechingly at Aldwin. A lump formed in Aldwin's throat. He nodded and helped Zeander push the first boulder off of Paraphin. They slowly moved onto the others.

As Zusie, Saphina, Chrystalina and Janilli arrived with several villagers, they looked fearfully at the mass destruction before them. It instantly reminded Saphina of Zeander's village when it had been raided by the Longtooth Grosshairs. They frantically looked about for their friends. Janilli, seeing the Tara Aquians in a circle, declared simply that she was needed. Zusie and her daughters understood and nodded their heads. The circle of Tara Aquians was so large they could not see who was in the middle of it; they were saddened all the same. They had become close to all the Tara Aquians over their journey. It was heartbreaking to know that one or more of them were injured, or worse, lost to them.

Saphina anxiously looked around for Aldwin. Seeing him, she called out his name and quickly ran to him. Zusie and Chrystalina followed. Upon seeing her, Aldwin shook his head, indicating that he did not want her to come forward. She did anyway. Seeing Paraphin under the boulders, she immediately started to push the nearest boulder off him.

"Saphina...," Aldwin started to protest.

"Don't," Saphina interrupted. She looked at him crossly as she pushed at another boulder.

"Will you at least push the smaller ones, please?" Aldwin implored anxiously as he thought about their unborn child.

The night before the Rapcicors' attack they had felt the baby move in Saphina's belly. At the time it had been a joyous occasion. However, it had not moved since. Orliff had declared that both she and the baby were fine, but Aldwin fretted all the same. Seeing the troubled expression on his face, she moved to a smaller boulder. Zusie, Chrystalina and a couple of the Elsbrier villagers had come over and immediately started moving the rocks off Paraphin. When they were all rolled away, Zeander knelt down and closed Paraphin's eyes. He sniffed loudly as he looked down at his dear friend.

"Leave us," Zeander asked. He did not need to look at the others to know that they too were saddened by the loss; he could hear their sniffles behind him. However, he wanted time alone with his friend. There were things he needed to say to him that he did not want the others to hear. When they did not move away he whispered urgently, "Please!?" The others looked sadly at him, not wanting to go, but complied and slowly walked away.

While Aldwin and the two villagers moved on to see if anyone else needed help, Zusie and her daughters walked over to the Tara Aquians. As they came closer, the silent vigil around whoever lay in the middle of the circle erupted into a mournful tune. Zusie and her daughters quickened their pace. The Tara Aquians let them pass through and they were stunned to see Barton on the ground. Gando's hands were on his head, Aldus' hands were on his feet and Lindrella was knelt beside his waist. Her palms faced upward.

A bulbous light formed between the three of them and enveloped Barton in a cocoon. It looked like the large bubbles that had transported Zusie and her daughters through Lake Kellowash on their visit to the Golden City of Awnmorielle. This however was made of light where their bubbles had been made of water. They looked curiously at Janilli who stood just behind Lindrella. She mentally spoke to Saphina. Over the journey to the Whipple Wash Valley, Saphina had learned to harness her powers of telepathy and was able to converse with Janilli.

"It is called *The Last Journey*," Saphina heard Janilli say. "It is Barton's wish that with his last breath he would speak with his brother Duntar. They are transporting his soul to Duntar so that they may say their last goodbyes." Zusie and Chrystalina looked curiously at Saphina as she inhaled sharply. She quickly calmed her nerves. She could sense the Tara Aquians' displeasure for the interruption in the ceremony. She slowly shook her head towards Zusie and Chrystalina, preventing them from asking what was wrong. They looked over at Janilli who glared at them in warning. They knew they needed to stand still and not say a word.

Several minutes passed by. The tune from the Tara Aquians grew louder as the bubble rose above their heads, glowing brightly. The bubble held a shape similar to Barton's in it. Like a flash of lightning, it flew into the sky and quickly disappeared.

The humming from the tune slowed. Aldus and Gando relaxed but kept their hands on Barton. Lindrella relaxed her arms and brought them to her side. They bowed their heads and waited for Barton's soul to return. Several minutes passed by before a disturbance at the edge of the circle made its way inward. Gando, Aldus and Lindrella looked up as the soul of Duntar, not Barton, walked to the center of the circle and knelt down beside the motionless body of his brother. Duntar's last wish, it would seem, was to speak with his brother as well.

Even the staunchest of the Tara Aquians looked shocked at Duntar's soul. Kerchot must have performed the ritual; he was the only other Tara Aquian who was strong enough. Slowly, as was custom, they all turned their backs and closed off their minds so that the brothers could have their last moments on this earth, in this realm, in peace. Out of respect Zusie and her daughters turned as well.

Several moments passed before the Tara Aquians turned back again. This time however, they joined hands and started to hum a different tune. Zusie, Saphina and Chrystalina could not help but look down. Barton's eyes were open. His soul had returned to his body. He looked at Janilli with such pain it hurt them to watch. Tears dripped down his face and his chest heaved as he strained to take his last breaths. In her mind Saphina could hear what Barton was saying to Janilli. "He has loved you from before time began and will love you beyond the end of time." Janilli cried out. Barton had taken his last breaths to give his brother's message to her. She never knew how deeply Duntar had cared for her. She looked at Barton and mouthed *Thank you.*

Barton nodded his head stiffly in response. He then looked at Zusie. With the last bit of strength he had left, he wheezed out, "We lost. Canvil has breached the mountain. Prepare." Barton's massive chest quivered as the last breath escaped his lips. Zusie and her daughters looked at him in shock. He had taken his last moments to find out news that might help them in their fight against Canvil. They watched with horrified fascination as Barton's soul, like a willowy wisp of smoke, left his body. The Tara Aquians' humming turned triumphant as Barton's soul floated towards the clouds. Their harmonic voices rose and reached the furthest parts of the clearing.

The fairies, hearing the tune, knew instinctively that Barton had passed over to the other side. Without words, they huddled together and sent a tearful prayer to the Light of Goodness that Barton's journey to the valley of sweet bliss and tranquility would be swift and uncomplicated.

*

From the top of the great stone stairs, Lord Canvil looked down to the boats that were anchored and tied to the shore. Their sails billowed in the breeze and their wooden oblong forms swayed slightly with the waves. They were primitive compared to the ships he was used to, but they had served their purpose.

Monto's assumption of the Tara Aquians had been correct. They had not harmed them while Canvil held a knife to Queen Faywyn's throat. He and his army crossed the lake without mishap. They were also able to walk up the stairs that led to the clearing before the Hollow of Rock without interference. However when they reached the ledge, they noticed that a landslide blocked the entrance to the crevice. Right afterwards, shouting and screams of rage could be heard from the men Canvil had left to guard the boats. The Tara Aquians attacked and a battle ensued. Several of his men had died, but then so too had many of the Tara Aquians.

It had been a clever move, Canvil thought. Kerchot had allowed them to cross the lake knowing that they would not be able to use the Hollow of Rock to pass through the mountain. If they had gotten control of the boats, Canvil and is men would have been trapped. Canvil knew that Kerchot would have the upper hand and to survive he would have had to forfeit Queen Faywyn to him. But Canvil was a devious warrior and studious when it came to battle strategies. He had enlisted the help of the Jawbrenders. They were large ugly fish with long thick whiskers that stuck out on either side of their large gaping mouths. They could walk on land and breathe out of water for hours on end. The Jawbrenders were no friend of the Tara Aquians and when they attacked, they were ruthless. The battle was over not long after it began and Queen Faywyn was still under his guard. However Canvil was not pleased. He looked down at the fallen that bobbed in the water with the bodies of Jawbrenders that had died as well. The Tara Aquians that had died, he noticed, were nowhere in sight.

His mind raced with thoughts of his next move. His army had dwindled considerably with the fight against the Tara Aquians. He had a reserve but they were camped in a valley that was a week's ride from Boswick. Spiedrux had infiltrated its borders over two years ago. They had reported back that if Canvil took Boswick he would have a way into the Whipple Wash Valley. He had ruled against it however and decided to go over the mountain range, which he was now regretting.

A cold breeze blew across Canvil's face. Winter would soon arrive to the valley. If they stayed, the remaining Tara Aquians may figure a way to steal Faywyn away from him. If they left the valley and met up with the reserve, which was his best choice, they may find a way to follow. He needed to stop them. He looked over at Ibisha and Egreta who returned his look thoughtfully; an idea quickly formed. As he hastily descended the steps, he ordered Rishtoph to bring the prisoners. Ibisha and Egreta followed.

As they neared the bottom stairs Canvil he shouted, "We are leaving. We will meet up with our comrades in the east. If we take Boswick we will have a clear path to the Whipple Wash Valley from there. But before we go take those bags," he said pointing to bags that sat in an open chest; Padmoor stood beside it. "And place them along the shoreline; several hundred feet on either side, and position them half way up the stairs." The bags he spoke of had been filled with tubes that had been joined together with a thin rope. The tubes were filled with a liquid that when ignited with fire, exploded.

The clear liquid inside the tubes had been Padmoor's concoction- a potion that he had happened upon quite by accident. He was simmering a pot of bloodleaf bark with the strained sap from a fever brush tree. While stirring it, a bit of the potion had dripped down the side. When it reached the fire it exploded, knocking the pot clear off the burner it was simmering on. It had taken some time for him to get the correct amount of each ingredient before the potion was stable to use and carry without incident.

Several of the Venom Horde came forward and carefully took a bag from him. They had used the tubes before and knew how dangerous the potion inside of them could be. Even though Padmoor had told them it would not ignite with fire, they were still wary of it.

"You mean to bring down the mountain?" Rishtoph asked in disbelief as he stepped onto the boat and shoved the prisoners forward. Canvil looked at his son irritably. Out of all his sons Rishtoph was the most anxious but the least qualified to take over the Kingdom. He would have killed him long ago if it had not been for the fact that only two of his sons remained. Jaja was the most qualified to run the Kingdom, but was the least bit interested. He preferred to travel the lands and spy for his father. Canvil was proud of his son's accomplishments even though he never told him so.

"Don't be ridiculous," Canvil said before clicking his tongue in annoyance. "I do not have enough power to bring down a mountain. However, I can destroy the entrance to their underwater caves before we leave this valley. If that is where Kerchot and his band of rebels have taken their dead, they will be trapped there with no chance of escape. The rotting flesh of their deceased will soon decompose and

Kerchot and his men, with no fresh air or way of escape, will die as well."

"You are a despicable monster," Queen Faywyn shouted as Ibisha and Egreta tied her and Summeria to the main mast in the center of the boat. Ibisha raised her arm and backhanded Faywyn in the face for being disrespectful to her liege. Summeria cried out and tried to come to Faywyn's aid as Ibisha raised her arm readying it to strike again. Egreta stopped Summeria though by grabbing her hair and smashing the back of her head against the post. Summeria's head lulled to the side as she tried to remain alert, but the blackness took over and she fell unconscious.

"Enough!" Canvil yelled.

Ibisha and Egreta immediately looked remorseful. They quickly bowed their heads and stepped away. Canvil walked over and knelt in front of Summeria. He looked her over quickly before he stood. A large bump had formed on the back of her head; she would be fine, but would have a headache once she woke.

"There," he sneered at the maidens as he pointed to the other side of the boat. They hurried to the other side and huddled together shaking with fear. Rishtoph looked at his father in surprise as he ordered one of the men to finish tying the prisoners to the mast. It was the first time his father had raised his voice at the elder maidens or ordered them around with such scorn. Rishtoph's look then changed as he wondered if his father had fallen for the witch woman. He was conniving and kept the assumption to himself, banking the information for future use.

After the bags were placed the men climbed back into the boats and pushed off from shore. "Take us out far enough away so that when the bags ignite we will not be caught in the downpour of rocks, but close enough so that you can still fire arrows at them," Canvil ordered.

The others were caught up with rigging the sails and manning the oars. No one saw the slight movement of blinking eyes on a ledge fifty feet up on the stone face. Covered from head to toe in grey coloured mud, Bablou stood motionlessly. He had overheard everything that Canvil was planning. He had to find Kerchot and warn him. He walked quietly and stealthily along the ledge then disappeared through a crack.

Once safely inside he took no time making his way down a long flight of stairs that led to a hidden door. The door entered into a passageway that branched off in two directions. The one on the right led to his home while the one on the left lead to the Golden City of Awnmorielle. Bablou took the passage to the left and quickly continued down it until he came to another door. He unlocked the door with a key that was on a chain around his neck. He moved a tapestry that hung over the door to the side as he silently slipped into a dark room. The crystals that hung from the ceiling lit up and illuminated the room in a soft glow.

This had been Desamiha's sitting room. Bablou quickly walked by the large chair that sat in the middle of the room. He noticed that a green robe was neatly draped over the chair. The bookshelves that lined the room, the tapestries and the chairs were all covered in a thick layer of dust. The room had been untouched by the Tara Aquians in reverence to the one they called Desamiha, who was really Janilli; sister to his friend Zusie. His heart panged at the memory of her pleading with them to leave the mountain and come with them. He thought with certainty that Canvil could not hurt them, but he was wrong. Whatever was in those bags could cause mass destruction. Canvil was more devious and cruel than Bablou ever imagined someone could be. There was no honour in the way he conducted himself or the things he ordered his men to do.

Time was of the essence however and he quickly made his way down a long hallway and through the throne room. He had come this way once before just after Zusie and the others left for the Whipple Wash Valley. He had carried a note to

Kerchot from Lindrella that had explained who he was and that they had made it safely to the other side. As he entered the throne room the first tremors from the exploding bags rocked the Golden City of Awnmorielle. He quickened his pace.

Just ahead he could hear hurried footsteps scrambling around as a second wave of tremors rocked the large golden walls. The tiled walls cracked. Bablou ran towards a large group of soldiers who had been chanting in a large circle. In the middle of the circle were the bodies of their comrades. No one looked up as Bablou ran past them.

The great city began to crumble as another wave of tremors hit. Bablou was knocked to the ground as he ran past the statue of Awnmorielle. The crystal statue teetered on its stand as water sloshed out of the fountain that surrounded it. The benches that surrounded the fountain rocked with the next tremor and toppled over. Bablou jumped over them and ran to a large archway. How he knew that that was where he would find Kerchot he would never know. It was as if someone was guiding him to the stone ledge at the entrance to the city.

He found Kerchot kneeling and chanting beside the body of Duntar. Bablou was saddened; Duntar had been his interpreter to Kerchot and his friend. How he was going to convey what he needed to say he did not know. Without thinking he ran up to Kerchot and grabbed his arm. Kerchot awoke from the chant and immediately grabbed Bablou by the throat. He stood, bringing Bablou with him. Kerchot was several feet taller than Bablou and held him in midair. Bablou immediately kicked at Kerchot's midriff and pounded his fists on Kerchot's arms as he tried to break the vice-like hold. Kerchot however could not be budged and he only held on tighter. Kerchot then brought Bablou face to face with him. Bablou watched as a light shone in Kerchot's eyes as he realized that it was Bablou that he had in a death grip. He immediately released him. Bablou fell to the ground and gasped for air.

The large stone pillars on either side of the entrance started to crack as another tremor hit. Kerchot had been deep in the *Burlyum Chant* and had not realized what was happening. He looked curiously at Bablou as he stood. The last tremor had weakened the city's structure enough that great boulders began to fall.

Bablou cried out, "We must leave!" He grabbed for Kerchot's hand trying to drag him forward. The stone ledge cracked open just twenty feet from where they stood. A large chunk began to slide into the water. Duntar's body had been on that slab. As his body fell into the water Kerchot cried out. He ran to the edge but Duntar's body had already slipped under the water.

"Kerchot we must leave!" Bablou bellowed. Kerchot understood and followed closely behind Bablou. Kerchot knew he had to get the rest of his men to safety. As they passed the statue of Awnmorielle, it teetered then fell forward, narrowly missing them. They ran as fast as they could to the eating chamber where the injured had been taken.

Kerchot immediately ordered that they were to follow Bablou. The Tara Aquians picked up their injured and followed Bablou. They maneuvered around large chunks of blocks that had started to fall from the walls and ceilings as the inner city began to crumble around them. They did not have enough time to run back through to Desamiha's chamber. Instead Bablou lead the Tara Aquians up a set of stairs to the healing chamber. The crystals that hung from the chamber ceiling flickered and began to fall as another tremor rocked through the city. Several of the Tara Aquians at the back of the group screamed out as the sharply pointed crystals dropped down on top of them, running them through.

Kerchot looked back as he heard their cries, but his fellow soldiers pushed him forward. Bablou guided them through an outer chamber that led to the great throne room. Instead of going through the door to the room he ran to a tapestry that hung on the wall. He motioned for Kerchot to move the tapestry to the side. Kerchot was surprised to see that there was a door behind it. Bablou took the key from around his neck and unlocked the door. The Tara Aquians followed Bablou through it. They quickly ran down a dark passageway. The further they got away from the city the less they could feel the tremors. When the tremors ceased altogether they slowed their pace. They walked for several hours down the passageway that not only curved dramatically but also ascended and descended steeply. Bablou had no problem maneuvering through it; the Tara Aquians however, often bumped their heads on the low ceiling. Just when they thought they could not stand it anymore the passageway grew larger and brighter as crystals in wall sconces lit their way.

They traveled silently for another hour or so. All the while Kerchot went over and over in his mind what had happened. Guilt took over as he thought of the men he had lost. Tears welled up in his eyes as he thought of Duntar and Barton, who had come to say goodbye to his brother, only to find that he too lay at death's door. He thought of the Jawbrenders who had ruthlessly attacked them in droves. They had no chance. He gave the command to retreat, but not before Duntar had been surrounded by a band of the ferocious fish. All Kerchot could do was kill as many of them as possible while arrows rained down on them from Canvil's men. He was able to pull Duntar away but could tell instantly that he would not make it.

Overwhelmed, tears blurred his vision as he thought of the men who had been trapped in the city. He wanted to go back for them, but knew that it was too late for them as well. Dread began to take over his mind and creep into his soul. He wondered fervently who would sing the *Burlyum Chant* that would send their souls on their last journey to sit in the arms of the All Mother, Awnmorielle. His mind raced with questions that he could not answer. What was he going to do with the injured that moaned in pain behind him? How was he going to care for them? How many more men was he going to lose? How was he going to save Queen Faywyn and return her home? He remembered the look of fear on her face as Canvil held the knife to her throat. Great emotion welled up and cried openly. He was a mighty warrior, none could match his skill and strength, but even mighty warriors felt heartache. What were they going to do? How were they going to rescue Queen Faywyn and help the fairies win the war against Canvil's invading army with no weapons to protect themselves? Quietly he mumbled the *Repentance Chant* to Awnmorielle and urgently asked her to show him the way.

Just up ahead a bright light shone from a large arched doorway. Kerchot rubbed the tears away from his eyes with the back of his hands as Bablou stepped through the arch. Kerchot followed but then stopped when he stepped onto a large landing. He looked around in surprise at the large cave. It was lit with bright crystals that hung from the ceiling. A waterfall cascaded out from a large hole in the rock face and flowed down into a pool on the cave floor. Plants in several shades of green cascaded over the edges of large landings that were connected by staircases. Members of the Boulder Clan looked up from the cave floor and waved enthusiastically at Bablou and the visitors.

"Welcome to my home!" Bablou said with pride as he looked up at Kerchot.

Kerchot looked down at Bablou and smiled weakly. He and his comrades followed Bablou down the many sets of stairs to the cave floor. Upon reaching it the injured were taken to the infirmary and all but Kerchot was taken to the dining hall where food had been set out for them. Bablou motioned for Kerchot to follow him. They walked down a long hallway and came to a door. Bablou opened the door and stepped to the side. Kerchot looked around in disbelief. He then looked down at Bablou, wondering if he had read his mind or understood the words of the *Repentance Chant*. Bablou had led him to a fully stocked armory with every weapon known to man. Kerchot picked up a finely made sword off a shelf next to the door and swung it in a large arc before he thrust if forward. *Perhaps*, he thought, *all is not lost.*

Chapter 23
Compromised

A group of volunteers from Elsbrier walked about carefully as they cleared the rubble around the Cropping of Rocks. The large boulders that had not been broken in the blast were rolled back to where they had stood for thousands of years. The broken pieces were put in carri-shifts and transported to the Pixies who would break them down further and use them for the pathways that wound their way through Elsbrier.

Another group of volunteers were in the village helping the Pixies clean up as well. The vibrations from the explosion had reached the village; planters had been knocked to the ground, some of the vendors' stands had received damage and one of the bridges had collapsed and fell into the Grandiflora River.

When the explosion happened, several citizens and visitors to the village came running from all directions into the clearing. Elder Enyce immediately took charge and started to yell out directions. The injured had been taken to the Mediplace. The dead were taken to the Forest of Glen where the Cross Over Point was located. Their bodies would be set in the Galadome Fire Pit that sat just outside of the forest and their ashes later would be spread on the forest floor like all the ashes of those who had gone on before them. A candlelit night vigil would be conducted in three days' time. *The Light Remembrance* chant would be sung while the Elders spread the ashes. The Tara Aquians chose to take Barton's body and would conduct their own cross over ceremony in private, but had agreed that he would have wanted his ashes to be spread next to his friend Paraphin.

Just as Obwyn and Nayew were instructing the volunteers to go home to their families, a group of armed men riding massive black roans could be seen crossing the clearing. A large covered carriage pulled by a team of impressive white roans followed them. Several smaller carriages came afterward pulled by two brown coloured roans each. Six covered carri-shifts, pulled by pokeys, brought up the rear. Nayew looked quizzically at Obwyn.

"I suspect it is Lord Warden and his Hawkeye team," Obwyn said. He then asked one of the villagers to let the Elders and Hamy know that Lord Warden had arrived. Obwyn and Nayew stayed to greet them.

When the carriage pulled up alongside them they looked speculatively at it as neither had seen anything quite like it before. The deep purple carriage was decorated with ornately carved white peacocks. Gold overlay outlined the peacocks' tail feathers and the eyes were made from gold jewels. As the carriage stopped, one of the two footmen jumped down from the back of it. He was lavishly dressed in white pants and a jacket. His shirt was a deep purple and had a gold band around the collar and cuffs. He walked to the carriage door and pulled out a set of steps that were hidden under the carriage. He latched the steps into holes on either side at the bottom of the door. He then opened the door, bowed and said grandly, "The Lady Rosetta Regina Balacourt."

A woman dressed in the finest gown either of them had ever seen before stepped to the door and held out her gloved hand. Obwyn wiped his hands on his shirt then immediately stepped forward and helped her down the steps. The woman had pale skin and pale blonde hair that cascaded in ringlets down her back. She was delicate in facial features and the gloves she wore were of finely weaved lace. In a whisper she thanked him then smiled lightly before walking away. Her voice was soft. As she walked across the grass, her pale gold coloured gown swished softly. It was embellished with an intricate floral pattern made of fine thread of gold. A faint scent of flowers lingered in the air behind her; Nayew smirked as Obwyn stared after her.

Next to be announced was Lord Warden. He stepped down from the carriage with agility. He was a handsome fellow with dark features, blue eyes and a cheeky smile that the women loved. He was dressed in a finely tailored suit. A dark purple cape hung to his feet and was held together with a gold and jeweled clasp. Upon seeing Nayew and Obwyn he immediately walked over to them and shook their hands firmly. Although they had never seen the woman before, they knew Lord Warden well. It had been four years since last they seen him. Not much had changed; he was still as physically fit as before. There was however a streak of grey in his sideburns and he had a goatee that hadn't been there before. They had all aged over the years and although Nayew and Obwyn's hair had not started to turn grey they did have aged lines at the corners of their eyes.

Next to be announced was Herb Marrona, Captain of the Boswick Trappers. He bounded from the carriage and enthusiastically shook first Obwyn's hand then Nayew's. He was a handsome young man with dark features, dark eyes and was too good looking for his own good. He was as ruthless and competitive on the playing field as he was socially. He had a cocky smile that the young women fell for and when he winked and smiled at them they nearly swooned into a faint at his feet.

Lord Warden looked quizzically around him before he addressed them, "It looks like you have had a bit of trouble here. Have the Orhem Raiders arrived before us?" Lord Warden asked.

"No," Nayew said plainly but did not offer any explanation. The Elders had told them what the Radeks had seen and heard the last time they had been in Boswick. Neither of them was sure who they could trust. Lord Warden looked speculatively at them both for moment before he nodded.

"As you heard this is the Lady Balacourt. She is sister to Sir Nicholi Balacourt," Lord Warden said plainly as if Nayew and

298

Obwyn knew who he spoke of. However they looked back him questioningly. "Ah yes, I forgot. He goes by another name here doesn't he?" Lord Warden looked at Herb for assistance.

"Hamy," he said with a big smile. "They call my cousin Hamy."

"Yes, yes that is it. What a deplorable name," Lord Warden said snootily. "But he is heir to a Kingdom. I suppose he can call himself whatever he likes."

"It is a name given to him by our father when we were children," Rosetta said in defense. "He was quite funny as a child, always hamming it up for our parents." Her face was sad as she mentioned her parents; a look that Obwyn did not miss nor did Nayew. Something was amiss.

"Hamy is waiting for you. I believe he has your rooms ready," Nayew said. "Do you care to walk into the village with us or ride?"

Rosetta was about to answer but Lord Warden gently took her by the elbow and led her back to the carriage. "We will ride," he said over his shoulder. "I would hate for Rosetta to twist an ankle on this rubble." Rosetta looked back and smiled an apology to Nayew and Obwyn. Herb bowed to them and leapt back into the carriage after Lord Warden and Rosetta entered.

Obwyn waited for the last carri-shift to go by them before he spoke. "Do you get the feeling that something is not right?"

"Yes indeed," Nayew said, and then he looked up at the sky. "The sun will soon set. I believe Rayley has invited us for dinner. I think it wise to tell them that we suspect something is amiss with our visitors," Nayew said.

"I agree," Obwyn replied as they began to walk towards the village. The rest of the clearing could wait till morning to clean up. "Did you see Lady Rosetta's face when she mentioned her parents?" Nayew nodded his head. "I hope she does not have bad news for Hamy. Today has been hard enough on all of us."

"I am sure he will let us know if something is wrong," Nayew said.

They walked the rest of the way to the Tree in silence. Just after they bowed to the Tree for permission to enter, Zan called out their names. They both sighed and turned around to see Zan, Arnak and Jopha running up to them. They were coming from the part of the village that had small boarding houses and cottages that visitors could rent. As the Tree closed its limbs Nayew and Obwyn walked back down the hill.

"He's not there," Zan said breathlessly. Just as Obwyn and Nayew looked at him questioningly Shanata and her sisters came running up as well. They had come from the direction of the Vendor Market.

"He's not in the square either," Shanata said.

"Nor the library," Mariela said.

Just as Obwyn was about to ask who they were all talking about Elder Andi, Phinney and Athia came from the newcomers' encampment.

"Neither is in the Mediplace or the newcomers' encampment," Elder Athia said.

"He isn't in the Gnome Gardens either," Elder Andi said.

"Nor is he in the Evergreen Forest," Phinney said. "I have the Pixies and Wood Spirits looking for him."

"What do you think this means?" Mariela asked shakily. She was more nervous than the rest of them.

Everyone started to talk as once. Nayew and Obwyn looked at each with bewildered expressions. They had no idea who they were talking about. The conversation quickly came to an end when Obwyn whistled very loudly. "If all of you can calm down for a second perhaps we can help out with whoever it is you are looking for," Obwyn said.

"Don't you know?" Elder Andi asked.

"Know what?" Nayew said with great agitation. "We have been at the Cropping of Rocks all day. If you are talking about Jaja we told you he took flight on the back of a black

Avidraught. I doubt he would be stupid enough to come back to the village. It has been a very long day. If you don't mind we would like to wash up and get something to eat!" Nayew was not one to get riled up easily so when he yelled at Elder Andi she did not take offense; it indeed had been a very long day for all of them.

"Sorry Nayew," she said calmly. "We thought you would have been told." She looked at her sisters who only shook their heads and shrugged their shoulders; obviously no one had thought to speak with Nayew and Obwyn. "Enyce asked to speak with Xander. She thought perhaps he could shed some light on what Jasper has told us about Jaja." Nayew and Obwyn both nodded their heads at the same time.

"And no one can find him?" Nayew asked.

"Who saw him last?" Obwyn asked. Everyone standing around could tell that they both were thinking the same thing they had thought when they couldn't find him. That Jaja and Xander were one in the same.

"I saw him two days ago in the library," Mariela said nervously as tears started to form in her eyes. "He was talking about books and their binding. How some of the older ones desperately needed to be fixed and that he would get onto it right away. I, I told him about *The Book* and that it was in need of care." Mariela stopped talking when she heard the Elders gasp. Everyone else looked at her questioningly; no one knew what book she was talking about.

"Please tell us you did not give him *The Book*," Elder Andi asked anxiously. Mariela began to cry.

"Leave us!" Elder Phinney said angrily as she looked at Zan, Arnak and Jopha. "And talk to no one about this." The three of them nodded and left in a hurry taking the path that led to the Vendor Market. The Elders and fairies immediately started to walk up the hill, Nayew and Obwyn followed them.

"What book?" Nayew started to ask.

"Not out here!" Elder Andi said tersely. The Tree let them pass and no one spoke until they were in the Gathering Room.

The rest of the Elders were there waiting for the others to arrive. Mariela wailed loudly. The Elders looked questioningly at the other sisters.

"Oh do shut up!" Elder Andi shouted as she looked with scorn at Mariela. Elder Rayley instantly stood.

"What is going on here?" She asked as she looked from the angry expression on Andi's face to Mariela who was trying to control her emotions as Shanata comforted her.

"We have been compromised sisters," Andi said and walked briskly to the table. She sat down with a thump next to Sianna. "I told you," she looked accusingly at Enyce, "that giving her *The Book* was a bad idea."

They all voiced their opinions that perhaps Mariela was too young to understand its contents or be trusted with the knowledge found within. All but one Elder immediately started to scold Mariela. The only one who didn't was Elder Rayley. Mariela would have preferred her scolding than the look of utter disbelief that quickly turned to despair. Mariela sank down in her chair and started to cry again, but quietly.

"That is enough!" Shanata said angrily as she looked at the Elders with scorn. The other fairies stepped forward and stood behind their sister. "Can't you see that she understands how wrong it was?"

"Wrong? Wrong!?" Elder Andi said angrily. "It was more than just wrong. She had no right to take *The Book* out from its safe place, let alone give it to our enemy."

"What are you all talking about?" Obwyn asked angrily.

"If Jaja is Xander and Xander is Jaja and he has *The Book*, then we are all doomed," Andi said sweeping her hand grandly in front of her. "And she put it right in his hands." The fairies immediately came to their sister's defense. They began to yell at Elder Andi. The other Elders took offense and started to reprimand the fairies.

A loud bang startled everyone into silence. They looked with shock down at the end of the table; Nayew had pounded his fist on the table so hard a chip of it had flown off and landed somewhere on the floor behind them. Obwyn stood beside him with his arms crossed angrily in front of his chest.

"What has gotten into all of you?" Nayew asked angrily. "What is this book you are talking about?" He bellowed then looked at Sianna. She looked inquiringly at her sisters, who all nodded in agreement.

"Why don't we all sit?" Sianna said. "It has been a very trying day for all of us. We are all emotionally charged. Perhaps having something to eat will calm our nerves and then we can talk about *The Book*," she finished saying. She looked at Rayley.

"Yes, I prepared a meal. It's in the warming oven. Perhaps Mariela and Shanata can help me get it while the other fairies set the table," Rayley said. Mariela stood and walked with Shanata to the kitchen. The other fairies immediately went to the side board and started to take out the plates and cutlery. "Make sure you set a place for Orliff," Rayley added as she followed Mariela and Shanata into the kitchen.

"Nayew, why don't you and Obwyn wash up?" Enyce suggested. They nodded their heads and left for the bathing chamber.

"I will go and get Orliff," Sianna said.

"I will come with you," Phinney added.

The rest of the Elders helped the fairies set the table. No one spoke as they walked politely around each other. The day had indeed been a trying one. It was as if a dark shadow of anger had descended on them and rubbed everyone's nerves raw. Perhaps food and a calm discussion would dissipate the shadow and lighten their spirits.

*

Sometime later Nayew, Obwyn and Orliff sat in shock as Elder Sianna finished her explanation of *The Book*. It was an accounting of the Elders and Queen Faywyn's time in the valley and how they got there. It explained where they came from and who sent for them. It also explained about the constant warring between the two Supreme Beings, Chaos and the Light of Goodness. It went into depth about the Whipple Wash Tree and how it came to be, and why it was so important to keep it safe. It also told of a plague upon the world that would infect the souls of men and bring them to their knees. The very last chapter of the book spoke of the heroes that would be born and save mankind from the evil plague.

"*The Book* is written in an ancient language that only Mariela and I can decipher," Sianna said. Mariela looked up from her hands that she had clasped in her lap throughout Sianna's accounting. She then looked with surprise at Elder Rayley.

"For some time now we have suspected that your special power is linguistics," Elder Rayley said. She then smiled as Mariela's expression went from surprise to disappointment in a manner of seconds. "This information displeases you?" Rayley asked.

"No, well yes, just a little," Mariela said as she looked at her sisters. "I was hoping it would have come in a grander way like my sisters had. I didn't even know that I received it." The Elders laughed lightly.

"Well that is because you have had it for quite some time," Elder Rayley explained. Mariela looked at her questioningly. "You have been reading books well beyond your years and in different languages since you knew how to walk." The fairies looked at their sister with surprise. All the times she talked about the books she had read, they had no idea that the books had been written in different languages.

"But I am sure my sisters," she started to say then stopped when they shook their heads.

"I know a couple of languages from my travels with the Radeks," Shanata said. "But not well enough to read books written in them." Mariela then looked around the table and smiled broadly. She had her special powers.

"I am to be the interpreter?" Mariela asked.

"Yes," Rayley said. "You girls will need someone who can decipher languages, codes, and hieroglyphics. You will also need someone who can quickly learn new languages. Little is known of the Kingdoms south of the Guardian Sea; you will need a linguist." Mariela smiled brightly as her sisters clapped her on the back and the Elders applauded her. Nayew, Obwyn and Orliff were the only ones not rejoicing. Frowns had furled their brows and turned down their mouths.

"If Sianna and Mariela are the only ones who can decipher *The Book* then why are you so worried that Jaja will give it to Canvil?" Orliff questioned.

"You don't understand," Elder Enyce said. "Lord Canvil is very old. He has been on this earth for a very long time and possesses powers that no other human being has."

"Are you saying he is not human?" Nayew asked. Enyce looked at her sisters.

"No more secrets!" Nayew commanded. "We are all on the same side and if we are to battle against Canvil we will need to know everything." The Elders nodded in agreement.

"We suspect that he is a direct descendant of the Supreme Being Chaos," Enyce said gravely. "If that is true, then it makes sense why Xander, Jemas, Jaja... whatever we are calling him latched himself to Mariela." Mariela looked with shock at Enyce. "It is not your fault dear. Like the rest of us, you had no idea who he was at the time."

Mariela thought back about all the time she had spent with Xander, talking about the books she had read and what her favorite ones were. He had been so interested; she had never been suspicious of it. She instead thought she had simply found someone who loved books and reading as much as she did. Now it made sense as to why he always asked her to read to him. He couldn't read the books that were written in a different language. She looked apologetically at the others and then smiled when she came to Zee.

Zee was trying to stifle a yawn behind her hand but failed.

Within seconds of yawning, her sisters and Elder Jolise and Athia yawned as well. Enyce saw the weary faces of her sisters and the fairies. She stood and suggested that it was time to end the day and they would meet again first thing in the morning.

"But we have further things to discuss," objected Obwyn.

"Is it imperative that we deal with it tonight?" Enyce inquired.

"No I suppose not," Obwyn conceded. The suspicions about Lord Warden and Lady Rosetta could wait until morning. He then stood up as did Orliff and Nayew. They started to make their way to the stairs. As they walked to the steps Obwyn turned back and looked questioningly at Zee.

"What is the matter?" Orliff asked as he too looked back at Zee.

"Zee, where is Jasper?" Obwyn asked. Zee looked puzzled at him for a minute before she answered.

"I haven't seen him since...," she had to think for a moment longer, "Since we found out about Paraphin and Barton." She looked sadly at the others. "He had been quite upset; angrier than I have ever seen him before. I suggested that he come back here and sit for a while." She quickly got up from her chair and ran to her room. She came back into the Gathering Room with a note in her hand and gave it to Mariela. Scribbled on it was a short message written in a language that Zee could not understand. The hand writing was poor, but Mariela was able to decipher it:

Dear Zee

I have gone to help Rhethea find Jaja. Please do not worry about me.

Love Jasper

"Oh no!" Zee cried out. Mariela instantly dropped the note and started to comfort her. Shanata, Enna and Ashlina quickly ran to her side to do the same. The others in the room looked on with worried expressions, wondering if Zee would try and follow him.

"Zee, listen to me!" Enna said. "Jasper is a warrior. Look what he has accomplished on his own. He escaped from Lord Canvil, rescued the Elfkins, Meadow Imps and Tara Aquians from certain death, made it through the Hollow of Rock and survived the attack by the Rapcicors. He is stronger than you remember."

"I know he is," Zee said. Surprised at her reaction her sisters stepped away from her and the Elder's looked quizzically at her.

"He will be in good hands. Rhethea is a warrior as well!" Zee said nodding her head. Her sisters sighed. "We have things we need to do here. I trust in the Light of Goodness that Jasper will return unharmed." The others standing in the room also sighed in relief.

"Well then, gentlemen we will talk in the morning," Enyce said to Obwyn, Orliff and Nayew. They nodded and said their goodnights. "Girls off to bed with you then," Enyce said. "We will talk about today's events in the morning." The fairies said their goodnights and went to their rooms.

When all was quiet Zee came out of the kitchen dressed in riding clothes. She packed a bag full of food and swung it over her shoulder along with her sword and a quiver of arrows. She tied the knife Obwyn had given her to her waist and firmly held onto her bow. She quickly and quietly walked up the stairs and out of the hollow in the Tree. When she came to the leafy vines they would not part. She whispered for the Tree to let her pass through; it however did not budge.

"Going somewhere are you?" Shanata asked as she and the other fairies came out from behind the trunk of the Tree. Zee whirled around.

"You are not going to stop me...," she started to say before noticing her sisters' attire. They were dressed in their armour

307

and like she, had a sword a quiver of arrows and a backpack over their shoulders.

"You will need these if you are coming with us," Enna said as she threw Zee's armour to her. Zee dropped what she was carrying and quickly got dressed.

"How did you know?" Zee said as she buckled the belt at her waist and re-adjusted the knife in the sheath so it sat on her right hip.

"We are your sisters. We knew you would try and rescue Jasper," Mariela said. "Besides I have some questions of my own to ask Jaja," Mariela said with a sneer.

"Well let's just hope Rhethea hasn't run him through before we find him," Ashlina said.

Enna walked up to the leafy vine like limbs and looked expectantly back at the Tree trunk. When it did not open for her she growled menacingly at it. The Tree sighed and the vines slowly parted. Each of the fairies said thank you as they passed through.

They quickly made their way down the hill and into the village. As they came up to *The Baron's Den* a movement at one of the tables startled them. A dark figure came forward and the fairies raised their swords. When the figure came into the light they at first looked in shock at who it was. They smiled as another figure came forward and stood beside the other.

"Where might the five of you be going this late at night?" Zeander said as he looked up at them. Bauthal stood beside him; his arms where crossed in front of his chest.

"We are going to find Jasper," Zee said. Zeander raised his left eyebrow in question. "He went after Jaja."

If surprised Zeander did not show it nor did Bauthal. They had both seen the drastic changes in Jasper over the journey. Although at times he could be emotional he had matured as well. He had argued with Zusie when she insisted that he fly away and bring back help during the attack by the Rapcicors.

Jasper, they of course knew, had been afraid. Not from fear however, but from worry that when he returned with help it would be too late and they would all be dead. He still believed that if he hadn't left his brothers after the Venom Horde had caught them spying and tied them to the posts that they would still be alive. No matter how much encouragement he received from Saphina that he had done the right thing, he still blamed himself for their deaths.

"Well I guess we will be going with you," Zeander said as he and Bauthal walked forward. "I have my own questions to ask Jaja." The fairies knew that if Zeander had the chance to confront Jaja he would not ask him any questions.

"There will be no arguing," Bauthal added as he looked with resolve at the fairies.

"Alright then," Shanata said. "But keep up."

"How are you going to find him? Didn't he leave on an Avidraught? You gave your Avidraughts to the Jarrell brothers. How do you expect to follow them?" Zeander questioned.

"We know exactly where he is going," Mariela said assuredly. She had remembered Xander asking about the outlying communities. He had been very interested in Dunaster.

"It still doesn't explain how we are going to get there," Zeander said.

"With these," a voice said from the shadows.

The fairies immediately raised their swords, Zeander drew his knife and Bauthal bared his teeth. Upon seeing who it was they lowered their weapons. Hamy walked forward and handed each of the fairies a lead that was attached to a white horse that had already been saddled.

"Where did you get these?" Mariela asked.

"They are Lord Warden's. He won't need them for a couple of days or so," Hamy replied. Mariela smiled but upon seeing his face she frowned. Hamy's eyes were red and puffy. It looked like he had been crying.

"What is the matter?" She asked.

"It can wait until you return," he said. "Go on now. You are wasting time."

The fairies mounted the horses. Hamy picked up Zeander and put him in front of Shanata. He then helped Bauthal to sit in front of Enna. As Hamy walked back into *The Baron's Den* the fairies started down the path that led south out of the village. They would follow it for several miles until they reached the fork in the road. West would lead them to the Gnome Gardens; east would lead them to Dunaster.

Elder Enyce and Athia stood silently in the shadow of the *Village Voice*, not far from *The Baron's Den*. Datoka stood beside them. "Follow them," Enyce said. "But don't let them see you." Datoka nodded his head and took off after them.

"How did you know?" Enyce asked as she watched Datoka disappear into the shadows.

"Something in Zee's eyes," Athia said plainly. "I just knew."

Enyce nodded her head. As Shanata's mentor she knew when things were bothering her and sometimes what her next move was going to be even before she made it.

"Why did you let them leave?" Athia asked. "Aren't you worried about them?"

"The time of worrying about the fairies has come to an end." Enyce said. She started to walk towards the hill and the Whipple Wash Tree; Athia followed her. "The fairies will soon leave on their journey. We will not be there for them. They will need to make decisions on their own and trust that they are the right ones." Athia nodded in response. "We have taught them all that we can teach them, sister. It is their time now." Athia nodded her head again.

As they walked pass *The Baron's Den*, neither of them saw the slight movement from the curtains that hung in the window on the second floor. Behind it Lord Warden sneered as he watched the sisters walk towards the hill. He had been listening to the conversation Hamy had with the fairies. He angrily walked over to the table in the middle of the room. On top of the table sat a large object that was covered with a blanket. He whipped the blanket off and stepped back. The blanket had been covering a large metal cage. Inside the cage a firefly immediately jumped when the blanket came off. She grabbed the bars of the cage and pulled as hard as she could on them. She screamed but her cries were muffled by the cloth that covered her mouth.

"Ahh, you are a feisty one," Lord Warden drawled. "But you will soon see that there is no fighting the effects of the *Essence of Blue*. You will soon do my bidding." The firefly stopped rattling the bars and stood in the middle of the cage. She breathed deeply as she calmed her nerves. Lord Warden walked around the cage, looking closely at her. He had captured her on their way to Elsbrier. She had been dazed when one of his footmen had knocked her to the ground. He had yet to see what she actually looked like.

She had Pixie like facial features and body shape. Except for the rear end of her torso; it was elongated. Her body was covered in a skin tight suit. Her small bare feet only had four toes and her hands only had three fingers and a thumb. Her small ears were pointed and her short hair stuck straight up in a point. Her wings were delicate and iridescent. As he looked at her, her skin began to turn orange.

"Oh no you don't," he said and picked up a bucket of water that sat under the table. When the skin of a firefly turns red it burst into flames and torches everything in its path. A bucket of water will not only douse out the flames, but can kill a firefly as well. They won't drown from it but they could go into a thermal shock when the cold water hits their flaming skin. The firefly calmed herself down and her skin immediately turned yellow again. "Now, I have a mission for you," Lord Warden said. The firefly immediately crossed her arms and turned her back on him.

"Like I said there is no resisting the *Essence of Blue*." He went to the dresser by the window and pulled out the top drawer. He picked up a small wooden box and took out a vial that had a blue liquid in it. He walked back to the table. Seeing the vial the firefly instantly tried to run away from it. But with nowhere to go she looked pitifully up at Lord Warden a he tipped the bottle over. Three drops fell onto the firefly's head. Her eyes immediately glazed over and she marched to the center of the cage and stood erect. Lord Warden opened the cage door and held out his hand. The firefly stepped onto his hand and stared straight ahead as he carried her to the window.

"I have a mission for you," he repeated as he as he untied the cloth from around her mouth. "Find the one they call Jaja, and let him know that the fairies are on the move." The firefly nodded in obedience. Once Lord Warden opened the window she flew out of it and instinctively made her way south. Lord Warden smiled ruthlessly as he closed the window. All was going as planned.

Chapter 24
Rhethea's Revenge

The sun was setting on what had been a busy day in the village of Dunaster. Travelers who had not reserved a place in Elsbrier for the upcoming Hawkeye Games had found rooms there. Located at the top of the bluffs that line Lake Toriona, the village was growing by leaps and bounds. It almost had the same accounting of citizens as Elsbrier. It however was nothing like Elsbrier.

Instead of a quaint village setting that sprawled out into the countryside, Dunaster was a third of the size. The center square was surrounded by a labyrinth of narrow roadways that curved in and around the village. The buildings that lined either side of the roads were three and four stories high. A series of rickety looking staircases that spanned the height of the buildings gave access to balconies on each of the floors and rooftops. The vendor's shops were on the main level of the buildings and shoppers had to actually go inside to make their purchases. It wasn't like the vendors in Elsbrier who put their wares outside their shops under canopies.

Dunaster had become a major port for ships taking cargo across the Sister Lakes. Lake Toriona was the largest of the five lakes that were interconnected with large waterways. The bluffs reached as far west as Pleasantland and as far east as Warfdorte which sat nestled at the tip of Lake Iree. Dunaster, like Elsbrier, was busy even at night. With so many visitors arriving, the vendors stayed opened well past the time they would normally have closed. Street keepers lit oil lamps which sat on tall poles every fifty feet or so along the roads.

Rhethea, who had arrived in the village the previous morning, was walking out of one of the shops. She had boarded Mitch's Avidraught, Alwim, in a stable located just outside the village. She wore a pale blue hooded cloak over her clothes. The large hood hid most of her face from view. She wasn't known in Dunaster, but she didn't want to take the chance that someone might recognize her. Her search for Jaja so far had been fruitless. She had gone to each of the stables and asked if anyone had boarded a pure black Avidraught anytime over the past several months. The answer had been no. She couldn't give anyone a description of Jaja, because if Jasper had been correct Jaja would change his look for each place he stayed in. The black Avidraught however would be a little harder to disguise.

As she walked onto the next shop she had an eerie feeling that someone was watching her. She turned around quickly, but there were so many people walking by her she couldn't tell if anyone was spying on her or not. She continued to walk down the road towards the center square. By the time she reached the third shop she was positive someone was following her. She stopped in front of the next shop and pretended to look with interest at what the vendor had displayed on the other side of the window. However she was actually using the reflection of the window to look behind her. She glanced to the left then right; no one looked suspicious. A quick fluttering movement above her made her look up. Someone was staring down at her from the second story balcony on the other side of the road. She quickly turned; Jasper was sitting on the metal rail of the balcony.

"What are you doing here?" She asked. "Get down here right now." Rhethea put her hand out and Jasper landed on it. "Explain yourself."

"Perhaps it is you that should explain yourself," a gruff voice called out. Rhethea whirled around in shock. Coming up the road from the center square were her brothers. None of them looked too pleased to see her.

"That is a rhetorical question Mitch. You know what I am doing here."

"I know sister," Mitch said. His voice became softer. "You

didn't have to steal my Avidraught..." he started to say, but Rhethea interrupted him.

"Alwim is not yours to steal," she said defiantly, which made Mitch sigh.

"Yes I know, but if you had only asked I would have given...I would have asked him to take you," Rhethea looked at Mitch in surprise, and then looked at her other brothers; they all nodded their heads. Rhethea sighed heavily. Her departure had been rash; of course her brothers would want to talk to Jaja as well.

"How did you get here by the way?" She asked.

"Let's find a place to talk and get something to eat," Mitch said. "Then I will explain how we got here."

"There is a place across the square that's probably not too busy this time of day. It belongs to a friend of mine," Rhethea said. "Jasper, pocket or shoulder?" She asked and ignored the puzzled look on her brothers' faces when she mentioned she had met someone. Jasper looked around; the crowd in the square was getting denser.

"Pocket," he said and then curled up his snout. Rhethea opened the pocket on the left side of her cape and Jasper jumped in it. He wriggled around so that he was facing the front. All one could see was his head and shoulders as his hands clutched the thick band at the top of the pocket.

"A friend?" Aro inquired as they all started to walk towards the square.

"You've only been here for a day!" Yan said.

"And you have already made a friend?" Reg asked. Mitch and Ody smirked at their brothers comments but kept silent themselves.

"Well yes, but you know him too," Rhethea said as she led her brothers through the crowd of people.

As they walked passed a stage in the center of the square the brothers looked questioningly at each other. When they didn't speak, Rhethea looked back and seeing their puzzled expressions she explained, "Remember the Manker family?"

The brothers nodded. The Manker family had lived in Elsbrier up until ten years ago. Their father started a shipping company and moved his wife and their six children three sons and three daughters, to Warfdorte. The brothers had heard that they had been doing quite well for themselves.

"Well," she said, "Lendar moved here about three years ago and opened a little eatery and a boarding house."

"Lendar," Mitch said. "Isn't he the youngest son? He's your age right?" Rhethea could hear her brothers snickering behind her. She knew what was coming next so she stopped dead in her tracks just fifteen feet from the eatery and confronted her brothers.

"All right, get it over with now before we go in," she said as she stood with her hands on her hips. Jasper looked up at her with a worried expression. He knew her temper well and was second guessing his choice to ride in her pocket.

"Well, I was just remembering the last time we saw him," Mitch smirked.

"Yes I think we were picking him up off the ground, weren't we?" Yan said.

"I believe you're right brother," Aro said.

"I do remember this, didn't I carry him to Orliff?" Reg asked.

"Yes I think you did," Ody chimed in.

"I don't think I know this story!" Jasper exclaimed.

"Well, let me tell you about it," Reg said as he looked down at Jasper. "The day before the Mankers moved, Lendar tried to steal a goodbye kiss from our darling little sister."

"She would have none of it," Yan butted in. "And knocked him clean of his feet. I think he flew ten feet in the air."

"He did not," Rhethea said. "Jasper, don't listen to them. It's all lies."

"She hit the little blighter so hard; she knocked out his two front teeth," Aro said then chuckled.

Rhethea bit her bottom lip; she had knocked out his teeth. "There was so much blood and poor Lendar was in such a fit of hysterics I had to carry him to Orliff," Reg continued.

"You did not have to carry him to Orliff!" Rhethea retorted.

"Oh yes I did!" Reg said. Ody who was standing beside Reg nodded his head.

"It's a wonder he's even talking to you. If it had been me, I would never speak to you again!" Yan said indignantly. The brothers all laughed at the look on Yan's face. Jasper even laughed.

"Well, he's more than speaking with me, I slept here last night," Rhethea said then chuckled as she looked down at Jasper. When she realized what her words implied she immediately looked up at her bothers; they were no longer laughing. "Oh for goodness sakes," Rhethea said. "I slept in one of the boarding rooms; alone!" She emphasized.

"Yes, well that better be the case," Mitch said as he pushed his way past his sister and walked with purpose to the small eatery that was simply named, *Mankers On Market Square*.

*

The following morning Rhethea, her brothers and Jasper said goodbye to Lendar. He had been a wonderful host, fed them well and gave them each a room to sleep in without charging them. The brothers didn't even mind when Lendar gave their sister a longer hug than was normally acceptable. Each of the brothers shook his hand before they left and said that they would be back again for a visit.

The seven of them quickly made their way to the stables where they boarded their Avidraughts. After paying the fee they made their way to a place just outside of Dunaster. It was located on a beachfront about two miles down the shoreline of Lake Toriona. It was a small fishing port called Dover Point. It had a large dock that stretched out over the lake for several hundred feet. There were several outer buildings that housed boats and fishing gear. They were closed up for the winter.

Lendar suggested they look there for Jaja as there were also small cabins located in the forest nearby. Dover Point was a secluded spot this time of year. If someone wanted to hide out it would be a perfect place to do it in.

The Avidraughts quietly touched down two hundred feet from the first cabin. Mitch whispered to them to spread out and stand guard. If Jaja was there and got past the brothers they would need the Avidraughts to stop him from taking off. Farley whispered back that they would stop him at all cost. Mitch ordered Jasper and Rhethea to stay with Farley. Rhethea would have none of it and before her brothers could stop her she started to creep up to the first cabin. Jasper followed her.

"Don't even think about," Mitch said harshly as he pointed at Jasper. "If we fail we will need you to take a message back to the Elders." Jasper nodded that he understood and fluttered down onto Farley's back.

Rhethea and her brothers checked out each of the six cabins. No one was there and they looked like they had not been disturbed after the owners of them had closed them up for the winter. There were also no footprints on the soft ground surrounding the cabins either. Jaja hadn't been there or he had been very thorough with covering his tracks. They were just leaving the last cabin when Ody put up his hand for them to stop. He smelled the air and then hushed his brothers. He smelled the air again and walked to the corner of the cabin and peered around it. Through the trees he could see another cabin and relayed this to his brother with hand signs. Mitch motioned for Farley and the Avidraughts to circle around and come up behind it. Farley nodded that he understood and as they circled around, Rhethea and her brothers made their way to the front of the cabin.

Twenty paces away, Ody put up his hand for them to stop. He had come across tracks; several of them. Everyone squatted down and took a closer look at them. There were two distinct Avidraught prints in different sizes and several smaller prints that look like oversized bird tracks. Ody looked at his brothers and sister as he mouthed *Rapcicors*. The brothers and Rhethea immediately looked warily about. The Rapcicors were not known to come this far south and one never knew for sure how many there were. They worried more however about the second set of Avidraught prints.

They quietly crept up to the cabin. Although the cabin was smaller than the others it was basically the same. Stairs led to a porch that spanned the width of the building. In the front of the cabin there was a door on the left side and a window on the right. As Ody and Rhethea crept up the stairs their brothers went around to the sides and back. If the cabin was indeed like the others there would be windows on the two side walls, a door on the back wall and another small window.

Ody crawled over to the door while Rhethea crawled over to the window. She slowly raised her head to peer inside. It looked empty. When they heard the crash of the backdoor and Mitch call out they immediately stood and went inside. The place was indeed empty, but it hadn't been for long. Yan checked the embers in the small cooking stove; they were still warm. Reg checked the small bedroom while Aro checked the bathing chamber. Both were empty but they too had been used as recently as that morning.

Someone had stayed there, that was for sure. Although there was no evidence that it was Jaja, they knew it was him. There were Avidraught and Rapcicor footprints outside. It was not common for anyone else to ride the Avidraughts and the Rapcicors never associated with anyone outside of their own kind, up until the battle with the Elfkins and the other newcomers that is. Rhethea had heard from Shanata that Zee had seen a hooded stranger with the elder Rapcicors.

At the time of course neither she nor Shanata had known it was Jemas. As she looked around the place he had stayed at while he was away from Elsbrier, the thought that he stood by while innocent people were being hurt turned her stomach and fueled her anger.

"Rhethea," Yan said. "Are you ok?" Rhethea looked over at him when she heard her name. Yan was looking not at her face but her hand with a concerned expression. Rhethea looked down at her hand. She had drawn her sword and was holding the hilt in a tight grip.

"Yes I am fine," she said as she sheathed her sword. "What do we do now?" She asked to no one in particular. Before her brothers could answer her, Farley came to the back door.

"Felon and Amos picked up a trail leading south through the forest to the beach. There are footprints leading from the edge of the forest east along the shore." Rhethea was the first to jump into action.

"Do you want to ride Farley or Alwim?" She asked Mitch.

"Alwim," Mitch said.

"Perfect, I will go with you then if you don't mind," she asked Farley. He nodded his head and backed away from the door to let them out. Jasper flew off Farley's back and hovered in front of them.

Rhethea and her brothers mounted the Avidraughts and quickly picked their way through the forest towards the beach. Jasper flew beside Rhethea. They traveled along the beach for some time following the two sets of Avidraught prints and the several Rapcicor prints. Obviously Jaja wasn't worried about being found out. They continued on until they came to a section where the bluffs jutted out into the water several feet. The footprints separated; the Avidraught prints were no longer visible, and the Rapcicor footprints followed a path that gently sloped up the side of the bluff.

"I think we should take to the air. Perhaps we can spy them from up there and see what direction they went in," Mitch suggested. The Avidraughts took flight. Just as they crested the bluff they could see in the distance the band of Rapcicors running in a northern direction. They looked in the air for Jaja and the other rider, but could not see them.

"There!" Ody said. He pointed to a spot in the distance. A lone rider was making his way along the top of the bluffs.

Even from this far away Rhethea could tell that it was Jemas.

"Where is the other rider?" Mitch asked. The brothers and Rhethea looked around in the air first, but couldn't see the other rider. They checked the ground, but couldn't see him there either. "Perhaps they left at different times," Mitch suggested.

"That's quite possible," Ody said. "So who do we follow? The Rapcicors or Jaja?"

"Seriously," Rhethea said. "You needed to ask that question." Without waiting for Ody to reply she urged Farley to go eastward. Her brothers and Jasper followed her.

"What do you think she is going to do to him when we catch up with him?" Ody asked as he flew beside Reg.

"I am not sure," he said. "But I do know I wouldn't want to be in his shoes when we do." Ody started to laugh until Mitch hissed at him.

"Do you want to give away our position?" He said crossly. He then quickly made hand signals for them to split up. Ody and Reg started to fly north east, Yan and Aro flew south east and he, Rhethea and Jasper flew due east. They started to catch up to him just as he entered a forest that was longer than it was wider. However, it was full of underbrush and would take Jaja some time to pick through.

On the other side of it was a grassy knoll that sat next to a raging river whose current was treacherously swift as it made its way to Lake Toriona. On the other side of the river was another forest. Mitch motioned for his brothers and sister to land on the river side of the knoll just before a wooden covered bridge that spanned the river. After they dismounted they looked up at a large sign that hung down from the bottom cord of the truss:

BEWARE OGRE COUNTRY

No man no fairy no beast
should cross this bridge,

unless they wish
to come to their demise
as our midday feast.

"Ominous and poetic, how lovely," Rhethea said with a worried look on her brow. The bridge was entrance to the Greens of Totarrian; home to the Ogres. If the sign was not enough of a deterrent, the forest itself was filled with oddly shaped trees that had twisted trunks and canopies that looked like mushroom tops. As far as anyone knew this was the only the region the trees grew in.

"I thought they were illiterate," Reg said.

"Obviously not," Rhethea replied.

"Why is he headed for the Ogres home?" Yan asked as everyone dismounted their Avidraughts.

"You don't think they are in leagues with him, do you?" Rhethea asked Mitch. If the Ogres were in leagues with Jaja and his father the fairies would need to know. It was to be their first stop on uniting the Kingdoms.

"I know as much as you do about this," Mitch said with irritation.

"So do we let him go and follow," Aro said. "Or stop him before he crosses the river?" The brothers and Jasper looked at Rhethea. She gave them her answer by drawing her sword.

"Right then," Mitch said. "Farley you and the other Avidraughts stay here. Keep an eye out for Ogres." Without waiting for Farley to answer, Mitch crouched towards the crest of the knoll. Just before reaching it he dropped to the ground; he crawled the rest of the way to the top. His siblings followed suit; Jasper fluttered just above their heads.

Upon reaching the crest they lay flat on their bellies, peeked over the top and looked for Jaja. The river behind them was so noisy they couldn't hear if he was coming, but they would be able to see him. It didn't take long before they spotted him. He was about thirty feet from the edge. He was moving very slowly, taking his time. Mitch and Aro looked curiously at each other.

"What is he doing?" Mitch whispered. "Why is he moving so slowly?"

"It's like he is stalling for time," Aro said. Rhethea and her brothers looked curiously at each other.

"Aro, you and Reg go that way," Mitch said as he pointed to the left. "Yan, you and Ody go that way," he said. "And circle around. Rhethea and I will meet him head on." The brothers nodded in agreement.

"But you all understand he is mine, right!" Rhethea said pointedly. Her brothers nodded that they understood. They would not interfere unless it looked like Jaja was going to win.

"What about me?" Jasper asked.

"Stay here," Mitch said. "And keep an eye out for Rapcicors." Jasper nodded.

The others got into position and waited for Mitch's signal. He and Rhethea walked down the knoll. Just as they reached the bottom of the small hill Jaja emerged out of the forest; the black Avidraught followed behind him. He looked the same as he had when he was disguised as Jemas.

Mitch once again looked curiously over at Aro, who returned his look. Jaja was not surprised to see them instead he looked calculatingly at them.

"You are not surprised to see us?" Mitch asked. Jaja did not answer; instead he looked back at him with a calm expression. As Aro and Reg came forward the black roan pawed the ground with his heavy foot. He was a brute of an Avidraught; as tall as Farley but more muscular and wild looking. His mane and tail were long and his ears tweaked at each new sound. When Reg and Ody came forward he pawed the ground again. Jaja ignored the roan. Mitch had a sneaky suspicion that the Avidraught could not speak like Farley and the others.

"So it is to be the six of you against me," Jaja said with a drawl. "That doesn't seem quite fair," he added. With one fluid movement he took his sword out of the scabbard that hung from the belt around his waist. The sword was long and the hilt had thick twisted steel that fit loosely over his wrist. It protected his wrist and gave him free range of movement.

"No," Mitch said with a drawl imitating Jaja. "We are only here for the show." As Rhethea unsheathed her sword and stepped forward her brothers surrounded Jaja and the Avidraught. The Avidraught nickered and pawed his foot on the ground again.

"Stay," Jaja said and walked forward. "Rhethea, my love, you really don't want to do this do you?" He asked.

The endearment fueled her hatred for him and she raised her sword. Jaja was not surprised that she could wield it. One night while out walking, they had talked at length about her fighting skills. She had been practicing sword play with her brothers since she was a little girl. After hearing that, he challenged her to a match. He had found her skillful, but not someone he needed to worry about. At the time however she was fighting against someone she was falling in love with; a person who had only treated her with respect and kindness. She was hoping he would ask Osborne for her hand. Of course she wouldn't show him the extent of her skill for fear of injuring him or scaring him off. It had been her experience that men, no matter the age, didn't like women who were more skillful than they were. Especially at sword play and other things that were deemed male-orientated.

However, he was not who he portrayed. Underneath his handsome features, loving eyes and gentle smile was a heartless demon that had no remorse for the pain he inflicted or the lives he took. She would not hold back. Visions of the area around the Cropping of Rocks, the injured as they rolled on the ground wailing in pain and the blood that had quickly stained the ground came to the forefront of her mind. She let the last vision of her home fuel her purpose for revenge as she engaged him in battle.

Their swords clashed as they danced effortlessly at first around the area. Worried about the noise of swords, Farley and Felon galloped up the slope and stood at the top beside Jasper. He looked fretfully down at Rhethea and her brothers. Farley and Felon watched with relief however as Rhethea expertly countered every strike that Jaja made. The time slipped by quickly as her brothers encouraged her on. Jaja had nicked her twice; once on her left arm and once across her chest. She did not stop even though she could feel blood trickling down from the wounds. She ducked down from a strike. As she stood she twirled out of the way of another blow and slashed down with her sword. The twirl had caught Jaja off his guard and the tip of her sword split open his left arm from his shoulder to his elbow. Ignoring the blood that immediately started to wet his shirt, he looked appraisingly at her.

"You are better than you let on," he said.

"Yes. I suppose we were both pretending to be someone we're not," Rhethea retorted.

She looked quickly at his arm and felt no remorse for doing it. How quickly she had fallen out of love with him. She looked into his eyes and knew that it had been all a ruse and wondered if he had used magic on her, as she now hated him with a vengeance. No one had told her though that the opposite of love was not hate, but indifference when concerning the affairs of the heart. If she hated him, she still loved him and that could be to his advantage. As if he could read her mind, he said something that he had said to her once before while he tried to console her. The words spoken had had the desired effect and she had calmed down. Right afterward he kissed her so passionately it made her knees weak.

"You are beautiful when you're angry," he said. She paused for a minute giving him the advantage he needed. He knocked her sword from her hand. Rhethea cried out as pain shot up her arm and she fell to the ground. However she was not done and as she rolled away from his next strike she kicked his feet out from under him. Jaja fell hard on his back and his sword dropped to the ground. Mitch quickly ran forward and stepped on the sword, preventing Jaja from raising it.

Jaja quickly took his hand out of the circle of metal. As he was halfway to standing Rhethea tackled him. Again he was flat on his back, but this time Rhethea was on top of him. While she pressed her right knee into his throat, she bent his right arm backward over her left leg. Just as she was about to push down, which would break his arm, he brought his leg up and kicked the back of her head. Dazed, she rolled off of him; he rolled in the opposite direction. They both quickly stood and began to circle each other. Jaja kicked out and landed a blow against her hip. She winced as the pain shot down her leg, but she didn't falter in her stance. She waited for his next move. He kicked out again, but she blocked it with her arm. She then kicked out, but he moved just before it made contact. They circled again and when he came at her he kick out once again, but she moved just in time and his foot grazed her ear.

"Finish him!" Mitch growled.

Annoyed, Jaja advanced on Rhethea. Before he could reach her she kicked out with her right leg and it landed hard against his chest. He stumbled back and she advanced with a punch to his face with her left fist. She connected and his head swung to the side, giving her the opportunity to deliver an upper cut that sent his head backwards. Jaja stumbled once again and landed on his back. Rhethea immediately jumped on his chest; her knees were on either side, pinning down his arms. The weight of her leg on his opened wound made his head dizzy from the pain. He tried to ignore it and gather his wits, but he wasn't fast enough and she began to pummel him. Her fists were swift as she delivered blow after blow. All the while she was screaming that she wasn't beautiful and great tears dropped from her eyes and onto his face.

The black Avidraught advanced and before her brothers could warn her, it knocked Rhethea off Jaja. Farley immediately charged down the hill towards the Avidraught. Felon called out as she ran after him, but he didn't stop. Just as the Avidraught stood up on his hind legs, Mitch and Aro ran forward and dragged Rhethea out of the way. Farley ran into the Avidraught before he could stomp down and knocked him to the ground. The Avidraught fell hard and just missed landing on Jaja.

Chaos broke out as the black Avidraught got to his feet and stepped in front of Jaja to protect him. Reg and Ody came forward, but the Avidraught struck out and tried to bite them. They stepped back out of its reach. The Avidraught would not let them near Jaja. Farley and Felon started to attack the Avidraught, but he had gone wild with rage. He tried to bite them too and kicked out at them. Several blows landed on Felon. Just as Farley advanced he heard Amos yell, "Ogres!" He turned and watched as Amos and the others raced down the hill; Jasper quickly followed them.

"Ogres!" Amos yelled again as they came to a quick stop.

"Ogres?" Mitch questioned.

"Yes. We saw them coming through the forest towards the bridge; they should almost be there now." Amos said anxiously.

"What do we do about those two?" Ody asked. The black Avidraught still stood in front of Jaja; the extra Avidraughts had not deterred him from protecting his rider. Jaja, they noticed, was very slowly getting to his feet. There was no getting past the Avidraught without one or more of them getting injured.

"Something is wrong," Jasper said breathlessly as he caught up to the group.

"Yes we know," Mitch said with irritation. "The Ogres are coming."

"No," Jasper said. "Something is wrong with the fairies."

"The fairies," Rhethea said. "You can sense them this far from home?"

"No," Jasper said. "Zee sent me an image. They are surrounded by Rapcicors."

It didn't take long for everyone to realize that they had been had. Jaja wasn't in cahoots with the Ogres. He probably didn't even know they lived this close. Rhethea looked at Jasper as he nervously fluttered back and forth. Of course she thought. Somehow Jaja knew that Jasper would follow her and that Zee would follow him. Shanata and the other fairies would not let their little sister leave without them. It had all been a clever scheme to get the fairies away from the village.

"You," Rhethea said as she whirled around and stared at Jaja. He was trying to put his foot in the stirrup. "You were stalling us from going home, weren't you?" Jaja did not look at her as he winced in pain and tried to put his foot in the stirrup again. His silence was her answer. Enraged Rhethea rushed forward, but her brothers held her back. The black roan snorted, bared his teeth and pawed menacingly at the ground. "You are despicable!" She yelled at him. Jaja lifted his leg and swung it over the Avidraught. He winced again as he grabbed for the reins. Then he looked at her.

"This is war Rhethea, what did you expect!" Jaja said with a sneer as he stared back at her with a sinister glare. Rhethea looked aghast as Farley came up to her.

"We have to go now. I will leave without you if you don't come now!" Farley said. Rhethea nodded. She and her brothers quickly mounted the Avidraughts. As they took flight they saw the Ogres coming over the crest of the knoll.

"You're too late," Jaja said quietly as he and the dark roan took flight. They flew over the knoll several feet above the Ogres' heads. Jaja looked down at them. An Ogre who was taller than the rest returned Jaja's stare. He had an intelligent look in his eyes. Jaja sensed that he was their leader. He made a note to seek the Ogre out when his wounds healed.

Jaja flew east. He had a small place near Warfdorte and would rest there while he nursed his wounds. The loss of blood from his injuries made him weak. He laid down on the black roan's neck and closed his eyes. A vision of Rhethea came to him and he sighed. She really was quite beautiful when she was angry and could fight better than most of his men. *Too bad,* he thought, *she was fighting on the wrong side.* With his eyes closed Jaja did not see the Ogres follow Rhethea and her brothers.

Chapter 25
An Unexpected Discovery

The Ogres ran across the countryside with heavy footsteps. Tuffs of grass flew up behind them. They jumped over large boulders with ease and crashed through outcroppings of trees and bushes, not caring that they broke the limbs of thousand year old trees or crushed delicate vegetation under their feet. Elder Enyce and the Wood Spirits would be horrified if they saw the destruction the Ogres left in their wake. Just as they entered another cropping of trees their leader slowed. When they came to the edge of the small forest he put up his hand for them to stop. Their breathing, although heavy, was not laboured considering how fast and long they had been running. The leader looked shrewdly at the battle that was taking place in a large clearing on the other side of the trees.

The ones they had followed were fighting next to five young females. They desperately fought off a band of Rapcicors that had surrounded them. He was surprised to see that a little man rode on the back of a dogee and fought quite well considering the birds were several sizes larger than him. Beside him a large badger grappled a Rapcicor to the ground and grabbed it by the throat, ending its life with one quick snap. The Avidraughts that he saw take flight with the woman and the five men were also fighting off the Rapcicors. They either stomped on them or kicked them into the undergrowth. Several of the large birds lay dead or severely injured on the ground around them, but they kept coming out of the forest in droves of twenty or more at a time.

The leader of the Ogres instantly understood the strategy; tire out their enemy until they could no longer fight. It was a heartless strategy because several of their own kind would die in the process first. But by sheer numbers, the Rapcicors would eventually win. The Ogre leader listened carefully to a conversation that was going on in the small circle of defenders.

"Shanata it is time you and your sister leave," Mitch said. "Get on your Avidraughts and go."

"No!" Enna said as she cleaved off the heads of two of the Rapcicors. A third she knocked in the head with her shield. When it dropped to the ground she stabbed it in the heart.

"Farley, at least take Zee and get her out of here!" Mitch yelled.

"No!" Zee yelled back as three Rapcicors came at her. She jumped over their heads and landed lightly on her feet behind them. Surprised they came to a skidding halt and looked behind them. Farley instantly turned around and kicked two of them with his hind legs. They went flying over Zee's head and landed with a bone cracking thud against the trunk of a tree. Zee ran the other one through with her sword.

The leader of the Ogres smiled; the little girl had a warrior's heart as did the others. But their hearts were also kind for they would not leave their friends to battle alone. His right ear twitched violently and he looked east. Something was coming through the forest and fast. Not three minutes later a band of Rapcicors ran into the clearing; a hundred fold or more. The leader took less than a second to decide and raised his arm; indicating that they would join in the fight. The Ogre standing next to him looked crossly at him.

"Fielddegard, this is not our fight. Let the humans figure this out on their own," he said.

"I am making it our fight Rojon," Fielddegard said. "There will be a time when we will all need to take a stand. Pick a side brother."

Rojon did not wait to choose and spoke instantly, "I fight beside you brother!" He said. Fielddegard nodded then raised his arm again. The small band of Ogres ran into the clearing.

"What in the world are those?" Rhethea asked with shock as the Ogres ran towards them.

"Ogres!" Mitch and Shanata said in unison as each dispatched a Rapcicor.

"Shanata, Mitch there!" Mariela cried out. They looked across the clearing towards the band of Rapcicors that barreled down on them.

"Ogres and Rapcicors!? How are we to fight them all?" Ashlina cried out as she came up to fight next to Zee; Arturo followed her. He and Farley kicked two more Rapcicors into the trees.

"I don't know," Shanata said as she looked with worry at Mitch; he shook his head and looked with worry at his siblings. How were they going to fight the Ogres, they were so large.

As the Ogres neared they swerved around and headed full tilt towards the large band of Rapcicors. Upon reaching them they immediately started to swing their large metal spiked clubs. With one swipe they took out several birds at a time. The birds whizzed through the air for several feet before dropping to the ground with a dull thud. The Ogres spread out and stood with their backs to the fairies and the others. Seeing this Enna yelled out commands just as another band of Rapcicors came out of the forest to the west.

"Spread out," she said. "Stand with your backs to the Ogres. Farley you and the others stand behind us and take care of any birds that might get by us or the Ogres." Zeander, Datoka, Bauthal, Farley and the other Avidraughts took up ranks behind the fairies. Beside each fairy a Jarrell brother stood. Rhethea stood at the end beside Zee. With the Ogres on their side it did not take long before they heard a loud honking noise coming from the east side of the forest. The noise came again and the Rapcicors immediately stopped their advancement and ran back into the forest. Enna, Ody and Reg all yelped for joy at the same time making the others laugh. Their laughter quickly subsided however when they heard heavy foot steps behind them. They turned and looked up at the Ogres.

Fielddegard knelt down on one knee while his men stood behind him. Mariela cautiously stepped forward. *"I am Mariela,"* she said in the language of the Ogres. Fielddegard understood and nodded. *"We are the Whipple Wash Fairies and these are our friends; the Jarrell brothers and their sister Rhethea. These three are Bauthal, Datoka and Zeander."* When Fielddegard nodded they all nodded a greeting in return. *"Do you understand Elfish?"* Mariela asked.

"Yes," Fielddegard said. Mariela sighed gratefully. She knew their language, but had never spoken it at length. She was not sure of the exact pronunciation of many of the words.

"I am Fielddegard and this is my brother Rojon. These are our cousins, Kenkale, and Kevink. This is Bearl, his brother Arlesk and their sister Buneve." The fairies and Rhethea looked at Buneve with surprise expressions. She looked similar to the other Ogres, but her features were slightly finer. Although she wore clothes similar to her brothers they could tell that underneath she was shaped like a woman. When she took off the helmet she was wearing, they smiled. Her thick hair was braided. The braids stuck out from her scalp in all directions. The ends were tied off with colourful bands.

"Thank you for helping us!" Shanata said as she stepped forward and stood beside Mariela. She held out her hand. Fielddegard held onto it lightly and shook it. Her hand was engulfed in his, but he was gentle. "I don't know what would have happened to us if you didn't show up when you did!" She said. Fielddegard nodded.

"How did you know where to find us?" Shanata asked.

"We followed your friends from the grassy knoll before the river that borders our lands," Fielddegard said. "We heard fighting and came to see what it was about." Shanata and her sisters looked at Rhethea and her brothers.

"We found Jaja," Rhethea said. There had been no time before to tell them. The fairies looked at them in shock.

"Yes," Mitch said with pride. "Our dear little sister handed him his backside."

Aro stepped forward and put his arm around Rhethea's shoulder, "I daresay Jaja will be nursing his wounds for days to come!" He said as he gave her shoulder a quick squeeze. She brushed off his arm as her cheeks turned red.

"Are you alright?" Shanata asked Rhethea.

"I have a couple of cuts and will have some bad bruising but I will heal," she replied.

"That is not what I meant," Shanata said with concern.

"I know," Rhethea said. "I will heal," she repeated.

"How did you know we were here?" Mariela asked.

"Jasper received Zee's message," Yan said. Everyone, including the Ogres, looked at Zee.

"You sent a message to Jasper?" Shanata asked.

"Yes I thought if he had found Rhethea and her brothers they might be close enough to help out," Zee said. "I wasn't sure it would actually work."

"Excellent," Shanata said and clapped her sister on the back. "Well done!" Zee looked around; everyone was smiling at her.

"Where is Jasper?" Zee asked with concern. Mitch looked towards the forest and called out Jasper's name. Jasper flew out from behind a large tree towards the group. Upon reaching them he landed on Zee's shoulder. He looked warily up at the Ogres.

"I told him to take cover in the trees," Mitch said. "If we did not make it out alive he was to go back to Elsbrier and warn the Elders."

"I am glad I don't have to make the trip back to the village by myself," Jasper said and leaned his head against Zee's cheek.

"So are we," she replied.

"I think it is time to leave," Shanata said as she looked up into the sky. By where the sun was positioned it was just past noon. They were still at least a day's ride away from Elsbrier if not more. The only settlement between them and home was

Little Springs. If they rode they would make it there just after nightfall.

"Where are the Avidraughts you rode here on?" Mitch asked as he looked around the clearing. When they arrived they were so worried about helping the fairies they didn't think to look for any other Avidraughts.

"We didn't bring Avidraughts," Shanata said. "We rode Lord Warden's horses." Mitch looked around for the horses. His brothers and Rhethea would ride them back to Elsbrier.

"Don't bother looking for them," Enna said as she sheathed her sword. "They got spooked when the Rapcicors attacked and they fled."

"They left you here to fend for yourselves?" Amos said with disgust. "Horses!" He said then snorted as he looked at the other Avidraughts. None of them would have left the fairies, even if they ordered them to.

"You've got that right!" Enna said as she patted Amos's neck.

"Yes, well you can double up if you like," Farley said. "We can't fly for long with two of you on our backs, but we can walk quite a distance."

"Alright then," Shanata said. "Ashlina, you and Arturo scout ahead." Because Arturo was small he would not be able to carry two of them. But he and Ashlina could fly ahead and make sure that no other Rapcicors laid in wait for them.

"Can I go with them?" Jasper asked from Zee's shoulder. He had felt useless as he watched the battle from the tree line.

"Yes Jasper that is an excellent idea. That way if Ashlina sees anything you can fly back and let us know," Shanata said. Her words made him feel better and he puffed out his chest a little. Zee smiled at him as he flew off her shoulder and hovered beside Ashlina who had already mounted Arturo.

"Zeander can you, Datoka and Bauthal run up ahead as well?" Shanata asked. Zeander nodded. He had been surprisingly quiet during their ride to the clearing. She meant to ask if he was alright but then the Rapcicors had attacked and there was no time. He was probably missing Paraphin and did not know how to talk about it. She would make a point of asking him while they walked back.

"Rhethea," she continued to say. "You ride with Mitch, Ody you go with Mariela, Yan you with Zee, Reg you and Enna, and Aro you can ride with me." The brothers nodded in agreement. Yan walked up to Farley and cupped his hands together and bent down to help Zee up. There were no boulders for her to stand on. Zee however walked away and tried to pick up one of the Rapcicors. He was too heavy for her to lift so she dragged him over to another one.

"Zee what are you doing?" Yan asked. Her sisters immediately turned in Zee's direction. She dragged another bird across the grass.

"I am putting the Rapcicors in a pile for the *Healing Chain*," Zee said as she laid the dead bird next to the other two. Fielddegard looked at her curiously before he looked at his brother and cousins. The fairies, Zeander and Bauthal immediately understood and started to drag Rapcicors to the pile Zee had started. The Jarrell brothers looked at their sister for explanation.

"It is something the Tara Aquians taught them," she said. "It will cleanse their sorrows of taking a life, but also send the souls of the Rapcicors to their next destination. Once they are in a pile they will set them on fire and sing the Healing song." Her brothers looked curiously at each other for a moment before they too joined in. The Avidraughts followed suit.

"Leave them," Fielddegard said. The fairies looked up sharply, so too did the others when they realized he was talking to them.

"Excuse me?" Shanata said.

"My cousins will take care of them," he said. "They will take them back to our village. We will strip them down and dry the meat. The feathers we will use to fill our mattresses and pillows, and the bones we will make into flutes and use for darning needles."

Everyone looked with surprise at the Ogres. Zeander however understood. It was the same for the Meadow Imps; they used every part of an animal and threw nothing out. Shanata nodded as she remembered something that Obwyn had taught them about killing animals, '*You only kill an animal if you are going to use all of it. You do not kill for sport*'.

"Alright then," Shanata said. "We will make pole-shifts and help you take them to your village." She looked around at the others who all nodded.

"That won't be necessary; my cousins will be able to handle it," Shanata looked at him curiously, she did not miss that he was not including himself or Rojon.

"Are you coming back to Elsbrier with us?" She asked. He looked at her cleverly and then smiled. His teeth unlike the others were evenly spaced apart.

"Yes, my brother and I will come back with you. I think it is time that we speak with Elder Enyce and her sisters." At the mention of Enyce's name Shanata's left eyebrow rose.

"You know the Elders by name?" She asked.

"Of course we do," he said. "We live in the same valley. Why would we not know their names?"

The fairies looked at each other. No one had taught them about the Ogres yet. It was to be their last lesson before they left on their journey. The only thing they knew of them is what they heard from the trappers. The Ogres lived in seclusion and were never seen outside their borders. Ronan and Ronan were the only ones they had seen up close, but then they were only half Ogre and remembered nothing of their past.

Everyone mounted the Avidraughts. As Aro climbed up behind Shanata he whispered, "They live in a village and sleep in beds?" Shanata shrugged her shoulders. Obviously what they had heard about the Ogres was not true. The trappers had made them out to be illiterate barbarians that lived in the open air and only grunted when they talked.

Although Fielddegard was the only one who had spoken, he was quite articulate in speech and obviously intelligent. Shanata looked at her sisters with an inquiring stare. They nodded and smiled back. Their last lesson they would learn firsthand as they walked back home. Wouldn't Elder Enyce be surprised when they told her they didn't need the lesson after all? As Arturo took flight Ashlina called out over her shoulder, "Make sure you tell me everything." The sisters chuckled.

Shanata then looked up at Fielddegard as he walked beside her. Before she asked her first question she wondered what the Elders would say when she and her sisters returned home with not one but two Ogres. The firefly who had watched them from a nearby tree flew in the direction of Elsbrier. There was news to report.

*

The sun had risen and Elsbrier was busy as usual with all it comings and goings. It had gotten busier however in the three days that the fairies had been away. The Orhem team had arrived and so too had several of the other teams. It was obvious that everyone wanted to get in extra practices before the tournament and perhaps appraise their competition.

The grand prize was quite high this year. Lord Warden contributed the largest prize to the winning team. He had sectioned off several plots near Boswick for each player of the winning team. As well, a two story house would be built, along with a barn. The house would be furnished and the barn would have pens for livestock and a corral for horses, which he would also gift the players with. It was the richest pot yet and every team wanted it for themselves, even though it meant moving to Boswick. This year's competition was going to be fierce.

Several of the traveling vendors had arrived as well. Their brightly coloured tents were set up along Vendors Row. In a week's time it would be filled from the stadium right into Elsbrier.

A dozen Minstrels, three troupes of acrobats and all manner of artist had also arrived. Even the author Thurston Field had arrived early. He was staying in one of the small artists cottages near the theatre. On that particular morning he and J.Z. Jones walked down Vendors Row. They stopped to watch the Hawkeye Teams as they worked out. Three of the nine teams had got up early to do their morning workout in the meadow next to the stadium. It was a cool morning; the temperature had dropped several degrees overnight. Everyone who stood around was bundled up in overcoats or wore heavy sweaters over their day clothes. However the team members were dressed in short pants and short sleeved shirts that showed off their lean and muscular bodies. Several of the young women in the village had come to watch the workout as well. The coaches of the teams had been adamant that they stand on the edge of the road so they did not distract their players. Their girlish giggles however could be heard clear across the meadow.

"Who will you be rooting for?" Thurston asked as he shivered. He took out a pair of gloves from one of the pockets in his overcoat and quickly put them on.

"The Eagles of course!" Miss J replied enthusiastically.

"Ah yes, your brother plays for them doesn't he," Thurston said.

Miss J nodded as she waved at Jarrott. He and his team mates were not far from the road. Coach Edward shouted crossly at them; Miss J and Thurston stopped to listen.

"What in the world is wrong with you boys this morning?" Edward asked. The boys were not taking their workout seriously. They were lagging behind Jarrott's moves as he led them into their morning routines. Edward knew the reason why, but he didn't feel sorry for them. When they heard what had happened at the Cropping of Rocks and that Rhethea had gone after Jaja they were all worried sick over it. If she had stopped to ask, each one of them would have gone with her. They stewed over it for a night until the Orhem team had arrived. They were a lively group of young men who made any excuse to party; birthdays, anniversary, holidays. They even made up holidays so that they could party. When they heard about what had happened at the Cropping of Rocks they invited the players from the Eagles to have a drink with them at *The Den*. One drink turned into several and a wild party ensued. The partying got so out of hand Obwyn and Nayew had to break it up because Lord Warden had complained.

"I have no sympathy for you. If you boys want to win this tournament you better get your priorities straight, now lift those arms!" Edward scolded them.

Fifty paces away players from the Boswick team also worked out while Lord Warden and Lady Rosetta sat on chairs watching them. A small fire burned in a stone pit in front of them and a man servant served them a light breakfast on trays which he placed on their laps. When a couple of his players snickered after hearing Edward scold his players, Lord Warden looked over at the Boswick coach. They had not joined in the previous night's festivities; mostly because their coach would exempt them from playing or worse Lord Warden would can them from the team and force them to pay back the retainer he had already fronted them. So when their coach, Graphin Ruchi looked their way, they immediately stopped snickering. However it was too late, he had heard them.

Graphin was short in stature, but powerfully built and he could and had fought men three times his size. Lord Warden had heard about him and hired him to coach his team after they lost the finals four years ago. Graphin had been a task master and worked the players until they were conditioned in a way that Lord Warden saw fit. Graphin was paid very well and he took his duties seriously. So when he pointed at the group who had broken their concentration they immediately stood at attention.

"You three drop and give me fifty," Graphin ordered. "Herb, count it out."

Herb Marrona walked up to his teammates. He stood before them with his legs apart and hands behind his back. The scowl he gave them spoke volumes; this would not be the end of it. They immediately dropped and he started the count for fifty push-ups.

"One arm," Graphin called over.

The players did not dare moan, but they looked up at Herb. "Do it," he sneered, "or forfeit your place."

The players immediately put one arm behind their backs as Herb started the count again. The players did not stop even when they heard a high pitched scream coming from the road side. Herb did not even turn around until he saw the others players stop what they were doing and looked wide eyed at the stadium. Graphin turned as well and for a moment was as dumbstruck as his players. The Eagles and the team from Pleasantland also stopped and looked with shock at the corner of the stadium. Miss J and Thurston turned as well. Miss J immediately gasped and held her hand over her mouth in fear.

The fairies had come around the corner. Their appearances were quite strange and disturbing. Their hair looked as though it hadn't been combed in several days. Their faces were bruised and their armour was soiled and bloody. The small entourage that followed them was stranger still. Shanata was in front riding on Felon while Rhethea rode beside her on Alwim. Rhethea looked worse than the fairies. She had several dark bruises on her bare arms. A large bandage was wrapped around her left arm. The front of her top had been sliced open and a bandage could be seen under it, just below her neck. The other fairies rode their Avidraughts behind them. The girls laughed easily at something that Bauthal had said.

Rhethea's brothers walked several paces behind them. They looked quite a mess as well; blood and dirt stained their clothes. Datoka walked beside them. Zeander rode on his back. However it was not their appearance that made the young woman scream, it was the two Ogres who walked behind them. Fielddegard and Rojon looked strangely over at the young woman; she was the only one screaming. Everyone else looked fearfully up at them, but no one had run away.

Shanata called over her shoulder to Zeander and Datoka and asked them to fetch the Elders. They instantly ran down the road towards Elsbrier. Rojon looked quizzically at the young woman as Datoka ran past her.

"Jasper," Rojon said as he took a sideways glance at his shoulder. "Do the women of your village always scream like that when you come home?" His question had the small entourage laughing with ease.

"No, only when Ody comes home," Jasper said cheekily. Everyone chuckled. Ody had been the brunt of many of jokes over the walk because he was the only one of the Jarrell brothers who had not married. Rojon had teased him, stating that perhaps it was because he was so ugly.

"Ah yes! Master Ody. He does have looks that would make a woman scream, and not from delight I am sure!" Rojon said then screwed up his face like he had just eaten something sour. The fairies, Rhethea and her brothers looked up at Rojon and laughed at his expression. Fielddegard was the only one who didn't laugh.

Over their journey to the village he had been, although kind, the more serious of the two. Rojon however was quite the character. He told countless stories and jokes that he embellished with great theatrics. It had eased the tension of what they had endured at the hands of Jaja and the Rapcicors. His likeable personality had instantly endeared him to the group. They even liked Fielddegard, even though he was more serious. It was quite unexpected to discover that the

Ogres were the complete opposite of what the trappers had made them out to be.

"I have no problems with the ladies," Ody said confidently as he puffed out his chest. "Perhaps Ogres don't find humans good looking."

"Oh no," Rojon said. "I find Yan to be quite good looking." Everyone, but Ody and Fielddegard laughed again. When Ody walked by the young woman that had cried out, Rojon bent down and sneered at her from behind Ody's back. The young woman screamed hysterically again and crossed her arms in front of her face before she dropped to the ground.

"See," Rojon said. "You are just too ugly for human kind. You should come and live with us; perhaps you will find a mate with one of our women. They are as ugly as they get, but not as ugly as you though." Everyone laughed again. This time even Fielddegard had a smirk on his face.

"Oh do stop that will you!" Thurston said scathingly to the young woman. "They are only Ogres after all." Hearing his words Fielddegard looked down at him and nodded. Thurston nodded back at him as they walked by.

"You know them?" Miss J asked. She had been concerned until she heard the fairies' laughter and saw that although they looked a mess they were quite well.

"Well not them personally," Thurston said loud enough for everyone to hear. "But when I researched material for *The Beast Within Us*, I did go and live with a group of them in the Fresar Region along the Denyth River. Quite lovely they are and very gentle really, even though they could chew you up and spit out your bones with one bite." He looked scathingly at the young woman again. She had stopped screaming when he yelled at her, but now she looked near to fainting; it was a good thing she was sitting on the ground. Miss J slapped Thurston on the shoulder and tsked at him before she went to console the young woman. Thurston immediately took out a pad of paper and a pencil from the other pocket in his coat and started to scribble an idea for another book entitled, *The Maiden and the Ogre*.

Seeing that all was fine the Boswick and the Pleasantland teams went back to their workout. The vendors went back into their tents and everyone else cautiously went about their business, steering clear of the Ogres. The fairies may not have problems associating with them but that didn't mean they had to be okay with it too. Three players from the Eagle team however were not afraid and immediately ran forward, even though Edward called for them to come back. He understood that they had been worried about Rhethea so when Jarrott started to go after them Edward raised his hand to stop him.

"Let them be. They are no good to me this way," he said. "I will make them work out again later today. Finish with the workout Jarrott." Jarrott nodded.

Edward looked with concern over at the Boswick team. They had improved considerably under Graphin's coaching. They had been a good team before, but now it was like watching soldiers. Each of their movements were precise and methodically thought out. Edward felt someone staring at him and looked over at Lord Warden who raised a cup in the air. Edward nodded at him then looked away. He had a strange feeling that Lord Warden had come with his team to spy on the Eagles. As he looked around the clearing he noticed that several of the other teams had arrived in the clearing to work out as well. He looked thoughtfully at a group of young women who laughed girlishly when the three Eagle teammates walked past them. *Perhaps,* he thought, *it's time to find a more secluded place to work out; one with no distractions.*

"Rhethea, are these Ogres bothering you?" Skye Bilonnettes asked as he and the other two stepped right in front of them making the fairies rein in their Avidraughts. Skye was a rather tall strapping young man with blonde hair, blue eyes and a quick smile. He and Marcus were Lead Guards on the team. He was a bit taken with Rhethea ever since she joined the team. However he was wary of her brothers and he never once tried to speak to her about anything before. At the time she also only had eyes for Jemas. He never thought he would actually get the chance to engage her in conversation.

"No, I am fine thank you Skye!" Rhethea said as she looked with surprise at him. She smiled. Encouraged, Skye immediately stepped forward. He however had only taken one step when he heard a grunt from both Yan and Mitch. When he looked at them they scowled menacingly at him. Even though he was taller and more muscular than they were, Skye took as step back and looked sheepishly at the ground.

"Perhaps maybe I could help you then Rhethea," Dale Vocke said with a cheeky smile. Dale was not tall in stature, but he was handsome with dark brown hair and dark brown eyes. He always had a bit of stubble on his chin that made him look rugged. He and Luke were the Fore Runners on the team.

"No Dale I am fine, really. Thank you though," Rhethea said then chuckled nervously. Her teammates had never once approached her with interest. She found it a little bit uncomfortable. So when the next teammate opened his mouth to speak she snapped at him. "No Hawns, I am fine. I really do not need any assistance!"

Hawns Temmet was the Gate Keeper for the team. He was a tall young man with a muscular build and had dark brown hair that he kept cut short. He had hazel coloured eyes, and his ears were slightly pointed. His grandmother had been a Pixie.

"Actually," he said, "I was wondering if Shanata needed help with anything." Rhethea looked at him in surprise, then at Shanata. Shanata was taken aback at the gesture and the gentle smile on his face. None of the young men in the village had ever quite looked at her that way before. Although cordial to the fairies and helpful when asked, they stayed clear of them. So when Hawns held out his hand to help her down from Felon's back, she blushed. To mask her embarrassment she got down on her own. She quickly composed herself before she turned and spoke.

"Actually," she said repeating his word with an air of authority. "You and a couple of your teammates can carry our saddles back into the village. I see that the Elders are on their way. We have much to talk about and the Avidraughts need to get home to their families." Everyone but Hawns looked toward Elsbrier. They could see that the Elders were indeed quickly making their way up Vendors Row; Nayew Obwyn and Orliff were with them. Shanata could feel Hawns watching her and she blushed. Encouraged he smiled broadly. As the fairies and the others walked towards the Elders, Hawns started to take the saddle off of Felon's back.

"I think she likes me," he whispered into Felon's ear.

"Don't be ridiculous!" Felon said as she nipped at him.

"Easy girl!" He said and patted her neck. Shanata looked back at that moment. She hadn't heard their exchange of words and she smiled inwardly, thinking that Felon liked him.

Rhethea looked at her and smiled. She and Shanata often talked about what would happen after the war when the fairies got home; would they take mates and have children of their own. Neither of them ever spoke about the reality that they may not succeed in their mission, lose the war and not come home at all. It was a reality neither of them wanted to think of, let alone lend fearful words to.

"Come on," Rhethea said as she put her arm around Shanata's shoulder and gave it a quick squeeze. "The Elders are waiting."

Chapter 26
Lizbeth and the Day of Remembrance

The evening after the fairies returned home with Fielddegard and Rojon, a soft glow from a hundred candles lit up the Forest of Glen, which lay a half hour walk northwest of the Whipple Wash Tree. A procession, led by the Seven Elders, had walked in a uniformed march from Elsbrier to the small forest. The time honoured ritual was normally only attended by Queen Faywyn, her daughters, the fairies, and the family and friends of the deceased. This ceremony however was attended by several hundred as every Elkin, Meadow Imp and Tara Aquian came to say their last good byes to their friends. Several of the villagers came to pay their respects as well.

Earlier that day the Tara Aquians had said goodbye to Barton in their own way not far from the Lily Pond. Afterward they brought his body to the Galadome Fire Pit and his remains were burned after Paraphin's had been. Once cooled their ashes were put into crystal vases that now sat on a hand carved wooden table. The Seven Elders stood beside the table and waited while the rest of the procession entered the clearing before the forest. Everyone quieted down when Elder Enyce and Rayley stepped forward. Enyce looked at the fairies who also stepped forward. As Rayley picked up the vase containing Paraphin's remains and Enyce picked up the one carrying Barton's, the fairies began to sing the *Light of Remembrance* while Homsa played the mandolin:

On this day of remembrance and forever more
Shall your ashes dwell on the forest floor
Nurturing the life of your own special tree
From the roots, through the trunk, to the leaves

May the Light of Goodness find you walking here
Among your loved ones and friends from far and near
Sharing stories and laughter of times gone by
Until long after the sun has set and the last owl doth cry

While your spirit soars freely up above
Find peace in knowing you are greatly loved
And we shall meet again and again
Here as we stroll through the Forest of Glen

Together Enyce and Rayley walked to two holes that had been dug nine feet apart at the edge of the forest. Two, three foot tall saplings sat directly behind the holes; beside them was a mound of dirt, a large bucket full of water, and a small hand held shovel. The Elders sat the crystal vases next to the holes and knelt down in front of them. Carefully, as the fairies continued to sing, the Elders poured the ashes into the holes. They then took three shovelfuls of dirt and mixed it in with the ashes. Once they were done they slowly poured water into the holes from the buckets. They each clasped their right hand over their heart, looked up into the sky and whispered a few words before they stood. Carrying the shovels they walked back to the group that had gathered.

Obwyn and Nayew came forward. Each picked up a sapling. They placed the saplings into the holes and held them steady. Elder Rayley bent down and handed her shovel to Zeander. It was almost as tall as he was. Saphina took a step forward to assist him, but he shook his head. He dragged the shovel over to the mound of dirt beside the sapling that Nayew held onto and was able to dig up a shovel full; he placed it in the hole. Zeander looked down into the hole and sniffled.

"I will never forget ya, ya big dolt," he whispered. He stood for a minute, looking into the hole; a great sadness overcame him. The tears quickly came, but he didn't brush them away nor did he care that everyone saw him crying.

Zeander let the tears drop into the hole as he whispered his goodbye. A couple of minutes passed before he was able to control his emotions enough to drag the shovel back to the Elder Rayley. Saphina came forward and knelt down beside him.

"He loved you as much as you loved him," she said as she took the shovel from his hand. Her eyes were full of unshed tears.

"I know," is all Zeander could muster to say. Lillian came forward and hugged him tightly to her. The tears came in great gulps again as he held onto her.

Elder Enyce handed her shovel to Lindrella; her hands were shaky when she accepted it. She walked over to the sapling that Obwyn held. She dropped a shovel full of dirt into the hole and like Zeander stood for a moment saying her last goodbye. She walked back and handed the shovel back to Enyce.

"This is a wonderful tradition you have. Barton truly would have understood the sentiment behind this," she said. "In our city, the Golden City of Awnmorielle, there are no trees. Over our journey from the mountain to here, Barton often talked about how wonderful it would be to sit under a tree and relax while listening to the breeze rustles the leaves. He was very enamored by our new home and looked forward to our new adventure in it."

Lindrella was not normally one to show emotion and tears welled up in her eyes. She was remembering the last time she and Barton had spoken. It was the night they had arrived in Elsbrier. Once everyone was settled they sat under the tree beside the Lily Pond with Airam Andiela and they talked of their home and the journey with her. She had told them of a series of abandoned caves in the escarpment on the other side of the Lily Pond and that she would be delighted to show it to them. Barton was looking forward to it.

"Thank you," Rayley said. She could see that Lindrella was

about to cry and put her hand on her shoulder. "You will see him again."

"I know," Lindrella said as she controlled her emotions. She looked curiously at the smile on Rayley's face.

"Sooner than that," Rayley said. "During the Solstice and Equinox Celebrations the spirits of our loved ones return here to the Forest of Glen; it is a Cross Over Point. That is what the benches are for, so that the living can sit with the spirits of their Dear Ones."

Upon hearing her words Zeander stopped crying and he, Lindrella, the Elfkins and Meadow Imps looked around at the nearest trees. They hadn't noticed upon arriving that every tree had a bench beside it. Lindrella and Zeander both looked to the right of Obwyn. Two wooden benches sat side by side. Zeander and Lindrella walked over to them. Something had been inscribed into the top rail of the bench.

Zeander read first:

"Here rests Paraphin, the last of the great Abo Snakes. He is a fierce warrior with a kind heart and is best friends to Zeander." Zeander sniffled loudly as tears came to his eyes again.

Lindrella read next:

"Here lies Barton a friendly giant who loves all people with care and understanding. His heart is as big as his compassion for the helpless and less fortunate than himself."

As the others came forward and placed a shovel full of dirt into the holes, Elder Rayley walked over to Zeander and Lindrella who looked curiously at the benches.

"You wrote of them in the present rather than the past," Lindrella said. "Why is that?"

Rayley thought for a moment before she answered; not everyone readily understood the spiritual power derived from

350

the Forest of Glen. It had been a bit of a shock to the Elders and Queen Faywyn as well when they had first heard of it.

"When we arrived in this valley we made a home in the Whipple Wash Tree as instructed by the Supreme Being; the Light of Goodness. One summer's eve while sitting in the branches of the tree, Phinney saw a radiant glow not far from the tree. She immediately alerted us to it as we had seen no life in the valley other than the wildlife. We walked over here with candles to investigate. A large crystal jutted out from the ground. As we got closer to it we noticed that someone was leaning against it. The person was a woman with dark curly shoulder length hair. She was dressed in a long flowing white-gold gown. She looked more like a ghostly vapor than she did human. Upon seeing us she smiled and her body transformed from vapor to solid mass. When we reached her she welcomed each of us with a warm embrace."

"We learned that her name was Lyneve," Elder Athia said. Lindrella and Zeander turned around. All the Elders but Enyce, who stayed to watch over the procession with the fairies had come over. "And that she is half-sister to the Light of Goodness." Athia finished saying. "She explained that the crystal was the Cross Over Point, a portal for the spirit of the, 'Dear Ones' as she called them, to travel from this realm to the next. Four times a year the Dear Ones can return, if they wish, to visit those who they shared time with in this realm." Lindrella and Zeander looked questioningly at them. "A tree is planted for those who wish to return and a bench is made for them."

"The first row of trees is connected directly to the crystal's root. The trees surrounding that row are connected to the tree in front of them and so on. Because the trees take years to grow their root system may never reach the crystal so being connected to the tree ahead of them ensures that they are connected to the crystal as well." Lindrella and Zeander nodded indicating that they understood.

Zeander looked questioningly over at the tree that had

been planted for Paraphin. Aldwin was putting dirt into the whole that was now almost full.

"Where do the trees come from? How do you know which one to use?" Zeander asked. "And who takes care of them?"

"Zila, her brother Kale, and a group of dedicated Pixies look after the trees. The saplings are grown in a field just on the outskirts of the village. We also use the trees in our gardens and on the pathways that wind throughout Elsbrier," Elder Phinney said. "I choose the tree; well not really me, I am more guided to the tree. It is not often that we have two pass at the same time," she said thoughtfully. "On occasion however we do but I am not guided to trees of the same species. For reasons more than I will ever know they both have maple trees."

"Why do you think they both have the same tree?" Zeander asked.

Elder Phinney looked down at Zeander before she looked at her sisters. Elder Enyce had come over to stand with them and when she looked at her she could not answer the question. Zusie, Janilli, Chrystalina and Saphina had also come over to stand with them and had heard Zeander's question.

"There are some things in this life that we are not meant to understand," Janilli said. "They are what they are and we may never know the reasoning why." Zeander looked up at her and Jasper who sat on her shoulder. He understood what she meant. So many things had transpired since Jasper had flown into their valley. If he had not listened to his brother Jopha or had not found the courage to persevere or had not landed on Lizbeth's doorstep they might all be dead right now. In his mind there had been too many coincidences for it not to have been engineered for a higher purpose. But perhaps Janilli was right- it would always be beyond their comprehension why things had played out as they had.

A hushed whisper steadily grew louder among the group of bystanders. Everyone standing around the benches looked back at the group. Marla came running forward and grabbed Zusie's hands.

"Zusie, it's Lizbeth," Marla said. Seeing the tears running down Marla's face Zusie instantly thought the worst. Before she could move however Marla smiled broadly, "She is here!"

Zusie gasped as did Saphina and Chrystalina. They looked toward the group who had started to part. They could see Orliff's head and shoulders above the heads of the Elfkins. He was stooped over slightly and looked to be pushing something. Zan and Arnak followed behind him.

"Sorry we are late," Orliff said as he walked towards the trees that Nayew and Obwyn were still holding. "But someone was adamant about coming here." He was pushing a wheelchair and in the chair covered in a warm blanket was Lizbeth. She looked small and frail in the overly large wheelchair. Zusie noticed that someone had taken the time to pull her hair up neatly into a bun. Her cheeks, although drawn, had red blotches on them. Her eyes were lively with the glint of life shining in them. Zusie cried out her name, ran over to her and fell to her knees in front of the chair. She clasped Lizbeth's hands in hers, hung her head and cried. Saphina and Chrystalina followed quickly after her. Jasper flew off Janilli's shoulder and fluttered just above Saphina's head. His eyes were full of tears as he looked down at Lizbeth. Lizbeth smiled warmly up at him and winked. Jasper sighed heavily; she was not upset with him.

"Shh now Zusie, there will be time for this," Lizbeth said in a breathless whisper. Her voice although quiet held an edge of authority to it. She hadn't lost her spirit while she lay for months in a coma. "For now I must say goodbye to a dear friend."

Zusie looked up in surprise as had everyone else who stood around. "You two," she said looking at Zan and Arnak. "Help me out of this chair will you." Arnak and Zan frowned as Zusie got up off the ground and stood to the side. Saphina and Chrystalina standing on either side of her each put their arms around their mother and hugged her tightly.

"She might be little," Zan said as he walked forward. "But she is very forthright."

"Forthright? She is a bit of a bully if you ask me," Arnak said as he came to her other side. Even though their tone was harsh they helped her to stand. "And she hasn't stopped chattering since we left the Mediplace."

The Elfkins that were close enough to hear what they said smirked. Lizbeth had always been forthright even when she was a young underling. But they also knew she had a kind heart and would give you the clothes off her back if you needed them. Lizbeth ignored their comments as they helped her stand. She took a tentative step but her legs were not strong enough to hold her. She would have fallen to the ground if Zan had not caught her around the waist. Without asking he picked her up gently and carried her to the nearest tree. Arnak followed behind them with her blanket. She looked at the tree for a minute and shook her head.

"I believe that one is Barton's tree," Lizbeth said as she pointed a slender finger at the tree that Obwyn was still holding steady. Every Elfkin and Meadow Imp looked at Lizbeth with shocked expressions; the Tara Aquians and Janilli had not. The journey from the Hollow of Rock had been long. Barton, out of his own admission had chosen to protect and take care of Lizbeth. Even though she had been in a coma, he could sense that she knew he was there taking care of her. Over the journey they had formed a bond greater than friendship. Barton had often talked to Janilli about what he sensed and although she could not confirm it, she knew that he was right in his assumptions. Tears welled up in her eyes as Arnak placed blanket down in front of Barton's tree and Zan sat her on top of it.

Zee came forward and handed Lizbeth the shovel, but she was too weak to hold and it dropped to the ground. Zan moved to pick it up but Lizbeth stayed him with words. "Leave it," she said. "Can you unclasp the necklace around my next for me please?" Zan untied the necklace. It slipped down the front of her gown and dropped to her lap. As everyone stood looking at her curiously Lizbeth started to take the dirt out of the hole. She was only able to cup two handfuls when her arms became weak from the effort.

"You don't have to be so stubborn, what is it that you want to do?" Zan asked.

"Can you uncover the root ball for me please," Lizbeth said. Zan parted enough of the dirt so that the root ball was showing. He then looked expectantly at Lizbeth for his next direction. However she looked up at Zusie. Zusie took the necklace she had made for Willham from around her neck and handed it to Zan.

"Please tie the necklaces to the base of the trunk and make sure they are touching the root and then fill in the hole again." Zan did as she asked.

"Thank you," Lizbeth said as Zan patted the earth down around the tree. "Is Paraphin's tree ready as well," she asked. Nayew nodded the earth had been patted down around the tree. "Please stand back a pace or two," she said looking at Zan, Nayew and Obwyn. They immediately looked at Elder Enyce who nodded her head. They stood back from the trees and Zan stood back from Lizbeth. Curious as to what she was going to do, everyone else took a couple of steps forward. Nayew and Obwyn immediately put up their hands to stop them. On several occasions they had witnessed the special powers of the Elders and the fairies, and knew when a magical gift was going to be used.

Lizbeth rubbed her hands together vigorously and whispered words that no one had heard her use before. A soft glow formed between her two hands, seeped out and enveloped her hands with a golden glow. She opened her hands and laid them flat upon the soil around the trunk of the tree. The Elfkins looked on in genuine surprise; they had never witnessed her do this before in the Greenwood Forest. Zusie knew that Lizbeth was special, but even she looked on in awe at her friend's ability. The Elders looked at her suspiciously.

"For Horman, my mate who I lost to soon, for Willham a loving mate and father, for Barton, the son I never had, and for our dear friend Paraphin; I ask of thee the Light of Goodness to shine down on their remembrance trees, giving strength and vitality to the roots so that they may grow strong, tall and live for an eternity here in the Forest of Glen."

Everyone but the Elders looked on in astonishment as Barton's tree slowly grew a foot taller. The few leaves that hung from its limbs turned golden. Just after the last leaf turned gold Paraphin's tree grew a foot taller. When the last leaf turned gold everyone watched in amazement as a gold line made its way to the nearest tree. It had been planted five years previously. When the leaves on that tree turned gold everyone exclaimed in delight and clapped their hands.

Lizbeth took her hands away from the tree and sat up straight; she looked up at Zusie who had tears in her eyes and smiled. Willham would be able to come for a visit during the Winter Equinox Celebrations. As Zusie looked down at her, Lizbeth swayed and her vision became clouded. Zusie quickly knelt next to her, but there was nothing she could do as the darkness took over. Lizbeth fainted. Zusie cried for Orliff as Lizbeth leaned heavily against her arm. Everyone stopped clapping and immediately looked at Lizbeth with worry as Orliff examined her.

"I told her this might happen," he said." But she refused to listen to me." He gently laid Lizbeth down on the blanket. "She has just over exerted herself and fainted. She will be fine." Everyone sighed as Orliff started to speak. He looked at Zan first, "Lower the back rest will you." Zan immediately went to the wheelchair and lowered the back rest while Orliff picked Lizbeth up off the blanket. "Fold that in half will you," he said to Zusie who immediately picked up the blanket, shook of the dirt and folded it in half. "Place it on the wheel chair." Zusie again did his bidding. When she placed the blanket on the chair she took the top half of it and held it up while Orliff placed Lizbeth on the bottom half. He took the blanket from Zusie and tucked it snugly around Lizbeth.

"I am sorry, but I have to get her back to the Mediplace. The night has grown cold and I don't want her to catch a chill," Orliff said.

Zusie nodded. "I will come with you," she said.

"We will as well," Saphina said as she, Aldwin and Chrystalina stepped forward. Orliff took one look at the resolved expression on their faces and nodded his head.

"Yes, if you must," he said. He didn't wait for them to answer however and immediately started to push Lizbeth towards Elsbrier. He had argued with her when she said she wanted to attend the ceremonies. She had only been awake for a few hours and was in no shape to leave. She had not listened however and when his back was turned she got out of bed and made her way to the front door of the Mediplace. Zan and Arnack were just bringing back a wheelchair that one of the vendors had asked to borrow after twisting his ankle. He was well enough now to walk with a cane and no longer needed the chair. When they entered the Mediplace, they had found Lizbeth leaning against the wall. They insisted that she sit in the chair before she fell. She only obliged after Zan had called out for Orliff.

Orliff looked down at Lizbeth and smiled, she was a feisty one that was for sure. No one he had treated before had quite so much energy after coming out of a coma induced by the sting of a Hummingmoth. Thankfully they had been few and far between and like Lizbeth's had been by accident. The other patients however were not coherent for several days after he administered the antidote. Lizbeth had been quite the opposite. Not only was she quite lucid, but chatty as well. Even though her voice was husky from lack of use, he understood her perfectly. She immediately wanted to know where she was. When he told her she was in Elsbrier she didn't blink an eye. Instead she merely nodded her head like she knew that that is where she was. When she asked to see Zusie and the others she became quite irate when Orliff told her she couldn't because they were attending the *Light of Remembrance Ceremony*. Again she didn't seem miffed by the information, but demanded that she attend it.

He had gone to the storeroom to prepare her a tonic to ease her nerves, when she had fled. How she actually made it out of bed and to the door he had no idea. Only on her assurance that she would listen to him for the duration of her stay in his care did he concede that she could attend the ceremony. Orliff looked at Aldwin and Zusie thoughtfully; he knew the excellent care they had given her over the journey had kept Lizbeth alive. But her recovery seemed to be happening in leaps and bounds. He looked quizzically down at her and frowned as he watched her eyes flutter open. She looked thoughtfully back at him and smiled.

Perhaps he thought to himself, especially after witnessing what Lizbeth was capable of doing, that there was more to the Elfkins than he first thought. Orliff was soon to find out however that a power far greater than what Lizbeth possessed had kept her alive and gave her abilities she had never possessed before.

Chapter 27
The Eavesdropper

The next day the sky overhead was gloomy with dark clouds. It had turned cold overnight and snow could be smelled in the air. The vendors walked around in warm overcoats and gloves as they opened their shops. Many of them decided not to set up the tables in front. Anyone wishing to purchase would have to do so inside the shops. The dreary cold weather however had not diminished the excitement that buzzed around Elsbrier. Word that Lizbeth was awake and performed magic in the Forest of Glen had everyone talking about it. No one more than Lizbeth however was surprised at it, as she had not had such powers before she had fallen ill.

While everyone theorized as to how she gained the power, the Elders were waiting for Orliff and Aldwin to finish examining Lizbeth. She was back in the Mediplace, laying down on the bed that was assigned to her. The curtains were drawn and the Elders stood calmly while Zusie paced back and forth.

Lizbeth had stayed in the Mediplace all night after they brought her back from the ceremony. Even though she was tired she was quite ravenous and joked that she could eat a whole river of fish in one sitting. Orliff however had limited her food to soups and dry crackers. When she complained that soup was all that she had been eating for months and that she would really like something more substantial to sink her teeth into, he conceded that she could have a sandwich.

Lizbeth groaned but ate the sandwich Alamat brought for her as well as two bowls of soup and several crackers. When Alamat brought her a tea with honey and lemon in it Lizbeth exclaimed with delight that it was the best thing she had ever tasted. She had not stayed up for long after her meal and had slept comfortably right through the night.

However, as it was her custom to wake up with the dawn, she had been sitting quietly for some time thinking about all that had transpired the night before. As Keeper of the Woods, she had certain skills with plants and often talked to them, which she knew helped them to grow, but she was not able to make them glow gold or grow a foot taller by just touching them. She looked down at her hands with wonder; turning them this way and that. They didn't look any different nor did she feel any different. Actually, despite being asleep for several months she felt quite fine and was eager to get on with the day. Not one for patience she moved restlessly in her bed. The pillow she was leaning against fell onto the side table and bumped the tea cup. It fell to the floor. Zusie heard the crash and woke instantly. She was sleeping in the bed next to Lizbeth's. She jumped out of bed and opened the curtain that had been drawn closed.

"Lizbeth," Zusie started to say anxiously, but then stopped as she looked curiously at her.

"What is it?" Lizbeth asked as she stared back at Zusie.

"You look wonderful," Zusie said as she continued to look at Lizbeth. The colour was back in her cheeks and she looked quite fit.

"I feel wonderful," Lizbeth said as she swung her legs over the side of the bed.

"Oh, no you don't," Zusie said as she walked to the bed. "Stay where you are while I fetch Orliff. I mean it," she said before she went in search of Orliff. Lizbeth did as she was told and that is how Orliff found her; sitting up, legs dangling over the side of the bed, hands clasped in her lap and looking impatient. Seeing how quite well she looked he asked Alamat to get the Elders and Aldwin.

For an hour the Elders and Zusie stood outside the closed curtains waiting for Orliff and Aldwin to finish. When the curtain was drawn back Zusie rushed forward. Orliff and

Aldwin came out from behind the curtain with scowls on their brow.

"What is it?" Zusie asked anxiously.

"Nothing," Aldwin said. "She is quite fine." He looked back at Lizbeth who smiled at him. Her recovery was almost full, and it perplexed him. According to Orliff she should still be quite fatigued, but Lizbeth was raring and ready to go. Aldwin and Orliff, of course, were at a loss as to why she had healed so quickly.

"I told you I was," Lizbeth said. "Orliff, could I possibly have something to eat. I am just famished."

"Yes," Orliff said. "I will ask cook to prepare something for you."

"It's not going to be soup is it?" Lizbeth asked which made everyone smile.

"No," Orliff said. "If Aldwin agrees, you can have something more substantial." Aldwin nodded. "I will ask Franny, our cook, to prepare a plate of scrambled eggs, honey home biscuits and a bowl of fruit, if you like."

"That sounds wonderful!" She paused, "What are scrambled eggs?" Lizbeth asked.

Orliff looked surprisingly at Aldwin and Zusie, who both shook their heads. They did not know what scrambled eggs were either.

"I will leave the Elders to educate you on what they are and I will ask cook to prepare you both a plate as well," Zusie and Aldwin both said thank you.

Elder Phinney quickly explained where the eggs came from. Zusie, Aldwin and Lizbeth looked curiously at her. None of them had heard of bastions before, so she explained what they were as well. Zusie and Aldwin were not quite sure they wanted to try the eggs; Lizbeth however looked enthused to try them. She was also wondering about the bastions and that you could fry, bake them and put them in a soup. She was looking forward to the frying and the baking of them, but if she never ate soup again she would be happy.

While they waited for their breakfast the Elders began to ask their own questions. They were all very curious of how Lizbeth gained her new found powers. Obviously it had not been from Jasper stinging her as no one who had ever gained powers from it before. Something else, they were sure, had influenced it.

"Zusie, please tell us about the journey here, especially anything out of the ordinary where Lizbeth is concerned," Elder Enyce said.

"Nothing really extraordinary happened, other than she was in a coma for the duration of it," Zusie said. "She traveled mainly in a trolley, except for a portion of the trek through the Hollow of Rock." Zusie faltered for a minute before she continued, "She rode in a sling on Barton's back." Everyone looked at Lizbeth at the mention of Barton's name.

"He was wonderful," Lizbeth smiled. "He spoke to me and quite often. I couldn't understand a word he said, but his voice was gentle and calming; it gave me comfort."

"Do you remember the journey?" Elder Rayley asked.

"Oh yes," Lizbeth said. "It was really quite an odd sensation. I could hear everything around me, but I couldn't respond to it. I couldn't open my eyes or move my legs and arms. I wanted to, but I couldn't. It was like I was paralyzed."

"Yes, we have heard that description before," Elder Enyce said. "No one however has been in a coma as long as you."

"Anything else?" Elder Rayley asked.

"No," Zusie said. She looked at Aldwin who also shook his head. "Do you think she will always have these powers?"

Enyce looked at Rayley who shrugged her shoulders. They both looked at Sianna. Out of all of the Elders she was the one who had traveled extensively; perhaps she had heard of something like this happening before. She however only shook her head. She had not heard of anyone acquiring powers that they were not born with.

"Well then, perhaps it is a mystery we will never solve," Elder Enyce said. She then addressed Lizbeth. "Lizbeth we welcome you to Elsbrier and look forward to having you share your knowledge of plant life with us."

"Oh yes," Elder Phinney said. "Once you are well enough to move about I would love to give you a tour of Elsbrier and our greenhouses." Lizbeth looked at her questioningly as she did not know what greenhouses were.

"And," Elder Andi added, "the Gnome Gardens; the harvest is now done, and most of it has been placed in the underground storage bunker, but there is still plenty to see. I think you will like the Gnomes very much." Lizbeth also looked at her strangely as she had no idea what Gnomes were.

"As well any information you can add to the books in our library would be wonderful," Elder Sianna said.

"Now, now there, don't be giving her work to do. I have yet to fatten her up," Everyone turned when they heard the voice, and the wheels of a trolley making their way down the hallway from the kitchen. Franny was pushing a trolley that was full of food and hot tea.

"The poor dear has just woken and needs some nourishment. The lot of you will have to wait until she is better," Franny said. The Elders smiled at Franny. She was an upfront woman who could put someone in their place without even speaking; a look was all it took. She had been the one to convince Homsa to stay in bed a week longer than he wanted to, by threating that she would live with him if he did not. She even went as far to pack a suitcase and set it on a table at the end of his bed. He conceded. He liked her, but he did not want her coming to live with him.

Franny was a robust woman who was quite tall, had dark brown eyes, a bulbous nose and dark brown hair that she wore under a crisp white cap. No one ever saw her without a white apron tied around her waist. Even though she was a forthright woman she had a kind heart and when she wasn't cooking in the Mediplace kitchen she baked lovely cookies and cakes that she gave out to anyone who was having a birthday.

"I agree with her," Aldwin and Orliff had both said in unison which made Lizbeth sigh. She was hoping she could tour her new home after she ate. Orliff had followed Franny to Lizbeth's bed with a wheelchair.

"For how long," is all Lizbeth said as Franny placed a tray on Lizbeth's lap. She quickly filled it with a plate of food and a warm cup of tea.

"At least a couple more days Lizbeth," Aldwin said. Lizbeth sighed in annoyance.

"If you behave yourself," Orliff added as he placed the wheelchair at the end of the bed. "Perhaps Zusie can take you for a stroll around the Mediplace and the gardens outside, but only if it warms up."

Lizbeth smiled, frowned and then smiled again as she looked at Elder Sianna, "If I have to be stuck in this bed could you bring me a book or two to read?"

"Yes of course," Sianna said.

"Oh that reminds me Lizbeth," Zusie said. "We found your journal and brought it with us. I hope you don't mind but Marla and Chrystalina have been keeping accountings of all that we have seen in it."

"Oh that is wonderful," Lizbeth said with a bright smile. "I would love to see it." She took a forkful of the scrambled eggs and her face lit up, "Oh these are delicious!"

"Try the biscuit, it's a homemade recipe passed down from my grandmother," Franny said with pride and a satisfied smile as she handed Aldwin and Zusie a plate of food. "I will come back for this," she said pointing at the trolley. "I have cookies in the oven," she said before she promptly made her way back to the kitchen.

"Oh that reminds me," Zusie said as she took a bite of the biscuit on her plate. "Along with some of the scrolls we found in the Crystal Cave we brought your golden statues with us."

"You did what!?" Elder Andi shrieked. The room went immediately silent as the Elders looked in astonishment at Zusie. Their expressions then turned to frowns.

"The scrolls and the statues, they are yours are they not? They look like each of you; I thought you might like them. They traveled in Lizbeth's trolley with her," Zusie said.

The Elders looked with anguish at each other before they began to talk rapidly. The food Franny had brought went untouched as Zusie, Lizbeth and Aldwin listened in on the Elder's conversation.

"That is how he was able to breach the valley," Enyce said.

"And conquer the Tara Aquians," Rayley added.

Andi chimed in. "That also explains Lizbeth's recovery."

"And powers," Rayley said thoughtfully.

"And that is why the Rapcicors attack failed," Phinney said.

"You know what this means don't you?" Athia exclaimed.

"That we are protected," Jolise said. "He will not be able to wage war here."

"At least not in Elsbrier," Athia finished. "Who knows how far reaching their power will cast."

"They didn't protect us from the explosion," Phinney said.

"Yes, but that was different," Andi countered. "They only protect from outside forces, not forces from within."

"Where will the war be then?" Rayley enquired. "We assumed here and have been making preparations for it." The Elders shook their heads.

"This will change the fairies' journey," Enyce said. "It will have to be mapped out again."

"But like Rayley said, we assumed it would be here," Athia retorted. "If not here what destination do they give to the troops they rally into battle?"

"Sisters," Sianna said calmly as she looked at the worried expression on Zusie's face. "You are frightening our new friends."

"Zusie we are very sorry," Enyce said. "You did not know that we left the statues to watch over and protect the Valley of NeDe and the Lost Tribes of Old." Zusie, Aldwin and Lizbeth looked at each other. They had never known the name of the valley they had lived in.

"It is I who should be sorry," Zusie said as she put her plate of food on the trolley. "We had not deciphered in the scrolls that the statues were there to protect the valley."

"You were able to decipher the scrolls?" Sianna asked.

"Yes my daughter Chrystalina is very adept at it. She reads the stars as well," Zusie said with pride. Lizbeth puffed out her chest as it was her that taught Chrystalina how to read the stars.

"I am impressed," Sianna continued. "There are very few who can read the language of the ancients. My sisters, our mother, myself and Mariela are the only ones in Southern Kingdoms that know how."

"Saphina and I can as well," Zusie stated, "but it is Chrystalina who is very keen on it."

The Elders looked at each other and all wondered the same thing- Was it because of their relationship to Canvil that Zusie and her daughters knew how? The language of the ancient was no longer used and forgotten by all nations, Northern and Southern, a long time ago. Canvil was not as old as Queen Faywyn and her daughters, but the language was still spoken when he was young.

"You said you carried some of the scrolls with you," Sianna said. "What of the rest of them?" She worried that if Canvil had taken over the Elfkin village he more than likely was able to breach the Crystal Cave as well. If he got his hands on the scrolls he would be able to decipher more than just the language.

"They are safely hidden in a cave behind the waterfall," Zusie said. Before Sianna could voice her concern that they would be damaged by the moisture from the waterfall, Zusie continued. "We put them in crystal line crates to keep them dry." Sianna nodded; yes that would preserve them. She hoped that Canvil had not found the cave behind the waterfall.

"Will you take us to the statues?" Enyce asked.

Zusie nodded. "I will check in on you later," she said and gave Lizbeth a kiss on her forehead.

"Don't forget my journal," Lizbeth said. Zusie nodded again.

"Zusie, will you tell Saphina that I won't be back until dinner. I want to spend some time with Orliff. There is much I need to learn," Aldwin said as he ran his fingers over the stethoscope that Orliff gave him.

Zusie nodded before she and the Elders made their way down the long hallway to the front door. She did not see the speculative look that Lizbeth gave Aldwin or hear her whisper "It's about time." She had surmised that Aldwin and Saphina were now mated.

It seems that she had missed quite a bit while she lay sleeping. She could hardly wait to get her hands on the journal to read all about it. She looked at the wheelchair and wondered; if Aldwin was going to be busy with Orliff perhaps she could make her way into the chair and out the door. However Orliff saw her looking at the chair and took the wheelchair with him. Lizbeth sighed heavily. What was she going to do to pass the time until Zusie came back? Sleeping was out of the question.

A movement in the rafters caught her eye and she looked up. Sitting on one of the beams was a creature unlike anything she had seen before. The creature, yellow in colour, with a fairy-like body, looked intently at the Elders and Zusie as they walked to the front door. Lizbeth heard the door open and watched as the creature stood and took flight after Zusie and the others. She called out to it but the creature never acknowledged that it heard her.

"Well that was quite rude," Lizbeth said. She wondered fleetingly if the creature had been eavesdropping on their conversation or was it coincidence that it wanted to leave at the same time.

"What was quite rude dear?" Franny asked. She had come back for the dirty dishes.

"There was something sitting..." Lizbeth started to say, but Franny interrupted her.

"Oh look you have company," Franny said. "I will bring some more tea and biscuits."

Lizbeth looked towards the front door as Franny walked quickly back to the kitchen. A bright smile lit Lizbeth's face. Jasper flew towards her; the fairies followed. They wore thick, brightly coloured sweaters with matching gloves and hats. Lizbeth thought they looked lovely. They each carried a couple of brightly wrapped packages. Lizbeth looked suspiciously at them. She was soon to find out that the fairies had stayed up all night with Bethel and Chrystalina, altering garments for Lizbeth. She had new tunics and undergarments, pants and shirts, a large thick sweater, gloves, and a matching scarf and hat set like the kind the fairies wore, as well as several pairs of socks and a pair of boots. Lizbeth was so elated to have company; all thoughts of the strange creature in the rafters were forgotten.

The creature slipped out the door just as it was closing behind the fairies. It kept to the canopies of the trees as it made its way quickly to *The Baron's Den* and Lord Warden.

Chapter 28
An Ogre's Tale

By the next day Elsbrier was a buzz again when the news of how Lizbeth had gained her special powers was discovered. However the villagers no longer talked about her powers. Rather they discussed if the Elders' assumption about the statues were correct. The statues were now in the cubby holes in the Gathering Room under the Whipple Wash Tree. They also speculated as to where the war would be fought. To stop Lord Canvil from his reign of tyranny and heal the Northern Kingdoms there was no doubt that a war would have to take place, but where?

Some argued that the Northern Kingdoms should fend for themselves and the Southern Kingdoms should not interfere. But the arguments always ended with; Canvil still had Queen Faywyn and he would not give her up without a fight. For the rest of the day everyone speculated on what actions the Elders and fairies would take. Come the following day however they would have something new to talk about.

When the Elders agreed that Fielddegard and Rojon could stay for a few days it had caused quite a commotion, but more so with Lord Warden than anyone else. Since arriving he barely spoke to the Elders unless it was to complain about one thing or another. He did so in a condescending manner that always ended with, *'this is not how I do things in Boswick.'* He suggested in a pompous manner that it was wiser to ask the Ogres to leave. When they did not agree with him, he made snide remarks about the Ronans and Orliff.

The Elders immediately took offense, because they loved and respected the Ronans as much as Orliff did. It was Elder Rayley whoever that put Lord Warden in his place. She had become very angry and told him if he didn't like how they ran things in Elsbrier he could take his team and leave. Lord Warden argued back that he was the lead benefactor of the tournament and was not about to pull his team from the competition. Elder Rayley then suggested that his team could stay and he could leave. He argued that that was ridiculous; he would not leave his team behind. She then suggested that he keep his opinions to himself and let them run Elsbrier as they saw fit. She also added that at any time they could cancel the games and there was nothing he or any of the other visiting royals could do about it. Lord Warden marched off in a huff and hadn't spoken to them since.

When he saw the fairies walking with the Ronans he overheard them tell Hamy that they were going to meet Rojon and Fielddegard. He cringed inwardly, but said nothing. Instead he made his excuses to Lady Rosetta and marched up to his room. He walked to the cage with the firefly in it and commanded her to eavesdrop on the Ogres. His plan to get rid of the Ogres with the Elders' help had failed, but that didn't mean he couldn't rid the village of them himself. An allegiance between the Ogres, Elders and the fairies was not in his plans and he would end it by any means possible. While he watched the firefly stealthily make its way towards the Whipple Wash Tree he plotted out his next move.

The Ronans had been wary about meeting the Ogres; Orliff and the Elders were all the family they had ever known. Neither of them remembered anything about the life they lived before they came to Elsbrier. However with encouragement from the fairies and their assurance that it would do them a world of good, they did. Orliff met up with them just as they stepped onto the path that led to the tree and beyond. As they turned a bend they could see the peak of the large tent behind a grouping of trees. The Ronans slowed their pace and the fairies walked on ahead of them. As they turned the next bend they saw a fire glowing in a stone lined pit. It was several feet from the tent. Sitting beside it on a large log was Fielddegard; Rojon was nowhere in sight. Three other logs sat around the fire as well. Fielddegard stirred something in a large pot that sat on a metal grill over the fire. They had refused the Elders' invitation to eat their meals in the Great Hall, stating that it had been so long since either of them had been camping. They were looking forward to cooking outdoors.

Zee and the fairies walked straight up to the fire pit and greeted Fielddegard warmly; the Ronans and Orliff stopped a few paces away. Fielddegard greeted the fairies warmly in return. When he began to ask where Jasper was he stopped midsentence when he spied Ronan and Ronan looking at him curiously. He stared back at them. He then gasped in astonishment. He dropped the large ladle into the pot which caused the fish stew that was cooking in it to splash over the sides. The flames greedily leapt up the sides of the pot, catching it on fire. Without thinking he immediately grabbed the handle of the pot and picked it up. Although his was as thick as rawhide the hot metal seared his hand. He yelled out with a great roar. Not wanting to spill the contents of the pot he carefully put it on the ground next to the fire. As soon as he let go of the handle however he jumped up and down as he grabbed at his hand.

His jumping shook the ground around them. The tent poles collapsed onto themselves. His roar alerted the Elders who came running down the hill, Jasper followed quickly behind them. It had also alerted Rojon who came running past the collapsed tent carrying an armful of wood. As he skidded to a stop, Fielddegard pointed at Ronan and Ronan. He was as shocked as Fielddegard and dropped the armful of wood onto his feet. Rojon roared out as Fielddegard had, and jumped up and down. The vibrations from his stomping knocked Zee clean off her feet and she landed bottom first on the ground with a dull thud. She immediately screwed up her face, leaned over and started to rub her bottom.

The Elders ran towards Orliff and the fairies. Several villagers along with Obwyn and Nayew ran in just behind them. Each of them brandished a sword. They thought the Ogres had been under attack, but hearing laughter they holstered their swords and walked to the circle. Enna was laughing hysterically at what had just happened and Ashlina quickly followed as she helped Zee to her feet. Shanata and Mariela hid snickers behind their hands. Elder Andi asked what was going on. Shanata quickly explained what had happened and everyone but Orliff looked from the Ronans to Fielddegard and Rojon. He immediately went up to them and ordered them to sit down on the logs so that he could take a look at their injuries. They did so, but looked inquisitively at the Ronans; which made the Ronans feel uncomfortable.

Seeing that everything was alright Obwyn told the villagers that they could leave. As they walked back towards the village they passed Miss Casey who was being pushed in her wheelchair by Miss J. They had been out for a stroll when they heard the roar. Miss Casey insisted that Miss J take her to the Ogres. One of the villagers told them that all was well, but Miss Casey wanted to see for herself.

"Are you okay?" Elder Enyce asked.

"I was just about to ask the same thing," Orliff said as he looked up at Rojon. Rojon seemed to be in shock as Orliff spread a salve on the tops of his feet. Fielddegard however was not in shock. As Orliff wrapped his brother's cuts with a filmy gauze, he addressed the Ronans rather than answer Enyce's question. "Come closer and tell us your names?"

"My name is Ronan Black."

"And my name is Ronan Brown."

Fielddegard looked at his brother. The shock at seeing the Ronans had passed and he was now looking at him with a hopeful expression. Fielddegard nodded at him and smiled; Rojon nodded and smiled as well.

"No," Fielddegard started to say as he looked at the

Ronans. "You are Nary," he said pointing to Ronan Black. "And you are Rayn" he said to Ronan Brown.

"How do you come by this information?" Orliff asked as he put a large dab of salve on Fielddegard's hand and quickly wrapped it with gauze.

"Because our last name is Ronan," Rojon said. "And these two are our sister's long lost sons."

A gasp of astonishment could be heard around the clearing as everyone looked from the Ronans to Fielddegard and Rojon. The Elders came forward and looked carefully at their features. Even Orliff looked more closely at them. There was no denying it. They had similar facial features. The shape of their eyes was identical right down to the length of their lashes and the arch of their eyebrows.

The clearing grew quiet. All that could be heard was the squeaking of wheels as Miss J and Miss Casey entered the clearing. "Did we just hear right; the Ronans have found their kin," Miss Casey asked. She immediately started to write on a pad of paper. Everyone turned in her direction when she spoke.

"Ladies," Elder Enyce said with irritation. "Nayew and Obwyn will you please escort them back to the village." Miss Casey was about to argue that it was newsworthy, but seeing the stern look on Enyce's face she looked towards Sianna instead.

"Yes, if it is alright with the Ronans...I mean Nary and Rayn I will come by tomorrow and give you the scoop on the story," Nary and Rayn nodded that it was alright with them. They both looked over at Fielddegard and Rojon.

"There is no need for that. We don't mind if they stay," Fielddegard said. "Please, won't you all sit while we tell you our tale of how we are kin to Rayn and Nary?"

Everyone picked a spot on one of the logs that surrounded the fire pit. Jasper fluttered down and sat on Zee's shoulder. Miss J pushed Miss Casey into the space between two of the logs. Before she sat down on the log she took the scarf from around her shoulders, folded it in half and spread it on the log. The Elders looked at her in disbelief before they turned to Fielddegard. Fielddegard cleared his throat before he began.

"Our sister Anajian met up with and married a trapper named Blackthorn," he started to say.

At the mention of Blackthorn's name everyone's back stiffened and they looked cautiously at Nary and Rayn.

"Henry was a kind man who loved our sister dearly," Fielddegard said. Relieved that it was not John Blackthorn, everyone turned back to Fielddegard. "Henry loved her so much that he had forsaken his own family when they condoned his marriage to our sister. When our parents heard how upset Henry's family was about their union, they asked Henry and Anajian to make a home in Pharynthorn or one of the smaller hamlets nearby. They however were not worried about their safety and moved to a cottage in the woods."

They had lived there quite happily for a number of years and had two sons. One day after the spring thaw Rojon and I went to visit them. It was our custom to see how they fared through the winter. And we also brought them gifts from our parents," Fielddegard faltered as a lump of emotion formed in his throat. Rojon finished the tale for him.

"We found their cottage burned to the ground," he said as he too tried to keep the emotion at bay. Everyone could tell however that their tale was continuing to get more difficult to tell. "Anajian and Henry were dead within it, and they had been so for several months. Our nephew were nowhere in sight," Rojon controlled his emotions before he continued. "We buried them in a small clearing beside their cottage before we set out to look for their sons. We had combed the forest surrounding the cottage, but because the snow had already melted there were no tracks to follow. We gave up the search for you," he said as he looked apologetically at Nary and Rayn. "But we never gave up hope that we would one day find you."

Nary and Rayn were caught up in emotion and could only

nod their heads. They understood how futile the search would have been. They held no ill feelings towards them. Fielddegard and Rojon smiled with delight. They were indeed their sister's sons. She did not have a mean bone in her body either and would have forgiven them too.

"How did you come to live in Elsbrier?" Rojon asked.

Orliff looked at the Elders who nodded their heads. Because they never found Blackthorn it was best that Fielddegard and Rojon know about him. He might still be out there biding his time. As Orliff explained what had transpired those many years ago Fielddegard and Rojon became steadily angrier. And when Orliff explained the extent of Rayn's injuries Rojon pounded his big beefy fist into his hand. When they heard of how Nary stood up to Blackthorn they looked at him with pride.

They had heard about Henry's brother and how cruel he could be. They had also heard that he had been the angriest of his family and vowed to get back at Henry for choosing an Ogre over his own kind. When they had come across the cottage they had thought the fire had been an accident, but when they heard Orliff's story they knew that wasn't the case.

Seeing that his uncles were getting more upset as time went by Nary stood and abruptly asked everyone to leave. He stated that he and Rayn would like to speak with their uncles alone. The Elders agreed and everyone, even Miss Casey, left. Nary, Rayn and their newfound uncles sat around the fire and talked well into the night. None of them noticed the firefly sitting on a branch in the nearest tree, listening to everything they said.

Chapter 29
Shanata Takes a Stand

Several days had passed since the Ronans found out about their parents. The news had traveled quickly and for two days afterward Rayn and Nary were bombarded with questions. Even visitors to Elsbrier stopped by their shop and wanted to talk about it. Miss Casey stopped by as well and interviewed them for the *Village Voice*. The Elders commissioned a visiting artist to draw a portrait of all four of the Ronans together; it was to be a gift for Rayn and Nary's grandparents.

The news however subsided as Elsbrier became busier with each passing day. All of the Hawkeye teams, their coaches, visiting dignitaries and fans had arrived. Those who didn't find lodging in Elsbrier traveled the short one hour ride to the Hamlet of Baryn located southwest of Elsbrier along the Grandiflora River, and the Village of Lochtaryn located not far from Baryn. Unlike Dunaster, these communities were small, with only a couple hundred residents each. In preparation for the Hawkeye games large boarding houses had been built to help with the overflow from Elsbrier.

Elder Sianna had visited the communities at the beginning of the summer and reported that this year's games were to be well attended if the feedback they were getting from the Southern Kingdoms was accurate. When the Council of Elders that governed both communities complained that they could not afford to build the boarding houses, the Seven Elders gave them the money to buy the materials and hire carpenters. When they asked for the Jarrell brothers they were told that they were too busy building the Mediplace and helping out with the fairies' combat training. The Council of Elders were disappointed. The Jarrell brothers were the finest carpenters around. They then asked if Osborne Jarrell could design the houses for them and oversee the projects. It was agreed upon that he would design them and travel one day a week to oversee their progress. He after all had a shop to run as well. Without a hitch the houses were built and were now filled with visiting dignitaries and their entourages.

Elsbrier, Lochtaryn and Baryn were not the only things filled to overflowing, Vendors Row was as well. From Elsbrier straight through to the gates of the Stadium vendors lined both sides of the road. More vendors than normal arrived and Elder Phinney mapped out the area surrounding the road. Tributaries, several hundred feet long, were added off the main road and vendors now lined each side of them too. Spirals of smoke coming from small portable chiminea fireplaces could be seen throughout the day and night. The air smelled of burning wood and sage, as the herb was used to soften the odour of the burning wood.

Elsbrier was a commotion of chaos from sun up to well after the sun set. With all the new strangers walking about it was difficult for Obwyn and Nayew to oversee the protection of the village. Jaja's deceit had not been forgotten and everyone was considered a potential enemy. The extra precaution had not diminished the festival spirit however, and everyone was looking forward to the Hawkeye games which were just a few days away. The only ones not looking forward to or getting excited about the games were the Elfkins. They were too busy helping the Jarrell brothers with the build of their new homes. Old Barty had overseen the plans for the Elfkin homes. Although they looked similar to the ones they once lived in, these homes were made with superior materials.

The Elfkins were fascinated with the addition of glass windows and indoor bathing chambers. Many of the Elfkins thought the glass was ingenious, because it would allow for light to come in eliminating the use for candles throughout the day. They were also given the choice of a covered porch off the front door, which most of them opted for. In the spring, bastion coops would be built, vegetable gardens would be sowed and weaving, pottery and drying huts would be built closer to the river.

At first it seemed that the Elfkins would not like their new home, especially after the death of Paraphin and Barton. However once Lizbeth recovered she comforted with her presence. The Elders had also taken every precaution to ease them into their surroundings and the advances in everyday living. It was quite different from what the Elfkins were used to.

Each day a group of them were taken into Elsbrier for a tour that was conducted by Jopha and Zan, who proved to be both knowledgeable and witty. While they sat comfortably in a four wheeled trolley pulled by a team of pokeys Jopha and Zan drove them around the village. They would occasionally stop and let the Elfkins out to wonder in and out of the shops in the Vendor Market. For the first time the Elfkins bought goods. The Elders had given each family a pouch of money that would last them throughout the winter season. Zan and Jopha also showed them where the Mediplace was, the Lily Pond and the stadium. Those interested were taken to the Gnome Gardens where they picked up bushels of vegetables, fruit and herbs. All in all their new surroundings were quickly becoming home to them.

They also became use to seeing Fielddegard and Rojon walking among them. At first Paramo and her group of friends had complained about them; saying that the sight of them would give their underlings nightmares. However, they had offered their assistance with building the Elfkin homes, which the Jarrell brothers appreciated greatly. When Paramo saw how hardworking they were she stopped complaining about them. Everyone wondered if perhaps it was because Martan had spoken to her. He had been released the day the fairies had brought home the Ogres. He had been well enough to help with the build and worked side by side with Rojon and Fielddegard. Zeander and Bauthal had formed an instant kinship with Rojon and Fielddegard on the walk back from fetching Rhethea. On Zeander's word the Meadow Imps and Tara Aquians, who also helped out with the Elfkin build, befriended them too.

Lord Warden was the only one left in the village who didn't like that they were there and in defiance refused to socialize with anyone. Lady Rosetta and the Boswick Trapper were they only ones out of Lord Warden's entourage who were social. Lady Rosetta was often seen speaking with Miss J as she loved the theatre as well. She was looking forward to the performance of *A Stab in the Park*. It would be presented on the open stage so that more of the visiting countrymen could watch it. Lady Rosetta had taken quite a liking to Obwyn, who seemed to like her just as much. On several occasions they were seen walking through the village together. They enjoyed sitting at the cafes, listening to the visiting minstrels and laughing at the acrobats and jugglers. It was the first time that Obwyn had shown interest in a woman since his wife had passed away several years ago.

The Boswick Trappers, especially Herb, had made quite the stir with the young ladies in the village. They followed him wherever he went and made all sorts of excuses to have lunch at *The Baron's Den* where Herb often sat with a couple of his teammates. This day had been no different. He was sitting at one of the tables when Mary walked in. She was wearing a lovely floral dress and a hand knitted sweater, matching scarf and hat set that Rishley had made. Her long hair was plaited in one braid that hung over her shoulder. A small pink ribbon was tied in a bow at the end of it. When she came up to a table that Zila was sitting at, she smiled prettily at Herb. He smiled back at her which made Mary giggle. Zila looked at Mary with a scowl on her face then over at Herb. He had tried to engage her in conversation while she waited for Mary to arrive, but she had ignored him.

"Mary, you are making a fool of yourself, do sit down will you," Zila said. Mary did not take offense to her friend's words. When she sat down she waved lightly at Herb, who winked at her and smiled; which caused her to giggle again.

"You do know he does that with all the girls," Zila said. She looked strangely at Mary's attire. "What are you wearing?" Zila was dressed in long pants, and a thick sweater that her mother had knit for her. Under the sweater she wore a long sleeved shirt. Placed over the back of her chair was a coat; a scarf lay over it. She had dressed for the weather. Mary on the other hand was dressed as if it were still summer.

"Yes of course I do," Mary said. "I am not an idiot you know. He is just so dreamy and what's wrong with what I am wearing?" Mary looked down at her dress. "I think it is quite lovely. I just finished making it last night."

"I agree, it is quite lovely," Zila said. "But isn't it a tad light for the weather we are having?"

"Well yes, I was cold walking over here, but I am inside now and it is quite cozy in here," Mary said as she looked over at Herb again and smiled prettily at him; he returned her smile with another wink. Zila looked over at Herb than scowled and tsked; he had winked at her as well. He was handsome she would give him that and muscular as well. But he was way too self-assured and brazen for her. She was attracted to men who were confident, intelligent, and quick witted, but gentle too. As she looked towards the entrance just such a man entered. He waited for his eyes to adjust to the dim light before he walked over to a table that had two Elfkins sitting at it. She looked at him and smiled.

"Would you like me to introduce you?" Someone said.

Startled Zila looked up; Shanata and Rhethea were standing next to her and were smiling at her. She hadn't noticed that they had walked in the door as well.

"Um, do you know him?" Zila asked.

"Yes," Shanata said as she sat down. Rhethea sat down next her. "His name is Septer; the two he is sitting with are Rangous and Marla." Would you like me to introduce him to you or are you just going to stare at him." Without waiting for Zila to decide Shanata walked over to the table that the Elfkins were sitting at and started talking with them.

"What is she doing," Zila whispered. Just as Rhethea looked over Shanata was pointing at their table.

"Looks like she is asking them to join us," Rhethea said as she opened the menu that was sitting in front of her. Zila moaned as Shanata walked back to their table, the Elfkins followed her. Shanata quickly introduced the Elfkins to Mary and Zila; Rhethea already knew who they were.

To cover her embarrassment Zila stood and started to pull another table over so they could all sit together.

"Here let me help you with that," Septer said. Together he and Zila moved the table in place, while Rangous and Shanata moved the chairs over. They all sat down but before any of them could say anything they heard raised voices coming from across the room. They looked over; Hamy was there, so too were Lord Warden and Lady Rosetta.

Lord Warden stood very close to Hamy and pointed his finger at his chest while he yelled at him. The dining room became hushed as all eyes were on the three of them.

The night Rosetta had arrived in the village she told Hamy that his father and mother had died in a carriage accident. Their father's brother had taken over control of the small Kingdom of Bridge Camryn. It was a fifth of the size of Boswick and they often shared resources. Hamy's uncle was overseeing the Kingdom until Hamy's return. Hamy had refused his sisters request to return home saying that he had made a home in Elsbrier and was not going to leave. When Lord Warden heard of his decision he was quite upset and told Hamy in no uncertain terms that he was to return right after the Hawkeye games. Hamy however refused. Lord Warden was not going to let it go easily and every chance he got he spoke to Hamy about his duties to the people. Hamy chose to walk away rather than fight with Lord Warden. It would seem that this time however he chose to stand his ground and the argument escalated.

When Lady Rosetta grabbed Lord Warden's arm and stepped between him and her brother, Lord Warden became furious. He raised his arm to strike her. He quickly lowered his arm however when he heard the gasp that echoed around the room. Several men stood, Septer and Rangous were among them. Rhethea and Shanata stood as well. Shanata quickly made her way across the room; Rhethea, Septer and Rangous followed her. She stood beside Hamy and Rosetta and smiled at Lord Warden. Lord Warden scowled in return.

Lady Rosetta had changed since arriving in Elsbrier. It was partially due to the friendships she had formed. She stopped reporting where she was going and often ditched the guards he had assigned to her. Each day she became more insolent to his demands and Lord Warden did not like it in the least. That is what the argument had been about. He had approached Hamy about it.

Even though Lady Rosetta was older than Hamy by several years he was now as head of the family. Lord Warden thought Hamy should take control over his sister's antics. Heated words had been exchanged. Hamy didn't think he had the right to reprimand his older sister; Lord Warden was furious. When Shanata reached out her hand to Lord Warden, he was still quite angry. Without thinking he grabbed her by the arms and shoved her backwards. She slammed into Lady Rosetta, knocking her to the ground. Shanata lost her footing and toppled on top of her. In the process Hamy, Septer and Rangous fell over as well.

Members of the Elsbrier Hawkeye team entered the inn just as Lord Warden shoved Shanata. Hawns immediately ran over to her; Dale and Skye quickly followed. Zila suggested to Marla that she leave in case things got out of hand. Marla looked down at her belly and nodded. Zila walked her out the door and told Marla that she was going for help. Zila suggest that Marla not enter the inn until things had settled down. Marla however only half listened. She opened the door to the inn so that she could keep an eye on Rangous and Septer.

They were so much shorter than everyone else in the room; she worried what would happen if a fight broke out.

Once Hamy got to his feet he started yelling at Lord Warden, who immediately yelled back. Septer and Rangous got to their feet and helped Lady Rosetta up. While Hawns assisted Shanata, a group of players from the Orhem team stood up and made their way over to stand with Hamy. Seeing this, the Boswick team stood and walked over to stand behind Lord Warden. He no longer shouted at Hamy. Instead he looked menacingly at the members of the Orhem team for interfering.

In previous years he had made no bones that he thought the Orhem team did not belong in the games. He disliked the Lord of Orhem, who did not come from a long line of royalty like he did. Lord MacNaryn was a self-proclaimed Lord. He had taken over Orhem from its rightful leader who had been a distant kin to Lord Warden. However the Orhem team had won a spot fairly and the Elders would not disqualify them on such trivial matters. The Kingdoms of men often changed hands from one power to another. The Whipple Wash Valley, Boswick and the Greens of Totarrian were the only Southern Kingdoms that hadn't.

After Shanata thanked Hawns for helping her, she reassured Hamy that she was fine and she walked over to Lord Warden, who continued to sneer at the Orhem team. He was about to say something to them when Shanata spoke instead. "Lord Warden that will be quite enough out of you for today," she said with an air of authority. Everyone quieted down instantly. Lord Warden looked at her in shock as did the members of the Boswick team. No one other than the Elders had spoken to him that way before. Everyone else however looked at her with pride. Lord Warden went to say something again, but Shanata held up her hand.

"Enough," she said and took one step towards him. She stared him straight in the eye. Lord Warden's shocked expression turned to one of contempt, however Shanata did not back down. With a calm and controlled voice that held an edge of intimidation to it, she spoke to him but only loud enough that those standing right next to them could hear. "My sisters and I have been quite patient with your lack of respect for us and the Elders. However, if you ever lay your hands on me or any other person in this village again, I will escort you out of Elsbrier myself. The Hawkeye games be damned."

"I have…," Lord Warden started. Shanata once again interrupted him.

"Yes, yes we all know how much it cost you to get here and how wonderful the prize is that you donated to the winning team. Do you really think anyone would want to leave their home to live in Boswick? I know for certain no one from the Elsbrier team would."

"How dare…," he sputtered.

"How dare I what, Lord Warden," Shanata said. Her voice had risen and because the room was quiet everyone could hear her speak. "All you think about is the Hawkeye games. But what about the war that is on the horizon. My sisters and I leave in a short time to rally the Sothern Kingdoms to fight against Canvil and his army. Not once have I heard you or members of your team talk about it. Have you made plans, are you arming your men or do you think that the Kingdom of Boswick will not be affected by the war. As the most northern of the Southern Kingdoms, Canvil will most likely strike there first. Have you even prepared your people for it? Have you even picked a side?"

A gasp could be heard around the room. Everyone assumed that every Southern Kingdom would fight against Canvil and his invading army. The Elders knew that that would not be the case. That is why they insisted that the fairies learn combat training.

The door to the inn closed with a loud bang. Everyone but Shanata and Lord Warden jumped. They both however looked over at the door. The Elders and Obwyn stood with their arms crossed; behind them were Zila and Marla.

"Shanata, is everything alright?" Obwyn asked. His sword was drawn; when she nodded he sheathed it. Elder Enyce stepped forward and looked around the room. She had seen enough to know that the situation with Lord Warden had escalated. She too looked at Shanata, however she nodded at her. Shanata understood and spoke again to the room at large. "We are finished here. Please return to your meals," Shanata then looked at Lord Warden. He did not say anything to her, but gave her a look that spoke volumes. She had not heard the last of him. Without a word to anyone he walked past the Elders and out of *The Baron's Den*, his team followed after him. The tension in the room eased as everyone went back to their seats.

"Drinks are on the house," Hamy said. The Orhem team whooped with joy; Hamy groaned. He then smiled however. They had chosen to stand with him and Shanata. Their support was worth what they would drink in mead. Shanata and Rhethea walked over to the Elders and Obwyn. Obwyn made his excuses and went over to Lady Rosetta who was sitting in a chair beside Hamy; she was thanking Rangous and Septer for helping her. Marla and Zila walked over as well and sat at the table. Mary joined them.

Zila looked up at her as she approached the table, "Are you still interested in Herb?" She asked.

"No, of course not," Mary replied.

"Good; it will save me from teasing you that he was named after a plant," Zila chuckled.

Mary looked crossly at her for a moment then burst out in laughter, "Yes, I definitely couldn't date someone who was named after a plant; a tree perhaps, but not a plant that you could squish under your feet." Everyone sitting around the table snickered.

Hamy thanked Rangous and Septer for helping out and told them their food and drink order was on the house. He then looked at the rest of the table and said that theirs was as well which made them all smile happily. Across the room the Elders looked curiously at Shanata.

"From what I seen and heard you handled that quite well," Elder Enyce said. Everyone who heard what she said nodded in agreement. "How do you feel?"

"I feel fine," Shanata said. "Why do you ask?"

"Because you are glowing dear," Elder Phinney said.

Shanata looked down at her hands and turned them this way and that. She could not see them glowing. Elder Phinney put her hand on Shanata's shoulder.

"Wait for it," she said. Shanata waited for a minute. A tingling sensation spread out from Phinney's hand to Shanata's fingertips. She looked down at them in awe; they were glowing gold. She looked up at the Elders who were all smiling at her. No one else in *The Den* seemed to notice, not even Rhethea who was standing right next to her.

"What does this mean?" Shanata asked.

"It would seem that you found your powers," Rayley said.

"My powers," Shanata said. "But I don't understand." She then looked questioningly at the Elders as a thought formed. They smiled at her again. "I am... the leader of the group," she contemplated.

"That is correct," Elder Enyce said. "And you have always been. You are wise and have inner knowledge of things that we did not teach you. You are protective of your sisters, us and the villagers. I gather you didn't think twice of confronting Lord Warden. Intuitively you knew it was the right thing to do."

"I sense something about Lord Warden that just doesn't sit right," Shanata said with a worry frown on her brow. "It's the same feeling I had when the Radeks and I had visited Boswick. There is a shadow behind his eyes," Shanata stopped then as she looked at the Elders; they had seen it too.

"Come," Elder Enyce said. "Let us find your sisters and tell them the good news."

"How do you think they will react to you being their boss?" Rhethea asked.

"Not a boss Rhethea, but a leader," Elder Enyce said.

"They are two very different things," Elder Rayley said as she opened the door. "And our Shanata comes by it quite naturally."

As they left *The Baron's Den*, the firefly who sat in a corner of the rafters stood and made her way along the beam that stretched the length of the dining room. Once she reached the end, she climbed into a hole. She crawled along on her hands and knees until she got to a section that was tall enough where she could stand. She walked between the floor joists of the rooms on the second level of the inn. She came to a section that veered off in two directions; she took the left. When she came to another section that veered off in two, she took the right. When she got to a large hole that was partially covered by a metal grate she reached up, pushed the grate to the side and climbed up. She stood for a minute and looked around; Lord Warden was standing beside the window. He must have come in through the back entrance. He heard the grate move, but did not look around; he was expecting the creature to return. Instead he watched as the Elders and Shanata made their way to the Tree; Rhethea took the path leading to the Mediplace.

"Well?" Lord Warden enquired.

"It would seem that they all have their powers now," she said. He could tell by her voice that she was holding something back.

"Anything else," he asked as he turned around to look at her.

"They are unsure of you," is all she said.

Lord Warden walked across the room. He picked up the firefly and placed her in the cage.

"You mean they mistrust me little firefly; as well they should. But no matter, everything has been put into action. They will not be able to stop me now. Soon, very soon, the fairies will be no more and all the Elders' plans will come to an end. Lord Canvil will reign over all and I will be right there by his side." Lord Warden laughed wickedly as he locked the cage door and threw the cover back over it.

Chapter 30
A Stab in the Park

The sun had set on the day before the Winter Solstice. No clouds obscured the brilliant display of stars overhead or the new moon. No one in Elsbrier however was looking up at the sky. They instead were looking with anticipation at the thick red curtains with gold trim that were closed on the stage. While they waited for the play, *A Stab in the Park* to begin, they talked excitedly among themselves. The open stage was set not a hundred feet from a sloping hill just outside of the village. Not far in the distance they could see the small cottages and the grand theatre. As expected several hundred villagers and visitors to Elsbrier were in attendance. Set at a forty-five degree angle to the stage were two rows of five tiered benches. They were set up for the visiting dignitaries' entourages. The first five rows of chairs that faced the stage were reserved for the dignitaries themselves. Everyone was sitting and waiting, everyone that is but Lord Warden.

Since the altercation with Shanata he no longer came out of his suite of rooms. His meals were delivered to him by one of his guards. The team's progress was reported to him by Graphin. They were ordered not to associate with any one from the village or the other teams. The guards assigned to watch over Lady Rosetta were told to desist. She was thankful for it. Still fearful of Lord Warden's anger, she packed her bags and moved into the small cottage that Hamy owned. Noticing that Lord Warden no longer came out to the practices, many of the visiting dignitaries questioned the Elders about it. They however refused to talk about it. Unrest had descended upon the village and the Elders had no idea how to ensure everyone that all was fine; especially since they did not believe it themselves. For tonight however, the excitement for the Winter Solstice Celebrations and the opening of the Hawkeye games eased the tension.

The area surrounding the stage was brightly lit with shuttered lanterns. They would be closed once the play began. Lights were set on the front of the stage and strung on rope above it so that everyone would be able to see the actors. Although the day had been warmer than the previous, the night was cool. Everyone was dressed in warm coats and had brought blankets with them; even the dignitaries had blankets placed across their laps.

The crowd hushed as the Elders, the fairies, Miss J and Thurston Field entered the area. They sat in chairs just to the right of the stage. Not far from them Lady Rosetta sat with Obwyn, Orliff, Nayew, Nary and Rayn. Some of the Elfkins had attended as well; Lizbeth sat with Zusie, Chrystalina, Janilli, Saphina and Aldwin. Behind them were Marla, Rangous and Septer; Zila sat next to him; her brother Kale sat beside her. Next to him was Bauthal and standing on the last chair was Zeander. None of the Tara Aquians were in attendance. Since the Crossover Celebration they had not left the Lily Pond. They were preparing for winter and had taken Airam Andiela's recommendation that they make their homes in the abandoned caves. They had been busy preparing the caves with simple furnishings and stores of food, blankets and clothing that the Elders had given them. Within the crystal lit caves there was a waterfall that cascaded down into a large pool. From there it emptied into a river that traveled to the Lily Pond. It reminded the Tara Aquians more of the Boulder Clans' home than theirs. And although it was not the Golden City of Awnmorielle it would do, at least until spring.

Homsa and his *Band of Players* sat just to the left of the stage. The Elfkins smiled and waved. Old Barty was there, he was in the flute section. When Elder Enyce nodded at Homsa he raised his baton, Old Barty and the rest of the players raised their instruments and began to play a mournful tune.

The curtains drew back just wide enough for an actor to

step out. His name was Gyn Avery and he lived in the Hamlet of Baryn. He often acted in the plays that Miss J directed. Gyn was a tall man with long white hair and beard. He had a deep voice that was slightly accented. He was dressed in a black, floor length cloak. Upon his head he wore a gold and red feathered black hat. He waited until the music lulled to a whisper. He then spread his arms forward as he recited the opening lines of the play:

In the still of a darken night an evil rose
Like mist it encompassed all that it touched
Fearful the hearts of man became
As the darkness within their souls
Fought to overcome the light
But death be to those that fear
For strength of conviction will overcome
The battle that has not begun
And the war that has yet to be won
Tally up to the bar, friend and foe
And listen closely to the sad tale of Maradilyn

Everyone clapped as Gyn took a dramatic bow. The music rose again as he walked off the stage. The lanterns surrounding the area were closed, leaving the stage lit in a soft glow that added to the eeriness of the play. The curtains drew back and there in the middle of the stage a woman sat in front of a headstone. She laid flowers on it and wept for the death of her mate. But as the play continued the audience learned that the mate, who had left her his journal, had been living a double life and his death had been no accident. The woman followed the clues that he had left to fish out his murderer and bring him to justice. For an hour the crowd was entertained and at the end Thurston Field's play received a standing ovation, as did Miss J and her troupe of Actors.

The Baron's Den hosted a gathering after the play was finished. Everyone exclaimed that it was the best play they had ever seen. The costumes that Annie Dee had created had been lovely and everyone praised her for the costumes and the set which she had also designed. The festivities were winding down and the fairies walked out of *The Den* with Rhethea, Zila and Mary. The night had chilled and everyone pulled their coats closer to them.

"Tomorrow is going to be exciting isn't it," Mary said as she put on her gloves.

"Oh yes," Shanata said in a monotone way. "The opening ceremonies and the first game will be very exciting." Mary saw that her smile did not quite meet her eyes. She looked at the other fairies. They also had glum expressions.

The fairies had been quiet all evening and even though they seemed to have enjoyed the play as much as everyone else; they looked like their thoughts were a million miles away. Mary looked at Rhethea and Zila; neither of them had to explain what the problem was. In ten days the fairies would be leaving. While everyone else watched the games they would be preparing for their journey. They would only attend the opening ceremonies and the first game. The Elders told them they would have to learn the route by heart because they were not going to have a copy of it for fear that they would be separated or the map would fall into enemy hands. The fairies' journey was paramount to winning the war against Canvil.

They were still planning to visit the Ogres first. With the Elfkin and Meadow Imps' homes built, Rojon and Fielddegard had left before the play had begun. No one else in the village except for Nayew, Obwyn and Orliff knew in what direction they would travel next. The Elders feared that there were still spies in Elsbrier and wanted to make sure that no one was able to thwart their efforts.

After learning that Chrystalina, Lizbeth and Bauthal knew how to read the stars the Elders decided that the fairies would have a last lesson after all. Each night they would be tutored by the three of them. With no map to travel by they would need to know where each of the most southern Kingdoms was located by the position of the stars. They would also need to know how to find their way home.

"Are you alright?" Mary asked as she put her hand on Shanata's arm.

"Yes of course," Shanata said. "I am not ready to go back to the Tree yet. Why don't we walk you all home?" The other fairies nodded that they too were not ready to go back. Mary, Zila and Rhethea indicated that they would like the company.

"I will just let the Elders know what we are doing," Shanata said.

The Elders were still in *The Baron's Den*. When Shanata came back out Jasper was with her. He landed on Zee's shoulder and they all went down the path that would take them to Mary's house first. Next they would drop Zila off at hers. It was in the forest not far from where Rhethea lived. She had finally decided that she would like a house in the clearing where her brother's lived. But because of the time it took to build the Elfkin and Meadow Imps' homes they would have to wait until spring to build hers.

They dropped Mary off at her home and made plans to have breakfast together at the *Little Café* next to Awna and Ira's bake shop. They took the path that would lead them to forest where the Pixies lived. As they walked the night grew steadily colder and dark clouds rolled in.

"It smells like snow on the horizon," Ashlina said after she sniffed the air. Everyone looked up. The clouds did look thick, but they had an eerie tinge of purple and green to them.

"Odd," Zila said as she looked at the others. "Clouds don't normally have that green to them this late in the year."

"And I have never seen purple clouds before," Ashlina said.

"What do you think it means?" Zee asked. Jasper shook nervously on her shoulder. "Are you cold?" She asked him. Jasper however didn't say anything as he looked nervously up at the sky.

"Jasper what is it?" Shanata asked. "Jasper, Jasper," she said again as he continued to look up.

"I've seen clouds like this before," Jasper said nervously. "The night I blew into the Elfkin village the sky looked just like this."

"Jasper that was a long time ago and far away," Mariela said. "You are home now; there is no need to be afraid." Jasper however looked at her with a worried expression.

"The winds blew me around like they were trying to kill me off,' he said as he thought back on that terrible night. "It was like something was guiding the winds, forcing them to blow with such force. "

The winds suddenly picked up and blew at the tail end of everyone's coat. Jasper hung desperately onto Zee's Shoulder.

"Here," she said quickly and picked up Jasper. "Curl your snout please." Jasper curled his snout and Zee put him in her pocket. "There," she said, "see there is nothing to worry about. You are safe little one. Nothing can hurt you now. It is only the wind. There is nothing to worry about." Her words eased his emotions as he looked at the others. The fairies and Rhethea looked reassuringly at him, however when he saw the concerned frown on Zila's brow he knew that there was indeed something more to worry about.

"Why don't you take Jasper back to the Tree," Zila said. "I will walk Rhethea home."

"No," Shanata said. "We will walk you both home. If a storm blows in we will stay at Rhethea's until it is over."

"What about the Elders?" Zila asked.

"Zee can send a message to Elder Andi to let them know," Mariela replied.

At the mention of her name Zee did not look at her sister. She instead looked behind her, then to the left and then quickly to the right.

"Zee what is it?" Enna asked with concern as her sisters looked at her. Shanata and Mariela had seen that expression on her face once before. It was the day they fought with the

394

Jarrell brothers. The Whipple Wash Tree had warned her about Enna.

"Zee, what is it!" Shanata said with authority that had Zee looking at her.

"It's warning me, something about the park near the open stage," Zee said as she concentrated. Zila and Rhethea looked at her curiously and wondered what "it" was.

On the other side of the sloping hill before the open stage a small park sat. It was the spot Edward decided was good for the team to practice in. It was just outside of the village and was rarely visited. There were several parks in Elsbrier that the villagers preferred to stroll through. This one was surrounded by forest on three sides and only had a few benches to rest on. It had been cleared and a hard packed earth pit had been prepared for the players to practice in.

Everyone looked at Rhethea, "There is no practice tonight or else I would be there. Coach Dee gave us the day off."

"Well, let's go and see what it is all about,' Enna said.

They walked quickly along the path that led to the open stage. As they did the wind picked up and the clouds overhead grew darker and thicker. Jasper began to shiver in Zee's pocket as memories of his flight from the Venom Horde flooded his thoughts. Zee who was still listening to the Tree didn't realize that Jasper had begun to shiver with fright. The Tree had now suggested that she send for help. Immediately she sent a message to Elder Andi, who did not respond. She sent a message to Farley instead, who responded immediately. He told her that they were on their way and would stop in the village for help. Zee told him that the Elders were at *The Baron's Den*.

"I have sent word to Farley who will stop by *The Baron's Den* for the Elders."

"Why didn't you just contact Elder Andi first?" Enna asked. She had been walking beside Zee and looked crossly at her.

"I did, but she hasn't responded yet," Zee said defensively.

Shanata and Rhethea who were walking beside each other looked back at Zee.

Shanata looked down at Zee's pocket, "Jasper can you contact Elder Jolise?"

Jasper did not answer her; he looked to be in a daze as he regarded the sky with a fearful expression. Shanata noticed the state he was in and looked worriedly at him; something was up; something was very wrong. She hurried her pace along the path and everyone followed quickly behind her. Several feet from the open stage they heard not one but several blood curdling cries and then all was silent. Everyone stopped abruptly in their tracks and looked at the hill. The lanterns that had lit the area earlier that night had already been taken down. The hill was in complete darkness.

"Should we wait for help?" Rhethea asked.

Everyone looked questioningly at Shanata for the answer. It was Enna however, who spoke. "Are any of you carrying weapons?" She asked.

Her sisters quickly opened their coats and pulled out the knife that Obwyn had given them. When they arrived back in the village after getting Rhethea he had taken them aside and gifted them the knives that Jonas had made specifically from Obwyn's design. They were sheathed in a Lea-Ther pouch that Airam Andiela had made, again from Obwyn's design. Enna then looked at Rhethea and Zila. They each pulled out a knife.

In a short amount of time the tranquil, peaceful village had changed. Once, not so long ago, everyone walked the pathways throughout Elsbrier and went where they wanted without fear that some evil would befall them. But since Jaja's arrival in the village, that had changed.

Enna looked sadly at her sisters and her friends. She wished she was carrying a sword. It would protect them more than the knives would. But they would have to use what they had if something evil lurked about on the other side of the hill. Together they crept up to the top of the hill and lay down on their belly to take a look. Zee took Jasper out of her pocket and set him down next to her.

The clouds separated; light from the full moon lit the area. Everyone stopped themselves from gasping aloud. A line of bodies littered the clearing. A tall, darkly clothed stranger walked along the line. He kicked at the bodies to see if they groaned or moved; none did. Standing behind the bodies were seven men. They wore dark clothes as well. The moonlight shone off the steel of their swords. A yellow creature fluttered by the stranger's shoulder; upon seeing it Jasper could not help himself and he gasped. The tall stranger immediately looked to the top of the hill, but the clouds covered the moon's rays again and he saw nothing.

"Tell him the deed is done," the stranger said to the yellow creature; it nodded and flew north towards Elsbrier. Shanata looked over at Ashlina who nodded before she quietly made her way down the hill. She would track the creature and find out who the creature was reporting back to.

The others watched closely as one of the men broke rank and walked forward. "Why do we do his dirty work Blackthorn," the man said. "Eliminating players from an opposing team, just so his team can win the games. War is coming and he is worried about winning the Hawkeye games." Blackthorn did not hesitate and grabbed the man by his throat.

"We follow his orders until the time comes when our Lordship tells us not to. Do you understand?" The man gurgled out his reply; Blackthorn released him. He fell to the ground and gulped in air as he clutched at his throat. Blackthorn looked at the other men; none challenged him.
"Make it look like they have had too much to drink and killed each other." Blackthorn continued, "These Orhem scum are known for killing each other over such trivial matters." The men nodded and began to set the scene. However, overhead the clouds gave way again. Just as it did the fairies heard a rush of wind behind them and the thudding of

hooves on the ground. They quickly turned to see Nayew, Obwyn and six armed guards landing just behind them. The men in the clearing had heard it as well and ran towards the forest. Blackthorn was the first of them to slip into the shadows.

"Blackthorn," Shanata yelled and pointed to the clearing. Nayew and Obwyn ran to them and looked over the top of the hill. They saw the bodies lying on the ground and just made out the men running into the woods before the covered the moon again.

"Explain," Nayew said as Rhethea, Zila and the fairies stood.

Shanata quickly explained what had transpired since they had left *The Baron's Den*. She left out however the part that it was the Whipple Wash Tree that had warned them. No one other than the sisters knew that the Tree spoke with Zee. Instead she said that Zee had a premonition.

"What was the creature Jasper?" Obwyn asked.

"A firefly," is all Jasper said as he fluttered beside Zee's shoulder. Everyone looked at him warily. Someone had brought a firefly into the village; the Elders were not going to be happy about this turn of events.

"Where is Ashlina?" Nayew asked.

"She tracked the yellow creature, the firefly, to see who it was reporting to," Shanata said.

"By herself?" Obwyn snapped. He tsked loudly before he leapt onto Arturo's back and took off towards the village, one of the guards followed after him.

"How do you know it was Blackthorn?" Nayew asked.

"One of his men called him by name," Mariela said.

Nayew growled before he turned to the guards, "John and Matt take Rhethea and Zila home, and go together. I don't want anyone out tonight by themselves."

"Do you not want us to follow Blackthorn?" John said.

"No, a storm is brewing and Blackthorn knows these woods better than anyone and all of its hiding places. You will

never find him. When you are finished meet us back here."
They nodded. Rhethea and Zila hugged each of the fairies
before they left with John and Matt.

"Your Avidraughts will take you back to the village,"
Nayew said. "Find Orliff first and let him know what has
happened. We need him here. And then let the Elders know.
They have returned to the Tree."

"What of them?" Shanata said pointing to the bodies on the
ground.

Nayew looked at the bodies and knew that none of them
had been left alive. He shook his head and grabbed for Felon's
reins, "Go back to the village Shanata."

"My duty...," she started to say but Nayew interrupted
her.

"Your duty is to see that your sisters are safe. Go back to
the village and make sure nothing has happened to Ashlina. If
one firefly is in the village there may be more. If so we need to
stop them before anyone else is hurt."

"Come sister," Mariela said. "Nayew is right, Ashlina
needs us."

Even though Shanata could not see who lay on the ground,
she had liked all the players on the Orhem team. She
remembered them with fondness from the first time she had
seen them on her travels with the Radeks and was looking
forward to watching them sing their anthem and rally the
crowd into a frenzy. A tear slipped down her cheek. She
wiped it away with the back of her hand as she took the reins
from Nayew with her other hand.

"Orliff first and then the Elders," Nayew repeated his
instructions. The sisters nodded.

Not long after the fairies left a group of Avidraughts
landed- riding them was the Jarrell brothers. Matt and John
had dropped Rhethea off first and came back with them. The
brothers had been visiting their grandparents and Rhethea
told them what had happened.

"Is it true?" Mitch asked as he dismounted from Alwim. "Blackthorn has returned and did this." He looked down at the bodies in the clearing. Nayew nodded his head. The news would travel fast and he needed the Lord of Orhem to know before anyone else in the village found out.

"Mitch, you and Yan go to the Orhem camp and bring Lord MacNaryn back with you; I don't want him finding out from anyone else. Make sure an armed guard comes with him."

If someone hated Lord MacNaryn enough to kill members of his Hawkeye team they may take a stab at him as well. Mitch and Yan nodded and immediately took off for the Orhem camp on the other side of the stadium; a fair distance away. Nayew looked at the rest of the brothers with pride as they dismounted their Avidraughts. They never hesitated to help out when needed and rarely had to be asked. He, Obwyn and the Elders had talked in length about what role the brothers would play in the war against Canvil and as of yet had not decided.

He started down the hill; the brothers and their Avidraughts followed him. As Nayew expected none of the players had been left alive. They walked around the clearing looking for clues as to who the men were that Blackthorn had brought with him and waited for Orliff and the others to arrive.

Chapter 31
The Journey Begins

Ashlina stood at the corner of the *Tri Pepary Cheese Shop* located across from *The Baron's Den*. She had tracked the yellow creature there. It had stayed in the shadow of the trees as much as possible. Ashlina understood how easy it had been for it to go undetected; it was a very clever little thing and only moved when it was sure that no one was watching. However her special power was tracking and not even this creature could outwit her.

As she watched it fly to a window that had been left partially opened on the second floor she wondered how long it had been in the village and who had sent it. Lord Warden had rented all the rooms and even though he had been acting strangely, she didn't want to think that it was him. *Perhaps,* she thought hopefully, *it was one of his guards.* She waited for a lantern to be lit but none was. Maybe the partner in crime was not in his or her room; Ashlina wondered how long she would have to wait for them to show themselves. She would wait all night if need be. She leaned against the corner of the shop.

A light thudding of hooves behind caused Ashlina to turn around quickly; her knife was ready in her hand. She sheathed it however when Obwyn dismounted from Arturo and Jon, a member of the Guard Squad, dismounted from an Avidraught that was unknown to her. Obwyn quietly walked up to Ashlina and without a word Ashlina conveyed where the creature had gone. Obwyn nodded that he understood. When he asked if she knew whose room it was she shook her head. Obwyn motioned for Arturo to stand watch while he, Ashlina and Jon started to creep forward. The door to *The Den* opened and they ducked behind a couple of trees. Peering around the trees they saw Hamy making his way towards them. It looked as if he was on his way home.

When Hamy walked by the tree that Obwyn stood behind, Obwyn grabbed him from behind and held his hand over Hamy's mouth. Hamy began to struggle, but settled once he saw Ashlina; she held her index finger to her lips. They walked to the corner of the cheese shop, but Obwyn didn't stop. Instead he walked to the back of the shop; everyone but Arturo followed him.

"What is this all about?" Hamy questioned them irritably. It had been a long day and night. The last of the patrons had left not fifteen minutes before. He was eager for his bed as the morning would come sooner than he wanted it to. With all the extra visitors to Elsbrier then in previous years he was running out of food stores and the cellar would soon be bare of mead and wine as well.

The Orhem team had depleted his supplies faster than he thought they would. At first light he had planned to travel to Baryn and Lochtaryn. Although they were small they were both famous for two things, their mead and wine. Nearly everyone in the two villages either worked in the fields or the brew houses. He made arrangements with Arnak and Zan to travel to Dunaster for the rest of the supplies. When Nary and Rayn heard that they were going they chose to go with them as well. They would wait until Hamy came back from fetching the wine and mead.

"Whose room is that?" Obwyn asked and pointed toward the window where Ashlina saw the creature enter.

"That is one of Lord Warden's rooms, why?" Hamy asked suspiciously.

Obwyn and Ashlina looked curiously at each other.

"What is this all about?" Hamy asked again. His voice rose and Ashlina once again shushed him. Before either of them could answer him they heard a light beat of wings above them, all three looked up and saw the fairies flying overhead, they separated however; Enna and Mariela flew west towards the Mediplace. Shanata and Zee flew towards the Whipple Wash Tree. Obwyn looked at Ashlina. He didn't have to speak. She knew what he wanted her to do. She ran over to Arturo and leapt onto his back. They flew off in the direction of the Tree. Obwyn squatted down and pulled Hamy down beside him. He looked at the window to Lord Warden's room.

"Are you going to explain what this is all about," Hamy said in a hushed whisper as he too looked at the window.

"An incident occurred earlier this evening, a terrible ordeal that involves Blackthorn and a creature that flew to that window." At the mention of Blackthorn's name Hamy looked with shock at Obwyn and Jon. Everyone knew the tale of Blackthorn and the Ronans. "We are not sure at this time if Lord Warden is involved, but we cannot take the chance of spooking him into running if he is."

"What do you want me to do?" Hamy asked.

"Nothing for now. But tell me, do you have a list of everyone who has rooms." Obwyn whispered.

"Lord Warden, his entourage, Graphin, his assistants and the players are the only ones renting rooms." Hamy paused. Obwyn looked at him curiously. "There are a couple of rooms empty, but Lord Warden insisted that he rent all of them." Obwyn's eyebrow rose with concern. "That specific room," Hamy pointed, "is Lord Warden's sitting room; his bedroom is the one to the left."

As Hamy spoke a lantern in the bedroom was lit and they could see Lord Warden as he paced in front of the open curtains. He had had a fair bit of wine to drink and needed assistance to his rooms; Hamy was surprised that he was standing. Obwyn looked curiously at him; someone else was in the room with him as he kept looking back and talking, but he could not see who it was. He crept closer, darting from tree to tree, trying to keep in their shadows. Hamy and Jon followed him. They were close enough now that they could see that Lord Warden was furious as he paced and talked. The window had been ajar, but they could barely make out what he was saying. He violently grabbed something off the dresser and tossed it across the room. They heard it crash against the wall.

"I hope that didn't belong to *The Den*," Hamy said harshly." He'll pay extra for that."

Obwyn looked at him crossly and then turned his attention back to the window. Something flew around the room. Lord Warden cursed at it. The creature made a dash for the open window, but Lord Warden was quicker. He reached it before the creature and slammed the window shut. Hamy winced, thinking that for sure the glass had cracked.

Lord Warden swatted at the creature as it flew around the room. He missed it however and it flew towards the open door to the sitting room and ducked inside before Lord Warden could close the door; he followed it. Obwyn groaned. The light was not on in that room; they could not see what was happening, but they could hear things crash to the floor. Angry, Hamy immediately stepped out of the shadows. Obwyn tried to grab his arm to pull him back, but Hamy was too furious to stop and pulled away from him. Obwyn and Jon had no choice but to follow.

Hamy quickly made his way to the back door of *The Den* and unlocked it. Obwyn motioned for Jon to keep watch. Obwyn knew that a set of stairs went up to the second floor from just outside of the kitchen and thought that Hamy was going to use them. He however walked through the kitchen to the dining room and towards his office; Jenni O'Grady would be there.

When Obwyn asked what he was doing he explained in a harsh whisper. "The Gnome Vegetable Stand has closed for the winter, and I offered the O'Grady sisters a job. They have been helping out with all the extra work. Anni and Dani help Mrs. O'Shay in the kitchen and Jenni helps me and the Finny sisters in the dining room. But because Arnak and Zan are leaving for Dunaster tomorrow, I asked Jenni to take over Arnak's shifts as the Night Clerk until his return."

Obwyn looked curiously at Hamy. He hadn't been concerned about Lord Warden breaking things, he was worried about Jenni. Hamy opened the door. As he feared, Jenni was not there. She must have heard the ruckus and went to investigate. He ran across the room to a locked cupboard and opened it with a set of keys that he had in his pocket. He took out a sword and a club. He ran out of the room and to steps that led from the dining room to the second floor. He took the steps two at a time; Obwyn followed closely behind him.

The long hallway that curved to the right was dimly lit with lanterns; Hamy rushed by them and turned the corner at the end of the hall. It led to the front of the building where Lord Warden's rooms were located. As they approached they heard angry voices cursing and a lot of shuffling; Jenni lay on the floor just outside of the door that led to Lord Warden's sitting room. They could see blood coming from a wound on her head. She was motionless, but breathing. Hamy went to rush to her side, but Obwyn held him back. Hamy struggled but Obwyn would not let go.

"You will do her no good if you are hurt as well," he whispered urgently. Hamy struggled, but Obwyn held tight. "Calm yourself, let's think this through." Before Hamy could agree a half dozen of Lord Warden's guards came up behind them and struck them both on the back of their heads; they crumpled to the floor. Hamy was out cold, but the knock had only dazed Obwyn. He lay motionless however; with his eyes shut he listened as the guards called out for Lord Warden.

"Lord Warden, what do you want done with these two?" A man asked with a gruff voice that was heavily accented. Obwyn could not pinpoint its origin.

"What two?" Lord Warden asked. As he stepped out of his room he noticed Obwyn and Hamy on the floor. "What have you done!?" Lord Warden yelled.

"We caught them spying," the man with the gruff voice said. "Would you like us to kill them?"

Obwyn thought of Hamy and Jenni's safety. It was he could not to jump up and skewer the man with his sword. He however continued to lay motionless and listen.

"No," Lord Warden said. He stepped between the man and Hamy. "That is Hamy heir to Bridge Camryn and that is Obwyn. If you kill them there will be a manhunt and we will not make it back to Boswick alive."

"Well, what do you want us to do with them then?"

"Leave them," Lord Warden said. "Come in here and help pack my things." The men walked over Hamy and Obwyn and went inside the room. Lord Warden followed. "This has gotten out of hand." Obwyn heard him say. He knew that Lord Warden was now talking to someone else.

"You knew the consequences when you embarked on this journey Lord Warden." The last bit was said with such scorn it shocked Obwyn. He recognized the voice. It was Graphin.

"You would do well to know who you are speak...," Lord Warden started to say but Graphin interrupted.

"No Warden, you would do well to know who you are speaking to. I serve one Lord and it is not you. You created this mess by forgetting who you serve. Lord Canvil will not be happy to hear that you have once again foiled his plans to invade this Kingdom."

"How many times do I have to tell you he cannot?" Lord Warden began. "The Elders have protected this Kingdom and now they have extra protection that those half-lings brought with them from the valley of NeDe. He will not breach these borders."

"But he has breached them, Blackthorn and I are here." Graphin stated. His patience for Lord Warden was waning quickly.

"No, you and Blackthorn were here before the half-lings arrived. Blackthorn was in the Firelog Forest and you were in Dunaster with Jaja. I am telling you his Lordship will not be able to cross into these borders." Lord Warden added as an afterthought, "And if Canvil thinks that he can, he is just as witless as the Seven Elders are!"

A scuffle ensued and Obwyn heard a heavy thud and then a moan. He took the chance to squint open his eyes. Lord Warden lay on the floor moaning and holding his jaw. Graphin stood over him; his right hand was in a tight fist and his left hand held a sword. He pointed it at Lord Warden's throat.

"If you ever insult my Lordship again, I will cut you from sternum to stem." For effect Graphin ran his sword down the front of Lord Warden's chest. The sharp blade cut open his expensive vest and shirt and left a red mark on Lord Warden's skin. Unafraid, Lord Warden swatted the sword aside. Graphin smirked as he looked menacingly down at him.

Just then Herb ran passed without looking down at Obwyn and addressed Graphin, "Sire, the Elders are coming with a platoon of guards. We must leave!" Graphin growled loudly. He had wasted too much time with Lord Warden.

"Help him up," Graphin said pointing at Lord Warden. Lord Warden slapped Herb's hand away and got up on his own. "Where is the creature?"

"Under the floorboards," Lord Warden said as he pointed to the metal grate that partially covered the hole. Graphin looked with disgust at the floor. If Lord Warden had not insisted on bringing the stupid creature with him they never would have been found out. Everything had been going to plan, but because he needed to know what was going on at all times, the fairies had seen the creature and tracked it back to the inn. A thought formed- it had been spying in the village for weeks and had never been seen; perhaps it wanted to be found out. Clearly the blue liquid was no longer effective.

"Clever," he said. "Burn it down."

"What of him," Lord Warden said pointing to Hamy.

"Leave him and your things, we don't have time to bring them."

"I will not leave my thi...." Lord Warden began to protest.

"You will do as you are told, or I will inform Lord Canvil that you were the one who foiled our plans, again. He will not be so easy on you this time," Graphin smirked as he walked over to the fireplace. He rolled the burning logs onto the floor with a poker. He kicked one over to the window where Lord Warden's bags sat. The flames ignited the material and the floor length curtains on the window. The flames rushed up the curtains and smoke rolled across the ceiling

"Sire, they are almost here!" One of the guards who watched from the bedroom window cried as he entered the room.

"Where are the areondraughts," Graphin asked Herb.

"The back door sire, quickly we must go."

Obwyn continued to lie still as Graphin and the others ran past. He waited until he heard the last guard turn the corner before he stood. He quickly closed the door to the room and then ran over to Hamy and shook him. Hamy gingerly opened his eyes.

"Get up son, they have set *The Den* on fire, and I can't carry both of you. Get up!" Obwyn implored.

Hamy winced as he got up and leaned heavily against the wall. He looked around; Obwyn was picking Jenni up off the floor.

"Quickly!" he said as he ran past Hamy. Hamy looked behind him; the hall was filling with smoke and the fire was burning through the walls and doors. He groaned loudly with rage before he too ran. He caught up with Obwyn and followed closely behind him. Obwyn ran down the hall to the stairs that led to the dining room. They descended the steps quickly but carefully as the room filled with smoke. Graphin must have set the kitchen on fire as well.

Hamy cursed loudly as they reached the bottom step. He ran past Obwyn and opened the door; Obwyn ran past him. Just as he was about to follow he heard a scream coming from the rafters. He looked up and just had enough time to open his hands as a creature fell into them. Without thinking he brought it to his chest, shielding it from the cold blast of air that blew hard against them and ran to Obwyn; he had carried Jenni to a patch of grass nearby.

When Hamy arrived Obwyn had taken off his coat and was laying it over Jenni. Before he could ask if she was okay they were quickly surrounded by the Elders, fairies and two dozen villagers. Several other villagers had arrived with one of the water pump stations and started to hose down *The Den*. Hamy looked sadly at *The Den*; it was nearly all engulfed in flames. He knew there was no hope for saving it. As the second water pump arrived he yelled over to the men manning it to hose down the nearby shops.

"How is she?' Hamy asked. Obwyn shook his head; it didn't look good. She had lost a considerable amount of blood and the thick cloud of smoke they had to run through didn't help her condition. Everyone looked down at Jenni with worry, except for Shanata. Her aura began to glow blue and without hesitation she stepped forward and knelt down beside her.

Shanata briskly rubbed her hands together then clapped them sharply; sparks of bright light flew out in every direction. She then splayed her fingers out wide and held them just above Jenni's head. She began to chant in a low whisper as she weaved her hands in a circular motion. Everyone looked at her in surprise as Shanata's aura shone down from her hands and soaked right through Obwyn's jacket. She continued with the circular motions from Jenni's head to her toes and back up again. She did so several times, all the while chanting words that only Elder Enyce recognized.

Several minutes had passed when the crowd standing around stood aside. From every direction several Wood Spirits walked into the circle. Elder Enyce indicated that everyone was to stand back. The Wood Spirits formed a circle around Jenni and Shanata and held hands as they too began to chant the words that Shanata was saying. The blue light from

Shanata's hands oozed out from beneath Jenni. It made its way to each of the Wood Spirits in little rivulets. They soaked it up and their wispy bodies took on a pale blue hue that transformed into white light that traveled back in little rivulets to Jenni.

Everyone watched in astonishment as Jenni's chest rose. She took in deeply a huge breath of air and as she exhaled she coughed; a terrible hacking noise escaped her. When she finished coughing, a dark grey wisp of smoke came out of her mouth and evaporated. Jenni coughed again and another wisp of smoke lighter than the last came out. It did so another seven times. Each time her cough got better and better until it was just a tickle in her throat. Shanata and the Wood Spirits' chant had become quieter and quieter with each cough until it was just a whisper. Everyone clapped with joy as Jenni opened her eyes.

Shanata looked up at the Wood Spirits and bowed her head; they bowed their heads in return. They then turned and looked at Elder Enyce and bowed their heads; she bowed her head in return. The Wood Spirits left the circle as they had come into it; in different directions. However they did not return to the forest. They instead walked to the nearest tree and disappeared inside of it.

Everyone even the Elders looked in bewilderment at Shanata who laid her hand on Jenni's forehead and smiled. Jenni looked curiously at her and watched in amazement as her aura changed from blue to gold and then disappeared.

"You saved me," Jenni whispered.

"Not really, I channeled the Wood Spirits that is all," Shanata said as she stood.

"Do not take what has transpired here lightly Shanata," Elder Enyce said. "You called the Wood Spirits to help you heal Jenni. You instinctively knew that you did not have the power to do it on your own."

"I didn't realize that I had," Shanata said as she looked at her sisters. "I just did what I thought was right. So am I the leader or the healer?"

"Why can you not be both?" Elder Rayley asked.

Before Shanata could answer they heard a set of hooves followed by wheels making their way to them. Everyone turned to see Alamat and Niella. They were riding on a covered carri-shift, a team of pokeys pulled it. Niella reigned in the pokeys and jumped down from the seat of the carri-shift; Alamat followed her.

"We saw the smoke and got here as quickly as we could. Is anyone hurt?" Niella asked.

"Well," Obwyn said. "Jenni was very badly injured, but Shanata healed her."

Niella and Alamat looked down at Jenni and could see the dry blood on her face and the paleness of her skin. But her eyes were bright and her breathing was easy. They then gave each other a knowing look.

"What was that look for?" Shanata asked as Niella knelt down beside Jenni to examine her.

"Well, out of your sisters, you are the one who excelled in the classes that I taught you," Alamat said. "Don't get me wrong. You all did well, but your sister here, just seemed to know things before I taught them to her. I suspected that you were a spirit healer and mentioned it to the Elders. They told me however that we would have to wait until you were ready to receive it."

"It was quite difficult, we might add, not telling you what we suspected," Niella said.

"I suspect your confrontation with Lord Warden is what started it. Are you feeling oddly?" Alamat asked. Shanata shook her head.

"Obwyn do you mind picking up Jenni and placing her in the carri-shift," Niella asked. She then looked at the Elders. "She looks well, but I think it best if we take her to the Mediplace and keep an eye on her for tonight. Orliff will want to examine her as well."

"That sounds wonderful. Shanata would you like to go with them?" Elder Enyce asked. Shanata nodded that she would like to go.

"Oh that will be splendid. We have a couple of books for you to read," Alamat said.

"Oh wait, can you look at this as well before you go?" Hamy asked as he opened his coat. Everyone thought perhaps that he had been hurt too. When he opened his jacket however and showed them the creature, which was still unconscious. They gasped.

"Where in the world did you find that?" Elder Phinney asked.

"It fell down from the rafters as we were exiting *The Den*," Hamy replied with concern.

Obwyn had walked back from placing Jenni in the carri-shift. Seeing the creature in Hamy's hand, he ran up to him. "That must be the creature Graphin was questioning Lord Warden about," he said as he looked at the creature closely. "Is that what you tracked Ashlina?"

"Yes it is," she said.

Elder Enyce stepped forward, but instead of looking at the creature she stood in front of Hamy and addressed the crowd that had come when they had seen fire, "I think it is best that you all return home." A collective moan could be heard among the villagers, but no one argued as they walked back to their homes.

"Elder Enyce," Henry Rosso called out. He was chief of the fire brigade. When they heard his call everyone turned, gasped, and then looked worriedly at Hamy. *The Baron's Den* was nothing more than a pile of charred and smoking rubble. Luckily none of the other buildings in the area had been damaged.

"I will handle it," Elder Rayley said. She walked to Hamy and put her hand on his shoulder. "We will rebuild it, and make it better than it was." Hamy could only nod as Rayley walked away.

"Here Hamy, why don't you give me the creature and I will take a look at it," Niella said.

"Don't touch it," Jasper said scathingly. He had flown off of Zee's shoulder and was hovering above her head. "Let it die!" His words had everyone looking at him sharply.

"Jasper," Zee said.

"What? It's firefly. They killed my brothers, and countless others! Just let it die." Jasper clenched his fists in anger.

Everyone gasped again. Hummingmoth messengers were not cruel by nature and Jasper had been the kindest of all of them. To hear his open hatred for the firefly was disturbing. The creature twitched in Hamy's hands. Seeing this, Jasper's unfurled his snout. The creature however was still unconscious.

"Jasper," Elder Jolise said. "That will be enough." Jasper did not take his eyes off the firefly as he re-curled his snout. "Zee, take Jasper back to the Tree," she said. "Ashlina and Enna go with her please. We will be there shortly." Each of them nodded and left for the Tree.

"Shanata, I think it best if the two of you come with us," Enyce said. "You can get the books from Alamat in the morning. We would like you to explain to us again what happened this evening." Shanata and Mariela nodded. "Farley you and the others may go as well, there is nothing more you can do here."

"Do you want us to track down Lord Warden and the others? They were on horses. It will be easy enough to pick up their trail," Farley said.

"No they weren't," Obwyn said. "They were on areondraughts… whatever that is."

"Areondraughts," Farley said. "Are you sure?"

"Yes that is what Graphin called them." Obwyn said plainly.

Farley looked at Felon and the others. They each looked with concern back at him, "Do you want to explain what they are?" Felon asked.

"Is this something that can wait until morning?" Elder Enyce asked. "I think there are more pressing matters to discuss."

"Yes of course," Obwyn and Farley said in unison.

"Good. Why don't you and Hamy take the firefly back to the Mediplace for Niella and Alamat? You can keep an eye on it while getting yourself checked over; you both look worse for wear." Obwyn and Hamy looked at each other. Their clothes were soiled from smoke, and blood streaks smeared the side of their faces. They looked back at the Elders and nodded. The covered carri-shift was too small for them to all ride in, so Farley and Amos offered to carry them. Obwyn and Hamy agreed and left with Alamat and Niella.

The Elders, Shanata and Mariela had only taken a few steps when they heard someone else calling for Elder Enyce. She sighed heavily. With all that had happened they had forgot that Orliff and Nayew had been in the small park taking care of the bodies of the Orhem team.

They all turned around and were surprised to see that Nayew and Orliff were accompanied by not just Lord MacNaryn, but Lord Farenell from Pleasantland as well. The Jarrell brothers followed them with two wagons that were covered in a white cloth.

Orliff and Nayew both looked at the charred remains of *The Baron's Den*. "No one was hurt," Elder Enyce said.

"Someone was," Elder Rayley said sadly as she rejoined the group. "Henry found Jon near the back entrance. He had been run through."

"Jon? No!" Obwyn said disbelievingly. "I had him stand watch as Hamy and I entered *The Den*." The colour in Obwyn's face drained. Nayew put his arm around Obwyn's shoulder. They had both grown close to Jon and the other members of the Guard Squad over the last few weeks. Jon, his brother Paulo and their two cousins, Jeb and Milo had been invaluable to the crew.

Nayew turned to Mitch, "Will you go with Yan and get

Paulo please. He is standing guard by the Stadium. He will need to know about his brother's death." Without a word Mitch and Yan left for the stadium.

"You say no one was hurt?" Lord MacNaryn said angrily. "Four of my men and three of Lord Farenell's are dead. Neither of us now have enough to play in the games."

"The games? The games! Are you serious?" Elder Andi shouted as she stepped right up to Lord MacNaryn. She did not notice that he had drawn his sword. It shook in his fist. "Lord Canvil has infiltrated our home and left death and destruction in his wake. He has bent the will of a men we once called friends. They nearly killed an innocent girl in the process. Your men lay dead in those trolleys and you are worried about having enough men to play in the games? Shame on you Lord MacNaryn! I expected better of you."

"Sister," Elder Rayley said calmly and laid a hand on Andi's shoulder. Andi looked back at her and slumped her shoulders. As Elder of the Gnomes she knew Jenni and her sisters quite well. It was she that suggested to Hamy that he ask them to help out at the inn.

When Lord MacNaryn had brandished his sword, the remaining Jarrell brothers dismounted their Avidraughts and came forward with their swords in hand. Nayew had brandished his as well. Mariela and Shanata held their knives in their hands. Lord Farenell had taken several feet back. He was not one for violence.

"Lord MacNaryn, Lord Farenell," Enyce said as Andi and Rayley stepped back. "We are sorry for your loss and understand that you are under duress. With your permission we will take the players to the Mediplace where you and your remaining teammates can visit to say their last goodbyes. If you like we can bury them in the Forest of Glen or you may take them home with you."

"Take them home? That is ridiculous! There are nine days of games...," Lord MacNaryn began.

"The games are cancelled Lord MacNaryn," Enyce

interrupted him. She took a step forward when Lord MacNaryn looked like he was going to argue with her. She stared him straight in the face with an expression that caused him to take a step back. Without a word he stormed off, Lord Farenell followed him.

"We have not heard the last of this sister," Rayley said.

"I know," Enyce sighed heavily. She turned and looked at her sisters as the others looked on.

"What next?" Athia asked.

Enyce looked at her briefly before she answered, "Call a Council of the Elders for first light. Invite the visiting dignitaries and the coaches of their teams. If Lord MacNaryn has not already told them he soon will." She then looked at Nayew, "Round up the remaining members of the Boswick team. Take the Jarrell brothers with you, there may be resistance. Put them in the holding cells until we have a chance to speak with them." She then addressed Orliff, "You and Obwyn can take the bodies to the Mediplace." Obwyn and Orliff nodded and quickly left.

"Cancelling the games is not going to go over well," Rayley said.

Enyce thought for a split second before she called after Nayew, "Nayew, afterwards send the Guard Squad to board up the main gate to the stadium and stand guard at each of the entrances. We will deal with the backlash before the meeting." Nayew nodded at his mate with a grave expression before he and the Jarrell brothers left.

"What would you like us to do?" Shanata asked as she and Mariela stepped forward.

Elder Enyce looked at them for a moment before she spoke. "Go back to the Tree and pack."

"Pack?!" Mariela and Shanata both said in surprise.

"But we don't leave for nine days!" Mariela implored.

Elder Enyce looked at her sisters before she responded to Mariela. Each of them nodded at her, "You will leave in the morning before the Council of Elders meet."

"In the morning?" Mariela said in disbelief. "But what of the Winter Solstice Celebrations? Are they canceled as well?" Mariela and her sisters were looking forward to the celebrations. Annie had made them lovely costumes and with Miss J's help they had secretly arranged a song that they would perform.

"Mariela there is no time," Rayley said sadly. "You and your sisters need to leave on your journey as soon as possible. We are sure that Graphin and Lord Warden are on their way back to Lord Canvil. We need to gather as many forces as we can before they reach him."

"What of the lessons of star mapping with Lizbeth and Chrystalina?" Mariela asked. As if on cue everyone looked up at the sky; dark clouds still obscured the stars from view. Rayley looked questioningly at her sisters.

"Jasper will go with you," Jolise said. Everyone looked questioningly at her. The Elders nodded while Shanata and Mariela still looked confused. "Jasper was able to find his way home," she explained. When they continued to look bewildered, she went on, "As you know Hummingmoths have an incredible memory. That is why they make such wonderful messengers, they never forget. They are able to recall conversations that took place years ago with clarity. Because of their excellent memories they are also able to backtrack. They are able to find their way home without maps or reading the stars."

"But they had never traveled that way before," Mariela said. "And yet Jasper was able to find his way home; how?"
"Yes, well we wondered about that too," Jolise said.

"We determined that perhaps Elsbrier is a beacon of sorts and the Hummingmoths are attracted to it," Phinney said.

"Not Elsbrier, but the Tree," Zee said.

Everyone turned in surprise to see Zee, Enna and Ashlina walking towards them; Jasper flew just behind them. Behind him walked Farley and the other Avidraughts; they were laden with the fairies' backpacks.

"What is going on here?" Rayley asked.

"Well," Enna said. "I think it would be to our advantage to leave tonight rather than in nine days. We will have to gather as many allies as we can before Graphin and Lord Warden make it back to Lord Canvil." The Elders looked at her with impressive expressions. "Our bags are already packed."

"That is wonderful," Elder Andi said with pride.

"That is not all," Enna said. "While Ashlina and I packed, Zee climbed to the top of the Tree. She spied a large mass coming from the north, it is almost here!"

The Elders looked questioningly at Zee as they wondered why she would climb the Tree so late at night.

"It is time they know Zee," Shanata said as she and Mariela walked forward and stood beside their sisters.

Agitated, Elder asked angrily, "It is time we know what?"

"I...," Zee hesitated because of the angry look on Elder Athia's face. Enna bumped her with her shoulder and whispered *go on.* Zee continued, "It... talks to me."

"What talks to you?" Elder Athia asked.

"The Tree does," Zee said, nodding her head.

"The Whipple Wash Tree?" Elder Rayley asked. Zee nodded again.

"Since when and why didn't you tell us?" Athia commanded as she looked sternly at Zee.

"There is no time to explain that right now. A large mass, quickly coming this way, don't know if they are friend or foe," Enna said cheekily. "Perhaps we should call for the guards."

"Yes of course," Enyce said as she waved her hand in the air. But before she could say more, two people walked towards them. One was rather short and the other rather tall.

"There is no need for that, we are friend," Everyone sighed in relief at Bablou. He was accompanied by a rather large Tara Aquian.

"It is good to see you old friend," Elder Enyce said as she stepped forward and hugged Bablou. He hugged her warmly in return.

"This is Kerchot," Bablou said. "They have come to help."

Before anyone could respond several people entered from the east side of the village. It was Lindrella, Airam Andiela, Ellda and nine Tara Aquian guards. Lindrella must have been conversing with Kerchot and knew that he would stop in the village first before joining them at the Lily Pond. Without preamble Lindrella ran up to Kerchot and hugged him warmly. The fairies and Elders were taken off guard by the show of affection. From what they saw and knew of the Tara Aquians they were reserved and showed little emotion. The only time they had seen a display of it was during the Crossover Ceremony for Barton and during the *Healing Circle*.

As Kerchot and Lindrella stepped away from each other, others entered from the west side of the village. The Jarrell brothers, Rhethea, Nayew, Orliff and Obwyn dismounted from the Avidraughts they were riding. Each of them looked in surprise at Bablou and Kerchot before Nayew spoke, "It is done," he addressed the Elders. "The rest of the team is in the holding cells; they swear however that they knew nothing of Graphin and Lord Warden's plans." He then looked questioningly at Farley and the other Avidraughts, and the packed saddles on their backs.

Again before anyone could respond to what he said people entered from the south side of the village. Rayn and Nary came into the light with Lord Warden's carriage. It was pulled by the team of white horses that had abandoned the fairies several weeks ago. Amos spoke quietly to Enna, "Look who decided to return. Psh. Horses." He said in disgust. Enna chuckled at his reaction to seeing the horses. The door of the carriage opened; Zila, Mary, Zan and Arnak stepped out of it.

"What are you all doing here?" Enyce questioned.

Everyone began to speak at once explaining why they were there. They all talked loudly over each other and no one could understand what anyone was saying. It all stopped however when a loud whistle pierced the night air. Everyone turned and looked at Enna as she brought two fingers out of her mouth. They then looked at Shanata; she had mounted Felon and was holding loosely onto the reins. Enna, Mariela and Ashlina mounted their Avidraughts and they sat quietly waiting for Zee. She stepped back several feet and was about to execute her running and jumping mount when Kerchot picked her up from behind and carried her over to Farley. He gently placed her on the saddle. She whispered a thank you to him. Jasper floated down and sat on her shoulder. Kerchot smiled at him, Jasper returned the smile.

The fairies and the Avidraughts then turned to the group that had gathered in a semi-circle around them. The Tara Aquians and Bablou stepped to the side. They first looked at Airam Andiela, Rhethea, Zila, Mary and Ellda. They had been their friends for as long as they could remember. Never did they treat the fairies other than kindly. Each of them had tears in their eyes. The fairies quickly looked away from them to the Jarrell brothers.

"You are ready for this," Mitch said and rubbed his jaw. The sisters chuckled as they looked at each of the brothers who all nodded and smiled.

When the fairies looked at Obwyn and Nayew, tears filled their eyes. They had been tough on the fairies while training them, but they had also been fair and just. The fairies had learned a great deal from them. When they looked at Orliff more emotion caught in their throats, but they fought it back.

"Do you have everything?" He asked as Rayn and Nary came up to stand beside their father.

Shanata looked at Enna. She and Ashlina nodded. "Yes Orliff we have everything," she said.

"Do you need food?" Nary asked.

"Or coin perhaps," Rayn said as he dug in his pocket.

"No we are fine, really," Ashlina said. "The Elders have provided us with enough coin for the journey."

"Right then," Orliff said sniffling.

When Zan, Arnak and Hamy stepped closer and reached out their hands, the fairies smiled as they shook them. The fairies looked at each other cautiously before they looked at the Elders. Queen Faywyn and her daughters had been like mothers to them; teaching, guiding and comforting them. It was hardest to say goodbye to them. The tears in their eyes spilled over and ran down their cheeks as they looked at the expression of love on the Elders' faces. Yes it would indeed be hard to leave them.

"May the Light of Goodness keep you safe," Elder Enyce said. Her sisters were visibly moved by the moment and held back tears as the fairies said their last goodbyes.

"And you," Shanata said. She then looked at her sisters who all gestured that they were ready. "Come sisters a grand adventure awaits us."

Shanata then looked at Enna and nodded. Enna raised her sword in the air and her sisters followed her. "May the Light of Goodness prevail!" They yelled.

Everyone joined in the hail as the fairies left not in flight, but trotting towards the Whipple Wash Tree. They had one stop to make before they embarked on their journey. For how could they leave home without saying goodbye to the one that had given them life?

The End

Epilogue

The day had risen on Pharynthorn and the Ogre village was alive with commotion. Several Ogres stood outside the large wooden doors of the Council Lodge, speculating as to why an urgent meeting of the Chiefs was called. Kenkale and Kevink stood on the last step before the doors. Bearl, Arlesk and Buneve stood on the first step that led to the doors. Fielddegard had asked them to bar anyone from entering the Lodge. They looked stonily at the onlookers. When asked what was going on, they refused to answer.

The fairies and Jasper had flown all night and arrived in the village just before dawn. They had sought out Rojon and Fielddegard, whose homes sat across from each other at the very edge of the village. When Shanata explained what had happened in Elsbrier the brothers immediately called for a council with the Chiefs who had grudgingly agreed. The Avidraughts waited at Rojon's home while the fairies walked with Rojon and Fielddegard to the Council Lodge. The meeting that was now two hours long, unfortunately was not going well.

"We tolerated your association with humans Fielddegard, but we will not tolerate your insolence towards us by inviting them here," Belfagard the eldest of the Chiefs said as he looked sternly at Fielddegard. Although he looked similar to Fielddegard he was taller and his muscular youthful physique was in contrast to his aged facial features. Dark lines creased the corners of his eyes and around his mouth. He was clean shaven, had short stubbly hair on his head and his eyebrows were bushy. The other Chiefs, eight in total, looked quite old in comparison. They had long thin silver hair on their heads and chin. They had long strands of hair growing out of their ears. All of them were dressed in long muted grey robes. The thick sashes that closed the robes tight around their midsection were black, other than Belfagard's; his sash was a deep shade of red. It marked him as the leader of the Chiefs.

Much like the Elders of Elsbrier, they each wore a medallion. However these medallions were quite rustic looking and a bit barbaric. They had nine strands of thin branches weaving around each other in a large triangular shape. In the center of each medallion was a shrunken head. The fairies had learned from Rojon that the heads were of the Chiefs before them. He explained that a Chief picked his successor at the birth of the young'un; the name given to the Ogre children. The Chief could not pick a young'un from his own kin; thus giving each family-clan a chance to have a member of their family as a Chief.

When the young'un reaches nine summers old he leaves his home and lives in the home of the Chief and his family. The young'un, from then on is addressed by his name followed by *The Successor*. *The Successor* is tutored in the ways of the Chief and the ancestry of the Ogres. He also is responsible for writing the *Raige Tome* of the Chief. The book is a detailed accounting of the Chief's achievements; pre and post his successor's arrival. Upon the death of the Chief his successor enters into the *Ritual of Legacy* which is a month long ceremony involving the shrinking and mounting of the Chief's head, the making of the urn for the Chief's ashes and the reading of the *Raige Tome* to the Clan members. The Ogres believed that the heads of their forefathers brought insightful wisdom to their successors. They were also seen as a prosperity and good will talisman to their lands. The urns that had their names engraved on them sat on shelves at the back of the lodge. Their medallion sat on the urn. When the Chiefs entered the lodge they put the medallions on before they sat in council and took them off before leaving.

None of the nine Chiefs had looked at the fairies, nor did their successors who sat in chairs directly behind their Chief. On occasion however *The Successors* did look at Jasper who was flying nervously back and forth by the doors. He had refused to sit with Zee, even though Rojon had told him he would be safe. The meeting had reminded him of another meeting; the day he had met the Elfkin Elders. The Ogres reminded him of the big, harry and bucked-tooth visions he had while flying up the stairs to the Crystal Cave of Aspentonia to meet Zusie for the first time. Although Fielddegard and Rojon were kind like Zusie had been, Jasper chose to stay at the back of the room, keeping a watchful eye open for the first sign of trouble.

When Fielddegard and Rojon had returned home and told of their adventure, the only ones who thought that an alliance with the Elders of Elsbrier was a good idea were their parents and Fielddegard's band of comrades; the ones who now stood guard outside. If Fielddegard thought that guards were needed perhaps there was going to be trouble despite his assurances to Jasper.

"Chief Belfagard," Fielddegard said calmly, "as we explained, the fairies are on a diplomatic mission to unite the Southern Kingdoms. War is inevitable, we will need to pick a side and begin preparations for it, manning our borders and…"

"You will not school us on war tactics Fielddegard!" Belfagard interrupted angrily. However before he could say anything else there was a loud knock on the door. It was so loud it frightened Jasper. He flew directly to Zee's shoulder. The other fairies had jumped in their seats as well; even a couple of *The Successors* had jumped.

The door opened. Kenkale and Kevink stepped through and immediately stood to the side as Buneve, Arlesk and Bearl walked in. Walking closely behind were three visitors.

"What is the meaning of this?!" Belfagard bellowed. He then looked in shock as Nary and Rayn stepped forward; each of them bowed in greeting. When the fairies looked like they were about to stand, Rojon looked at them with a warning glare. They instead stayed where they were and stared forward. Orliff sat down behind them and stared forward as well.

"Chief Belfagard," Nary began. "I am Nary and this is my brother Rayn."

"Yes, yes, I know who you are," Belfagard said with a sneer. He remembered seeing the boys when they were young. They had come with their parents to visit Pharynthorn when they were only two and one summers old. That was the first and last time any of the villagers had seen them. He had been displeased when Anajian chose to marry a human; forever forsaking the line of Ronan from becoming a Chief. With no holds barred he spoke of his displeasure and loudly. The other Chiefs, although they had been displeased of her choice, had not verbalized it. Belfagard however had his own agenda. He thought that a young'un of Anajian's would make an excellent Chief. She was not only intelligent, but also regal in stature and articulate in speech. If she had married a warrior Ogre their male offspring would be destined to become a great leader of Ogres. Instead two half-lings stood in front of him; their faces and body structure were disfigured as they shared the genes of a human, which he thought were an ugly race.

"This council is finished," Belfagard said in anger. "We will not join you in battle. This is not our fight!" He looked at the fairies and Orliff with a smug expression before he stood.

"Chief Belfagard," Fielddegard implored. "Will you not at least hear what Nary and Rayn have to say?" His plea however went on deafened ears as the Chiefs stood and walked to the back of the room in a single file. They placed the medallions on the urns before they walked out of the large doors that Kevink and Kenkale held open; their successors quickly followed them. Only one of them was brave enough to nod at the fairies as he passed by them. Nary and Rayn looked apologetically at Rojon and Fielddegard.

"We are sorry uncles if our intrusion was the cause for the fail in these negotiations," Nary said.

"No, it was not your fault," Fielddegard said as he reached out his hand and grabbed Nary's shoulder. "It was not going well before you arrived." He looked apologetically at Orliff and the fairies. The start of their mission was not going as planned. The Ogres would not fight on their side as Fielddegard and Rojon had assured the Elders that they would.

"Well," Shanata said. "That did not go as we hoped, but one good thing did come out of it." Everyone looked at her curiously as she stood. "They are not going to join Lord Canvil either, so that is a blessing in itself."

"Well you do have seven of us," Fielddegard said.

"We are not an army, but we can hold our own," Rojon added.

"But Chief Belfagard said that the Ogres would not fight," Mariela said.

"No," Rojon said. "Not quite. We have free will to do as we like that is why our sister was able to marry Henry. Although the Chiefs may not like it, we will join you." He then looked at the other members of the band, they all agreed. He looked down at the fairies and smiled.

"Go home to your families," Fielddegard said. "Pack your things and say your goodbyes. We leave at noon for Elsbrier."

As the Ogres walked out the door the fairies smiled. Their first stop on their journey may not have gone as planned, but they did gather a few Ogres to fight with them, which was better than having to fight against them. They followed Rojon and Fielddegard to the door, upon reaching it Fielddegard looked at Nary and Rayn, "I think we have time for you to meet our parents before we go if you like?"

Nary and Rayn looked at Orliff. "Of course Orliff and the fairies are welcome to join us," Fielddegard said.

"We would like to," Shanata said. "But we must be on our way."

"Yes of course," Rojon said. "I will walk back with you to my home."

The fairies gave the others a warm hug before they left with Rojon. As Ashlina stepped off the last step she abruptly turned around and looked at the doors that Rojon was closing. "What is it?" Shanata asked.

"I am not sure," Ashlina said as she sniffed the air. "I smell something, something familiar, but I can't quite place it." The fairies looked at her curiously until she shook her head. "Perhaps it was just the scent of Orliff; the scent of home, perhaps," she said sadly.

"Come sister," Enna said as she put her arm around Ashlina's shoulder. "There is an adventure waiting for us. It is too early to be melancholy. We are not even out of the Kingdom yet.'

"Why actually we are," Mariela said as they all started to walk with Rojon through the Ogre village. "Pharynthorn and the Greens of Totarrian is actually a Kingdom on its own."

"You don't say," Rojon said dubiously, and then he laughed lightly.

The sisters laughed along with him. Even Jasper did as he sat on Zee's shoulder. However he looked nervously back at the Lodge. He had smelled something familiar as well, but then dismissed it.

While they sat in the council, a dozen fireflies listened from the large beams that held up the roof. After everyone left, they sat and waited for several minutes to ensure no one else entered the Lodge. They all stood systematically and walked along till they reached the end of the beams. Once in place they gradually changed colour from yellow, to orange to red. Once red, they burst into flames and swiftly ran along the beams to the other end. The dry wood quickly caught on fire. Just before the Lodge filled with smoke, they flew out of the ventilation holes in the roof and disappeared into the woods.

As the fairies flew east they did not see the smoke rising from the building they had just left not minutes before or hear the clanging of the fire alarm as it rang throughout Pharynthorn. Nor did they see Orliff, Nary, Rayn and

Fielddegard running through the big doors of the Lodge to rescue the urns and medallions of the past Chiefs.

*

In Elsbrier the morning was not going any better for the Elders. Nayew had awaken them just after dawn to warn them that Lord MacNaryn had gathered the teams and several of the visiting dignitaries together after he was dismissed. He had enticed them into action and now roughly two hundred people surrounded the hill. They however stood several feet back; Nayew, Obwyn and their team of guards had got there first.

From atop of the hill, the Elders noticed that the crowd was only comprised of visitors to Elsbrier. Lord MacNaryn seemed to be their leader. Unrest had settled among them. Where there was unrest Chaos would soon follow.

"Sister we have to address them," Rayley said as she walked over to Enyce. "Before they rush up the hill and get hurt."

The Elders had taken up stations around the Tree. They were not afraid for themselves, because the Whipple Wash Tree would protect them. It however would not look so kindly on the ones that would try to hurt the Elders; severe injuries or death would come to those who tried.

As Elder Enyce raised her hand for everyone to settle down, a commotion started at the back of the crowd. They could see the crowd quickly parting ways. Enyce smiled when Datoka and three dozen dogees walked to the forefront of the crowd. Zeander was riding on Datoka's back and Bauthal walked beside them. Behind them was Zusie, Chrystalina, Saphina, Aldwin, Marla, Rangous, Septer, Old Barty and Lizbeth. Each of them carried a quiver of arrows on their backs and a bow in their hands. Except for Old Barty of course; he had his walking stick.

"You are up early," Rayley called down to them.

"Yes, I heard a rumour that there might be trouble and I thought you may need some help with crowd control," Zeander called back to her. She and Enyce smiled down at him. "And I brought some friends with me to help."

A nervous energy started to make its way through the crowd. It was one thing to confront the Elders with Nayew, Obwyn and their guards standing around, but it was quite another thing to confront them when dogees stood guard as well. The Elders looked at Lord MacNaryn who stood right next to a dogee that was so tall he could have used him as an arm rest. It was all he could do not to squirm when the dogee sniffed the air and then growled lowly.

"I would ask that each of the Lords, Ladies and visiting dignitaries please join my sisters and me in the Great Hall for a meeting of the Elders," Enyce said as she tried to keep a smirk from rising at Lord MacNaryn's discomfort. "The rest of you please return to your families and pack your bags for departure. In light of what has transpired the Hawkeye Games have been cancelled."

A discontented murmur rang out through the crowd then suddenly stopped as screams pierced the air. Everyone looked in the direction of the other side of the hill. Elder Athia and Jolise ran out from behind the curtain of limbs and were staring up at the Tree. "I warned them," Elder Athia said harshly. "I warned them not to come near the Tree, but did they listen, no they didn't. They just rushed up the hill swinging their swords willy nilly."

"Who did?" Elder Enyce asked in surprise.

"Three of Lord MacNaryn's guards," Elder Jolise said. "The Tree has them."

Enyce and Rayley looked up as well. They heard more screaming and looked as Andi and Sianna came running towards them from different directions.

"Idiotic fools!" Andi said. "They didn't listen to my warnings, now the Tree has them!"

"Same here," Sianna said.

"How many?" Rayley asked. The Elders both replied the same number; three.

Elder Enyce looked scathingly at Lord MacNaryn. The death of his men would be on his head for not heeding their warnings. A cry rang out and everyone looked up as a man went flying forty feet up into the air then plummeted down towards the ground. Just before hitting the ground which surely would have killed him several limbs snaked out and caught him. The Tree placed him on the edge of the hill and gave the man a little nudge; he rolled down to the bottom of the hill and didn't stop until he came to a halt just before Lord MacNaryn's feet. Lord MacNaryn looked down at the man; he was in shock as he stared blankly at the ground.

Lord MacNaryn looked up at the Tree; eight of the nine men he ordered to rush the Tree were still missing. Several minutes passed while everyone watched as the Elders pleaded with the Tree to release the men unharmed. Finally it did so, but not before it had some fun with them. It threw them up in the air, passed them roughly through its limbs and tossed them from one limb to the other. As a result all of the men rolled down the hill after the Tree gave them a push. None of them however were badly hurt; frightened near to death yes, but no serious injuries more than bruises and scrapes. It was an experience however that none of them would soon forget or want to repeat.

The crowd had started to disperse after the first man was tossed down the hill. By the ninth man only the Lord, Ladies, dignitaries and their guards had stayed.

"We will meet you in the Great Hall in half of an hour," Elder Enyce said. "You will not need your guards. I suggest you send them back to pack your things. You will all be leaving before the days end." The Elders did not wait to see if anyone argued before they disappeared behind the curtain of limbs.

An hour later the Ladies, Lords and dignitaries of the visiting Kingdoms sat before the Seven Elders. Nayew, Obwyn and their guards were stationed around the room and outside of the building. Zusie, Zeander and the others sat in chairs to the right side of the room. Lady Rosetta and Hamy had joined them, but they sat off to the left of the main group. All the dogees but Datoka had left; he sat just behind Enyce.

The meeting had already begun and Enyce was trying to keep her composure as she spoke with Lord MacNaryn and Lord Farenell who seemed to be the only ones who could not grasp what she was saying. "As I have already explained, a spell was cast using the statues to protect the Valley of NeDe. Once they left the valley the magic changed. It has diminished and we fear it is unstable. To give each of you one of them would be reckless on our part. They will not protect your Kingdoms from Canvil's invasion."

"Then how are we to protect our lands," Lord MacNaryn said angrily. "It is fine that you can protect yours, but what of our people," he said accusingly. The Elders sighed; finally it seemed as if he understood. However his question now broached a more delicate dilemma that irked the Elders. It was all any of them could do to contain their composure. When Elder Andi stood to answer his question Lord MacNaryn actually squirmed in his chair from the glare she gave him. She however addressed the room at large.

"When we first learned of Queen Faywyn's abduction we sent word to all of you that we thought it was best to cancel the games and prepare for war. You and Lord Warden," she said looking accusingly at Lord MacNaryn, "were actually the two who insisted the most that the games continue."

"If you are accusing me of being in leagues with the likes of him," Lord MacNaryn stood hastily but then immediately sat down when Datoka growled lowly.

"My sister is not accusing you of anything, she is stating a

431

fact," Enyce interrupted. She then looked at the other Lords and Ladies. "Have none of you prepared for the coming war?" she asked.

They all shook their heads and then looked sheepishly down at their hands.

"None of you," Athia said with disgust. "You have had a year and half to prepare, what have you been doing?"

"We have been preparing for the games," Lord MacNaryn said defensively.

"The Games? The Game?!" Elder Andi yelled. "Are you that dimwitted? War is coming and you are worried about a silly game?!"

"It is not just a silly game," Lord MacNaryn said as he stood abruptly again. "For many of us it is a way of life. The men that were murdered last night have been preparing for the games since they were wee lads. They eat, sleep and live for Hawkeye. It is all any of them had. Many of us are but small Kingdoms and do not have the riches that you do, nor a higher being that watches over us."

As one could imagine the Elders immediately took offense. The Light of Goodness watched over all. It was the greed of men and their reckless use and disrespect of free will that impoverished their Kingdoms. It was no use explaining that to Lord MacNaryn however, as he would not understand. His outburst and a defense of his men and the Hawkeye Games however did squelch the Elders' suspicion that he was in league with Lord Warden and Lord Canvil. Enyce rose and walked over to stand with Athia and Andi. The rest of the sisters stood and joined them.

"The meeting of the Elders is adjourned," she said as she addressed the room. "We advise you to take your people home and prepare your Kingdoms for the coming war. Any of you that wish to join us in the fight may bring your people back here; we cannot guarantee their safety however. But perhaps by the sheer mass of numbers we will prevail against any attacks."

"I thought you said this Kingdom is protected and Canvil will not be able to invade it," Lady Rosetta said timidly.

"That is true," Rayley said. "However, unrest has entered the hearts of men. And when unrest is left to fester, Chaos will soon follow. Like a disease it spreads with every wrong deed, every mischievous thought and every retelling of false truth until it consumes the very essence of man." She paused for a few moments letting what she just said settle in the room. Many of the Lord and Ladies understood, however Lord MacNaryn and Lord Farenell did not.

"Perhaps a private counselling with them would help," Athia whispered as she leaned towards Phinney.

"Perhaps," Phinney whispered back.

"And by counselling I mean, a whack over the head with Old Barty's cane," Athia snickered softly. Phinney snorted but immediately stopped when Enyce looked crossly at her before she addressed the room again.

"For those of you who are not joining us in the fight against Canvil, we wish you luck. War is coming whether we like it or not; have prepared for it or not. If Canvil finds a way to cross into our borders and conquers our Kingdom, there will be nowhere you can hide in yours from his wrath. May the Light of Goodness shine favourably down on you. You may now leave." No one in the room moved. "Right then," she said. "We are pleased with your decision! We are now on high alert. You are to go home and bring as many of your people who wish to be under our protection back with you. Pack only the necessities and bring all the weapons and food stores you can carry. For those of you who live further away, we march on Boswick the first day of spring. If you do not have time to return here with your people send your army to Bridge Camryn. We will be waiting there."

"So close to the Boswick Borders, do you think it wise?" Lord MacNaryn asked. "Will Lord Boswick not be home by then? Surely he would have his borders manned by armed guards."

"Lord Boswick and Sir Graphin are not going back to Boswick. We are sure they are reporting to Lord Canvil first," Elder Rayley said. "Bridge Camryn will be safe enough."

"So be it then. We will see you there," Lord MacNaryn responded. The Cliffs of Orhem was the farthest Kingdom away from Elsbrier. They would not have time to make it there and back again, before spring.

"We wish you all a safe journey and may the Light of Goodness favor you," Enyce said.

"And you as well," the Lord and Ladies said before they filed out the door.

The Elders had less than a moment for peace before they were interrupted by Alamat who came running into the Hall, calling out for Elder Enyce.

"What is it Alamat?" Enyce asked anxiously. She waited while Alamat caught her breath.

"She is awake," Alamat said. "And she has requested a counsel with you; specifically you."

"Who, Jenni?" Enyce asked.

"No, the firefly," Alamat said eagerly. "She is Ephanie Erikus, Princess Erikus. And she wants to form an alliance with you."

The Elders looked at each other with wary expressions before they made their apologies to Zusie and the others. They walked briskly out the door of the Great Hall and ran down the path to the Mediplace. If it was true and the fireflies garnered an alliance with the Elders, then the tides of the war may very well favour them after all.

*

Far off to the northeast of Boswick a lone hooded rider landed and gingerly dismounted from the black areondraught he had been riding. Three guards instantly came forward and bowed as the rider took off the hood of his cloak.

"Lord Jaja, it is good to see you," one of the men said.

434

"Yes," is all Jaja said.

"Take my areondraught to the stable, bathe and brush him and make sure he gets an extra ration of oats," Jaja said as he patted the areondraught's neck. "He is worth his weight in gold." The men looked curiously at the way Jaja spoke-something about his manner had changed. It was not their place to question him about it so instead one of them reached for the large leather saddle bag.

"I will take that," Jaja said as he grabbed the saddle bag, and slung it over his shoulders. The guards did not miss the wince of pain that crossed Jaja's face. "Where is he?" Jaja asked. The guards did not need to ask who he spoke of.

"Lord Canvil and your brother arrived yesterday. They are over there," a guard said pointing towards a small forest. Jaja looked over and could see a steady stream of smoke rise from a chimney.

Without another word he left the men to care for his areondraught. He sighed as he made his way to the trees; the frozen grass crunched under his feet. He looked up at the dark clouds forming in the north. Winter was upon them and soon the ground would be blanketed with snow. He wrapped his cloak tighter around him and winced again. His wounds were nearly healed, but he still hurt badly, especially first thing in the morning. It didn't help that he hadn't had a sound sleep since his fight with Rhethea.

Upon reaching the small forest he noticed that several smaller huts had been hastily built. Two guards stood in front of one of them, no smoke rose from its chimney.

Jaja stopped at that hut and looked at the door before he approached it. The guards did not say anything as he turned the handle of the door and opened it. He waited for his eyes to adjust to the dim light. Sitting on the floor leaning against one of the walls was Queen Faywyn and Summeria. They were huddled together for warmth and a thin blanket covered their shoulders. The hut was bare of any furnishings and the pit of the fireplace was bare of wood. Two tin plates and cups sat neatly stacked by the door.

Jaja looked at the defiance in Summeria's eyes as she returned his stare. He was surprised however at the look on Queen Faywyn's face. It was a self-assured expression. She was not looking at him; she looked at the saddle bag. He unconsciously adjusted the strap as an odd thought entered his mind; she knew he carried *The Book* with him.

"The truth is a heavy burden to bear," she said as she looked up at him. She then cocked her head to the side as a shadow crossed Jaja's face. She smiled and whispered, "As is love."

"Guards," Jaja bellowed. "Bring these prisoners provisions, furnishings, clothing and a stack of wood for the fire."

"But Lord Jaja, your fath...," a guard started to say. Jaja however grabbed him by the throat and pressed his thumb against the man's windpipe as he let his anger boil to the surface.

"I will deal with my father," he said angrily and then released the man who crumpled to the ground. He however immediately jumped up and started for the main encampment.

"Have you had a change of heart Jaja?" Queen Faywyn asked.

Jaja ignored her as he addressed the other guard. "When he gets back make a fire for them as well," Jaja said. The guard looked at him questioningly, he had softened since last he seen him. But then the guard smiled with Jaja's next words. "If they freeze to death we will have nothing to bargain with," Jaja looked menacingly at Queen Faywyn before he left. She noticed that the shadow that had crossed his face was no longer there.

Jaja walked on through the forest towards his father and brother. When he came upon a group of commanders he ordered them to post extra guards around the prisoners; he did not wait to see if they followed his orders. He walked on. Just ahead he could see his father's cabin; a massive structure that took up nearly all of the clearing it was sitting in. Anxious to show him *The Book* he quickened his pace. He then hesitated and came to a stop as he spied a shadow leaning against the last tree before the clearing.

Jaja groaned and with heavy footsteps he walked towards the tree. The shadow had plagued him since the hours and days after his battle with Rhethea. He had nearly died and lay for days in and out of consciousness with fever. The areondraught was the only source of reality he had among the nightmares that plagued him. Visions of Rhethea laughing with Shanata turned to visions of Zee riding on his back as he walked through Elsbrier. They then turned to the look of shock on Obwyn and Nayew's faces and the blood that dripped for Rhethea's arm. The visions varied in nature, but one thing was always constant, the shadow.

It had grown bolder and now walked with him in broad daylight. As he past the shadow he did not look at it. He knew what it wanted of him. The shadow smiled as Jaja let the saddle bag slip off his shoulder to the ground. Jaja stepped out of reach as the shadow stretched out its arm to touch him. He did not fear the shadow, but he did not want contact with it either. Lord Canvil would be furious to know that the shadow of his father, Erebos, had chosen a side to fight on and was doing everything in its power to persuade his grandson to join him.

Jaja's decision not to show his father *The Book* waned as he looked down at the saddle bag. He however left it with the shadow and quickly walked across the clearing to his father's cabin. If he had but turned back, he would have noticed that Rishtoph had been watching him from one of the windows in the cabin. When Jaja entered the door at the front of the cabin Rishtoph went out the back door and straight to the saddle bag. He looked curiously about and wondered why his brother had left it. He slung the saddle bag over his shoulder and walked through the woods to his own cabin. He had no idea that the shadow of Erebos followed him and would do everything in its power to persuade him to fight for the Light of Goodness.

33554962R00254

Made in the USA
Charleston, SC
18 September 2014